# Stefi and the Spanish Prince

Books by Donna Freitas

*The Healer*

The Unplugged Series

*Unplugged*

*The Body Market*

*The Mind Virus*

# Stefi and the Spanish Prince

DONNA FREITAS

An Imprint of HarperCollinsPublishers

HarperTeen is an imprint of HarperCollins Publishers.

 For information, address HarperCollins Children's Books, a division of HarperCollins Publishers, 195 Broadway, New York, NY 10007.
www.epicreads.com

Library of Congress Control Number: 2023944248
ISBN 978-0-06-266214-9

For the sake of the reader's ease with the language and for consistency, I chose to use the Spanish translation of certain words, rather than switch back and forth between both Spanish and catalán during Xavi's chapters—even though in real life, Xavi would think in catalán and likely speak to his neighbors in catalán, while also speaking in Spanish to Stefi and Santiago, who do not speak catalán (or catalá, as the case may be, if Xavi was thinking the word in the language of his birth). Please forgive this difficult choice!

Typography by Chris Kwon
24 25 26 27 28 LBC 5 4 3 2 1
FIRST EDITION

To Barcelona, this city I love,
and all my wonderful neighbors in El Gótico.

PART ONE

# Welcome to Barcelona

# One

The open-air market was packed on a Saturday.

Abuelitas with their grocery carts trailing behind them lobbied to get the exact right chicken at the poultry stall, the one with the longest line and all the people shouting over each other. Locals filled their canvas bags full of gorgeous, colorful fruit, vegetables just picked from a nearby farm, bright yellow and orange peaches, so ripe they were nearly bursting. Tourists with their fresh-squeezed juices milled about with their fanny packs and sunglasses and baseball hats, wandering and marveling at the beautiful mountains of tomatoes, of plums, of red and green peppers, of counters filled with dozens of different kinds of olives, of stalls with barrel after barrel of nuts, rice, and beans. One stall displayed every kind of gumdrop imaginable, hill after hill of candy-colored beauty, watermelon pink, lime green, Mediterranean blue. American tourists especially loved to gawk at the more unusual fare for them: pigs' feet, pig snouts, the head of a small goat, the entire body of a rabbit, eyes and all, skinned and ready to go straight into the oven. If you liked that sort of thing.

As it turned out, Stefi did like that sort of thing. Rabbit was kind of delicious. But she wouldn't tell anyone with a bunny she thought so.

"You like the strawberries?" a man behind a wall of fruit asked Stefi in English. She had paused by his stall, always risky if she was not planning on buying. The people who worked here didn't like tourists who stared and snapped photos but didn't purchase anything. "They are the best in the whole market!" he shouted at her over the red and yellow and green hills of produce.

"No, thank you," she told him in Spanish, even though her mother was always trying to convince her that when she was here at La Boqueria, one of the most famous markets in all of Spain, she should practice her catalán. Everyone in Barcelona spoke Spanish, but the true language of this region and its people was catalán.

The man smiled and shrugged as though to say, *Your loss, you silly American*.

Stefi shrugged back, but this time she told him to have a nice day in catalán ("Adéu!"), and his eyes widened when he heard her speak like a local. She turned the corner of the aisle, headed toward her favorite cheese stall. "Where is it?" she muttered as she passed the giant wheels of manchego, the gooey Tortas del Casar, the orange slabs of membrillo that add a dab of sweetness to the sharpest of these Spanish cheeses. Stefi rubbernecked at all the deliciousness because she could not help herself. But then her attention snapped back into focus. Today she was looking for one place in particular, a tapas counter where last weekend she ate something so memorable, she hadn't stopped thinking about it since. Hence her return trip on a Saturday morning. Stefi was a connoisseur when it came to food, too—her dream was to be a pastry chef.

She was trying to remember the place's name, but it was eluding her. La Torta? No. El Pulpo? No. That was the word for octopus, and Stefi didn't remember seeing octopus on the menu. La Boca? Maybe. Maybe that was it. That would make sense. Boca was the word for "mouth," and she was fairly sure the name began with a *B*.

Stefi stopped near another stall that sold only cured pork products. Jamón serrano, jamón ibérico, fuet, black sausage. Even chocolate sausage.

It was amazing the different kinds of sausage you could find in Barcelona. A special kind of fresh sausage called butifarra unique to the region was filled with things like asparagus, mushrooms, even apples or figs or curry. Her own abuela loved to eat it and cook it at home and was always trying to get Stefi to try some strange new flavor. Last time it was butifarra packed with "mushrooms of death," and Stefi soon learned there was nothing like having some good death mushrooms in your sausage for lunch.

She looked around, trying to get her bearings. This place was big; it was easy to get lost.

"You should have paid better attention, Stefi," she told herself. Then she told herself to stop talking to herself.

The heat hung so heavy, the air almost shimmered. The day was bright and sunny and blue-skied, because it was always bright and sunny and blue-skied in Barcelona. So much that when it did rain, residents behaved as if it were a special treat, using it as the American equivalent of a snow day, reveling in the watery excuse to stay in bed or curl up on the couch and watch television for hours.

Then again, the sun might be hot overhead, but inside La Boqueria there was shade. A great waving metal structure soared above the market to block out the glare of so much light.

A woman working at a nearby stall was eyeing Stefi like she was some suspicious character, maybe a thief, from behind sloping hills of eggs. Eggs were sold one by one, white, brown, medium, large, extra-extra-large, all of them unrefrigerated. There were even eggs that were a pretty light blue. A person could buy two, three, seven—however many she wanted. They were so fresh that tiny feathers still clung to them. Stefi eyed them hungrily now. The eggs from this market were the best she'd ever eaten. The yolks were bright orange.

Stefi smiled, gave the woman a wave, and moved on. She stopped at the next cross between aisles and glanced left, then right, before heading into the circular heart and soul of La Boqueria, one of the sights that made it so famous.

Great beds of ice stretched and curved, one after the other, topped with amazing whole fish, yellow, blue, gray, so fresh their eyes were completely clear, still clinging to life. Stefi paused to admire a particularly large fish whose name translated to "raptor" in English—as in the ferocious dinosaur of Jurassic Park fame. Each time Stefi saw the mouth of the raptor gaping wide with its rows of sharp, scary needle teeth, she thought about how she would definitely not like to meet one while taking a dip at the local beach in La Barceloneta neighborhood. Stefi shuddered as she passed it, careful not to slip on the perpetually wet floor in this part of the market. She emerged from the market's fishy heart and was halted by a large group of French-speaking tourists. When they didn't seem like they'd be budging any time soon, she poked the back of one of the men. "Perdón. ¡Perdón!"

The man glanced Stefi's way but didn't move. People liked to complain about American tourists, but really, they were pretty nice as far as visitors went. They didn't dress as fashionably as most of the Europeans, but they were generally polite and well-meaning. The crowd of tourists finally shifted, and Stefi squeezed by.

There. There! Her destination.

La Buena. That was its name. Not La Boca. La Buena, as in "the good" or "the good thing" or even "the beautiful," depending on the translation. She should have known it was back here, where there were a series of tapas counters rounded by metal stools so people could sit for a quick espresso or a plate of boquerones in vinegar or, better still, some sliced jamón from the leg of it sitting on the countertop. Or these giant shrimp Spain was famous for that Stefi had never seen anywhere else. Stefi nearly swooned in anticipation of all the bounty she hoped was about to come her way, both human and otherwise, all of which she felt she'd like to eat. Yum.

La Buena was already busy this morning, except for one lonely stool that had Stefi's name on it. She made a beeline for the open seat and snagged it just before someone else, nearly crashing into the man sitting to the right. He gave Stefi a look like he was none too happy about his new neighbor, like Stefi was interrupting his Saturday-morning tapa, which he was washing down with a tiny glass of beer.

"¿Perdón?" she said, with a slight shrug and an *Oops, so sorry* smile.

He glowered a bit before resuming his inhalation of the Spanish tortilla in front of him.

The tortilla was the reason Stefi had come, the best version of that amazing gooey Spanish omelet that she'd tasted in all of Barcelona. Well, Stefi returned for the food, sure, but there was one other thing pulling her here that surpassed her culinary interests.

She raised her hand to try and get someone's attention. "Hola," she called to the woman working behind the counter. The woman was her mother's age, maybe slightly younger, with wild, curly hair and startlingly Barcelona-sky-blue eyes. The woman didn't seem to hear her. "¿Hola?" she tried again.

The woman turned around. "What would you like, my love?" she asked, her English perfect but with a glorious accent. Musical, mesmerizing, sensual like this market and all the food here. If only Stefi could be that appealing, maybe her summer wouldn't have started out so disastrously—with betrayal and heartbreak, followed by more betrayal and then a transatlantic flight.

"Tortilla with pan con tomate, please," Stefi told her.

"Of course!" The woman turned around to begin preparing it.

Unlike other places, La Buena served tortilla fresh and hot. Stefi watched her beating the eggs, pouring them into the well-oiled skillet, and adding the yummy potato-onion mixture at its center. She was impatient for a taste. But eventually her attention drifted to the door that led to a closet-like prep space. Stefi watched and waited, but so far, nothing.

Her other motive for coming today didn't seem to be panning out.

A motive who happened to take the shape of an extremely handsome, tortilla-making guy her age or close to that, if Stefi had to bet. She guessed he must be the son of the woman cooking her omelet. His hair was as wild as his mother's, though straight, not curly, and long, like he was some sort of hot Viking warrior who'd found his way to the gates of this old city, ready to conquer the ladies with his flashing blue eyes. And, boy, would Stefi like to be conquered by *him*.

As Stefi waited for her tortilla to be ready, she thought back to last weekend. Just like now, she'd been sitting at this very counter waiting for her omelet when she spied this gorgeous boy, a sighting that had inspired more than a few bodice-ripping fantasies like in the romance novels she read during her free time. At one point, this boy disappeared into the back room of La Buena, apparently to retrieve more eggs, and she'd half expected him to reemerge with a sword strapped to his back and proceed to ravish her. That, at least, had been her hope.

Alas, there had been no ravishing.

Except for in her imagination.

In her Viking-related fantasies over the past week, the boy always eventually swooped Stefi up onto his horse and they would ride off . . . through the busy streets of Barcelona full of tourists? Stefi wasn't picky, so this sounded fine. Then, when they arrived wherever they were going, usually someplace secluded and private—perhaps the beach or the far side of Montjuic, which was always really deserted—they'd get down from the horse so that plenty of bodice-ripping could ensue. She would finally get to run her hands through all that silky hair of his, and the boy would look her in the eyes and—

"Here you go!"

"Oh!" Stefi nearly fell off her stool as a round, bright yellow tortilla appeared in front of her. "Sorry, thank you."

The wild-haired tortilla-making woman smiled kindly. "Ah, so you were having daydreams. This is a good city for daydreaming."

If only the woman knew Stefi's daydreams were as hot as the tortilla on her plate and involved a boy who was likely her son. She felt her skin flushing all the way up her neck and onward to her forehead. Stefi bent low to inhale the delicious smell of the omelet and smiled back at the tortilla-maker. "Barcelona is a beautiful place."

The woman filled a small glass with filtered water and placed it on the counter next to Stefi's plate. "Are you here on vacation with your family?"

Stefi shook her head. The poor woman had no idea what a complicated question this was for Stefi to answer. "No" was all she said.

The woman's thick, dark eyebrows arched. "You're living here?"

"Sort of? For the summer, at least."

"Oh, so a summer-abroad program?"

Stefi's eyes dropped to her plate again. She picked up the tiny silver fork sitting atop the paper napkin. "No, not that either." She sighed. "My mom is Catalán, my dad is American. He promised my mom we'd come back here to live one day. Apparently that day has arrived. Maybe. The jury is still out if we'll stay past summer."

"Hmm, that *is* interesting," the woman said. "But you don't sound convinced."

The man Stefi had nearly toppled off his stool sipped his mini-beer and eavesdropped on the two women. The people to Stefi's right paid their check and left their seats vacant for some other happy patrons. Surely they would fill in seconds.

Stefi poked at the center of her tortilla. Soon she'd be able to eat it without burning her tongue. The middle was molten. The smell of something delicious but unidentifiable wafted toward her from the grill and she wondered what it was. Calamari, maybe? "It's hard to leave everyone and move halfway across the world," she said.

"Ahh, I see." The woman brushed a stray black curl from her face. "There must be a girlfriend or a boyfriend back home, yes?"

Red crept up Stefi's neck again; she could feel her skin burning. "That's a complicated question too." Stefi refrained from spilling any of the details, which were gory. They included a boyfriend of three years, Jason, cheating on his girlfriend with a best friend. The girlfriend would be Stefi; the best friend would also be Stefi's, and went by the name of Amber.

So before her family left for Barcelona this summer, Stefi lost the two most important people in her life in one go. In the romance version of her current life, while in Barcelona, Stefi would meet the boy of her dreams and forget all about the terrible situation that preceded this trip.

The tortilla-maker's eyes clouded with sympathy. "Relationships always are complicated."

"Yesss," she sighed heavily.

The woman patted Stefi's hand. "Endings make room for new beginnings, yes?"

Stefi smiled wide; she couldn't help it. "Yesss," she concurred again. The woman was right, and Stefi had thought of this as well. This summer could be an opportunity if she let it, a chance for her to reinvent herself. On the flight here, Stefi decided she was going to be daring this summer. She was going to do things people like Jason, her ex, and

Amber, her ex–best friend, would never imagine her capable of. If a boy with a sword and a horse wanted to whisk Stefi off someplace private, for example, Stefi was going to throw caution to the wind for once and say yes to all of it.

Stefi was about to say something else to the tortilla-maker about exactly this—well, not *exactly* this—when the two seats next to her were suddenly taken. The patrons spoke very fast in catalán. The only part Stefi caught was "Bon dia, Marta!" Both members of the couple leaned over the counter and gave the tortilla-maker a kiss on each cheek, because that's how everyone greeted each other in Spain. Stefi listened to their talk but caught only a word here and there. But one of those words made her perk up and listen harder: *fill*, which was "son" in catalán. Marta was the tortilla-making woman's name, Stefi learned, and she supposed the boy with the equally wild hair was the son to whom the couple referred.

Yeah. Him.

The tortilla was finally cool enough to eat, so Stefi took a bite. For a moment, all else was forgotten: Jason, Amber, beautiful boys who might work at tapas counters at La Boqueria, finding a way to meet such boys. The omelet was even better than Stefi remembered. The center of it was gooey with potato and onion. The eggs were perfectly cooked and seasoned with salt. How did this woman, Marta, do this? Not all tortillas were created equal, and this one proved it. No wonder La Buena was always so packed.

Marta was suddenly in front of Stefi again. "You were here last weekend, yes? Another time you'll tell me the story of what happened before you arrived, eh? Because you'll be back again, yes? You like the tortilla, yes?"

Stefi nodded in agreement to all of Marta's questions. Even if she hadn't loved the food, it would have been difficult to say no to this Marta. She was like some sort of benevolent fairy queen who'd put a spell on Stefi with her prettiness and kindness and, of course, her culinary magic. "Definitely," Stefi said and watched as Marta twirled away to attend to another new set of customers at the other end of the counter.

Her only disappointment was Marta's absent son.

*Oh, well. Maybe he'll be here next week.*

Stefi eyed her plate. Her tortilla already looked like it had been attacked by a desperately hungry animal. In barely a blink, she'd eaten half of it. Stefi decided she needed to enjoy the rest more slowly, so as she stabbed another piece with her fork and lifted it to her mouth, she closed her eyes to focus on the taste, which seemed to get even better the more it cooled. Stefi could only imagine the look on her face as she chewed, letting the flavors spread all over her tongue like her abuela, the original foodie in their family, had taught her. Eventually, Stefi swallowed. When she opened her eyes, once again she was startled. She was no longer alone. But it wasn't Marta returning for more conversation.

A pair of blue eyes were staring back at Stefi, and they were full of laughter.

The Viking.

"You're enjoying the tortilla?" he asked, also in perfect English. Of course his accent was nearly as attractive as his face. How could it not be?

Stefi tried to swallow again, but something caught in her throat and she nearly choked. She could feel her face getting red, and her eyes must have started to bulge because the Viking boy suddenly grabbed her glass, filled it with more water, and pushed it toward her. Stefi took it, gulped it down, and tried not to spit in the boy's face as she coughed and sputtered. This had not been part of Stefi's romantic fantasy of what would happen if she got the chance to meet this boy. She finished the water and he filled the glass again. Her right-side neighbors said something in catalán that she didn't catch, and the Viking cracked up. Probably about her. Ugh. She drank down the second glass of water and finally felt like her voice might work again.

"Thank you," she croaked.

The boy flicked his thick hair from his eyes in a practiced gesture, and Stefi once again wished she could rake her fingers through it. "So I take it that's a no?" he asked.

"No?"

"You're not enjoying the tortilla?"

Stefi's eyes widened. "Oh no! I mean, yes! I mean, I *am* very much enjoying the food your mother cooks. It *is* your mother, right? It's even better than I remember from last week." *And you're even hotter than I remember from last week*, her brain added, luckily silently. Her inward swoon was also, gratefully, invisible.

The boy smiled, a look of pride on his face. "It's true, my mother is an excellent cook. I was going to have to kick you out if you didn't like our tortilla."

The couple next to Stefi turned to her. "It is the best in all of Catalunya. We've been coming here for years to enjoy Marta's magic."

Stefi's other neighbor, the man sipping the tiny beer and eavesdropping, grunted. "Me too. But we try to keep it a secret from the tourists, so don't go taking photos and putting them on one of those stupid social media sites that end up ruining everything the locals enjoy."

"Be nice, Arnau," said the Viking boy to the cranky man. He grabbed the glass and filled it with beer again. "This one's on the house, all right?"

"Don't worry, I would never do that," Stefi told everyone around her. She refrained from mentioning how she was on a summer-long social media fast anyway, since she couldn't bear to witness the public blossoming of the relationship between her former boyfriend and her former best friend.

Another boy appeared from the tiny closet prep-space at the center of La Buena. He was around the Viking's age, and he was holding a giant bowl of cut-up potatoes. He was followed by an older but also handsome man; it was like the tiny room was a clown car full of good-looking people. Between the three men and the one beautiful woman cooking at the stove, the establishment seemed strangely glamorous.

The Viking placed his hands flat on the countertop on either side of Stefi's plate and stared at her boldly. Stefi would have been lying if she claimed she didn't notice the way it made the long, tan muscles in his arms tighten and expand. She would also have been lying if she claimed that she wasn't imagining right then what it would be like to have those arms wrapped around her. "If you promise not to spill the culinary secrets of this city," he said, "I'll give you another few places to try while you're here on vacation."

"I'm not—" Stefi started, but the Viking's mother swirled by, hip-checking her son.

"The girl's not on vacation, my darling, her family is living here," she said before delivering the two steaming tortillas in her hands to the newest customers to Stefi's far left.

Had Stefi detected a warning tone in Marta's voice?

But the Viking's eyes filled with mischief. "Oh, really?" He was about to say something else when the other young man appeared at his side.

"You've got to go, it's time," he said.

The Viking rolled his eyes at him, then looked at Stefi again. "You'll have to forgive my cousin, he can be very rude."

Stefi opened her mouth to say not to worry, but the cousin said to Stefi, "I definitely don't mean to be rude, but this one is needed in the back urgently. The onions are calling to him."

The Viking erupted into catalán. Even though Stefi couldn't understand the words, she could tell he wasn't happy. Before the cousin could physically pull him away, the Viking leaned over the counter where Stefi was sitting, captured her gaze, and held it. Not like this was hard, since Stefi was more than willing to gaze back. "I'm Xavi, by the way," he said. "And you are?"

"Stefi."

A low rumbling laugh erupted from his throat. "That's perfect," he said, more to himself than to Stefi.

She blinked at him. "Perfect?"

"Your name. Stefi, like Estefanía, right? It's the Spanish version of Stephanie, but its derivation is from the Greek for 'crown,'" he added before the cousin yanked Xavi into the prep room again.

Marta appeared in front of Stefi and took her empty plate. "I hope you have a very good summer," she said as if advising Stefi not to return to La Buena, even though moments ago she'd asked if Stefi would come back the following week. Stefi's fantasies of horses, swords, a summer of exciting escapades on private beaches with long-haired boys named Xavi began to fade. "Estefi," Marta added with finality.

Stefi put down the money to pay and slid off the stool startled, this time with disappointment. "Thank you for the most delicious tortilla I've ever had in my life," she said by way of goodbye.

Marta's expression softened. "You're very welcome. And Xavi is correct—there are many good places for you to try. You should do your best to enjoy them all. I wish you well. I really do hope you have a wonderful summer."

# Two

"I saw how you were talking to the girl," Marta said.

Xavi watched his mother pouring eggs into the tortilla pan for what must be the hundredth time, and it was only noon. Marta spoke to him only in English. She was forever making Xavi practice, even though his command of the language was nearly perfect. If it weren't for Xavi's thick Spanish accent, people would probably think he was a native speaker. Marta had made sure of this by sending Xavi to the special British international school, Queen Elizabeth's, in the tony heart of Barcelona's Eixample neighborhood. It was situated within a few blocks of some of the most famous buildings in the city designed by Antoni Gaudí, also the architect of the city's legendary unfinished cathedral, La Sagrada Familia. With its magical colors and whimsical sculptures, there were always endless lines of tourists waiting to enter it.

Instead of answering his mother, Xavi scooped the potato and onion mixture into the center of the tortilla Marta was making.

But he knew exactly the girl to which she referred. The eye-catching American he'd flirted with boldly this morning. Her long hair and those flashing eyes had captured his attention. Well, her eyes and hair, plus a pair of long legs and delicate shoulders, not to mention all those curves. She'd had Xavi imagining all the different ways he could convince her to let him kiss her even though they'd just met. He should have been less obvious about it, given that his mother had been standing right there watching him the entire time.

Marta continued to stare at her son.

"I'd better get those beers," he said and moved toward the tap at the center of the counter.

Marta and Xavi loved each other fiercely. He was grateful Marta fought for him to have every possible opportunity so doors might open in the future. He knew Marta loved their little tapas place, but his mother didn't want this life for her son. Financial need coupled with Xavi's academic promise had won him scholarships to attend Queen Elizabeth's, the school that attracted the children of diplomats and politicians and some of the richest families in all of Catalunya. This was also how Xavi ended up with friends who vacationed in Monaco and Ibiza, children of the rich who shopped for couture on Passeig de Gràcia, the Fifth Avenue of the city, instead of in the cheap fast-fashion stores like Zara and Primark like the rest of Marta and Xavi's circle. This was also how Xavi ended up dating Isabel de Luna, the most notorious of all the rich girls at his very wealthy school—notorious for about a million different reasons, among them that her parents were a marqués and a marquesa, actual titled Spanish royalty.

As Xavi was busy pulling a dozen cañas for some of their regular patrons, the small glasses of beer Barcelona residents often drank in the mornings with their breakfast, he felt his mother's gaze still on him as she cooked, waiting for him to say something.

Both Marta and Xavi could make La Buena's most famous tapa with their eyes closed. There were many possible translations of "la buena" in Spanish, but one of them was "the correct," as in "the right way." Marta had chosen this name for their restaurant with care and precision. How *exactly* to make the typical Spanish omelet had always been cause for fierce debate in this hot, sunny country on the coast of the Mediterranean: With onions and potatoes or with only potatoes? People fought about this in the food columns of newspapers, argued about it in instructional videos on YouTube, and judged each other ruthlessly depending on which side a person came down with respect to this eternal question. According to Marta, onions were an essential ingredient, so this was her way of announcing to the world that she had settled the question definitively. Her way was *the one*.

A perfectly round, smoldering omelet rose high into the air with an experienced flip of Marta's wrist, and she caught it again in the simmering pan without looking. "Xavi, I'm not going to let this go," she said.

Xavi was certain that she wouldn't. His mother could be relentless.

Meanwhile, the patrons at the counter watched Marta work with fascination. Her talent was evident, but so was her striking beauty.

Xavi finished pulling the cañas from the beer tap.

Marta elbowed her son. "Eh? The girl who was here just now? Don't think I didn't see."

*The* girl. Xavi noted Marta didn't say *that* girl, as though the American in question were someone random; she'd said *the* girl, as though she were the only girl who'd appeared this morning even though there had been plenty. Xavi often wondered why he'd had to end up with such an observant mother. Lately, she was on him for just about every move he made. He understood why, but he didn't have to like this shift in his mother's behavior.

He dealt out the cañas to the patrons who'd ordered them. "What girl?" he asked Marta with a shrug. Before she could press him further, he took advantage of the fact that the line for a seat at La Buena was now so long, it snaked through the other stalls in the market. He trotted off through the opening in the counter, pad and pen in hand, ready to take down names. If there was a brawl about who was next in line for a newly available seat and access to Marta's cooking, it wouldn't be the first time.

“Hey, wait up,” Santiago said, following Xavi, also with a pad in hand, to help manage the list.

Santiago had been standing behind the counter, taking orders from newly arrived customers and placing them above the stovetop.

Xavi was ignoring his mother and now Santiago too.

Santiago was Xavi’s long-lost “cousin,” and Xavi could barely take a step without Santiago trailing after him. Santiago was like the orange-colored membrillo Marta bought at the stall next door to serve with the cheese plate on La Buena’s menu—and equally sticky. The two young men came as a package deal now, because this was the job Santiago had signed up for; the title of cousin was his cover. Santiago’s arrival had caused a bit of a stir among Xavi’s friends because Santiago was tall, handsome, and muscled like one of the football stars for El Barça, with his broad smile and wide, dark eyes. The attention seemed to roll off Santiago, though. Xavi and Santiago didn’t know each other well enough for Xavi to ask him outright why this was.

Santiago was clearly comfortable chiding Xavi, however. “Your mother meant the American girl you were flirting with earlier,” he said before walking up to a couple in wildly patterned Bermuda shorts that they did not seem to be wearing ironically. Ah, tourists.

God, did *everyone* have to notice Xavi talking to her? Xavi was feeling stubborn, so he continued to play dumb. “And which girl was that? There are always so many and all they do is stare at you.” This was true, but it wasn’t the whole truth. Xavi knew they stared at him too.

Santiago shook his head, then went to take the name of the next woman in line. People jostled by, ogling the wares at the many stalls, marveling at the one that sold nearly forty different kinds of olives—spicy, pitted, big, small, stuffed with peppers, stuffed with sardines, stuffed with cheese, green, black, and one variety that was almost purple. Xavi tugged his sweaty T-shirt away from his chest, and a couple of nearby girls tittered. It was sweltering in here today, despite the shade above them.

Summer had officially begun at La Boqueria.

Santiago put a hand on Xavi's arm and leaned in close. "Chaval, you should head back and help your mother, I'll do this," Santiago said.

"Why?"

"You know why. Because you shouldn't be milling about out here in the market."

Another large group of tourists jostled them, and one person bumped into Xavi hard as though to prove Santiago's point. But Xavi wasn't having it. "Oh, because behind the counter I'm so protected?"

Two small abuelas squeezed between the two young men, shopping carts filled to the brim with their purchases. A recently plucked chicken sat atop one of the carts, fat green artichokes atop another.

"It's easier to keep track of you, yes," Santiago said.

"What if I don't want you to keep track of me?" Xavi shot back.

Santiago gave him a look of desperation. "Chaval, just get back there for once. I'll get the rest of these names." Santiago looked left, then right, and Xavi wondered who he was searching for. "Besides, I could swear I saw that ex-girlfriend of yours lurking. You should get out while you can. She won't dare come up to you if Marta's nearby."

Xavi narrowed his eyes, studying Santiago. Had he really seen Isabel or was this a ploy to get Xavi to do as he was told? Either way, if Isabel was around, Xavi didn't want to run into her. Their last meeting had ended in disaster. A drunken one, at least on Xavi's part. "You did not see Isabel," Xavi said a tad nervously. "Did you?"

Santiago shrugged, then cocked his head ambiguously.

Isabel and Xavi dated off and on for several months this past spring, even though Xavi had never thought of Isabel as his type. She was more the type of girl who'd date the son of an oil baron, the type a rich guy would take on a shopping spree to Loewe—the Chanel equivalent of luxury fashion in Spain. Not like someone Xavi would go out with, in other words. But it was also true that in the very beginning, Xavi wondered if Isabel might turn out to be special. Then he'd found out she'd manipulated him into thinking she was someone else underneath that hard, glossy shell. After Isabel backstabbed one too many friends, started cruel rumors about a few too many girls in their circle, plus made it clear that she was dating Xavi to piss off her parents, he ended things. Some people at school referred to Isabel as the Ice Queen, a nickname Xavi discovered was apt. Isabel was as reserved and glamorous as royalty and just as remote and cold. She collected secrets from people so she could use them like weapons. The last kind of person Xavi needed to be around right now.

Santiago was peering past a nearby stall selling every possible kind of gumdrop. "I just saw a very expensive short pink chiffon skirt fluttering through one of the aisles," he said. "A sure sign of your ex."

Whereas most women wore jeans and T-shirts, summer dresses, or shorts and tank tops as they walked Barcelona's streets and shops and visited the markets, Isabel dressed as though the entire city—La Boqueria included—were her own personal catwalk, and she was always toting some four-thousand-euro Loewe bag to complete the outfit.

Santiago's eyebrows arched as he waited for Xavi's response, and Xavi realized that Santiago was not going to relent. The tourists in line for La Buena were getting impatient, since the two boys had paused taking names.

"All right, fine." Xavi sighed. "I'll go back behind the counter."

Santiago smiled with relief.

Even though Santiago could drive Xavi crazy, he liked the guy. Over the past few months and despite the strange circumstances that had forged their relationship, Xavi felt like they were becoming friends. And Xavi didn't really want to make Santiago's job any harder, given that Xavi *was* his job.

Xavi tucked the order pad into his back pocket and headed along the endless line to La Buena, careful not to slip. By midday, the floor of the market was slippery with water from the circle of fish stalls at the center of La Boqueria. Along the way, Xavi waved at Josefina, who owned a nearby stall that sold only jamón ibérico. Josefina blew a kiss back from underneath at least twenty legs of the famous Spanish ham hanging above her head.

Xavi returned her kiss with a grin.

Like so many of the older women who worked at the stalls in the market, Josefina had been like a grandmother to Xavi since he was a boy. Only a few months ago, Xavi would have run over to chat with her, ask if she wanted a snack, maybe get her to slice some ham for his mother to eat. But Santiago was keeping his eye on Xavi and shaking his head no. So Xavi did what he was supposed to and slipped back through the opening in the countertop.

Marta was chatting with one of the regulars even though some of the other patrons clamored for her attention. Xavi waltzed over to his mother and followed her lead, ignoring everyone else. "Hola, Bonnie," he said to the woman with whom Marta was talking.

Bonnie's face broke into a smile. Her long gray hair was parted in the middle and tucked behind her ears. "Xavi, how's things?" she asked in her thick Scottish accent.

Barcelona was a mix of locals and expats. Some of the expats, people like Bonnie, had left colder, northern countries like Scotland and Sweden and Germany for the warmth of this city and the proximity of the Mediterranean Sea, and some had come from Latin or South America because Spain was the land of opportunity for many Spanish-speaking people.

Xavi once found it difficult to understand Bonnie's Scottish accent, but he'd gotten used to it over the years. She'd immigrated twenty years ago and spoke Spanish and catalán as well as English. Bonnie was the owner of a famous cheese shop in the neighborhood where they lived, and she closed the shop whenever she felt like it, usually when she got hungry for lunch. Xavi was sure this was the case today and that people would be arriving at her cheese shop and wondering where she was.

"Oh, you know, the same old," he told Bonnie. "Busy. Marta has got me working hard."

"Mamá to you," Marta said to her son, then drifted away to attend to a customer who looked about to climb over the counter to pull himself a glass of beer.

Bonnie watched their exchange, fork dangling over her plate. "She knows what she's doing, your ma."

Xavi nodded at Bonnie's half-eaten tortilla. "I didn't mean to interrupt your breakfast. Or your brunch?" It was still early for locals to be eating lunch. Lunch was usually between two and four in the afternoon, and it was barely noon now. Two more hours until La Boqueria closed for the rest of the weekend and Xavi and his mother would be free to do whatever they wanted. Maybe go to the beach, given the heat. "You look like you had a long night, Bonnie."

"Ah, well, I was talking to Lis after she closed down the bar." Xavi's eyebrows arched and Bonnie took a playful swat at him. "Don't get any ideas, you," she said.

"Okay, sure," Xavi said in a tone that told her he wasn't convinced.

In all the time Xavi had known Bonnie, she'd never had a partner, but lately he kept running into her in the street chatting with their neighbor Lis in front of her bar of the same name. The bar was tiny but beautiful, with old medieval stone walls and a gleaming marble countertop that curved around from one wall to the other, the ceiling arching overhead. It sat only sixteen people on the stools lined up along the counter, but the whole neighborhood packed themselves into the place to catch up about their days and hear the local gossip.

Bonnie was shaking her head at Xavi. "Let me finish my tortilla in peace, Xavier."

Marta appeared next to her son again. "Bonnie is right. Leave her be."

"Yes, listen to your mother," Bonnie said.

Xavi put an arm around Marta and grinned. "I always listen to my mother."

His mother huffed and looked up at her son. At eighteen, Xavi was much taller than she was. "If only," she said.

"I am going to go chop those onions," Xavi announced, deciding this was a good moment to get out from under the eyes of these women who still thought of him as a little boy. He pushed through the swinging door into the prep closet at the center of La Buena.

Jordi glanced up from his place at the metal table where he was peeling potatoes, his face expressionless. He nodded at Xavi but didn't say anything. Jordi had been helping out at La Buena for at least a decade, and sometimes Xavi wondered how Jordi felt about Santiago. He imagined Jordi wasn't thrilled that Santiago was suddenly helping to manage Marta's tapas place, which required hours of potato peeling and chopping and, worse, dicing onions, but which Jordi could certainly handle on his own.

Xavi plucked one of the onions from the bowl of water where they sat to take the sting out, an old cooking trick. He got to work cutting them and teared up only a little. He wished he could tell Jordi the truth about why they'd "hired" Santiago, but Xavi knew he wasn't allowed.

So he and Jordi fell into a companionable silence.

Occasionally, Xavi stole a quick glance at the man to his right and thought about all he was forbidden to say. Which made him think about the other man in his life, the one who lived in Madrid. His father.

Until a year ago, Xavi thought his father was dead.

Marta had allowed him to think this.

When Xavi was small, he'd had wild ideas about who his father might be. As a child, he fantasized that his father would turn out to be a garbage collector who drove one of the big noisy trucks through the streets in the mornings. Or, even better, a bombero who swooped to the rescue on a long red fire engine, sirens blaring. Then those images gave way to others, like a famous flamenco guitarist or an actor in one of his mother's favorite TV series. As Xavi got older, he simply wished to have a father, no matter who the man turned out to be. Someone like his mother, who loved Xavi more than anything. Someone there when Xavi needed a father, a man he could admire. For years, Xavi daydreamed about his father showing up one day at La Buena, about how he would take a seat and order a tortilla like everyone else, but when Xavi went to ask him if he wanted another beer or an agua con gas, he would look up at Xavi, and Xavi would look back at him, and they would recognize each other, because their eyes would be the same.

Eventually, Xavi learned to stop asking Marta questions about his father—who he was, where he was, if he was still alive. Anytime he brought up the subject, Marta reacted in a way that was utterly unlike the mother he knew, the mother who'd always been open with her son about everything. But when the subject of his father arose?

Marta would immediately tear up.

Or leave the room.

Or simply shake her head and change the subject.

Occasionally she would say something cryptic and maddeningly brief: "Your father and I had a complicated relationship," or "Circumstances didn't allow for your father and I to be together." And even, once,

"Sometimes the world conspires to keep two people apart." Then there was the time Marta simply answered: "Your father broke my heart."

One day when Xavi was fourteen, he gathered the courage to ask Marta the question that burned inside him but that he'd always been afraid to speak out loud:

"Mamá, is my father dead?"

Not only did she tear up, shake her head, *and* leave the room at this inquiry from her son, but before she disappeared, she cried out, "Your father can never be a part of our lives! Stop asking me about him!" This kind of reaction was so unlike Xavi's mother in every other way, he decided he needed to respect Marta's wishes and let the issue rest.

So Xavi came to accept that this man would never show up to claim him. Whether alive or dead, his father was gone from Xavi's world and from the lives he and Marta had built together; whoever and wherever his father was, he'd caused his mother such a painful heartbreak that even all these years later, she was still wounded.

Besides, Xavi always reminded himself, he had the most wonderful mother a son could hope for, and this was more than enough. And between Marta and all the adoptive grandmas, grandpas, aunts, and uncles in their neighborhood and here at the market, Xavi had a better, bigger family than one real father could ever provide. So Xavi made his peace with the notion that he would never know his father.

Until one day Marta shattered her son's hard-won conviction.

Xavi's father was apparently as alive as he could be and wanted to meet his nearly grown son.

This revelation caused a terrible month-long rift, especially after she informed Xavi that he was going to Madrid to meet this so-called father who was a total stranger. Well, sort of a stranger it turned out. There was no getting out of this trip, Marta told him.

This mandate did nothing to heal the standoff between Xavi and Marta.

The night before Xavi was to leave for Madrid, while Marta was down at Lis enjoying a glass of cava, in a fit of anger Xavi began searching Marta's room for evidence of his father. He wanted to find a photo, a poetry book dedicated to his mother, a souvenir from a weekend away—something. A clue to their romance, a reason for why they'd fallen in love. What Xavi did find was a letter. It was tucked so far in the back of a drawer in Marta's desk he nearly missed it.

And because he was so angry at Marta, he proceeded to do the unthinkable:

He read the letter from his father.

When Xavi was halfway through, he forced himself to stop. He didn't need to read anymore—it had been wrong to read any further. It had been wrong to read any of it at all. Carefully, he folded the note and placed it back into its envelope and returned it to its place deep in the drawer. Shame flooded Xavi for going through his mother's things and violating something so private. But Xavi had read enough to understand why Marta decided not to tell Xavi's father about his son's existence and exactly why she couldn't bear to speak of the man.

When Marta came home from the bar that night, Xavi apologized for how he'd been acting and gave his mother a hug. The two of them cried, grateful to have made up. But he didn't tell Marta why he'd suddenly forgiven her and was relieved when she didn't ask about his change of heart.

So the next morning, Xavi traveled to Madrid, and it didn't go well between Xavi and his long-lost papá. In fact, it was a bit of a disaster. How could it not be? This was the man who had broken his mother's heart so completely that she never loved again.

"Xavi?"

Marta had squeezed herself into the back room and Xavi didn't even notice.

"¿Sí, mamá?"

"I could use your help out there again," she said, the dark, black curls that framed her face wet with perspiration. "The line just never stops."

Xavi put his knife down on the cutting board and wiped his eyes with the back of his hand. Even after soaking the onions, they were still strong. "I'm coming," he said and moved to follow his mother, but not before he caught Jordi staring at her. Xavi wondered if Jordi had a crush on Marta. It wouldn't be the first time someone in Marta's proximity had fallen in love with her. Marta had left a trail of broken hearts all over Barcelona. Not because she'd actively tried to break anyone's heart but because his mother seemed impervious to the attentions of any suitor. *It's a lost cause, Jordi*, Xavi wanted to say but held back. Whether it was Jordi or another man, he wished his mother's heart would heal enough for her to find someone else.

Xavi pushed through the door, and when he was out in the market again, his eyes widened. The line to get a seat at their counter was as long as he'd ever seen it. He kept telling his mother they needed a bigger place, but she kept saying no. She liked La Buena just as it was and always had been.

He set up at the burner next to the one where his mother worked and started pouring eggs into a skillet. "Mom, I think you've become famous," he said.

Marta shook her head. "Someone must have put us in another online guide this month."

"Maybe," he said.

Santiago was back behind the counter again, attending to new customers as they took their seats, getting their orders to pass on to Marta and Xavi. One bonus of having Santiago in their lives was the extra hand. But

Santiago's presence also inevitably reminded Xavi that this life he loved, in this place where he'd helped his mother since he was practically old enough to walk, was about to come to an end. The thought made Xavi sad, then angry, then exasperated. And then another thought swooped in and pushed those others away.

The girl. The one who showed up this morning with that loud laugh and awkward manners. Xavi wondered if she might return again for more tortilla, and, if so, would he be working? He hoped so. If she did come back, he wouldn't miss the opportunity to ask her out. Besides, Xavi needed to move on from Isabel. Maybe he could invite the American girl to the beach. He certainly wouldn't mind the chance to see her in a bathing suit.

Marta interrupted these pleasant thoughts by elbowing her son. "Xavi, you are going to cut that hair of yours this week, yes?"

Xavi flopped his long locks so they fell to the other side of his face to make this point: "No way. I like it as is."

"You must cut it," Marta said. She'd been after him all spring to do it.

He shrugged. "It's part of my rebellion."

Marta sighed. "Your whole life is part of your rebellion, my darling. But the rebellion has to come to an end. August is the deadline."

"Yes, but right now it's only June. I've got plenty of time." As Xavi uttered these words, another image of the American girl flashed in his brain. That long blond hair that reached the middle of her back and those legs because, yeah, he'd watched her walk away in those short-shorts until she disappeared from La Boqueria. "Do you think we'll see her again?" Xavi asked his mother.

"Who?"

"*The* girl, Mom."

This time Marta closed her eyes. "Oh, Xavi. You know you can't."

"And you know you shouldn't say that because I'll only take it as a challenge." His tone had an edge, one that Xavi was sure his mother must notice. But his tone was not directed at Marta. It came from the place inside him that was hurt—no, *angry* that suddenly being his father's son came with the kind of rules and expectations that could change his life so drastically that it would soon be unrecognizable. The same father who once disposed of his mother like she had no value at all.

"Xavi," Marta pressed.

He swirled the eggs in his skillet before scooping the filling into the middle.

Xavi's mother took a deep breath. Eyes closed, she said, "You already broke one heart this spring—do you really need to break another?"

Marta was referring to Isabel, although Xavi was surprised to hear his mother speak of Isabel this way. Marta did not like her even a little.

Xavi flipped his tortilla expertly. "I'm not sure Isabel even has a heart."

When Marta opened her eyes, her lashes were wet. "Xavi. I am being serious."

Oh no. He hadn't meant to make his mother cry. "Ma?"

"You cannot forget who you truly are, my love," she said, her voice low. Marta's next words reached under her son's skin and into his center in a way that was terribly unsettling, most of all because Xavi knew her words were true. "You are the prince of Spain, Xavier," she said. "And soon you are going to have to start acting like it because the whole world is going to know."

# Three

Xavi was going to be the death of Santiago.

"¡Chaval!" Santiago called out as Xavi weaved his way quickly through the market stalls as though he wanted to lose Santiago. Which he probably did. The Saturday crowds lingered in La Boqueria, reluctant to leave even as the small kiosks were closing for the weekend. It was nearly two p.m., time for the workers to head to lunch at home or somewhere in the city.

"You should know your way around here by now," Xavi tossed over his shoulder as he disappeared around the corner.

Santiago picked up his pace. He knew his instructions well—no, his royal duty: stick to the newly discovered heir to the Spanish throne like fig jam to manchego. "Slow down."

"I don't want to leave my mother alone as she closes up," Xavi said, hair flopping over one eye. He brushed it away. "She needs those potatoes so we'll have them for Monday when we open."

Santiago looked at the mountain of potatoes rising up next to them at one of the many vegetable stalls in the market. "Can't you buy them over here?" He looked the other way and saw another, smaller hill of them. "There are potatoes everywhere!"

Xavi marched onward, barely glancing back as he took another sharp turn. "They can't be just *any* potatoes. They have to be from Alan."

The two young men reached the side of the market that spilled into a small plaza where local farmers set up carts a few days a week in the open glare of the sun. Xavi headed to the very last vendor and greeted the gray-haired man whose wares were nearly sold out. He was already packing up to go. Xavi reached over the remaining tomatoes and a few peaches rolling around in the cardboard carton and clapped the viejito on the shoulder. "Alan!" Xavi beamed. "I'm so glad I caught you before you left. Got any potatoes hidden in your secret stash? We were overrun today, and my mother is worried about Monday morning."

Santiago stood by as the older and younger man talked, sorting through what Alan had left to offer from the stores he held aside to supply the tiny tapas bars and kiosks encircling the market. Santiago's exasperation began to subside. Some of the señoras at the neighboring carts came over to greet Marta's beloved son with kisses on his cheeks and some lavish grandmotherly attention, patting his long hair and wiping away the pink and red lipstick they left on Xavi's face—kisses Xavi received with patience and kindness. Santiago leaned against the stone wall in the sliver of shade at the edge of the plaza as Xavi piled potatoes into a spare carton and chatted with all the abuelas.

Xavi would certainly cut a dashing figure as prince, Santiago thought. Unselfconsciously handsome and a natural with people, Xavi could talk to anyone. And he did talk to *everyone*, with a generosity and sincerity Santiago knew that Xavi's father, the king, would come to appreciate. The entire country of Spain would come to appreciate it eventually, once they got over the shock of learning that King Alfonso XIV had a son after all.

If only Santiago could keep Xavi under control for a few more weeks, until summer came to an end and, with it, life as Xavi had always known it. Easier said than done as far as Santiago was concerned. Obedient Xavi was not. Rebellious was more like it. Rebellious and maddening and unbelievably difficult, not to mention politically catalán in a way that might prove a problem, given the ongoing tensions between Madrid and this Spanish region always threatening to secede from the rest of the country. But Santiago chose to push these issues aside for now, since it was all he could do to keep Xavi in his sights. If Santiago hadn't liked Xavi so much as a person, he would have already asked the royal guard to switch his post. At nineteen, Santiago was only a year older than Xavi, so Santiago was meant to be a "soft introduction" to the young prince's new situation, a barely present reminder of Xavi's life to come and a resource for all he'd need to learn about the role he would soon play in the monarchy. It was a role, too, one that needed to be performed. Being a prince, a monarch, was a kind of theater, yet the curtain was always up. The prince of Spain would live on a perpetual stage with an audience that never took its eyes off him.

Xavi was receiving even more kisses now as the viejitas said their goodbyes. Soon he thanked Alan and then arrived in front of Santiago. There was a sack of potatoes and who knows what else thrown over his shoulder, a carton of fruit balanced along one arm, and his long hair was sticky from the heat and falling around his face. Even sweaty with oil stains and splotches on his shirt from cooking, Xavi was handsome. Under other circumstances, Santiago would be asking Xavi out and hoping he might say yes.

"Thanks for waiting," Xavi said with some remorse.

Santiago shook his head, but he was smiling. Despite Xavi's efforts to lose him in the market earlier, he always eventually felt bad that he made Santiago's life more difficult. Santiago also tried to keep in mind that Xavi was going through one of the biggest adjustments of his life. "It's no problem," Santiago said.

Xavi's thick eyebrows arched. "No?"

"Nah."

Xavi glanced around furtively, maybe to see if Isabel was lurking.

Santiago hadn't been lying when he told Xavi he thought he'd seen Isabel. In theory, Isabel de Luna would be the perfect girlfriend for a young prince, given that she came from one of the wealthiest titled families in all of Spain. Santiago occasionally tried to do more digging into why their relationship ended so badly, but Xavi's answer was always something like "No, no way, never again," or "I can't be with someone I don't trust and who manipulates even people she claims to love." Santiago wanted to quip, *Well, welcome to the royal family!* but always refrained.

"Are we good?" Santiago asked.

Xavi adjusted the sack over his shoulder. "Yeah. Let's bring these to my mother and get out of here. I told Diego I'd meet him by the fountain in the Plaça Reial at three, and I need a shower first. So do you, chaval."

Santiago's heart lurched.

They would be seeing Diego within the hour.

Xavi plunged back into the market, and Santiago followed him, distracted.

Compact, fit, with big blue eyes and swoon-worthy lashes, Diego was energetic and funny and smart and friendly. He was built like the most perfectly small package Santiago had ever seen, topped with a wild head of dark hair that Santiago dreamed of running his fingers through each night before he went to sleep.

Santiago was crushing on Diego hard, in other words.

*No, no, stop, you can't.* Santiago immediately course-corrected his thinking. But each time he saw Diego, this got more difficult to do. Santiago breathed in deeply, then out again, trying to still his pounding heart.

"Santiago? You coming or what?" Xavi stopped ahead of Santiago in the aisle to find out why he was lagging behind.

Santiago didn't even realize he'd come to a halt right next to one of the egg sellers as she closed up for the weekend. This was exactly why his crush on Diego was a problem. The mere mention of Diego, and Santiago was shirking his duties of managing Xavi and his safety. Plus there was the teeny-tiny problem of the conflict of interest Diego posed, given that he was the best friend of the person Santiago was assigned to guard.

"Sorry, I spaced out for a minute," he said.

Xavi grinned. "I didn't think that was possible. Tell me whatever caused it so I can remember when I need to lose you in the future for some alone time."

Santiago caught up to Xavi and glowered at him. "Ha-ha. Just go; it won't happen again."

They continued on, this time with Santiago sticking close. He couldn't help but wonder what the tourists would think as they swirled through the market as it closed if they knew the future king of Spain was brushing by them, carrying a sack of potatoes over his shoulder and a cardboard tray full of leftover fruits and vegetables.

Santiago had grown up in the halls of the royal palace.

He was born at the Palacio Real in Madrid. Technically, on the grounds of the king's private residence, La Zarzuela, with the assistance of one of the palace doctors. The residence was located on the outskirts of Madrid, and the king's own doctor had been called in to help with the birth. At the time, Santiago's mother, Sara, was the palace social coordinator, and his father, Carlos, was the head of the Guardia Real, the branch of Spain's military charged with keeping the king safe.

As a child, Santiago roamed freely through the magnificent Palacio Real, whose architecture had been inspired by the Louvre in Paris, with its central courtyard and its own parade grounds. With over three thousand rooms, the palace was as opulent as it was enormous, and whenever

Santiago could sneak away from the schoolteachers who educated the children of the staff, he made it his mission to discover every single nook and cranny. He snuck into the throne hall with its beautiful frescoes on the ceiling and the gigantic fifteenth-century chair where the king would sit for formal events and to conduct official business. He ran up and down the more than seventy steps of the palace's grand staircase, with its gold filigree garlands that ringed the ceiling, the painted angels looking down on its guests, its round, crystal, windows and the red royal crest of the monarchy that greeted people when they reached the top. But Santiago's favorite room might have been the royal chapel because of its display of violins crafted by the most famous violin maker in history, Antonio Stradivari. People came from all over to visit Madrid's magnificent palace, and Santiago got to treat it as his own personal playground.

As much as Santiago loved the grandeur of the Palacio Real, he loved the understated private residence, La Zarzuela, even more—well, understated in comparison. He'd often gone there while his father was working because King Alfonso was that kind of man. He understood that his staff and his guards were expected to go above and beyond for the crown, so he went above and beyond to reward them for this sacrifice, making sure their children could be nearby in the process. La Zarzuela had been the home to the king and queen of Spain since the early 1600s. Though smaller, it was still opulent, with carefully manicured gardens, a rose-colored-brick facade, and a sweeping fountain that stretched across the entirety of its front entrance like a waterfall.

But most of all, Santiago had grown to love Alfonso himself. He loved the king as though he were his own father.

His real father, Carlos, died defending Alfonso during an assassination attempt on his life just three years into Alfonso's reign. Santiago was only ten at the time. The attempt on the king was well known, but so were the heroic acts of Santiago's father, who had thrown himself in front of Alfonso and taken the six bullets meant for the king's body. At the funeral, Santiago remembered accepting on his father's behalf the royal saber given to any member of the guard who dies defending the crown, from the king's own hands.

"Your father paid the ultimate price for me." The king leaned down so he was eye level with Santiago. He looked pained for the young boy. "That sacrifice is not easily forgotten. I personally will make sure you are taken care of in this life. This is a promise, young man. I will always be your ally."

Santiago remembered hearing these words from the king on that awful day and feeling the sincerity that went along within them, but he hadn't understood what they meant until he lost his mother, too, to breast cancer.

It was then that the king began to take an active interest in Santiago—in his education, his future, even his health. The king started a tradition with the young boy whose parents had given their time and one of whom had given his life to the crown. Once a month, he invited Santiago for breakfast at La Zarzuela, just the two of them. It was also the king who encouraged Santiago to train to enter the Guardia Real like his father before him. The king's generosity to this young orphaned commoner made some sense—his parents had been devoted to him, and Alfonso never married and had no children of his own.

Or none that he'd known about until very recently.

As far as Spain was concerned, Alfonso was still the most eligible bachelor in all the nation. Soon they would find out there was a second-most-eligible bachelor, the king's newly discovered son, the Principe de Asturias, the official title of the heir to the Spanish throne.

It was because of Santiago's close relationship with the king that he was chosen to be Xavi's guard. Not long after Alfonso found out about Xavi's existence, he called Santiago in for a private audience in the chamber adjoining the king's formal office. Santiago arrived dressed in the traditional blue and red uniform of guard trainees, his black leather boots clomping heavily against the floor. When he entered the room, Alfonso was drinking his morning café con leche.

"I found out I have a son," the king blurted.

Santiago felt his jaw drop. Shock rushed through him like a river of ice, followed by a barrage of burning questions he dared not ask.

The king took a gulp of his sugary, milky coffee and looked up. The king's gaze was heavy upon him. "At the end of this summer, his existence will be announced. My son will need protection, but he will also need a friend. Accepting this new life as a royal will be very difficult and lonely. It's a great change for someone to transition into such a public life at age eighteen. This is where you come in, Santi. You are to become that friend and guard." The king suddenly seemed tired. "Will you do this for me?"

Santiago nodded. Like his father before him, he would do anything for the king, so of course it followed he would do anything for the king's son. It was an honor that the king had asked.

Santiago's subsequent conversation with Francisco Hernández, the jefe of the Guardia Real, was what caused him to worry. Francisco had been a friend to Santiago's father and had always been kind to Carlos's son. But he also had a reputation for being exacting in all the ways and places the king was known to be soft. It was Francisco's job to protect the crown, after all. Still, Santiago had been in Francisco's office many times as a child, playing on the floor as he waited for his father to return from some assignment and take him home to their residence at La Zarzuela, and he regarded the man like an uncle.

After a few pleasantries, Francisco got straight to the point. "I need you to ensure that by the time we announce Xavier Bas's existence to the public, he will be ready. On *every* level," he clarified. "You know what that means, yes?"

Once again, Santiago nodded. He understood very well what Francisco meant. By the time of the announcement, Xavi needed to arrive at the palace without any unwanted baggage in tow. No scandalous attachments, his slate wiped clean and ready to begin his new life. As Santiago walked away from Francisco and down the familiar halls of the royal residence with their portraits of former monarchs, princes and princesses and queens and kings, Santiago promised himself he would not let either of these important men down—not Francisco and certainly not the king—no matter what this would require of him.

What Santiago couldn't have known that day was that his own heart might be in the mix.

"Are you ever going to tell me the plan for this afternoon and evening?" Santiago asked Xavi as they rushed down Carrer de Ferran, one of the main streets in El Gótico. It took them through the plaza in front of Barcelona's city hall and spilled them out onto one of the wider streets in the old medieval neighborhood, lined with bars and shops and packed with tourists. "We've been over this. You have to apprise me of all attendees, all locations."

Xavi picked up his pace. "I'm not the prince yet, so no, I don't."

Santiago trotted to keep up. "Chaval, you must get used to these procedures. And yes, you are the prince. You have been since you were born, even if you didn't know it. It's who you are."

"Chaval," Xavi said back to him, rather mockingly. "You need to relax while you can. No one else knows who I am, so it's not like you have to be so worried."

In truth, Santiago was pressing Xavi about their evening for reasons other than royal concerns. He half hoped the only person on their agenda was Diego, despite how hard he tried to deny this to himself. Santiago needed to gain control of his feelings. Xavi was headed into what would be the greatest transition of his life and the life of the monarchy. Santiago owed it to his country and especially to the king to prepare Xavi for what lay ahead.

Xavi turned left under the archways that marked the entrance to Barcelona's Plaça Reial, with its palm trees and birds shrieking high up in the branches. Today it was alive with people enjoying their Saturday afternoon, eating long lunches at the many restaurants that ringed the square, their tables shaded by the porticoes above the outdoor halls. But Xavi headed straight to the fountain at the center of the plaza. He crossed his arms and leaned against the marble lip of it casually. The sound of the water falling into the pool below was soothing in the heat.

Santiago copied Xavi's stance.

The two young men enjoyed a moment of peace.

Soon Xavi would not be able to do things like walk this city anonymously and meet his friends wherever he felt like it. Santiago felt a pang of sadness for the future prince and the many changes he faced. A life where his friends would need appointments, extensive vetting, and special escorts, all so they could see Xavi for a cup of coffee that would likely occur in private quarters. No more meeting up by public fountains surrounded by tourists and Catalans alike.

Xavi raised his arm in a wave, trying to catch his friend's attention from across the plaza. "Hey! Vale," he called, using Diego's middle name.

Diego's eyes lit up in recognition, and Xavi's closest friend since childhood made his way to where they waited for him.

Vale, the nickname Diego's friends occasionally used in greeting, was short for Valentino. As in Valentine, the saint of love and lovers.

*Of course his middle name is Valentino*, Santiago had thought on the day he and Diego met.

Something rippled across Santiago's skin as he watched Diego approach, heat prickling across his body. The muscles in his back and arms tightened under his shirt. Santiago shifted from one foot to the other, tugging at his collar.

Diego arrived and hugged Xavi, the typical greeting for men in Spain, then reached for Santiago and gave him a hug as well. "Good to see you again," Diego said, his arms around Santiago, hands clapping Santiago on the back.

A thrill shot through Santiago, making him nearly dizzy. He cleared his throat. "Good to see you too." As Santiago blinked at the shorter, handsome young man, so much swirled within his chest. Amid everything else there was the certainty, however painful and inappropriate, that Santiago had it bad for Xavi's best friend.

# Four

"Abuela, let me get that for you!"

Stefi was scandalized. She'd returned to her grandmother's apartment building in El Gótico to find the woman dragging a heavy wheeled cart stuffed to the brim with groceries. One slow step at a time, her abuela was winding up the staircase. All four flights. Abuela's white-gray hair was slipping from its bun from the effort.

"Cariño, I've been doing this my whole life," Silvia said. Even so, she moved aside so Stefi could take over. Silvia put a hand to her chest as she tried to catch her breath.

The stairwell was narrow, the steps made of stone so old they'd started to crumble. Like so many places in El Gótico, with its labyrinth of medieval stone streets, Silvia's building dated back to the fourteenth century. Over decades, it had been updated and redone and rewired and updated and redone again to allow its residents to live contemporary lives inside homes centuries older than the United States, to do things like get Wi-Fi so they could have internet and watch TV series on Netflix. But the foundations of Silvia's building were even older than the structure. As with many places in Barcelona's medieval heart, there was a large, square glass panel built into the floor of abuela's lobby so visitors could see down into the Roman ruins. Sometimes Stefi went and stood at the center of the glass, marveling at what was literally ancient history beneath her feet. One time,

Stefi got down on her hands and knees to get a closer look at the rough-cut rocks that formed the remains of an oven and passageways through a forgotten city. The Roman walls that had surrounded Barcelona when it was founded in the first century BCE and called Barcino were only a block away from abuela's building.

"This is so heavy," Stefi exclaimed to Silvia, yanking the handle of the grocery cart upward, eventually getting the hang of it; the trio of wheels were designed to go up steps just like these. Great big artichokes sat atop the canvas bag. Stefi's mouth watered as she eyed them. Artichokes were her favorite, and the way Silvia prepared them was especially delicious.

The older woman and the younger one continued slowly up the many flights of steps. Silvia followed her granddaughter's progress until they reached the landing on the fourth floor, the ático where Silvia had lived since she was born. As with the Roman ruins in their basements, Barcelona's buildings were full of áticos, the name for the topmost apartment, usually one that boasted a terrace. Some áticos were tiny, barely more than a studio attached to an outdoor space. But Silvia was lucky—her family's ático was two stories of rooms, the top floor small but with a sweeping terrace surrounding it. The terra-cotta brick of its floors undulated in waves, having warped across the decades, but the family kept their furniture from wobbling with small wedges of wood and whatever else they could find and enjoyed the place all the same. The view of the city was breathtaking. The apartment was big enough for Stefi and her parents to live there with abuela for the summer while they decided what the future held for them. It was lucky Silvia hadn't sold the place back when so many local families were moving to the outskirts of the city. Lately, vacation rentals had the wealthy buying out older residents. Everyone wanted to make money off the gullible tourists who came for sun and sea and sangría, even though no local would ever drink sangría.

"I was thinking I'd make the artichokes for our lunch today, cariño," Silvia said when Stefi rolled the cart over the threshold of the apartment, out of breath herself. Abuela had on the typical sleeveless, loose housedress that so many women wore for their shopping in the city, this one a pale green. Abuela had lots of them, a different color for each day.

Even though Stefi was still full from the tortilla she'd eaten and a bit floaty thinking about the boy whose name she now knew was Xavi, she would never say no to her grandmother's cooking. "I think that sounds like a great idea, abuela." Stefi gestured toward the cart of groceries. "How do you do this on your own?"

Silvia gave Stefi a warm smile and flexed her biceps. "Your grandmother is a strong lady."

This made Stefi laugh, and the laughter felt good. After she left the market, Stefi had caved and done what she promised herself she wouldn't do all summer: She went on her former best friend's Instagram. The second she did, her heart plunged and crash-landed on the hard cold stone of the ruins below the streets, wounding her all over again. Her heart had been throbbing, hurt, ever since. Amber had posted a very intimate shot of Jason: He was lying in bed, shirtless, the sheets rumpled around him, looking at the person with the camera with what could only be described as *smoldering eyes*—that's how Stefi's romance novels would describe them, for sure. The shock Stefi felt when she'd seen the photo still hadn't worn off. The part about Amber and Jason sleeping together she'd already figured. But didn't Amber know better than to post a photo that private? And worse, didn't she worry at all that Stefi might see it and be upset? When had Amber become so heartless?

Silvia was watching her granddaughter. "¿Cariño?"

Stefi snapped out of the memory. Abuela was waiting on her. "Sorry!"

Silvia directed Stefi to bring the grocery cart into the kitchen. She rolled it through the entryway of the ático and into the living room, with its many sets of French doors that welcomed the air and sent cheerful sunlight streaming everywhere, all over Silvia's old, upholstered couch with its floral fabric and the wooden chairs that had been Silvia's mother's before her. But one of the walls was painted a bright Mediterranean blue, and big pink peonies were bursting from a sunshine-yellow vase on the kitchen table. Silvia usually left the French doors open, and today was no different. As Stefi moved across this room, her heart seemed to peel itself off the ground and float back upward into her chest. At the end of the living room was abuela's kitchen with its enormous cutting-board island that faced all those wonderful French doors. Stefi blinked as her heart settled again behind her rib cage, still wounded but trying to heal. She was feeling better already. All it took was a few flights of stairs with abuela and the thought of artichokes in her near future. Well, and maybe another romantic fantasy about what she and the Viking boy could do if Stefi got him alone for a few hours. Take that, she imagined saying to Amber.

Abuela fussed with the flowers on the table; she plucked one peony from the vase and placed it in a different spot where it had more room. Stefi wheeled the cart to the cabinets and the fridge and began to unpack it.

The artichokes went straight onto the cutting board so Silvia could prep them, and most of the rest went into the colorful bowls on the countertop of the island. Stefi lit up when she saw all the beautiful fruit. She knew Silvia bought it especially for Stefi. Her abuela often complained that Stefi's legs were too skinny and that she needed more meat on her bones. Silvia was never happier than when she was feeding people, especially Stefi. Stefi took after her grandmother in this way, since she was never happier than when she was baking for people she cared about.

Stefi inhaled sharply at this thought as she remembered all the cakes and cookies she'd made for Jason and Amber, the two most important people in her life outside her family. All that effort to show them how much she cared. But then Stefi let the breeze flowing through the apartment from all the open doors sweep these painful thoughts away.

Silvia finished fussing with the flowers and joined Stefi on the other side of the island. She headed straight to the sink. "Would you like a little coffee as a pick-me-up?" She was already pouring filtered water from a big bottle on the counter into an Italian espresso maker. Barcelona's water could be used for cooking but not drinking.

"I'd love some," Stefi said.

Silvia fitted the filter into the base, packed it with coffee grounds, and set it on the stovetop to heat. Then abuela took down an enormous pot from the cabinet, the one she used to make artichokes, and filled it with water. She set it on a burner to heat alongside the coffee maker.

Meanwhile, Stefi piled yellow and orange and deep purple plums of all sizes, some as small as cherries, into a big green bowl. Then she piled yellow, white, and doughnut peaches into another big bowl that was bright red. And finally she piled tomatoes—heirloom, Roma, grape, tiny ones on the vine—into a big oval blue bowl. The kitchen counter had become a riot of color, reminding Stefi of La Boqueria.

The sound of coffee percolating on the stove mingled with the noise coming in from the streets outside as Stefi and Silvia moved around each other in the kitchen. Lastly, Stefi dug way down into the bottom of the grocery cart and came up with the fish heads. Silvia used them to make the stock for paella. Stefi covered her nose with one hand and with the other held the bag of fish heads as far away from her body as she could toward Silvia.

Silvia saw Stefi's grimace and laughed. She plucked the bag from Stefi's hands without wincing and peered inside. "You can make all the faces you want, but you know those fish heads are the key to any good paella." Silvia dug even farther down in the grocery cart and pulled out the very last bag that remained, which was full of fish guts. She dangled the bag in front of Stefi for her granddaughter's inspection. "These too," Silvia said with a grin, then hid all of it away in the fridge. "You need to get used to dealing with them."

Stefi shuddered. "I know, I know."

There were reasons Stefi wanted to be a pastry chef and not another kind of chef. The kind of chef that handled fish guts, for example. But when Stefi arrived in Barcelona ten days ago, she'd told her grandmother she wanted to learn to make paella. She was feeling a little less sure now, given all the stuff that went into the pot. It was a better-not-to-know-how-they-made-the-sausage kind of thing.

Now that they'd finished unpacking the food, Stefi couldn't resist plucking a peach from the bowl on the counter. She brought it to the sink to wash it and dry it with one of the dish towels, careful not to break the skin. "Where's Mom and Dad, do you know?"

Silvia was already preparing the artichokes, carefully slicing off the pointy tops and the stems. "Your parents went on a picnic to Montjuic."

Stefi bit into the peach, so juicy she needed to eat it over the sink. She swallowed the sweet flesh and nearly groaned because it was that delicious. "Of course they did."

Stefi's parents, Ana and James, were still disgustingly romantic. They were always going on dates and walking around the city holding hands. This was exactly why Stefi hadn't told her parents what had happened before the family left for Barcelona. She particularly didn't want Ana to know, although Stefi usually told her everything. Stefi hadn't breathed a word about how she'd walked in on Jason kissing Amber a few days before she and her family got on a plane to come here. She'd refrained from telling her mom she hadn't spoken to either Jason or Amber in two whole weeks, something that would have been unthinkable until recently.

Initially, Stefi had resisted this family trip to Barcelona for the summer before her senior year. She didn't want to miss all the parties, all the going to the beach, all the hanging out with friends before their last year of high school began. To be totally honest, she'd worried that if she went away for the summer, when she got back—if her family decided to come back, that is—Jason and she would break up. He'd been hinting to Stefi that he wasn't thrilled about the idea of being long-distance for nearly three whole months.

But now, when Stefi thought about the magnitude of his betrayal and Amber's too, she felt only shame. Humiliation flooded Stefi's face and ran across all the skin of her body. Stefi was still too embarrassed and hurt by the whole debacle to confess to her mother why their family trip across the Atlantic suddenly couldn't come soon enough. Ana kept trying to pry out of her daughter what was wrong, but Stefi kept telling Ana everything was fine, that her mother was imagining things, that Stefi had simply discovered an urgent desire to practice her Spanish and better her catalán and to take pastry-making classes.

Stefi's pastry class would finally start this Tuesday.

People came to Barcelona from all over to enroll at Hofmann's, the famous culinary institute. Stefi had always wanted to learn to make croissants and see if she had what it took to be a real pastry chef, not just an amateur, and this summer, she was determined to find out.

Ana wasn't stupid, though. She kept asking Stefi if Amber was going to visit so the two girls could have some time together in Barcelona. Her mother had also wondered why Stefi and Amber weren't texting constantly as usual and why Stefi wasn't texting Jason either and also why in the world Stefi kept leaving her phone at home when she went out to explore the city. Amber had been a fixture in their family's house ever since the two girls became friends in kindergarten, and more recently, Jason was constantly there too.

Stefi threw the pit of the peach into the trash can under the kitchen sink as these awful memories moved through her. She washed her sticky hands and face.

Silvia turned off the gas under the coffee maker and finished chopping the garlic that would go into the already simmering artichoke pot. She tipped in the garlic from the cutting board and plopped the heavy artichokes, one by one, into the garlicky water.

"Cariño, what's going on in that brain of yours?" Silvia asked as she pulled down two small café con leche cups from one of the kitchen shelves to prepare their coffees. First, she poured in the espresso, then she filled the rest of the cup with milk. Some people steamed the milk first, but often during summer, the milk was poured in cold. This was as close as you'd get to iced coffee in Barcelona unless you found a Starbucks. Silvia pushed one of the cafés con leche across the counter to her granddaughter and waited for Stefi to answer her question.

Stefi dumped a spoonful of sugar into her cup from the nearby bowl and stirred. "Oh, nothing," she said overly cheerfully.

Her grandmother eyed her but apparently decided to let it go. "Would you get down the frying pan for me? The one above the fridge?"

"Of course, abuela."

Stefi grabbed a chair, dragged it over to the fridge, and climbed up to retrieve the heavy pan in which Silvia would fry the artichokes after they'd cooked in the water long enough to soften. After placing it gently on the countertop, she looked up.

Abuela was watching her with that worried look. "Cariño, you can tell me anything. I know something is going on. Ever since you arrived, you haven't been yourself."

Stefi opened her mouth, then closed it.

Could she really tell her grandmother *anything*? Even about that terrible day when she'd gone over to Amber's house to ask if she could borrow one of Amber's suitcases? Stefi had used her own set of keys to let herself in, the ones she'd had since middle school because that was the kind of friendship she and Amber shared—the kind where they could enter each other's houses like they were family. On Stefi's way up to the second floor and Amber's room, she kept yelling her friend's name and rambling about the suitcase she wanted to borrow. Stefi did knock on the door before she opened it. She knocked and she banged on it, but as usual, Amber's music was playing loudly. Too loudly for Amber to hear someone asking to enter. When Amber didn't answer, Stefi pushed open the door like she had a million other times when Amber's music was on and Amber hadn't heard Stefi's knocking.

"Hey, so, I need to ask you a favor," Stefi said as the door swung wide. But then she froze, her words dying mid-sentence.

Amber and Jason were lying on the bed where Stefi had slept countless times, so lost in kissing each other they had no idea that Stefi was standing there watching. After Stefi recovered enough to slam the door, cutting off the awful vision of her best friend and boyfriend together, she turned and ran. Back through the hall and down the stairs and out the front door and on to her own home and up to her own room to shut herself inside it, her heart pounding mercilessly.

A tear ran down Stefi's cheek, and she turned away from abuela.

*Ugh, ugh, ugh*. The hurt reared again in Stefi's body, searing her insides. She gulped down more of the coffee, which didn't do anything to cool it. But then Stefi reminded herself of the decision she'd made ten days ago as the plane was speeding down the runway and then lifting into the air on the way to Barcelona, and the sharpness of the pain subsided a little.

This summer, in Barcelona, Stefi was going to reinvent herself. Stefi was going to press the reset button on everything. She was going to try new things, things that no one in her life at home would expect her to try. She was going to defy expectations, even the ones she had for herself. She was going to take risks and see what happened, come what may. She was not going to be shy about anything, not about what she wanted, not about what she didn't want, not with her outfits or even her hairstyle. She was going to *live*. Over the next few months, Stefi was determined to find her voice and use it as loudly as she felt like. She knew it still existed deep down inside of her, but it had been muted for years in favor of those other, ever-dominant voices in her life—Amber's and Jason's.

Stefi felt a finger brushing across her cheek.

Abuela, tiny and wrinkled and fierce as ever, was wiping away the tears running down her granddaughter's cheeks and staring into Stefi's eyes with a fiery protectiveness and love. "Cariño, you are crying." She handed Stefi a tissue. "Whenever you are ready to talk, your grandmother is here to listen."

Stefi nodded. "I know."

Silvia pointed at the kitchen table. "You go and sit and let your abuelita get you something even better than these coffees while these artichokes finish cooking."

Stefi watched as Silvia reached up into another of her kitchen cabinets and pulled down two of her pretty glasses. She dropped a big round cube of ice into each one—it landed with a satisfying *clink*—then filled each glass with a good few inches of vermut. She plunked a slice of orange into the sweet, fortified wine, followed by an olive speared on a toothpick, and joined Stefi at the kitchen table.

"It's vermut hour anyway, cariño."

"Okay, abuela."

Silvia held her glass in the air. "Salud."

Stefi did the same. "Salud."

The older woman and the younger one clinked their glasses.

"Now, tell me what is wrong," Silvia demanded.

Stefi wiped her face again. She was about to burst out with everything when she remembered something else and her heart lifted. Just a little, but she could feel it. "How about I tell you something that is right instead?"

Silvia studied her granddaughter as though trying to decide whether to allow Stefi to continue to avoid talking about what was bothering her. But then she seemed to make up her mind. "Tell me the right thing, yes."

"I kind of met a boy in the market today."

Abuela perked up. She smiled. "Kind of?"

Stefi's heart swelled a little. She nodded. "And he's kind of hot."

Abuela sighed, then laughed. "You and your kind of. Either you met him or you didn't and either he's hot or he's not, cariño."

Stefi admired the deep red color of the liquid in her glass, the way it shone like rubies. She used the toothpick to swirl the ice. "Okay, fine," she said. "I did meet him and he is hot, abuela."

"Tell me everything," Silvia said.

As they sipped their vermuts, Stefi obeyed her grandmother and, as usual, soon felt better for it.

# Five

"Go, go, go, go, yeah!"

Xavi and Diego leaped up from their chairs, both of them with their arms high and fists waving in victory. The two friends hugged and clapped each other hard on the back. Then they turned to their neighbors at nearby tables and hugged them too. The night was cool, the bars were full, and all over the city, there was celebration.

Barcelona had just scored their first gol of the night against Madrid.

Xavi looked at Santiago, who was decidedly not celebrating. In fact, Santiago was scowling, his arms crossed over his chest. Or maybe he was pouting. "Oh, pobrecito," Xavi mocked, grinning like he had made the remarkable goal himself. "Madrid is losing and you're oh so sad? I'm very sorry, dear cousin."

Santiago's gaze drifted up to meet Xavi's as though he were not at all traumatized by the tip in the score away from Madrid and toward Barcelona. "I'm not worried even a little," he said. "I know who will be celebrating at the end of this night and it will not be you and Diego."

Diego placed a firm hand on Santiago's shoulder, and Santiago's scowl faltered. "Let me make it up to you, chaval. How about I buy you the next beer as a consolation prize? I know that total domination of your team is hard to watch."

Xavi pulled some monedas from his pocket and plunked them into Diego's palm. "Nah, let me cover this round, especially if you're willing to go and get the beers for us."

Diego sauntered off, and Santiago's eyes followed him. Then: "Sit down already. The gol is over," Santiago said to Xavi.

But everyone around them was still gloating; the sound of people *Cheers*-ing and clinking glasses bubbled along the street.

Xavi dropped into his seat again. "Only because I don't want you to start crying." He leaned back, stretched out his legs, and put his hands behind his head obnoxiously, still unable to wipe the grin from his lips.

Santiago rolled his eyes and shook his head at Xavi. "You're ridiculous."

"Ah, I just love a good Clásico." Whenever Futbol Club Barcelona and Real Madrid played each other, the game was referred to as El Clásico because they were Spain's biggest rivals.

Xavi looked around at his fellow Barça fans, sheer joy flowing through his body and everyone else's. As the game continued, people snacked on spicy patatas bravas and other popular game-night tapas. The streets were teeming with fans; they packed the bars and restaurants and overflowed onto sidewalks. Xavi never loved his city more than when everyone came together to watch Barça play. This place came alive on game nights with an infectious, irrepressible energy and camaraderie that Xavi had loved since he was a small boy. Barcelona's neighborhoods were full of sidewalk terraces, so in many of the bars and restaurants, staff had rigged up giant outdoor televisions, unfurling enormous screens on which to watch their beloved soccer team.

Santiago rested his head on his hand, elbow on the table, looking dejected.

"I think you're the only person at this bar who's unhappy," Xavi observed. He glanced inside through the windows but couldn't see Diego in the crowd. He must still be in line trying to get their beers.

The crowd yelled a collective "Oh!" as Barça almost made another gol, but the ball went slightly wide of the net.

Santiago looked relieved that his beloved Madrid narrowly escaped getting further behind in the game. Then he turned to Xavi and a small grin appeared on his face. "You know you're going to have to learn to root for Madrid."

Xavi stared at Santiago as if he had just suggested Xavi become an assassin because there was money to be made in murder for hire. For Santiago to suggest Xavi root for Madrid when he was a lifelong Barça fan amounted to sacrilege.

"No way," Xavi said, his voice choked with passion. "Never. There are some things that simply cannot be done no matter who I am."

Santiago was clearly enjoying this turn in the conversation and enjoying torturing Xavi with this so-called requirement of his heritage. "You do realize the full name of the team you loathe so completely is Real Madrid."

Real as in "royal." The team was literally named Royal Madrid.

Xavi rolled his eyes in an exaggerated manner.

But Santiago wasn't finished. "As in, when Madrid plays El Clásico at home, the king always sits in the royal box for the game. It's part of the job. It will soon be part of yours."

Yes, Xavi knew this. Of course he knew this. But that didn't mean he was going to accept it. Or comply with it. "I don't care if they rename the team Prince Xavi Madrid—I will never in my life occupy that royal box. Unless I'm allowed to root for Barça while I'm in it."

The two boys glanced up and saw Diego making his way through the crowd.

"Well, you will come around," Santiago told him. "The monarchy requires it."

Xavi stared at Santiago hard. Hearing his own name associated with words like *prince* and *monarchy* seemed even more impossible than him becoming a Madrid fan by the end of summer. Even after he'd had nearly six months to get used to the idea that he was the prince of Spain, the notion was still so outlandish as not to be true. But then a knowing grin returned to Xavi's face before Diego arrived with their celebratory beers—well, celebratory for two of them, not for Santiago. "Then the monarchy is going to have to change, isn't it?" Xavi said.

Xavi becoming a prince had happened like this:

Marta, Xavi's mother, went to college in the United States on a full scholarship. She'd randomly ended up at the same university where Alfonso, who was only the prince of Spain at the time and not yet King Alfonso XIV, was going to graduate school. One night, they met at a bar. Before Marta realized who she was talking to—she'd never followed the tabloid stories about the Spanish royal family, so she hadn't recognized the prince—she told Alfonso how much she loathed his home city, Madrid. This started a fiery conversation between Marta and Alfonso about which city was better, Barcelona or Madrid. In the middle of that ever more heated discussion, Marta's friend tugged on her sleeve and whispered, "You realize you're talking to Prince Alfonso, right?"

At which point, Marta's eyes grew wide—but not with embarrassment. She put her hands on her hips and turned her laser-sharp blue-eyed gaze up at the very tall man before her in the bar. "Are you seriously the prince? How can you live with yourself? The monarchy is full of arrogant people who drain money from the country's coffers and who don't let the catalán people live in peace!"

Only after Alfonso had recovered from being talked to like this by the tiny, stunning woman before him was he able to find the words he was searching for, which were these: "I'm sorry you feel that way. Marta, is it?

Perhaps you'd like to discuss your opinions further over dinner, just the two of us?"

Marta was not easily unsettled, but she did not expect the response from the prince to take the form of an invitation to go out on a date. "Well, yes, I would very much like to do that!" she said with as much fire as before.

Their first date went well.

One date led to another and then another. Soon after, Alfonso and Marta were in love. But they kept their romance a secret.

There were many reasons to hide their relationship. One was so the paparazzi wouldn't follow Marta around and try to dig up dirt on her life and her past and so Alfonso could have a girlfriend in peace. But another was that Marta came from a Catalán independista family, and Alfonso was a madrileño not only by birth but as part of the royal line. The two young lovers made for a scandalous pair, and they knew this. Catalunya was always trying to break away from the rest of Spain, and Marta's parents were diehard separatists, politically speaking. Regardless of whether Alfonso and Marta loved each other, they were never going to be able to stay together in the long term. Or at least, this was what they believed. The monarchy wouldn't tolerate it, and there was no way the rest of Spain would be able to wrap its mind around a catalán princess in the heart of Madrid and the royal palace. Plus, Marta's family would never allow their daughter to live among the enemy, so to speak.

But when it came time for Alfonso to return to the palace and resume his official duties, the couple found they did not want to break up. They talked in circles about all the ways they could defy expectations and remain together, and Marta began to believe that the love between them might win over what both had agreed were outdated constraints on the royal family's dating pool.

Then one morning after Marta returned home to Barcelona, she received a letter from Alfonso—the same letter that Xavi would find and read eighteen years later when he was going through his mother's desk. In it, Alfonso wrote of the tragedies of star-crossed love, but mostly, he talked of duty, the responsibilities of the crown, and the need to preserve the royal line. *His* duty, *his* responsibilities, *his* need.

By the letter's close, Alfonso ended their romance, and on a very permanent level.

He begged Marta never to contact him again and gave her all the excuses—it would be too difficult because they loved each other too much, they could never manage to be friends, the whole affair was doomed from the beginning, et cetera, et cetera.

But the letter was devastatingly clear: they were over.

Marta wept and cried and cried and wept. She was stunned, she was inconsolable, she was heartbroken. But she was also enraged. She felt humiliated and put in her place by this prince and his duty to the monarchy over her. Alfonso had reminded Marta she was a commoner and therefore unworthy of being with someone so far above her station. Worse still, Alfonso told her this in such a cowardly way, by letter; he was unwilling to face her and say all of it in person.

Marta decided that if Alfonso never wanted to hear from her again, she would give him exactly what he wished. Marta dried her tears, swallowed her sobs, held her head up high, and moved forward without a backward glance at the Spanish prince, this boy who was her first love.

Then, shortly after Marta received Alfonso's letter, she discovered she was pregnant. She had the baby and never told a soul who the father was, not even her own parents. Certainly not Alfonso. Not after that crushing letter. Besides, Alfonso's father suddenly became ill, and the whole country was holding its breath—within months, a new king would be crowned, and that king would be Alfonso. Now Marta could never tell Alfonso they were going to have a son together—it was awful enough to bear his rejection of her alone, but she refused to bear his rejection of both her *and* their baby.

Before Alfonso took the throne, he was supposed to get married—to a woman of his family's choosing. With Alfonso's father in the hospital, his mother and everyone else at the palace hurried to find him a suitable match. Alfonso did, in fact, get engaged to someone perfectly fit to eventually become the queen of Spain. She was beautiful, she had the right kind of pedigree, and she came with a champion social-climbing family. But the wedding was not to be. The day before the ceremony, Alfonso got on a plane to the Azores. He refused to return until his family and the rest of the royal advisers stopped trying to force him into a marriage he didn't want. Within months, his father passed away, and Alfonso took the throne—alone. He was the first bachelor king in Spanish royal history. And a bachelor he would remain.

When Marta learned that Alfonso had stood up his royal bride, she'd felt a moment of hope. There were even times when she fantasized he might show up in Barcelona at her home or at the tapas counter she eventually opened all on her own at La Boqueria, ready with a grand gesture of apology and love. It wasn't as though the king didn't know how to find Marta. But Marta never heard from Alfonso again.

Time passed and Alfonso never married, which also meant he never had any children.

Except that he did—he just didn't know this. His only son was born a mere month after he became king.

One day, more than seventeen years later, King Alfonso agreed to give an extensive sit-down interview to the most famous television journalist in all of Spain, María Moreno. This was not normal for the king. But scandal had been swirling around the royal family—Alfonso's younger siblings were fighting over the line of succession. They all wanted the throne to go to one of their children.

The day of the king's interview was epic.

Everyone in Spain planned to watch the live interview, even in Catalunya. The thing was, over the years, Alfonso had won the country's sympathy. He'd turned out to be the most popular king in all of Spain's royal history, known for his kindness, his generosity, his openness to listening to even the most independent of the independistas. What's more, Alfonso was still the country's most eligible bachelor. Entire series of romance novels were dedicated to the fantasy of King Alfonso finally meeting the woman of his dreams, falling in love, getting married, and making this woman his queen. Television producers even approached Alfonso and tried to convince him that they could help the king find love, that they would work tirelessly to locate the most eligible women the world over and bring them together so he could choose whomever he liked the best—if only they could televise the process. People tried to set Alfonso up, and the tabloids went out of their way to publish every single photo they could obtain of Alfonso standing in the same frame as another woman—any woman—in order to speculate whether perhaps she might be *the one*. To no avail.

So by the day of the interview, Alfonso was one of the most popular men in Spain.

Even Xavi planned to watch.

At the apartment where he lived with his mother, he made snacks and turned on the TV in the living room. But the moment he sat down with his glass of red wine and a big bowl of chips and olives, Marta marched up, grabbed the remote, and turned off the TV.

"Hey!" Xavi protested.

Marta seemed to breathe fire. "We're not going to watch that garbage."

Xavi rose from the couch and slipped the remote from his mother's hand before she could stop him. "I've been looking forward to that garbage!" He stretched out his arm and promptly turned the TV back on. The screen came to life and a voice announced the imminent start of the interview "the whole country has been waiting for!"

"Turn it *off*," Marta said, glaring at her son.

Xavi could see something pleading in his mother's eyes behind the anger. "What is your problem, mamá?" he asked softly.

"What is *yours?*" she shot back, her volume rising. "When have you ever cared about the monarchy?"

"Everyone I know is watching; it's no big deal!"

Marta just shook her head. She closed her eyes a moment, slowing down her breathing. Then she opened them again. "Fine, watch whatever you want," she said, and stormed out of the room and into the kitchen.

So Xavi did.

The familiar song announcing the start of the famous journalist's program filled the room, and Marta's banging around in the kitchen grew louder. It sounded to Xavi like she was rearranging the pots and pans. And maybe all the contents of the cabinets. Doors opened and slammed shut. The faucet went on and off. Metal clanged against the countertop. Xavi wondered what had gotten into his mother. But then Alfonso appeared on the screen, and Xavi made himself comfortable on the couch; he put his feet up on the coffee table, munched his chips, and sipped his wine. Marta was right—it wasn't like Xavi really cared about the monarchy, it was just that, like everyone else, he held a special place in his heart for Alfonso. The guy wasn't so bad.

*You know, you look just like the king.*

People had been saying this to Xavi his entire life.

*You could be the king's son.*

This was another popular comment.

Xavi would always shrug and laugh and make a joke about the royal blood in his veins. But in truth, it did create a sort of strange affinity in Xavi for Alfonso.

Soon the king and María Moreno appeared on the screen, Alfonso in an understated yet elegant gray suit, María with her hair pulled away from her face and wearing a simple blue dress. The two sat across from each other in a carefully lit room in the royal residence.

"Well, here we are," María said to begin the conversation.

"Yes, welcome to my home," Alfonso returned, ever polite.

The interview started simply, with questions about Alfonso's recent travels to Germany to meet with the chancellor, followed by inquiries about the upcoming vacation Alfonso planned for himself and his elderly mother, Lola, in Menorca—the king's well-known love for his mother adding yet another point ratcheting up his popularity. But soon the talk turned to succession gossip and the fact that Alfonso could have avoided these infighting problems if he'd found himself a queen and provided the country with at least one heir and hopefully a spare.

The banging in the kitchen came to an abrupt halt.

Xavi glanced toward the doorway but Marta was nowhere to be seen, so he turned his attention back to the screen.

This was the point in the interview when María prodded Alfonso about his love life. His *nonexistent* love life, which was the cause of so much speculation—and adulation as well.

"Your Majesty, why didn't you ever marry?" María leaned forward slightly in her chair. "Were you never in love?"

There was a long, dramatic silence—matched by the silence that fell across the apartment Xavi shared with his mother.

"I was in love," Alfonso finally said. "Once," he added with a heavy sigh. Then he reached a hand up to his face and wiped his eyes.

The king of Spain was crying.

Xavi heard someone creeping up behind the couch, but he kept his eyes on the television.

María Moreno managed to keep her expression impassive. "And, might I ask, what happened to this mystery person?"

"It was a very long time ago," Alfonso said.

María waited for the king to elaborate. When he didn't, she pressed him. "Is this person why you never married?"

Tears streamed down the king's cheeks. He opened his mouth, closed it, opened it again. Then he forced a laugh. "I think it's time we moved on to other topics," he said with finality.

María knew not to disobey Alfonso's wishes. He was the king, after all. Besides, she'd already gotten the scoop of the century, so she allowed the interview to shift to talk of politics.

Xavi heard sniffling behind him. He turned around. The look in his mother's eyes was faraway. "Mamá, are you okay? What's the matter?"

She jumped, startled, as though she'd forgotten Xavi was sitting in front of her on the couch. "Xavi!"

What was going on?

Once again, Marta went for the remote. She picked it up and turned the TV off. This time, Xavi knew not to argue with her.

Then: "Cariño, we must talk," Marta said to her son, tears streaming down her face, one after the other. "There's something I need to tell you. I've kept this secret long enough."

Xavi stared into space as he remembered the night his mother finally told him the truth. It seemed so long ago now. Meanwhile, Santiago and Diego were deep in conversation during the halftime break—or, more accurately, they were deep in conflict about Barça and Madrid.

Diego's voice rose along with his body as he leaned over the table toward

Santiago. "Well, why don't you go back to Madrid if it's so great!" Diego might be small, but he could be fierce.

Santiago looked at Diego like he was ready to pounce.

"Hey, hey!" Xavi said, coming to life and reaching his arms across the table between them. "We're all friends here, let's remember that."

There was a long, tense pause, then Diego and Santiago grinned at each other and burst into laughter. The tension faded as fresh bravas arrived at their table, steaming on a plate and covered in spicy sauce. Diego and Santiago shook hands and sat back down.

Diego raised his glass toward Santiago. "I suppose we can be friends until the second half starts."

Santiago glanced at the clock ticking down the minutes of the break. He raised his glass as well. "All right. For the next slightly over eight minutes, we can be civil."

Xavi shook his head, laughing, and joined in their toast.

But then his attention shifted, caught on something across the street.

Some*one*. The American girl. Could it be?

"Is that . . ." Xavi started, but before he could finish his question and, really, before he could even think, he was up out of his seat, weaving past the tables lining the sidewalk, then heading across the street like a Barça forward maneuvering to the goal. "Hey!" he called to the girl, but she didn't turn around. Her back was to him, and she was looking in the windows of a neighboring bar. "American girl!"

At this, she flicked her head to look behind her.

Xavi halted, disappointed. He put his hands up. "Sorry! I thought you were someone else."

The girl took him in and smiled, clearly pleased to find such an attractive pursuer. "Don't be sorry," she said, her accent decidedly American—at least he had gotten that part right.

She looked like she was going to say something more but Xavi turned around and went back to his table, knowing his friends would make fun of him. He slid into his chair again, dejected.

"What was that all about?" Diego asked.

Xavi didn't need to look at Diego to know he was grinning.

Santiago answered for Xavi. "An American girl who likes Marta's cooking."

"But don't all girls like Marta's cooking?" Diego asked. "I mean, don't all humans like it?"

"Yes," Xavi said, glancing at his friend with a grateful smile.

The second half began, and so did the cheering and shouting along the sidewalk. Even as Xavi joined in, he couldn't shake his disappointment. He'd found an American girl tonight, but not the one he wanted to see. He took a gulp of his beer. "Where do you think she lives?" Xavi asked, eyes on the screen as Madrid moved the ball down to their end of the field.

"Who?" Santiago asked.

"The American girl," Xavi said. "If you had to guess."

Santiago snorted. "Xavi, don't do it. Stop thinking about her."

Barça stole the ball from Madrid so Xavi dared a glance at his royal guard. "Why not? I get to have a casual fling, don't I? It's summer."

"Of course you do," Diego concurred, his eyes still glued to the screen. "Why wouldn't you have a fling? Why can't we all?"

"It's not a good idea," Santiago said to Xavi.

The crowd oohed as a Barça player went down and the med techs ran onto the field.

Diego popped up from his chair. "I'm going to take advantage of this break in play." He ran inside the bar, Xavi presumed to go to the bathroom.

Xavi crossed his arms, eyeing Santiago. "A fling is a great idea."

Santiago curled a hand around his beer. "Chaval, I saw the way you looked at her."

Xavi grinned. "Like I look at every other girl I've dated in my life?"

The young royal guardsman leaned close to the prince. "Don't make problems where there aren't any."

"How is this girl a problem? I don't even know her."

"Listen," Santiago said, growing serious. "You are going to quietly live out your last anonymous summer alongside your mother at home and at the market. Then you will head to Madrid to officially announce who you are to the rest of Spain, as meticulously planned by your father and his staff, to take up all the responsibilities that come with who you are and public life."

"When you put it like that," Xavi said, "it sounds like I'm headed to prison."

Santiago took a sip of his beer. "Being royalty is a bit like being in prison, yes," he told Xavi. "An exceptionally nice, ritzy prison, but still."

"And what does any of this have to do with me liking some random American girl?"

"Everything," Santiago said. "Honestly, you're better off with Isabel, someone whose family is titled."

"You're joking," Xavi spat.

"I'm not."

"That is never going to happen again."

The crowd burst out yelling and clapping, and the young men's attention returned to the screen for a moment. But once again, Barça missed the goal by barely an inch. Xavi caught a glimpse of Diego trying to make his way through the bar and outside.

Xavi looked back at his "cousin." "I am not letting my last summer be boring. You have to know that. Besides, who cares about a fling? It's not like I'd let things get out of hand. I mean, if I can survive Isabel, I can survive anyone. I'm impermeable."

Santiago looked at Xavi hard. He responded, but once more, the crowd erupted around the two young men, people jumping out of their seats and cheering because Barcelona had scored, nearly drowning out his words.

Still, Xavi managed to hear everything Santiago said as clearly as if the bar were silent. "No one is impermeable," Santiago muttered amid the din. "Not even the prince of Spain."

# Six

Santiago was staring and he knew it. Diego was turned toward Xavi. The angle allowed Santiago to admire the exact line of Diego's profile.

It was Sunday, midday, the Barça-Madrid game long over and the weekend marching forward to Monday. The three young men were at Xavi's place, as they often were, sitting on the terrace outside Xavi's bedroom. Xavi and Marta lived in a busy corner of El Gótico. They had more terrace than apartment, which wasn't bad in a place with weather like Barcelona's but certainly made for cramped living quarters. During the evenings when La Buena was closed, Xavi and Santiago often spent time on this terrace with its old metal table and chairs. Xavi had rigged up a sail shade on posts to provide relief from the hot sun during the day. Six stories below on the street, the sounds of bustling Barcelona were far away but unmistakable.

"Are you sure you want to go to that restaurant this afternoon?" Xavi asked Diego. "It's so over the top."

Diego gave Xavi a playful shove. "Come on, just because you don't want to run into Isabel doesn't mean we have to avoid every single summer party from school."

"But it's all the way up at the top of the Eixample," Xavi complained.

Barcelona's Eixample neighborhood, with its beautiful, modernist architecture and ritzy bars and restaurants, was one of the wealthiest areas of the city, and Santiago loved the place. It reminded him of Madrid. But it was also where Isabel's family had their penthouse, three entire floors of one of the most sought-after historic buildings in all of Barcelona. It sat right on the wide, tree-lined Passeig de Gràcia, the boulevard that was to Barcelona what the Champs-Élysées was to Paris. The correct pronunciation of Eixample in catalán was as elegant as the neighborhood itself: "Ahh-*shaahm*-pluh." And to Santiago's dismay, ever since Xavi and Isabel had broken up, Xavi made it a point never to go there.

"Like the Eixample is so far," Diego said with a laugh.

As Diego laughed and chided Xavi, Santiago admired the muscles in Diego's arms. He could never take his gaze off the boy: His big eyes and those long lashes framing them. That bright, mischievous smile Diego always wore on his handsome face. The row of fraying leather bracelets along his right wrist, a wrist Santiago longed to encircle with his hand. At least here, at Xavi and Marta's apartment, Santiago could relax. No one was about to scale the old medieval walls of the building to get to the young prince, because no one knew who Xavi was—not yet, anyway. The secrecy around Xavi's identity made Santiago's presence mostly redundant, just a check on Xavi's behavior and well-being before the big announcement. That is, as long as Xavi's identity *remained* a secret.

Diego caught Santiago's gaze as he plucked one of the blistered pimientos de Padrón from the plate on the table. He sucked the pepper down until all that was left was the stem, which he tossed onto a nearby plate. "God, I wish I were a cousin and got to live with Marta all summer and eat her cooking all day."

Santiago nearly swooned as he watched Diego eat that pepper, then nearly swooned again at the thought of Diego living in the same apartment as he and Xavi. That would be amazing. And total torture. It took every bit of wherewithal for Santiago to remain upright in his chair as he considered the possibility. Diego clearly had no idea how attractive he was as he ate.

Santiago was nearly dizzy with the sight of him. "Marta *is* amazing" was all he said.

"No kidding," Diego said passionately. He scanned what remained on the plate as he decided which pepper to eat next, some more seared than others, some with big flakes of delicious local salt clinging to their skins, some as tiny as a thumbnail. Every few peppers, a person was sure to get one with a tremendous spicy kick, and that was part of the fun of eating them.

Diego made his choice. Then Santiago plucked a pepper for himself and swallowed it down, managing not to choke. The pepper was delicious, but Santiago's throat was dry.

This was not good. None of this was good.

Santiago needed to gain control of himself. He forced his stare away from Diego and back to Xavi, even though doing so felt like trying to lift one of Barcelona's cathedral bells with a single finger. All but impossible. What was Santiago supposed to do when Xavi spent practically every waking minute that he wasn't working at La Buena with this guy?

As Xavi and Diego returned to their bickering about the afternoon's events, Santiago's brain drifted back to the Barça-Madrid game the other night and to his own bickering with Diego as they sat across from one another and gradually rose to standing as they argued about Madrid.

Santiago would have kissed Diego right then if they'd been alone.

Or he would have *tried*.

On the surface, they'd been fighting about fútbol, but really, this was flirting at its best. Sparks flew between them as they traded insults. Well, Santiago couldn't speak for Diego, but he certainly felt the flames stoked on his side.

It didn't help that Diego was single.

It was one of the first things Santiago had learned about Diego when he arrived for his "family visit" to Marta and Xavi's. Both Xavi and Diego were newly single, which they felt was an auspicious way to begin their summers. Diego's ex-boyfriend had moved away to France, but they'd been on the outs beforehand anyway, apparently.

Now Santiago made an executive decision. "There's three of us here. Don't I get a vote about our Sunday afternoon's activities?"

Xavi and Diego went silent as they turned to him, Xavi's eyebrows arched in surprise.

"Of course you do," Diego said with a smug smile on this face.

Could he tell what Santiago was thinking? Santiago sure hoped not.

The peppers were nearly gone. Santiago chose among the last of them and popped the tiniest one in his mouth. The sweet spiciness was out of this world, chased by that delicious, sharp salt. God, Marta could have a Michelin starred restaurant if she wanted. Sometimes he wondered if he should tell this to the king.

Xavi crossed his arms. "Well, cousin?"

"Let's go to the party," Santiago said with a shrug.

And just as Santiago had imagined, his agreement with Diego's wishes inspired the boy to give Xavi another playful shove on behalf of the win, and Santiago enjoyed every moment.

The bar was packed.

Xavi rolled his eyes. "Look at this place. I'll take Lis's any day."

"You're not wrong," Santiago muttered, leading the way through the Sunday-afternoon throng, eyes darting everywhere as he assessed the risk. But this was the kind of crowd that would fawn over Xavi if they knew who he was, not try to kidnap or kill him.

"I like it," Diego said happily, trailing behind the pair as he took in the scene.

What a scene it was.

People lined the bar, some with long, elegant flutes of cava in their hands, others clutching designer cocktails, glancing occasionally in the gilded mirrors on the walls, all of them dressed in their Sunday best, which for this crowd was elegant, designer, and, for some, couture. This was the spot the wealthy of Barcelona had chosen as their go-to for late nights and weekends.

Sunday afternoons in Barcelona were for eating out in general. All the stores were closed, including most of the supermarkets. For families, this meant gathering the kids and the grandparents for a nice long meal, upwards of three hours of drinking, eating, talking, relaxing on one of the many sidewalk terraces or at one of the traditional restaurants that served catalán fare. Whole fish over a fire, roasted rabbit, sometimes a big paella, or even arroz caldoso, "soupy rice," which was like paella but, well, soupier, the rice swimming in a delicious seafood broth.

But for people like Santiago, Xavi, and Diego?

Sunday afternoons were an opportunity to either sleep off the night before or party all day into the evening. In Barcelona, there were two kinds of restaurants. One was the neighborhood kind, like near Xavi and Marta's apartment—tiny, low-key, and with a pedigree as old or older than all those catalán grandparents.

The other kind was like this one.

El Beso Mas Largo. Translation: the longest kiss.

Perched high up in the Eixample on one of its toniest blocks, it was four entire stories of long, marble-topped bars, sparkling chandeliers, edgy design. El Beso Mas Largo was all glass and velvet and silk, filled with beautiful couches and chairs for lounging and boasting sweeping terraces on each of its four floors. The walls had pocket doors, so they opened fully to the outside. Places like this attracted Barcelona's poshest residents, la gente pija. Which was probably why the most pija of them all, Isabel, chose this place for today's Sunday hangout.

Santiago searched for Isabel in the crowd but didn't see her. She must be on one of the other floors. He began to relax. The only weapons in sight were champagne flutes and perhaps a jewel errantly flung from an ear after an overzealous hair toss. The only problem for Santiago and Xavi today might be that their attire wasn't quite up to El Beso Mas Largo's standards. Not true for Diego, though, who always managed to look stylish even in a T-shirt and jeans.

"Shall we get a drink first or go find everybody?" Diego asked.

Xavi eyed Santiago next to him. "I need a drink to handle this place, so let's start there."

The three young men pushed through the crowd to the bar.

As they squeezed their way to the front, Santiago did his best not to enjoy being pressed against Diego's side, to fail to notice the skin of Diego's arm along his own or the way Diego's chin nearly brushed the top of Santiago's shoulder as he moved to get the bartender's attention.

Nope. Santiago didn't pay attention to any of this.

To distract himself, he again scanned the room. He could tell this was not Xavi's scene and, interestingly enough, neither was it Xavi's father's, the king's.

One of the things Santiago—and his own father before him—had always loved about the king was that he never went to places like this. Not unless he had to for some royal reason or another. More often than not, the king preferred the kind of bar or restaurant that the locals favored. Alfonso always caused a stir when he showed up at one, but Santiago admired him for it, especially because of the long-term effect of the king's visit on the owners—which was a whopping net positive. Alfonso made sure to pose for a photo with the dueños in front of a table full of their food so they could proudly put it on their wall and boast about his visit. Alfonso would never do such a thing for a place like this one. The king cared about the people, and to him, *people* meant the working class. And this place was decidedly not for them.

"I'll get this round," Santiago offered when the bartender began handing out cocktails to their group. Which actually meant that the monarchy would get it. Santiago had a discretionary fund for Xavi's outings. But Xavi didn't seem to realize that when Santiago paid, it was not out of his own salary as guard. In any case, Xavi was still too proud to accept royal money—yet another thing he would need to get used to soon, since royal money was *his* money. Marta had also declined any financial assistance, though there was plenty of it for her. Enough to buy her and Xavi a place as nice or nicer than that of any of his friends from school. She was the mother of a prince, after all.

As Santiago paid, Diego passed the cocktails between them.

"Where do we think everyone is?" Xavi asked.

"Oh, on the rooftop, definitely," Diego said.

They wound their way up the staircase to the fourth floor. Each level featured a different color—a pale green, a masculine gray, a sunny yellow, and, finally, a cerulean blue to highlight the view of the far-off sea and the clear Barcelona sky above.

Diego pointed to the terrace. "There they are."

Santiago followed the direction of Diego's finger. Outside, at the head of a long table, sat Isabel, a glass of cava perched in a delicately positioned hand, her gaze hidden behind big round sunglasses. Tall silver buckets full of ice and bottles of cava stood alongside the table, and towers of shellfish—oysters, shrimp, scallops—climbed up and up in a series of round silver platters. As they approached, Santiago could see that people were in an uproar over something, chattering and passing phones around to share their screens.

Isabel's gaze landed on the three of them, one person in particular.

But Xavi hung back.

Santiago turned to look at him and saw how Xavi was avoiding meeting Isabel's eyes. So Santiago grabbed Xavi's arm and yanked him along.

As they arrived, the chatter grew among the group, in part because people were calling out greetings.

"What's everybody talking about?" Diego asked one of the girls; Santiago thought her name was Gemma. She held up her phone so Diego could see. Diego scanned whatever it was. If Santiago hadn't been paying attention to his crush, he might've missed the source of everyone's interest, but because he was watching over Diego's shoulder, he saw the headline.

A shiver went through Santiago despite the heat.

On Gemma's phone was a post from ¡Qué Fuerte!, the biggest of the gossip sites in Spain. The UK had always thrived on their trashy gossip rags, but it was only in the past decade that the people of Spain had discovered a similar hunger to know all things about celebrities and the monarchy, from who was dating who to who was seen eating what and where. Of late, the site employed influencers of all kinds, young and old, and it had amassed an enormous following.

Santiago cursed inwardly.

He yanked Xavi once again and gestured for him to look.

BASTARD PRINCE OF BARCELONA?

Santiago needed to read only a few lines for the blood in his veins to run even colder. *Rumor has it that the king has an heir after all and that he's been hiding in plain sight, in Catalunya, of all places. The only question is when the monarchy will confirm to the Spanish public what they deserve to know: Do they have a prince? And is he handsome?*

The post was from Leonora Valdez, one of the biggest influencers their age in all of Spain.

Diego shrugged at Gemma. "Every couple of years there's a rumor like this about some secret prince."

Gemma took her phone back and placed it on the table. Then she held out her glass so Diego could fill it with cava, and Diego, ever the gentleman, did so. "But what if this one is true? And what if he lives among us?"

Isabel called out from her place at the other end of the table, "Yes, what if he did? Wouldn't that be exciting?"

Santiago could feel the tension rolling off Xavi. "It's going to be okay," he whispered, though inwardly he was still cursing. "You need to act normal. Drink your cocktail and put a smile on your face. The best response is to be your normal arrogant self."

Santiago watched as the tension in Xavi's face melted into one of his signature grins; the way he tossed his hair as casual as ever.

Xavi buried his hands in his pockets. "Me, arrogant?"

Santiago laughed. For once in Xavi's life, he was taking Santiago's advice.

# Seven

Out of the corner of Xavi's eye, he could see Isabel paint a seductive smile on her face and adopt a carefully crafted relaxed posture in her chair as she waited for Xavi to notice her. Seconds passed and turned into a full minute.

Xavi refused to meet her gaze.

As usual, Isabel was holding court. A table full of the most beautiful girls from Queen Elizabeth's stretched along the fourth-floor terrace, Isabel at the head. They made for quite the sight, even for such a glamorous place as El Beso Mas Largo, the lot of them as sparkling as the crystal glasses in their hands. But Xavi knew Isabel's friends were afraid of her. Because of this, they came when she called. To refuse Isabel was to court social disaster and possibly worse, though Xavi so far had managed to emerge from her orbit mostly unscathed. Her friend Gemma was here today, and Lara and Josefina and Sofia and so on and so forth, the group of girls from school who always hung on Isabel's every word, watched her every move, and obeyed her every command.

Xavi tried to keep himself at a reasonable distance from all of them.

Even so, suspicion bloomed inside him. Those rumors about a Catalunyan prince in ¡Qué Fuerte! had Isabel de Luna written all over them. It was the kind of thing she'd relish doing if she'd somehow gotten hold of the truth about Xavi. But how could she have? Xavi shook off the thought. The answer was: She couldn't. Not as far as he knew.

So he kept that grin on his face steady.

Diego breezed past Xavi and up to Isabel. "Hola, guapa," he said, leaning down to kiss her on each cheek. "Salud." He clinked his cocktail glass against her champagne flute.

Isabel smiled at Diego, and batted her lashes. "I'm so glad you boys could make it," she said, loud enough so Xavi could hear.

"It took a lot of coaxing, but here we are," Diego said with a shrug toward Xavi. "You look stunning as always," Diego added.

Xavi watched as Isabel rose to show off her outfit, certain that this was not for Diego's benefit alone; she likely thought it was an act of kindness for everyone around her, Isabel generously offering a glimpse of her beauty to all nearby. Xavi also knew Isabel was trying to tempt him. And in truth, he found it hard to turn away.

Today she wore a blue strapless dress that was loose and flowing and fell all the way to her feet. As she gave a twirl for Diego, she managed to turn more than a few heads out on the sunny terrace of El Beso Mas Largo. "Thank you, darling," she said to Diego.

But instead of taking her seat again, Isabel made her way toward Xavi.

He could have turned around and walked away, but he didn't.

"Hello, Xavier," Isabel said, planting herself in front of him. She rose onto her toes and leaned in to kiss his cheeks. The first hit its mark, but the second brushed the edge of Xavi's lips.

"Isabel," Xavi said, doing his best to sound as cold as the ice in the buckets there to chill the cava. In the end, it didn't matter what Isabel said or did or wore or what tricks she might try, and she certainly had plenty of those. Nothing could thaw Xavi's heart where Isabel was concerned.

But she only smiled up at him, seeming perfectly content to wait as long as it took.

It was rather unlike Isabel to go for someone like Xavi. Everyone around them saw this, which meant it was even more unlikely that Xavi would look her way. He was not her type, so it took him a long time to realize she'd started to flirt with him. For one, Xavi wasn't rich. For two, dating someone like Xavi wouldn't gain Isabel anything—not social status or wealth or connections. At least not back then, before Xavi found out he was a prince.

So initially, Xavi was rather immune to Isabel's attention. In fact, her first attempt to seduce him failed spectacularly. She invited Xavi over to her house, which he'd been to many times with their friends from school. But Isabel hadn't mentioned he'd be the only guest that evening, and the plan was for the two of them to go swimming in the rooftop pool. When Xavi stepped off the elevator into the de Luna's massive penthouse, Isabel was waiting for him in a white cover-up.

"Where is everyone?" he asked, looking around.

Isabel ignored his question. "I thought we could go for a swim. It's still so hot out, isn't it?"

Xavi shoved his hands into the pockets of his shorts. He felt ambushed and considered leaving. He could see the outline of Isabel's very teeny bikini underneath that silky dress. "I didn't bring a bathing suit," he said.

Isabel had laughed. "It's very private up there. The only one who will see you is me."

Not wearing a bathing suit was apparently the idea. In truth, Xavi was tempted.

This was why, when Isabel beckoned him to follow her beyond the apartment's grand, two-story entrance hall with its enormous chandelier into the formal living room beyond it, he complied. He glanced all around at the beautiful surroundings, especially the massive Picasso on one wall and the Salvador Dalí on another. Yet Isabel took no notice of them, brushing by the paintings like it was normal to have the works of the most famous Spanish artists in history all around her—and Xavi supposed it was, since she'd grown up here.

Xavi kept thinking he should go, but soon they were climbing the stairs to the roof. When they arrived on the terrace, the night was hot but resplendent, and Xavi couldn't help admiring the place. The terrace was for Isabel's family's use alone and it boasted one of the few private pools in all the city, expansive and sparkling. They were on top of the world, with a view of Barcelona that stretched all the way to the sea and all the way up to the hilltops inland. The moon shone above, the stars glittered, and the water in the pool shimmered.

A perfect setting for romance.

Xavi shook his head. This was clearly a trap of Isabel's making—a trap set for him.

"I don't know about you," she said nearly immediately, "but I'm ready for that swim." She walked over to the edge of one of the sun beds, kicked off her sandals, and stepped onto the decking barefoot. Then she began to undo the buttons of her cover-up, one by one.

"Isabel," Xavi said, his tone full of warning. He knew he should leave, but something was keeping him there. He wasn't sure what. Curiosity? Maybe even a little desire? He was playing with fire by being here at all. As Xavi stood there debating what to do, Isabel slid the delicate fabric over her shoulders, down her arms, and all the way off. She tossed the cover-up on top of a lounger. Then she wandered over to the stairs at one end of the pool. Xavi didn't look away; he couldn't seem to make himself. One stair at a time, ever so slowly, she waded in, the surface of the water rising first to her shins, then to her knees, and onward to the middle of her thighs.

That was when she stopped and called out, "The water is perfect. Are you going to join me or what?"

Xavi hesitated. Then he shook himself out of whatever trance she held him in. What was he doing here? "Actually, no, I'm not. But you enjoy your swim."

"Xavi—" she called, but he didn't turn around. This time he kept going, back down the two sets of stairs to the first floor of Isabel's apartment, not stopping until he reached the elevator. Xavi knew better than to allow himself to get involved with Isabel de Luna, and he was annoyed he'd followed her up to the pool at all.

The night Isabel finally did manage to seduce Xavi, it was completely by accident. It was over a month later, after yet another party on Isabel's rooftop with all their friends. Her parents weren't home since they were never home, especially not in summer—a fact that always made Xavi a little sad for her. Xavi left the party with everyone else. He'd gotten all the way to the lobby when he realized he didn't have his wallet. He waved the rest of his friends on without him and went back up to the top floor and into the apartment. When the elevator doors opened, he immediately called out, "Hello? Isabel?" He didn't want to surprise her.

When there was no response, he began to navigate his way through the rooms. Soon Xavi saw her lying on one of the couches, alone and staring up at the ceiling. She wasn't on her phone, she wasn't doing anything, and she didn't seem to notice Xavi was standing there. Rather than announce his presence, Xavi found himself speechless.

A few moments before, Xavi had left a completely different Isabel, the cold, manipulative seductress Xavi had been dodging of late as she tried to convince Xavi they should at least hook up, if not date, and whose advances he continued to reject. Even though, in all honesty, Xavi was attracted to her. But on this night, he'd come upon a wholly different girl, one who seemed in possession of a softness Xavi had never seen before and who had cast a spell on him already. Earlier, Isabel was wearing head-to-toe couture, the kind of outfit that likely cost more than Xavi's mother's tapas place made in a month. Now she'd traded her runway attire for a ratty old pink T-shirt, the neck fraying and torn, like something had eaten through it. She wore a pair of loose purple sweatpants with holes over one knee. She was casual and unguarded and real. Xavi wondered if he was finally seeing the true Isabel, a person she kept carefully hidden behind that sophisticated facade and all that expensive fancy attire.

"Isabel?" he tried again, worrying he'd intruded on a private moment. "My wallet must have fallen out of my pocket. I came back to get it. I'm really sorry to bother you."

Her eyes found Xavi then, clearly surprised. She sat up quickly, swung her feet to the floor, tried to fix her hair. "Xavi, hi, you surprised me." She wiped her cheek with her hand.

Xavi detected sadness in Isabel's eyes. Even loneliness. He took a step closer. "Are you all right?"

She blinked and looked away, uncharacteristically quiet.

The French doors of the living room were open, and Xavi could hear the faraway sounds of people on Passeig de Gràcia floating in the air and the faint sounds of a jazz band playing.

He walked over to the couch and sat down next to her. Then he found himself reaching for Isabel's hand, wanting to comfort her, although it had never before occurred to Xavi that she might need comfort from anyone. When she turned back and looked at him, something about her in that moment reached straight into his heart. He leaned in to kiss her. Their lips touched. When he pulled away, the look on Isabel's face was one of clear-eyed surprise.

"Why did you just do that?" she asked.

"I'm sorry," Xavi said, stricken. "I shouldn't have."

She combed a hand through her long hair, and her eyes filled with confusion. "I've been trying to get you to kiss me for weeks."

He took her hand again. "Well, now I have."

Isabel choked out a laugh. "But I'm a mess."

"You are not."

"I am, though. I mean, I'm in my pajamas." Isabel sent her gaze sweeping down her front to her toes. "Look at me," she said.

So Xavi did. He stared at Isabel, unable to turn away. He'd never seen her so beautiful. *This* Isabel, Xavi wanted. "If you insist on finding a *but*, then fine, you're a breathtakingly beautiful mess, Isabel, and you should try being a mess more often because it looks good on you. I think I like this version of Isabel."

Xavi had meant for her to laugh, but instead, tears pooled in her eyes. She got up from the couch and started to walk away, wiping her face again.

"Hey," Xavi said, startled. He got up and followed her. He reached for her and pulled her close again. He lifted her palm to his lips and kissed it. "Don't cry. I didn't mean to upset you."

"I'm just . . . I don't know what to say," she said. "I'm surprised to hear you feel that way about me."

"That can't be true," Xavi said. "You must have guys telling you you're beautiful all the time. You must have everyone telling you that. You are beautiful, Isabel. Just because I haven't told you before now doesn't mean I didn't think it. Of course I see your beauty and I always have."

Isabel tilted her chin and gazed up at Xavi. "It's not that. It's that you think I'm beautiful right now. I'm not used to having someone want me when I'm just being . . . me. The *private* me." Isabel tugged at the neck of her ratty T-shirt. "No one ever sees me like this because I never let them. Not friends during sleepovers, not even my parents." Her laugh was strangled. "My mother would probably disown me if she saw me."

Xavi bent forward and pressed another light kiss to Isabel's lips. "Well, I like you this way," he said. "You clearly have no idea how gorgeous you are right now." Xavi's hands found Isabel's waist. "I think I need to kiss you again. Would that be all right?"

Isabel responded by reaching her arms up around Xavi's neck and kissing him like she was starving. Xavi kissed her back the very same way, and as he did, he felt something stir inside his heart. He wondered if Isabel felt it too.

But not long after that magical night, Isabel became Isabel again. Before Xavi knew it, everything between them had fallen apart.

It didn't occur to Xavi until much later that maybe Isabel had pickpocketed his wallet to lure him back to be with her because she'd figured out the version of herself that Xavi would actually want. Xavi hated having this suspicion, but by then he knew Isabel too well to think she would never go that far—she definitely would, of that much he was certain. This was the problem with Isabel: Even when Xavi believed he'd found the real Isabel underneath the facade, he couldn't be sure. Isabel could never be trusted.

"So what do you think about that new post on ¡Qué Fuerte!?" Isabel asked Xavi.

He could feel her eyes on him, studying his reaction. "I don't think anything," he said, refusing to notice the pretty flutter of her dress. "You know I could care less about the trash they publish. And the people who write it for them."

Before Xavi could excuse himself to talk to their other friends, to Santiago, to Diego, to absolutely anybody but his ex-girlfriend, Isabel continued. "What if this time the rumors are true, Xavi? And there's a prince among us here in Barcelona!"

It was as though Isabel could sniff out opportunity. He could just imagine what Isabel's social-climbing mother, Marine, would think if she found out Xavi was the Spanish prince.

Xavi only shrugged in response. "I don't find it exciting at all," he said to Isabel, and walked away, willing himself not to look back.

# Eight

Stefi was in heaven.

She was melting in the heat; she was sweating through her clothes; the hair that had fallen from her ponytail was plastered to the side of her face and neck; the hat on her head tipped to the side like some kind of failed soufflé, but none of this mattered. All Stefi cared about as she packed up her things to leave her pastry class for the day was the fact that her strict, grumpy teacher at Hofmann, Chef Arzak, had admired Stefi's layers! Layers of dough, that is.

Sorry, no—her *lamination*.

This was the correct word for the painstakingly tricky task of folding large rectangular slabs of butter one after the other into the dough that would eventually become a croissant.

"Your lamination technique is really coming along," the woman said and nearly followed this compliment with a *smile*.

Stefi's responding smile was so big, it nearly lifted her off the ground right there in the baking lab alongside all her older, more experienced fellow pastry-makers.

Nothing, absolutely, nothing could ruin Stefi's mood. She could care less that her T-shirt was greasy with butter and clinging to her skin from sweating in that hot kitchen all morning or that her long hair was tangled in knots. She was going to head the few blocks back to her abuela's, take a long, cold shower, and put on a fresh, clean everything. Then who knew what the day would hold? Maybe a walk to the beach? Maybe a wander in and out of the shops on Passeig de Gràcia? The rest of the afternoon was Stefi's to do what she wanted with, and the endless possibilities were wonderful.

She yanked the chef's hat from her head as she walked down the street and tried to shake out her hair, but it was so sticky it barely moved. As gross as Stefi was, her heart felt light.

Not even the photo of Amber and Jason holding hands that they posted on their profiles and that Stefi stupidly let herself look at *again*, even after she'd promised herself she would not look—she would *not*—could take her away from her current happiness. Clearly the photo was meant to announce to everyone Stefi knew at home that Amber and Jason were officially together. No—Stefi was living her new life and enjoying every sunny, buttery Barcelona second of it. Maybe one day she'd feel ready to post an image of her amazing time in Barcelona, but not yet. She was still getting her feet back under her, and she didn't want this to become a competition between her and Amber about whose summer was better and she knew it easily could.

Stefi turned the corner on Consellers in El Born to take the shortcut she'd found that led across Via Laietana and straight up to her abuela's in El Gótico, the path least clogged with tourists, when suddenly two tall people crashed into her. Stefi nearly went flying onto the cobblestoned street.

But then two muscular arms reached out and caught her.

"American girl!" the owner of those strong arms said. They were still wrapped around Stefi's sweaty, greasy self. "I mean Stefi—right? Isn't that your name?"

She looked up into the boy's face. "Yes? Oh!" The Viking! "You're Xavi."

Someone cleared his throat next to them. "And I'm Santiago, Xavi's cousin. Xavi, let the girl go," he commanded.

"Oh, sorry." He released Stefi.

Stefi was reluctant to step away. She would have been happy to stay all day in this boy's arms. She almost couldn't believe her eyes or her luck—to run into the son of the chef from La Buena, and right here on the street so close to her abuela's. Xavi was so good-looking, it almost hurt to see him standing there, hands stuffed in the pockets of his jeans, eyes alive and dancing, and that half grin on his face. He had an energy to him that was infectious. That was, well, flirtatious.

"It's so nice to see you, Xavi," Stefi said with more enthusiasm than she should probably allow to enter her voice. Then she remembered her current state, and embarrassment flooded her. She turned to the other boy, recognizing him as the person who'd been practically glued to Xavi at the market last weekend. "You said your name was Santiago, right? It's nice to see you too. I was just on my way home to shower and change. I was taking a class all morning and well"—she swept a hand across her body—"I'm obviously a mess."

Xavi laughed and pointed at the chef's hat hanging limply between her fingers. "What kind of class, exactly?"

"A class involving covering oneself in butter?" Santiago suggested.

"Well, kind of, yes," Stefi said. "I'm spending the summer learning to make croissants at Hofmann. And other things, too, obviously. But croissants are my priority." Inwardly, Stefi cringed. Had she actually just said that? God, she was such a dork.

But Xavi lit up. He whistled appreciatively. "Hofmann? Really? That's impressive. It's not like they let just anyone into those classes."

"I *was* pretty excited when I got accepted," Stefi admitted.

Xavi slouched against the gray stone wall next to him and tossed his hair in this way that made Stefi swoon. "I've tried to take a class at Hofmann a few times myself, but I've never gotten accepted."

"Seriously?" Stefi said. The shouts of children playing floated down the street and swirled around the three of them. "But you work at La Buena! That must count for something."

"Yes, but it doesn't help with pastry skills, as I'm sure you know. Baking is a whole other trade. Lots of excellent chefs can't bake a cake to save their lives. My mother included."

Stefi laughed and a thrill went through her. She and Xavi apparently spoke the same cooking language. She was so excited she nearly forgot that she was, as Santiago had mentioned, practically covered in butter and a total disaster, appearance-wise. Her hair, God, it must be disgusting. Good thing she couldn't see her reflection. Stefi's attention shifted to Santiago, who was clearly not enjoying Xavi and Stefi's back-and-forth or being seen on the streets of El Born with a girl who looked like she might have woken from a nap on the floor of a bustling restaurant kitchen.

"Chaval, we're late, remember?" Santiago said.

Xavi seemed to awaken at the sound of his cousin's voice. "Yes, I guess we are. But why don't you join us, Stefi? We're on our way to meet some friends for a drink after work—well, Santiago and I are, though none of the rest of our friends have ever worked a day in their lives." He rolled his eyes. "Anyway, would you like to come? The bar is only a few blocks from here. It's great. It has a really nice terrace and it's one of the prettiest spots in El Born."

Stefi glanced down at her shirt, and she could feel the sweat rolling down her back as they stood there in the sweltering street. She wanted to say yes, but she couldn't go anywhere dressed as she was. Disappointment flooded her. "I'd love to, but I really need a shower. Maybe another time?"

"Yes, maybe another time, perfect!" Santiago seemed inordinately pleased with Stefi's decline of Xavi's invitation and eager to get wherever they'd been heading before Stefi appeared and brought their progress to a halt.

Xavi narrowed his eyes at his cousin. A grin formed slowly on his face. "I have an idea. Cousin, why don't you go on ahead and meet up with everyone, and I'll accompany our new friend Stefi home and wait while she gets changed, then the two of us will join you later?"

A thrill went through Stefi again. Xavi wanted her to go so badly, he'd go with her to abuela's and wait for her to get ready. It almost sounded like he was asking her on a date. She was about to say yes, but Santiago got there first.

"Xavi, you know that's . . . not . . . something I should do," he said. "Um, what if I get lost?"

Xavi clapped Santiago on the shoulder. "I have faith in your sense of direction. Plus the wonders of GPS! Or you could always come with us and wait with me while Stefi showers."

Panic flickered across Santiago's eyes. What a strange, difficult person, Stefi thought. Handsome, definitely, but a bit odd. He was turning something that should have been easy into something entirely too difficult.

"Stefi hasn't even agreed to your plan," Santiago said. "And, really, people are waiting on us—"

"Yes, I have—agreed, I mean," Stefi cut in before Santiago could say anything else. To Xavi she said, "I'd love it if you accompanied me home." Then to Santiago, she said definitively, "And I think *you* should go on ahead to your friends since you're obviously worried about showing up late. You can apologize on our behalf and explain that we'll join you all very soon."

Xavi's grin got wider. "La mujer has spoken." Before Santiago could respond, Xavi swept a hand in the direction Stefi had been headed when they bumped into each other. "After you," he said.

And just like that, Stefi was walking up the street with the handsomest boy she had seen since arriving in Barcelona, the one she'd noticed on her first day in this beautiful city. Maybe soon she'd live out one of those fantasies from her romance novels after all.

"Nice to see you, Bonnie!"

"Hey, Francesc!"

"Oh, hi, Clara! Hey, Jaume!"

Xavi seemed to know just about every single person in her abuela's neighborhood; it was like he was the mayor of El Gótico. The last two people he greeted were standing outside a bar Stefi knew well already, since it was directly below her abuela's building.

"Xavi, nice to see you, how's your mother?" asked the man named Jaume.

"She's the same," Xavi said. "We're both working a lot this summer."

Clara shrugged. "Aren't we all?"

"This is my new friend Stefi," Xavi said again and again, introducing her to the people they ran into who were all clearly a regular part of Xavi's life. "She's here for the summer from the U.S." Xavi turned to her. "Stefi lives nearby, apparently."

"Welcome, Stefi," Clara said. "Where are you staying?"

"Actually," she began, and pointed upward, her gaze following her finger toward the sky. "We're here. I live in the top floor of this building. Well, my grandmother does." She let her eyes return to ground level and saw that Xavi's jaw had fallen open.

Jaume's eyes lit up. "You live above our bar?"

"Your grandmother is Silvia?" Clara asked nearly in the same moment.

Stefi smiled. "Yes—you know her?" A crowd of tourists moved through the usually quiet plaza where the four of them were gathered, then headed down one of the narrow streets connected to it, the noise from their chatter getting fainter as they moved away.

"We do," Jaume said. "She's un amor."

"I agree," Stefi said. "My parents and I are crowding her apartment this summer, and she is nice enough to let us live with her."

Clara waved off Stefi's remark. "Oh, I am sure she likes having her granddaughter and daughter here. It's hard to live alone, yes? Especially at Silvia's age?"

Stefi nodded. It was true; she didn't like to think of abuela by herself in that big apartment. She turned to Xavi. "I'm going to run upstairs and shower and change real quick." Stefi realized she was nervous about herding Xavi upstairs without any prior warning to Silvia or her parents, never mind knowing Xavi was in the living room while she was getting undressed just one wall away. "I'll be back before you know it!" Stefi hurried to the heavy wooden door that led up to abuela's. She took out the giant old key, fitted it into the even older lock, turned it, and pushed into the dark stone lobby. She flicked on the light in the stairwell and began to make the long climb. When she finally arrived on the fourth floor, she was huffing. She fitted yet another strange old key, circular and with spikes protruding from it, into another old iron lock. This one was even trickier, but it finally gave way and soon she was inside the apartment.

She dropped her keys into the bowl next to the door. "Hello? Anybody home?"

"Oh, hi, honey!" her mother called back.

Stefi made her way past the vestibule into the living room, where her mother had obviously been reading on the couch. The book lay open in her lap, but she was looking at her daughter.

Ana smiled. "Sweetheart, how was Hofmann's today?"

"It was great, actually," Stefi said. "I'm kind of in a hurry, though."

Her mother uncurled her legs from the sofa and placed them on the pale red terra-cotta floor. "Oh? Where to?" Her mother was doing that thing where she tried to sound uninterested in Stefi's life but in truth was *very* interested and clearly wanted details.

Stefi hurried through the open French doors to the balcony outside and glanced downward. There was Xavi below on the street, still talking to the people who worked at the local bar. She turned back to her mother. "Um, I met some people last weekend and ran into them today and they invited me out."

Her mother was already up from the couch and joining her at the balcony. "Hmm. By *people,* do you mean that handsome long-haired boy down in the plaza?"

"Mom, shhh," she hissed.

"Sorry!" Ana studied her daughter. "But Stefi, what about—"

Before her mother could say *Jason*, Stefi cut her off. "I need to go and clean up. We can talk about it later!" She hurried upstairs to her room and immediately started peeling off her disgusting clothes. For a brief moment, Stefi caught her reflection in the mirror and groaned. Her appearance was even worse than she'd imagined. But then, Xavi hadn't seemed to care. *Huh.* Well, Stefi wasn't going to question it further, she decided; she jumped into the shower.

As Stefi soaped up her hair, her thoughts returned to Xavi, and she wondered if his thoughts were on her right now too. She was suddenly glad that one of the first things she'd done after arriving in Barcelona was push through the jet lag and use her hard-earned savings from waitressing back home to treat herself to a shopping spree. It was part of Stefi's summer-reinvention plan. On her best days, she was able to tell herself that Amber and Jason's betrayal had done her a favor. It got the two most influential people in Stefi's life out of the way so she could finally remember who she was on her own. So she could try new things without feeling like she might be judged. Aside from her own family, the people Stefi met in Barcelona would have no idea who Stefi had been before her arrival here. Like Xavi. For all he knew, Stefi was the most popular, daring, awe-inspiring girl at her school, not the person who'd lived in her best friend's shadow for years.

On Stefi's first day in Barcelona, as she fought her jet lag, she'd wandered for hours up and down Portal de l'Àngel, one of the big shopping areas in the heart of the city. She'd even wandered up to Passeig de Gràcia, avoiding the fancy designer stores in favor of some of the more local boutiques. She came away with new tops and jeans and two summer dresses, one of which provoked a comment from her mother when Stefi wore it for the first time: "Well, look at you—I remember when my legs were that nice." Stefi rolled her eyes at Ana, but inside she'd been pleased her mother thought she looked good. And when a bright green bikini caught Stefi's eye in the window of a store, Stefi went inside and tried it on. She'd been surprised by the sight of herself in the mirror. Stefi had always worn tank suits for swimming. She'd never wanted to draw attention to her body at the beach or to how different it was from Amber's, especially when Amber was always spilling out of the teeny bikinis she favored. But soon Stefi was pulling out her credit card and plunking it down at the register to buy the green two-piece. After all, she no longer had to worry about walking on the beach next to Amber, because Amber wasn't here and wouldn't be coming to visit as they'd planned.

Stefi turned off the shower and grabbed a towel to dry her hair. She went to the drawer where she'd hidden away the new underwear she'd also bought during her shopping spree. She had yet to wear any of it. But today, Stefi chose a matching set she'd bought on sale, lacy white with a pattern of tiny yellow flowers. She could wear them for only herself, as the saleslady had said when she bought them. Stefi adjusted the towel around her, went to the windows of her room, and peered down again into the plaza.

There was Xavi, still chatting with the owners of the bar.

She put on the matching lingerie set, followed by one of her new dresses. Stefi could wear this for both herself and someone else. Because why not? This was Barcelona!

Stefi raced through the living room and out the door of the apartment so quickly her mother barely had time to shout, "Have fun!" before Stefi was gone, winding her way down the stairwell to the street below. She was sure her mother would have questions the next time she was home, but she needed to put that conversation off as long as she could. She still wasn't ready to tell Ana about Amber and Jason. Stefi reached the ground floor, pushed through the giant wooden door, and walked into the plaza.

Xavi was leaning against the wall across the way, arms crossed, staring right at her. "Hi again."

Stefi tried to catch her breath. She was suddenly aware of her outfit and what she'd chosen to wear underneath. Would Xavi somehow be able to tell that she'd put on lace underwear? And if so, would he think it was for him? "Hi again," she said.

"Feel better?"

Her heart was pounding. Was it the race down four flights of stairs or the sight of Xavi standing there that had it hammering? "Yes," she told him. "Much."

Xavi joined her at the center of the street and began to lead her back the way they'd come. "You know this is my neighborhood too," he said. "My mother and I live a couple of blocks from here."

Stefi fell into step with Xavi. This tidbit of information seemed promising, like maybe hanging out with Xavi this summer was part of Stefi's fate. If she'd believed in that sort of thing. They passed a tiny gallery selling oil paintings, a shop that refurbished furniture, and a narrow bar open to the air with a line of stools along the wall outside its windows. "That makes sense," she said, "given that you know every single person on the street and in the shops."

Xavi was smiling. "And I guess this means we're neighbors."

"I guess it does."

A café worker waved at Xavi and yelled out, "How's your mother?"

He raised his hand in response. "Same as always, working hard!" Then to Stefi, he said, "And since I know everyone, as you said, it follows that I should know you as well."

Stefi felt a little faint. "I think your math sounds right," she told Xavi. "That as neighbors, we should know each other."

"I'm glad you agree."

Xavi's arm brushed Stefi's as they walked and she tried not to swoon. "I do."

"Now let me warn you about the people you're going to meet where we're going," he said.

Stefi heard the caution in his tone. "All right."

"One of them might be my ex," Xavi said. "And she's likely to be . . . less than nice to you," he added. He went on to tell her about the girl named Isabel.

Stefi listened to Xavi describe this person and decided it was a good sign that Xavi wanted to give her a heads-up about his ex—wasn't it? Didn't it mean he must be thinking of her as someone to date? "I'm sure it will be fine," she said, though inside, she wasn't as sure as she sounded. She was curious to see what Xavi's ex-girlfriend was like. Stefi bet that she'd be beautiful.

The two of them crossed Via Laietana and headed back into the Born neighborhood. Everything—absolutely every shop, every bar, every street—was suddenly more beautiful with the transition. El Born was like this, so gorgeous it seemed magical. Stefi let the magic carry her along. As usual, her mind filled with romantic fantasies. Walking on one of El Born's narrow pretty streets, hand in hand with Xavi. Ducking into one of the dark little bodegas for a drink later in the evening. Kissing over candlelight. Catching Xavi staring at Stefi from across a terrace full of friends. As she glanced at Xavi next to her, she realized these fantasies were not that far from her reality.

Soon, they arrived at the very start of the Passeig del Born.

As usual, the sight of it stole Stefi's breath. She realized that Xavi was watching her.

"Beautiful" was all he said.

Stefi's heart fluttered. Had he meant the Passeig del Born or her? She turned her head and watched Xavi back. The afternoon suddenly seemed very promising.

"Yes," she agreed rather vaguely, meaning the neighborhood but also the boy standing next to her, looking like he might want to kiss her. Or even ravish her. Stefi wondered if she might burst into flames right then and there. *It would be a great way to go*, she thought.

# Nine

Xavi and Stefi sat at the far end of the table full of his friends from school, in prime terrace territory, right at the end of the Passeig del Born.

Far from Santiago and far from Isabel. This way, Xavi could enjoy the sight of the girl sitting next to him. A sight of her which making it a little difficult for Xavi to breathe. Stefi clearly had no idea how beautiful she was, which made her all the more amazing. It was as if she'd appeared out of thin air like some kind of exciting promise that his last summer of freedom might turn out to be fun after all. He had to find a way to kiss her before the end of the night. He hoped she would want to kiss him back. They had definitely already exchanged some flirty glances.

Across the table from Xavi, Gemma was eyeing him, then eyeing Stefi, who was chatting with Josefina next to her. "So what's the latest, Xavier?" Gemma asked, dark eyebrows arching.

Xavi looked up at his friend from school. "Nothing at all, Gemma," he replied. Then he grinned. Of all the girls in Isabel's entourage, Gemma was his favorite. She was pretty, like the rest, but she was also probably the smartest—book-smart, not socially manipulatively evil-smart like Isabel. Also, she was extremely nice, and she'd proved this by being nice to Stefi from the moment they'd met, nearly an hour before. Josefina was being nice too, which surprised Xavi more than a little. He hadn't been sure that Isabel's friends would behave themselves when he showed up with Stefi.

"Looks like it," Gemma said, matching Xavi's grin with her own.

"How are you, by the way?" he asked. Gemma had just ended a long-term relationship with a girl from one of the neighboring schools. Even though Xavi knew Gemma had done the breaking up, Xavi also knew breakups sucked no matter who made the decision.

"Oh, you know, surviving," she said. "Breakups are never fun."

Stefi glanced across the table at Gemma. "God, that's a truth if I ever heard one."

Gemma perked up. "You sound like you're speaking from experience."

Stefi nodded and seemed about to expand on what she'd meant. Xavi was eager to hear every word of Stefi's response, but he didn't because this was the moment Santiago chose to get up from his seat at the other end of the table and meander over to Xavi.

Santiago bent low and whispered in Xavi's ear, "Don't ever ditch me again. You're not supposed to go anywhere without me."

Xavi pretended to laugh as if Santiago had made a joke. "I'll take that under consideration in the future," he said, looking up at his royal guard. Xavi was going to have to find another way to lose him later so he could see where things went with Stefi. If they went anywhere.

Santiago made a strangled sound and meandered back to his seat between Isabel and Diego.

Stefi said something else to Gemma, then turned to Xavi again. She leaned closer. "Your cousin Santiago doesn't like me much," she observed.

Xavi leaned back in his chair and gazed at Stefi, trying to decide which version of this girl he preferred, the butter-covered post-Hofmann Stefi or the pretty sundress-wearing Stefi before him now. He couldn't decide, since both had their charms. "Nah, he's just a worrier," Xavi replied. "Don't take it personally."

"Santiago is a little hard to get to know," Gemma said. "But he's nice once he lets you in."

Stefi smiled. Gemma said something else cryptic about boys and their issues that Xavi didn't quite grasp but that made Stefi laugh—clearly a reference to their earlier exchange about breakups. Xavi wished Santiago hadn't chosen to approach him when he had. It was difficult for Xavi to imagine why any guy would be breaking up with the girl sitting next to him. Then again, it was hard for a lot of guys Xavi knew from school to understand why he'd broken up with Isabel. Besides, maybe Stefi had done the breaking. Either way, Xavi was happy with the outcome, because he was about 99 percent certain the girl was currently single. And into him. At least a little.

Xavi could tell how embarrassed Stefi had been earlier, running into him and Santiago right after her pastry class. Which meant she cared how she appeared to Xavi. But then she'd come downstairs after her shower transformed, that wispy yellow sundress flowing to the middle of her thighs and showing off those amazing legs. When she walked out the door and into the street, Xavi had wanted to kiss her right then. But in truth, seeing her before this, her clothes a mess and everything about her covered in grease and sweat, made Xavi like Stefi more. After all, how many times had Xavi left La Buena with his shirt stained and gross and run into someone from school who'd surely judged him for his appearance? He was not about to judge Stefi for the same. Besides, it meant Stefi was a girl unafraid to work, unafraid to literally get her hands dirty, who could maybe appreciate the kind of life Xavi and Marta led. Who might even admire it, as opposed to rejecting it in disgust, like Isabel.

But how long was that life going to last? It would be over with the summer, Xavi reminded himself. He pushed this upsetting thought away.

"Ibiza? Really?" Isabel shouted shrilly at the other end of the table.

She was talking to Josefina, while Stefi listened next to her. "I didn't think people like us vacationed there anymore. It's *so* much more cosmopolitan in Nice during the summers. The beaches are superior. My mother, the marquesa, would never set foot on that island, which is why we always go to the south of France. Or occasionally to Mallorca. The *non*-touristy side of it."

*People like us.*

The "us" Isabel meant excluded people like Xavi. Isabel always let Xavi know this. There were times when he fantasized about the moment Isabel found out she could have been with the prince of Spain but had done everything in her power to make Xavi feel like he was lesser and undeserving of someone like herself. The other day at El Beso Mas Largo, when Isabel brought up the rumors in ¡Qué Fuerte!, part of Xavi wanted to tell Isabel the truth and watch her face change as she took in the shock of such a reality.

Stefi was surveying the people sitting at the long table now, one by one, her eyes lingering on Isabel before she turned back to him. "So these are your, um, school friends?"

"You sound surprised." He studied Stefi's expression and saw there was an underlayer to her question. Really she was asking, *So this is your ex?* "It's complicated."

"I can see that," Stefi said.

Their attention drifted toward Isabel again.

Isabel did that—drew all the eyes nearby to her. Isabel took after her mother, Marine, who was always praised for her daring feminist style, since Marine chose clothes that "celebrated" the woman's body. *Vogue* had pronounced this very thing last summer in an eight-page spread that featured both mother and daughter in all their glamour. Maybe this was how things worked when your mother was a famous model and your parents were titled Spanish royalty—you appeared in magazines like *Vogue* and were admired by all.

"So, Isabel seems nice?" Stefi said, sounding like she really meant the opposite.

Xavi laughed. He and his friends were used to Isabel, but Stefi's eyes had practically fallen out when he'd introduced the two girls to one another.

Isabel had looked Stefi up and down like Stefi was some gauche American doll come to life, then she'd stuck out a limp hand and said, "Encantada," as though she were talking to someone's pet and not an actual person. Then she rose from her chair and parked herself in front of Xavi, making a show of getting on her tiptoes and leaning in to kiss him once on each cheek. "Well, isn't she just adorable," she whispered in his ear.

Xavi had looked right back at her. "I think so," he said.

Then, turning to Stefi, Isabel asked, "Where did you get that dress? Zara? Or maybe Primark?"

Stefi, nice person that she was, answered honestly. "No, I got it at Mango," she said, as though Isabel might want to go find the dress and buy one for herself.

That's when Xavi put a hand on Stefi's lower back. "Let's go sit over there," he said, pointing to the open seats at the other end of the long table, next to Gemma and near Sebastián, one of the nicer guys from school. Xavi guided her away from his ex, liking the feel of his hand pressed ever so lightly on her back. Xavi was relieved when Gemma popped up to give Stefi two kisses of greeting plus a hug.

"Why don't you sit near me?" Gemma said, and she began peppering Stefi with questions about life in the U.S. and why she was here for the summer.

Xavi appreciated this. It allowed him to both learn new information about the girl he'd brought along today and admire Stefi while he listened.

But now, as both he and Stefi turned their eyes on Xavi's ex, he found himself trying to understand how he had let himself fall for Isabel and how he might explain this to someone like Stefi.

"Isabel is . . . well . . ." Xavi trailed off, not knowing what to say about the girl at the other end of the table. It truly was like Isabel had put a spell on him for a time. That's what it felt like to Xavi now that Isabel's magic had worn off.

"Isabel is . . ." Stefi prompted, obviously wanting to know the story of how Xavi had ended up with someone like *that*.

But Gemma finished the sentence on Xavi's behalf. "Isabel is—and can be—a good friend when she wants to be. And she is deeper than she might appear at first glance. Not to mention, extremely attractive," Gemma added with a laugh, then took a long gulp of her cava.

Xavi studied Gemma, surprised by the unsolicited praise of his ex. He wondered what might be behind it.

"Most people are deeper than they appear," Stefi concurred.

Gemma was nodding.

Xavi glanced at Santiago at the end of the table. His "cousin" was currently deep in conversation with Diego. It looked like they might be fighting again, probably over Madrid and Barça. Xavi decided to seize this opportunity, even though he knew Santiago would make him pay for it later. Xavi put a hand lightly on Stefi's arm. "You want to go for a walk? I can give you a tour of the neighborhood."

Gemma's eyebrows arched at Xavi, but she turned to Stefi and said, "Xavi is a very good tour guide."

Xavi wanted to hug Gemma in gratitude. But all kinds of things flashed on Stefi's face, and Xavi wondered if she was debating whether to decline his invitation. She looked at her half-finished drink.

He wanted to reassure her somehow. "Don't worry, we don't have to be gone long."

Stefi turned her head; her long hair brushed across Xavi's hand, making him shiver. "No, it's just that I don't want to leave without paying. You're sure your friends won't think we ditched and left them to foot the bill?"

Xavi laughed. This was not what he'd expected Stefi to say. He studied the American girl who could rival Isabel in beauty but who was so unselfconscious about her appearance. How similar and yet how different two girls in his orbit could be, one concerned only for herself, the other deeply concerned for everyone *but* herself.

"I promise it will be fine," he said. Glancing again toward the other end of the table, he worried Santiago might turn Xavi's way before he and Stefi could make their escape. "Come on, let's go now, or my cousin is likely to follow after us. He doesn't like to be left out of anything, not even me taking a girl on a tour through the neighborhood."

To Xavi's great satisfaction, when he stood, so did Stefi. And before Santiago could notice, they'd stolen away down one of El Born's shadowy streets, the rows of sparkling twinkle lights shining high above them.

# Ten

When Santiago finally came up for air during his discussion with Diego, he glanced at the end of the table and nearly lost his mind. "Did you see where Xavi went?" he asked Isabel on his other side.

Isabel glared at him. "And why would I care about Xavi's whereabouts?"

Santiago rolled his eyes. "Right, why would you," he replied in a manner that was less than convincing and caused Isabel to huff at him.

Santiago wanted to kill Xavi. If only he weren't charged with protecting him, he might try.

"I'll be right back," Santiago said to no one in particular. He stood up and looked all along the Passeig del Born but didn't see Xavi anywhere. He walked away from the table and started down one of the narrow, neighboring streets, then turned left and started down a different one. Then yet another. There was absolutely no sign of Xavi or Stefi. The only people Santiago saw were tourists and locals stuffing their faces with pastries from Hofmann's nearby shop, licking ice cream from one of the many gelato establishments that dotted El Born, or drinking cava and cocktails at one of the gazillion terraced bars that lined the neighborhood's center. Oh, and there were a few couples making out in some of the more shadowy corners of the streets.

For the first time since landing in Barcelona, Santiago wondered if he needed to call the king.

Santiago filed weekly reports with Alfonso about Xavi, updating the palace about Xavi's activities. Because of Santiago's special relationship with Alfonso, he knew the king wouldn't mind if Santiago reached out to him directly. Alfonso would even welcome the communication, and expressly told him this before he'd hugged Santiago goodbye, after which Santiago had gotten on the royal private jet that flew him away from Madrid, his home city, for the longest time he'd ever been gone during his entire nineteen years of existence. But Santiago had always treated his closeness to the king with a delicate care, probably far more than the king needed—or wanted—him to. Besides, Santiago hoped to show the king he could be a professional like his father before him and that the king was right to entrust to Santiago with this complicated job. Santiago did not want to let Alfonso down.

But he was also starting to feel like he was in over his head. Xavi's resistance to all things palace-related was getting more pronounced, not less, especially given his recent propensity to take off without telling Santiago where he was going.

He pulled out his phone to see if Xavi had sent him a message.

Nope. Of course not.

His finger hovered over the initials ARE, which stood for Alfonso, Rey de España. But then he returned the phone to his pocket and hurried down yet another of El Born's busy streets.

Where could Xavi be?

Santiago had hoped Xavi would come around to his newly discovered origins, maybe even celebrate the tremendous privileges that came with finding out he was a prince, for God's sake. But Xavi was not only stubborn, he could truly be an idiot about the whole situation. He didn't seem to grasp—didn't seem willing to even try—how lucky he was that someone like Alfonso was his actual dad.

Santiago would have given anything for luck like that.

The first and only time Xavi visited the royal residence was a sheer disaster. The warm, kind, funny person Santiago had recently gotten to know as Xavi, had shown up in Madrid as an angry, suspicious young man dead set against seeing anything good in the king. When long afterward, Santiago demanded to know why in the world Xavi had acted this way, Xavi confessed to him about the letter from Alfonso that he'd found in Marta's desk. Santiago was surprised by what Xavi said of its contents, since it didn't sound like the king he had always known, and Santiago told him this.

Either way, Xavi had hardened his heart on his trip to Madrid, and it remained stony until he returned to his mother, Marta.

"I want to get to know you," Alfonso had told his son on that visit.

Xavi and Alfonso were sitting at the opulent breakfast table of La Zarzuela, surrounded by its fresco-covered walls and its grand gilded windows. Santiago was at the table with them eating his breakfast because Alfonso had invited him, thinking Santiago's presence might help Xavi relax.

Apparently, it did not.

Xavi's fork was all too loudly clattering against the fine china plate as he ate his eggs—eggs that he'd already commented were nothing in comparison to the ones made by his mother. "You forfeited that opportunity when you decided my mother wasn't good enough for you," Xavi said in response to the king's overture.

Alfonso closed his eyes.

Santiago winced upon hearing this exchange. He could see the king trying to breathe slowly, long inhales and exhales. Santiago had been around Alfonso his entire life and knew the king did this when he was feeling strong emotions to allow them to pass through him before he spoke again. Having lived in the public eye since birth, Alfonso was very practiced at maintaining his composure. But what Santiago couldn't tell, for once, was what the king was feeling. Anger? Frustration? Impatience? Some combination of all three? Or was it something more like sadness, even contrition, for the kernel of truth behind Xavi's accusation?

Santiago didn't know much about the history between Alfonso and Marta—no one did. It was possible only the two people involved would ever know exactly what had happened. But he was certain the reason things ended had everything to do with Alfonso's role as the ruling monarch of an important European country and Marta's decidedly unsuitable role as a modest tapas-maker from a region of Spain that was always trying to secede. Which would understandably be difficult for the son of that woman to forgive.

"But here we are now, Xavier," Alfonso said evenly to his son. "Life has given us a second chance."

"It's Xavi, and no, my mother gave us that chance by allowing you to know that I existed after you destroyed her heart," Xavi said, and Santiago saw the king's eyes widen and his mouth open, perhaps to protest or defend himself, but Alfonso never got the chance to speak because Xavi wasn't yet done. "And after spending my entire life wondering about my father, after a single weekend with him, I'm unsure whether she should have provided the opportunity for us to meet." At this, Xavi stood, chair screeching against the meticulously maintained Spanish-tile floors in a way that made Santiago wince again, this time along with the rest of the staff hovering at the edges of the room.

Alfonso shook his head. "I think you should speak to your mother about why things had to end."

Xavi's eyes narrowed. "I don't need to because I already know exactly why!" Then Xavi stormed off and started to pack his things.

Alfonso gave Santiago a pleading look.

Santiago got up and followed Xavi to try and talk some sense into him.

Xavi was banging around the room, snatching things from drawers and off hangers and stuffing them inside his suitcase in a way that would have them wrinkled and ruined by the time he reached Barcelona. Since they'd arrived at the palace, Xavi barely seemed to notice the beauty of his surroundings or the stunning details of the room where he'd been housed during this visit. Alfonso had interviewed Santiago for hours to learn the kinds of things Xavi liked: old Almodóvar movies, the color blue, absurdly large pillows and lots of them, the sight of a tree from his window, since in Barcelona's El Gótico, trees were rare. The king had gone above and beyond to outfit the room that would be Xavi's with anything the boy might like.

Xavi hadn't even noticed the king's effort. He was so angry he couldn't see what was right in front of him.

"You need to give Alfonso a chance," Santiago said to him from the doorway. "The king is a good man."

"No, actually, I definitely don't need to give a chance to a man who treated my mother so badly" was Xavi's retort.

*The king still loves your mother* was Santiago's immediate thought. But he didn't dare say such a thing out loud. For one, this was only a suspicion on Santiago's part, one he had no way of confirming without asking the king outright. But also, it was none of Santiago's business who the king loved, even if it was Marta, Xavi's mother. Santiago had liked Marta immediately upon meeting her and by now thought she would make an excellent queen of Spain, not to mention a wonderful wife to the lonely king. And after living with Marta for months, Santiago understood why the man might pine for Marta nearly twenty years. She was as kind and funny and smart as she was beautiful. Everyone who knew Marta fell easily and quickly in love with her. All this and she worked hard, proud of all that she had achieved in her life and on her own to boot.

Extremely admirable, in other words.

If only her son would open his eyes and not fuck up the possibility that the one person Xavi loved most in his life—his mother—might finally get to have the love she obviously still pined for. Yet another thing Santiago learned since arriving at their apartment in Barcelona was that, like the king, Marta had never dated anybody else again. There might have been terrible heartbreak between Marta and the king, and surely mistakes were made, but the past was the past, and Santiago had a feeling the king would do anything to move forward—with both mother and son. Alas. Xavi was determined to be a dumbass about the whole situation.

Santiago returned to the table full of Xavi's friends from school, defeated. "No sign of Xavi, right?" he said to the group.

He'd hoped Xavi might have returned by now. He saw Isabel doing her mean-girl thing with Josefina, Gemma and Sebastián deep in conversation, and Diego, who looked as handsome as ever, but no Xavi.

Worse still, Diego stared at Santiago strangely. "Xavi can take care of himself, you know."

"Yes, of course, b-but, well," Santiago stammered. "Um, I *do* know that."

"You worry about him a lot," Diego observed, not for the first time.

"Well, he's family," Santiago said.

Diego was still studying Santiago as if Santiago might be hiding something. "Yeah, but you worry about him *a lot* a lot."

"I am the older cousin after all, and I promised Marta . . ." Santiago trailed off because he had no idea how to finish this sentence. Diego knew Marta far better than Santiago, and he would know Marta was probably the most laid-back person in Catalunya. The only person Marta wasn't laid back about was the king of Spain, which Santiago knew from the few times he'd tried to bring up Alfonso and she'd uncharacteristically run from the room.

"You promised Marta what?" Diego asked with a laugh.

And Santiago thought to himself: Exactly.

"Marta has every faith in her son," Diego went on. "Trust me, I've known Marta practically my whole life. She's raised Xavi to be independent, confident, hardworking, self-sufficient."

Santiago was about to concur, but Diego got there first and said something that not only surprised Santiago but thrilled him.

Way. Too. Much.

"But if you *are* that worried about Xavi, why don't I help you find him?"

Santiago tugged at the neck of his T-shirt like he was worried he might overheat. "Really?"

"Sure. We'll look together. I'll come with you."

Santiago stared at Diego. "You will?"

Diego shrugged. "Who knows every single place Xavi might take a girl better than me?"

Santiago smiled. "True."

Diego stood up and gathered his things. "Of course, I never lie," Diego said, and flashed a sly grin at Santiago.

Was Diego flirting? A million feelings and thoughts and concerns and images rushed across Santiago from head to toe at this possibility, most of them conflicting, especially the image involving Francisco Hernández shaking his head no to Santiago from across his great big desk at the Palacio Real. But then a different one lingered after all the others.

Happiness.

Santiago was about to go off traipsing through the medieval quarter with Diego. Just the two of them. This person had not only offered to head somewhere alone with Santiago but might even be flirting with him. As they walked in the direction of El Gótico, which Diego assured him was where Xavi would eventually end up with Stefi, Santiago wondered how to understand Diego's chivalrous—well, generous—offer to help him. Was he misreading Diego's intent? Had Diego made the offer just to be nice? Or was it for other, far more exciting reasons, like the possibility that Diego might return Santiago's affection, even a little? Was Diego flirting or not flirting?

He glanced at Diego now. He was talking away about where Xavi might be with Stefi, but Santiago could barely absorb a word he was saying. The urge to take Diego's hand was so strong, Santiago thought he might faint with need. He breathed in deeply and then out deeply, just like he'd seen the king do his entire life, desperately trying to maintain his composure.

# Eleven

Xavi wound Stefi down yet another cobblestoned street, but Stefi didn't mind. They were all so beautiful, narrow, too, but this one especially so. A secret street, empty of tourists. Shadowy and quiet and romantic. Stefi loved this tour. It was perfect.

So was Xavi, she decided. If a photo of this boy was ever on the cover of one of her novels, it would surely be an immediate bestseller. Stefi would certainly buy it. Getting to spend so much of the afternoon with Xavi, walking around and talking to him for hours, had given Stefi a chance to really take him in, to study his features, everything about him, and boy did she like what she was seeing. She practically had Jason-amnesia as a result.

All good signs.

"Don't tell anyone," Xavi said now, "but this might be my favorite street in the city."

It was in El Gótico, but in a very different part from where Xavi and her abuela had their apartments. They'd left El Born a while ago, and it was clear Xavi had no plans to return Stefi to his table full of friends. Which was fine with her. The sun was setting and the day was giving way to evening. Stefi kept wishing she were daring enough to reach for Xavi's hand, but so far she hadn't mustered the courage.

He stopped, looked one way up the street, then turned and looked up the other. "I love this spot in particular," he told her. "The tourists never come here."

Xavi pressed a hand against the uneven stone wall to their right and pointed at the bookshop a little ways down, carved into the rock like a tiny cave. The yellow light inside gave it a charming glow, much like the place for tea and cakes diagonally across from it that was run by nuns. The people of the medieval heart of this city built their restaurants and shops into the walls that lined the neighborhoods, and the result was a fantasy made real.

She pressed her hand against all that history alongside Xavi's. The stone was cold under her palm despite the lingering heat of the evening. For a moment she wondered about all the people who'd touched this same place with their own hands. Who were they? Children playing, tired women carrying their wares home from the market, an old man steadying himself? Lovers entwined in a passionate embrace? Stefi could feel Xavi close to her, the unusual quiet of the street allowing her to hear his steady breathing.

"Stefi," Xavi said.

She felt Xavi's hand cover her own.

"Yes?" Stefi shifted so she could look up at Xavi, her back against all those centuries of history. Xavi's hand pinned hers to the wall. He looked down at her and she looked back up at him. The stone along her back sent shivers up her spine, or maybe it was the expression in Xavi's eyes that caused her to react this way. The leather bracelet Xavi wore around his wrist brushed against her skin, each simple touch opening blooms of feeling in Stefi's chest. Stefi allowed herself to examine the boy before her once more, the muscles that corded up along his forearm to his shoulder, the strong lines of his jaw that rose toward sharp, angled cheekbones. Looking at him made Stefi's whole body ache; her skin prickled with goose bumps.

Had she ever felt this way with Jason?

Jason had never made Stefi feel what Xavi was making her feel just by standing there, touching her hand, and looking at her. This was it, Stefi thought. This was her summer romance, just like it happened in all her novels. The sound of laughter spilled from a window far above them as Stefi tried to send Xavi a message telepathically: *Kiss me, Xavi. I want to be kissed.*

"We've already run into each other twice in one week," Xavi said.

Stefi's heart was galloping inside her chest. "The goddess of summer obviously wants us to become friends."

Xavi's mouth stretched into a smile. His hand slipped lower until it pinned her wrist.

Stefi felt she might slide to the ground; her knees grew weak. She wondered if Xavi would catch her. The thought of being in his arms made her knees even weaker.

"I can accept that," he said. "But she only wants us to be friends, you think?"

Stefi barely noticed another couple wandering by, their eyes elsewhere, offering the young couple privacy. They disappeared around the corner, and Stefi and Xavi were alone again. "Maybe she wants more than that."

Xavi's head bent closer. "I think she does."

His breath brushed across her skin. Her heart was so loud, she could hear it. "I have an ex-boyfriend," she said in a rush, feeling the need to warn Xavi about Jason. Though she wasn't sure why, exactly. "I'm still getting over him, so I'm not ready for anything new. Nothing serious. The thing with the boyfriend . . . it ended badly."

Xavi's mouth was so close, they were nearly kissing. "Good, because I can't get serious with anyone either. And as you know, I have a complicated ex."

*Isabel.* He meant Isabel. Who was so beautiful that if someone had told Stefi there really was a goddess of summer and Isabel was that goddess, Stefi would have accepted this without question. How could she possibly measure up? Stefi swallowed. She was having trouble breathing with Xavi's lips so close to her own. *Then again*, she told herself, *Isabel isn't here with Xavi—I am.*

Xavi slid the hand pinning Stefi's wrist over her palm and entwined his fingers with hers. "I'll also be gone from Barcelona before the end of summer," he told her.

This news entered Stefi's brain and went out the other side. She decided to focus on the moment. Why worry about the future? The old Stefi would have, but the new and more daring Stefi was living for the moment. And right now the moment looked a lot like a hot boy who wanted to eat her for dinner.

"I don't want another boyfriend," she said. "I've had enough of boyfriends. Boyfriends are the worst." With each statement, Stefi's declaration grew stronger. Yes, what she needed was a fling. A meaningless summer fling. A fling that, kiss by kiss, would rise like a wall between Stefi and all that had happened before she arrived in Barcelona until she could barely see that memory of Jason and Amber in her mind anymore. "I just want to have some fun. Distract myself from the heat wave on its way."

"Well, that's perfect, then," Xavi said. "Barcelona heat waves can be brutal."

"So I've heard." With her free hand, Stefi plucked at the front of her dress because she sure was feeling hot, a gesture that elicited a sigh from the boy looking down at her. So Stefi finally found the courage blooming inside her amid everything else and she rose up on her toes and kissed him.

# PART TWO

# Heat Wave

# Twelve

This heat wave was going to Xavi's head.

Or maybe it was the American girl he'd kissed the other night. They'd stopped at making out but she'd kissed Xavi like she was starving for whatever he had on offer. She definitely left him thinking about all the other things he'd like to do if they ever found themselves in private for an hour or two. Or even a whole afternoon.

Marta was waving a spatula in front of Xavi's face. "Mi amor."

"Yes, mamá?"

Marta pointed to the television screen. It sat high above the shelves at La Buena, which were stocked with bottles of agua con gas, tiny cans of Coca-Cola, tins of sardines, artichoke hearts, and other conservas typical of so many tapas places in Barcelona. "I can't find the remote anywhere. Can you reach up and turn the TV on for me?"

"God, it's not even eight a.m. and it's this hot already?"

"Unfortunately, yes," Marta said.

Xavi reached one long arm up and searched along the edge of the flat-screen for the on button. They normally didn't use the television at La Buena. It wasn't like it was a bar where people came to watch Barça play. In fact, the only time of year they turned it on was this one.

There. He found it and pressed it. The television came to life, and he went about finding the right channel.

Xavi looked behind him. Fellow shopkeepers at La Boqueria were already gathering around the counter, eager for what they were about to see: the first encierro of the season.

The running of the bulls in Pamplona.

All over Spain, people set alarms to make sure they were up and brewed their espresso so they could ready themselves to watch. People on their way to work would duck into a bar for a few minutes, and people already at work would pause to swipe their phones or tune in to the screen set up in a break room or central location so they wouldn't miss a single second. The people who ran the stalls and counters in La Boqueria were no different.

"There, you've got it!" someone yelled.

Xavi retracted his hand from the television controls, then stepped back to watch with his mother and Santiago and everyone else in the crowd, most of them sipping their coffees or beers in anticipation of what was to come.

The encierro was covered live with accompanying play-by-play commentary. That meant if a bull caught one of the runners—as often happened—the shocking scene was also broadcast live. Occasionally someone *died*. Afterward, there was always an extensive slow-motion replay, with close-ups of each bull knocking into someone or a horn catching a shirt or, well, a neck, followed by the official count of the injuries, how bad each injury was, and if it had sent someone to the hospital. The newscasters always covered this part with gusto.

"Seven fifty-five," Santiago said, checking his phone. He ran out from under the counter to stand farther back and get a better view of the screen. "Five more minutes and we're off."

At least Santiago was talking, if not talking directly to Xavi, he thought. He joined Santiago so he could watch without craning his neck too painfully.

The camera panned across the crowd of spectators cheering from their windows all over the city of Pamplona, then lingered on the bulls in their pen.

"I hear they're from Puerto de San Lorenzo today," someone near Xavi commented.

La Fiesta de San Fermín had officially started yesterday with the Chupinazo, the ceremony and party that marked the opening of the festival. Everyone gathered in the main square at the heart of Pamplona, wearing white and holding bright red kerchiefs high over their heads. Twelve rockets were sent into the air, followed by a special chant ("Long live San Fermín!"). Then the spectators tied their red kerchiefs around their necks and started popping bottles of cava and plenty of red wine. By the end of the day, everyone's white outfit was stained a dark red.

But today, July 7, was the *real* start of the festival. Just before eight a.m., and for the next eight days, the entire city would come to a halt to watch the hundreds of corredores chant in unison, first in Spanish, then in Basque, their prayer to San Fermín, whose statue looks down on them from its decorated perch in the wall. The runners asked the saint to protect them twice—as if this might help if a bull got hold of their shirts or, worse, a leg or an arm. Or ran right over people like they were roadkill. Then a rocket would go off, and a dozen giant, angry bulls would be released from their pen and chased down the street by men clanging cowbells and holding pointy sticks. Not like the bulls needed any encouragement.

Xavi loved it. He wondered if Stefi was watching too. If her abuela was the kind of person who tuned in every day and called to the whole family to come and join her or if she was disapproving of the tradition.

"Mi amor, turn up the volume, will you?" Marta asked Xavi.

There was only a minute until the start. Xavi ran back behind the counter and felt for the controls along the bottom of the screen again. At one point, he turned the sound down by accident and heard cries of protest from the crowd gathered around the counter. But then there was clapping when the volume went up and up.

Xavi hurried back to take his place between Marta and Santiago.

Santiago was not talking to Xavi, and he wouldn't look at him either.

If only Santiago hadn't found Xavi with Stefi the other night and been such a pain in the ass as he hurried Xavi away with some fake Marta-emergency, maybe Xavi would have gotten Stefi's number. Then he'd be able to text her to see if she was watching. Or tell her to turn on the TV. Or invite her to come down to La Buena to watch here and maybe even drink a mini-beer for breakfast to calm her nerves as she watched the crowd of gigantic bulls with the biggest, scariest, pointiest horns you'd ever seen chasing hundreds of fleeing humans down the streets like they wanted to kill a few of them. Technically, he could go and ring her abuela's bell to see if she was home like boys had done when his mother was young. This was Xavi's last resort, however.

Jordi wandered out from the prep space. He ducked under the counter to join their group, planted himself quietly next to Marta, and crossed his arms.

"I read that there are less than five percent women running this year," Jordi commented as the men in white and red on the screen—it *was* almost all men—jumped up and down and stretched as they got ready to run. There were a few women swirling around in the crowd, but not many.

Xavi wondered if Jordi was trying to impress his mother with his feminist statistics.

"That's because women are smarter than men," Marta replied, and Jordi laughed.

Thirty seconds. The chant to San Fermín asking for protection began. The camera again panned across the thousands of people cheering from the windows and buildings along the path through the old medieval heart of Pamplona that ended in the beautiful old bullring.

Xavi had hoped that maybe Stefi would surprise him and show up at La Buena at some point while he was working, but so far she hadn't. Xavi was sweating through his T-shirt, and not just because of his worry that Stefi might never reappear and he'd have to show up at her apartment like an old-fashioned suitor. Or, worse, a weird stalker. The heat was so heavy, Xavi could practically see it shining and swirling like oil in the air. The runners must be melting in their long pants.

"You know, next year, if you want to, you'll be able to see this live," Marta whispered to her son. "I'm sure they'd set you up in the best possible spot to watch."

Xavi looked around at the crowd gathered at La Buena, all the familiar faces of people he'd known since he was a little boy, plus the regulars who'd come in early to drink their morning beers and watch the tourists get gored by bulls with glee. "But then I wouldn't be here with everybody."

Marta sighed. "Oh, Xavi. No. I think that's the idea, mi amor. You are going to have to get used to it sooner or later. And you need to think about it as an opportunity, darling."

The rocket shot up into the sky, and the runners took off.

The camera showed the bulls as they rushed out of the pen. It always took a few seconds for the bulls to catch up to the runners, but when they did, Marta always covered her eyes and watched between the gaps of her fingers.

Xavi nudged his mother. "Mom, come on, nothing has happened so far."

As the bulls neared the runners, a few people fell and the bulls trampled right over them. Xavi would definitely not want to be stomped on by a thousand-pound animal. The crowd at La Buena let out a loud "Ooh" when one of the bulls crashed into the stone wall of the infamous treacherous curve, taking another runner with him. It was one of the most dangerous moments of the run because the bulls often stumbled and crashed and you didn't want to get caught underneath them or on top of them. The bull who'd smashed the man into the wall got up and continued on, running scary-fast and chasing after another unfortunate man who was on the slower side at the back of the crowd. Once the rest of the bulls cleared the area, the medics went to tend to the poor man lying curled up on the ground who was not looking so good.

"I hope he's okay," Marta said.

Jordi leaned in. "He didn't catch a horn, so he might just be a bit squashed inside."

Marta tsked. But Santiago chimed in, next to Xavi, "That is the deal, you know? If you run with the bulls, you might not leave with your life. It's always a risk."

"Yes, one my son will *never* take," she said.

"Of course he won't," Santiago said. "He's not allowed."

"I'm right here," Xavi reminded them.

By now the bulls were running smack in the middle of the crowd. A man turned his head and looked terrified when he caught sight of the long sharp horn next to his ear. There were famous runners who ran day after day, year after year—Pamplona residents raised to run with the bulls their entire lives. People might not believe it, but there was a technique to this, or, really, an art, and the men who knew what they were doing made the run look almost graceful, tapping the bulls with newspapers, patting them with their hands without fear.

One man was doing this now, running between the horns, constantly turning to monitor the bull behind him, patting the bull's head like it was a golden retriever. The crowd gathered at La Buena oohed and aahed. It was almost always the tourists who got injured, not people from Pamplona.

"Uh-uh!"

"Oooh, shit!"

Just before the narrow entrance to the bullring where everything would come to an end and the runners would celebrate their survival, a bull caught a runner and tossed him up into the air.

"I can't watch this!" Marta shouted and ran off to somewhere else in La Boqueria.

Jordi turned and followed her.

The rest of the crowd was rapt.

Eventually, the bull moved on, and people ran out to help the man.

The camera pivoted to the ring, where the crowds were standing and cheering all the runners as they spilled into the stadium; the bulls were drawn into the pen that awaited them. Now the runners could celebrate the fact that, at least today, they'd gotten out of the encierro with their lives. Survival equaled success in this festival.

"Well, that was exciting," Santiago said.

Xavi glanced at him. "So you're talking to me again?"

"I guess."

"Fine."

"Fine."

Almost everyone stayed to watch the first slow-motion replay, but eventually the crowd dispersed and Xavi shut off the television. Soon La Boqueria would be busy with locals trying to buy their groceries before the tourists were out of their hotels and Airbnb beds and clogging the aisles. A few people took seats at the counter so they could get a quick breakfast or a second café con leche before opening their stalls and suffering through this awful heat. Marta and Jordi returned to their stations now that there were no more threatening bulls to stress her out.

The temperature rose and rose as the morning passed. Xavi stood in front of the stove cooking and wondered if he might faint. But he was more worried about his mother. Maybe he should send her home?

Marta turned to her son. "Why don't you and Santiago go to the beach," she said, apparently thinking the same thing about him.

Xavi looked at his mother like she might have gone crazy. "What? But it's barely ten a.m."

"Yes, and it's already over thirty-six degrees."

"And what are *you* going to do?" Xavi asked.

"Close early, I think."

"But you *never* do that," he said.

"Well, maybe it's time your mother takes a break."

"What if *you* go to the beach today? I'm sure Jordi would go with you," Xavi suggested.

But Marta didn't seem to hear him. She had a faraway look on her face. "Maybe it's even time for your mother to take a vacation," she said as though Xavi hadn't mentioned the beach or Jordi.

"A vacation?" The shocks kept coming. First, his mother considering closing La Buena early because of the heat, and now Marta talking of going on vacation? Xavi considered asking his mother where and for how long she might go on vacation. He noticed that Marta hadn't said, *Maybe we should take a vacation*. Marta's plans, whatever they might turn out to be, seemed like they did not involve her son. Now all kinds of other questions popped up in Xavi's brain. Like: Did his mother have a secret boyfriend? Could she have been going out with someone and Xavi simply hadn't noticed? But he would have known, wouldn't he?

"I think a vacation is a great idea," was all Xavi told his mother. Marta always respected Xavi's privacy, so Xavi would respect hers too. "Just keep me posted, mamá," he added, and leaned down to give her a kiss on the cheek where she stood, sweating like everyone else, but more so because of the heat rolling off the stove. "Let's close, all right?"

"All right," she agreed with a sigh.

Xavi turned all the burners off, to the chagrin of the tourists in line, and told the patrons who'd just sat down at the counter that they were closing early.

Then, as he scrubbed the stovetop, something exciting occurred to Xavi. If his mother went on vacation, he would have the whole apartment to himself. Well, except for Santiago. But Santiago he could handle. Xavi could invite Stefi over. He could invite Stefi over and they would be alone. If he needed to go to her abuela's to invite her, it was well worth it, he decided.

Marta started to sing "Tanti Auguri," a celebratory Italian favorite by Raffaella Carrà that people often played when it was someone's birthday. Xavi joined in. He heard Jordi humming it through the open door of the prep space as he made his way through his own closing checklist. The song made Xavi feel like dancing even in the heat.

When they were finally finished, Xavi untied his apron and hung it up on its hook.

"¡A la playa!" he called out, excited for the unexpected day off.

Aside from that one article about a prince in Barcelona, ¡Qué Fuerte! had thankfully remained silent about Xavi's true identity ever since. His anonymity lived to see yet another day, and that day would involve the beach, ahora mismo. Right now. Immediately. Without a second's delay.

# Thirteen

For Stefi, the heat wave started with a kiss. Well, multiple kisses. Or more like full-on making out that left her completely breathless and disheveled—hair, lipstick, clothing.

Stefi let out a laugh as she walked down the street on her way to the beach. If only that cousin of Xavi's hadn't physically dragged him away, leaving Diego to walk Stefi home. What was with that guy? she wondered. She'd considered showing up at La Buena this morning to see if Xavi was working and to give him her number because this was what the new, bolder version of Stefi would do. But Stefi was too nervous about running into Marta, his mother, given the way she'd kind of shooed Stefi from Xavi last time. Much like Santiago kept doing, come to think of it.

Did they not want Xavi to date an American?

Maybe that was the problem. Which Stefi could understand, since Americans could be a lot of things, many of them not so good. She would just have to work to change their opinions.

Stefi crossed the street into La Barceloneta, getting closer to the beach with every step. Thank goodness. She'd be drenched in sweat by the time she arrived. She could practically feel the turquoise Mediterranean water cooling her off already. Mercifully, her pastry class had ended early. Her normally strict teacher had been undone by the temperature like everyone else and dismissed them after only an hour.

It was so hot today, Stefi could almost understand why there were signs in certain parts of the city showing the outline of a body and a line through it: "No Nudity." As in, "No walking the Barcelona streets naked." The city had passed an ordinance making it illegal to be in the city without any clothes because apparently this became a problem a couple of summers ago. Abuela told her this one day when Stefi asked about the signs. While nudity was common on certain parts of the beach, abuela explained, locals and European visitors knew that once they left the sand, they needed to put on their shirts and shorts or at least a bathing suit with a cover-up. Not so with some of the other tourists. Stefi had yet to see anyone breaking this city law, and she shuddered at the thought of running into a bunch of drunk guys her age who weren't wearing bathing suits.

Stefi zigzagged down the wide boulevard that ended at the beach, doing her best to follow the pattern of shade from the trees that lined the avenue. One seafood restaurant after the other dotted the street to her left, all of them packed with people sitting outside, waiting for their paella and their giant shrimp and their plates piled with grilled calamari and other fishy things. There were a few ice cream shops and little kids doing their best to lick their cones before they melted away in the bright hot sun. Boy, those ice creams looked good, Stefi thought. Maybe she would get herself one later. Soon she passed a few stores selling beach gear and then the bars near the sea. Everyone seemed to be walking in the same direction on the boulevard—toward the beach. It was the only sane place to be on a hot day like today.

Stefi came to a halt at the beginning of the boardwalk.

Whoa.

Turquoise-blue sea sparkling in the sunlight stretched toward the horizon. Magnificent. It was good Stefi was wearing her sunglasses. But between Stefi and the sea, the beach was jammed with people. She finally understood the meaning of the phrase *packed in like sardines*, especially now that she had opened more than a few sardine tins for her abuela. Stefi adjusted the brim of her sun hat against the glare and searched for an open spot in the sand. Was there one? When Stefi couldn't see anything in one direction, she turned in the other. There.

A small spot midway between Stefi and the sea opened up as a family got ready to leave. She hurried toward it before someone else could take it, the little beach umbrella her abuela had given her slung over her shoulder in a slim sack bumping against her hip. Sweat streamed down Stefi's stomach, across her neck, and along the side of her face. She had endured heat waves at home, but nothing like this, a blast of air coming up from Africa. Even so, people didn't really use their air-conditioning in Barcelona, even when it was available and even when the temperature topped a hundred. Stefi wondered what in the world it would take for abuelita to turn on the AC units in the apartment. Perhaps the city needed to be burning before her grandmother would cave and turn on that cold air. *It's better for the environment* was abuela's eternal answer, which Stefi knew was true, but still.

"Success," Stefi said gleefully when she reached the open spot without anyone beating her there. She dropped her bag to her feet, removed the towels inside, spread one out to lie on, and left the other standing by for after swimming. Stefi stuck the pointy end of the little umbrella as far down in the sand as she could manage, then opened it to provide some much-needed shade. Abuela had known what she was talking about when she insisted Stefi take it. Stefi slipped off the cover-up and shoved it away into the now-empty bag.

Finally! Stefi was at the beach in Barcelona!

Stefi had chosen to wear her new green bikini. She'd felt so daring when she put it on and looked at herself in the mirror. It sure was teeny.

But now, in front of her, behind her, to her left, to her right, no matter which way Stefi turned, she saw the very same thing. Women everywhere, the vast majority of them wearing only bikini bottoms, a few of them completely naked. Old women; middle-aged women; mothers with children; college-age women in massive groups of friends, drinking beer and lying in the sun; girls who looked to be around the same age as Stefi or slightly younger. So many women and girls sitting on their towels or taking walks down by the water or helping children build sandcastles or jumping in the waves, their hands waving high in the air, all of them topless. And the completely naked ones were the abuelas. Women with every kind of body imaginable, women whose breasts were big, small, round, perky, sagging, wrinkled. No one seemed worried about what they looked like or what anyone else might think of their bodies. Probably the only women who weren't topless were the American tourists and, maybe, the British ones. Surely there were some locals who didn't go topless, but they seemed to be at the other end of the beach, where Stefi wasn't able to find a place to sit.

Stefi swallowed and blinked, her hand inadvertently reaching to straighten one of the triangles of her bikini top, making sure it was exactly where it should be, which was covering up everything on Stefi's body that should be covered. Despite the No Nudity signs in the city, Stefi hadn't realized what this would mean for beachgoers. Stefi had plopped herself right in the middle of dozens of topless women and girls, many of them so beautiful, she felt it was scandalous to look. And yet, no one else seemed to notice anything amiss. Barcelona was part of Europe after all, Stefi reminded herself. Weren't Europe's beaches famous for all the beautiful sunbathing women?

Stefi sat down on her towel and reminded herself that it was actually pretty amazing to see so many women and girls walking around completely unconcerned about their bodies, even saggy grandmothers. What Stefi saw around her was a beach full of women comfortable in their own skin. Perhaps the most surprising part was that the men didn't seem to be doing any ogling, not even of the stunningly beautiful women who looked like they'd just walked off a runway. If the men noticed, they were polite enough to be discreet. This would never happen with the guys Stefi knew at home. Their eyes would be popping out of their heads, and Stefi was sure they'd be unable to behave themselves.

For a brief painful moment, Stefi thought that if Amber were with her now, she would be stripping off her bathing-suit top without a second thought and trying to convince Stefi to do the same, which Stefi wouldn't. Then Stefi would be stuck on the beach with Amber flaunting herself and Stefi covered up like a prude. She winced at the image. But then something dawned on her. Amber wasn't here. And neither was anyone else from home. Stefi's parents were off on a day trip, being their typical romantic selves, and abuela was playing cards at a friend's place, someone who was actually willing to turn on her air-conditioning. Stefi didn't know a single soul here. For all the people around her knew, she was just another girl from Barcelona. Besides, it was sweltering, even in her little circle of shade.

"Come on, Stefi, be like the Barcelonans," she said out loud to no one but herself.

Before she could decide otherwise, Stefi reached around her back, tugged the bow of her bikini top loose, and lifted it up over her head. She dangled it over the opening in her beach bag, then dropped it inside.

There. At any point, she could decide to put it back on.

Stefi looked around. Everything was fine. Totally and completely fine. No one was staring at Stefi in shock or pointing at her, offended. Not a single person even seemed to notice what Stefi had done. If people did, they certainly didn't care. Now Stefi was just another topless girl on the beach.

*No big deal, nothing to see here.* Stefi sat there awhile, upright on her towel, palms pressing into the sand, trying to decide how it felt to do something she'd never dare do at home. Men walked around like this all the time, so why shouldn't women? This was practically a feminist act, Stefi decided. Besides, how different was it to wear that tiny bikini top or go without it? It was barely there in the first place.

As Stefi sat there contemplating all of this, her gaze occasionally shifted down to her chest, and she wondered if anyone nearby was paying attention to it. Her body might not be quite like Amber's, but she'd been told before, and not only by Jason, that it was beautiful. Maybe this experience would be good for Stefi's self-esteem, good for her body image; it was like exposure therapy, a way for her to become more comfortable in her own skin. She wouldn't mind being more like the many women and girls who seemed so unselfconscious all around her, not at all worried about how they appeared to everyone else. If Stefi could reach that point too, it would be a summer well spent.

At that encouraging thought, Stefi rose from her towel. Like the other girls and women around her, she walked to the beautiful Mediterranean, head held high, relaxed and casual, and waded right in.

# Fourteen

Santiago might have been walking the beach with Xavi in the full light of this very hot day, but in his mind, he was reliving the other night.

Not the anger he felt about Xavi's ditching him twice in one day. But the silly, heady joy about his experience searching for Xavi through the medieval quarter on a beautiful Barcelona evening, just himself and Diego. And how, in the middle of that search, Diego turned to Santiago and said, "This looking-for-Xavi situation is making me parched. How about you?"

Santiago had swallowed. Was Diego asking him if he wanted to get a drink?

They'd stopped in front of the most adorable bar. This one was particularly lovely, with its updated modernist woodwork and its old-fashioned white marble bar manned by two mixologists with massively muscled biceps shaking up drinks. Better still, the moodiest of mood lighting gave the whole place a romantic glow. A battle erupted inside Santiago's mind and reached a crisis point. Santiago knew he should say no to Diego, that he should continue in his search for Xavi. This was what his job required, and this was what both the king and Francisco, the jefe of the guard, were counting on him to do. But there was also Santiago the teenage boy who knew beyond a shadow of a doubt that he not only had it bad for Diego but his crush was turning into a full-blown, one-sided love affair. The more he hung out with Diego, the more he liked the guy. That side of him was fighting hard for Santiago to say, *Yes, please,* to Diego's suggestion that they get a drink at this very romantically lit establishment only a couple of steps away.

Teenage-boy Santiago won the battle.

"Sure, I could use a drink," he said.

Diego's happy face when Santiago gave him a yes confirmed that he'd made the absolute right decision. For teenage-boy Santiago, at least.

Diego opened the door and ushered Santiago inside with an "Adelante." Which meant "After you," and was the kind of gentlemanly thing a person did on a date. Was this turning into a date? This was the next question that had spasmed through Santiago's mind and heart and nearly made him dizzy.

On the beach, Santiago looked ahead at Xavi. There was still a bit of tension between them, so Santiago kept a few steps behind him. Xavi's friends had chosen to sit on the posh side of the long curving C of sand, down near the W Hotel and the bars underneath it, where sometimes you ran into famous Barça players and their model girlfriends. But today, getting there was brutal. The walk was one unending oven-fest in this heat. He let his mind float back to his new favorite thing to think about: Diego.

"Let's sit at the bar," Diego had suggested when they'd walked inside that beautiful little cocktail spot in El Gótico. At first, Santiago didn't relish the idea of sharing Diego with the extremely attractively buff bartenders. But the moment the two young men sat down on the stools side by side, Diego swiveled toward Santiago, his knee pressed into Santiago's thigh.

"So what do you want?" Diego asked him.

*You, I want you*, Santiago's heart practically shouted. But thank God, out loud his only reply was "I bet they have good cocktails here. Why don't we see if there's a menu?"

Diego raised his hand to call the bartender and soon they were searching the list, trying to decide what to order. Diego had yet to move his leg. All of Santiago's sensory awareness seemed to be centered on the place where Diego's knee touched his thigh.

Diego looked up from the menu. "Do you trust me enough to choose for you?"

Santiago had been too distracted by Diego's knee to comprehend the menu, and now he was reeling because of Diego's offer to order on his behalf, which made this seem even more date-like. "Definitely," Santiago said, since reading drink descriptions was beyond him anyway.

Soon they were sipping delicious concoctions in beautiful glasses, and Santiago nearly forgot the reason they'd stumbled into this bar. For a while, he allowed himself to enjoy this temporary amnesia. Santiago let his thigh press back into Diego's knee a bit, and when Diego still didn't shift away, Santiago took this as encouragement and dared to say, "So, Xavi tells me you went through a tough breakup this spring."

Diego's gaze dropped to the cherry-colored liquid in his glass. "Yeah, a lot of us had breakups this spring. Xavi, Gemma, Isabel, me."

"Was it serious?"

Diego used the slice of lemon peel to swirl his drink, then set it floating in the glass. "You know, I used to think it was, but now I'm not so sure." Diego's eyes returned to Santiago's. "Every day that passes I realize maybe this person wasn't as big a deal to me after all."

Santiago's heart fluttered. "Is that a good thing or a bad thing?"

"I think a good thing." Diego held Santiago's gaze. "I promise I'll tell you as soon as I'm sure one way or the other."

Santiago smiled at this, and Diego smiled back. Were they having a conversation in code? He sure hoped they were. He shifted on his bar stool so his knee was now ever so casually positioned between Diego's legs. If they wanted to talk face to face, the stools were placed so this was their only option. Besides, Santiago's legs were very long. Santiago realized that with another slight shift in position, he could put a hand on Diego's knee. Or, even more amazingly, he could lean forward and give Diego a kiss.

Did he dare?

But then the decision was made for him with an ill-timed text that broke the spell that had fallen over Santiago and Diego the moment they happened on this bar and walked inside.

Diego showed Santiago the message from Isabel on his phone. **Are you two ever coming back? What about Xavi?**

*What about Xavi?* Santiago thought on seeing this, heart sinking. Santiago needed to go and find the guy, which meant his romantic moment with Diego was about to come to an end.

Diego studied Santiago. "You know, we don't have to leave yet."

But Santiago shook his head and finished the rest of his delicious drink. "Yes we do," he said and called for the check. "*I* do."

Diego shrugged. "All right. If you say so." He sounded disappointed.

But was it disappointment because Diego hoped the night would lead them elsewhere romantically? Or disappointment about Santiago's strange obsession with knowing Xavi's whereabouts at all times? Could Diego even be annoyed by this?

These questions lingered in Santiago's mind as he walked, causing him to sweat even harder in this awful heat despite the fact that he and Xavi were right now splashing through ankle-deep water as they searched for that damn spot where Xavi's friends from school awaited them. This place was as packed as Santiago had ever seen a beach in summer. He checked his phone, then searched in the direction the GPS told him to go to meet up with everyone. They should be close.

Then Xavi halted so suddenly that Santiago nearly crashed into him. "Watch it, Xavi," he protested.

But Xavi didn't apologize. He didn't even seem to register that he'd nearly tripped Santiago and sent him crashing into the wet sand and water. Santiago followed the line of Xavi's gaze and saw why the prince of Spain had been stopped so totally in his tracks.

"Joder," Santiago muttered.

Xavi didn't hear this from his royal guard either. He was too busy watching the very beautiful American girl emerge from the water.

Santiago sighed heavily. "Just go and say hello to her," he told Xavi, feeling generous for the moment. "I'll hang back at a discreet distance."

Xavi nodded but couldn't seem to find any words. Santiago nearly laughed as Xavi stumbled off to talk to Stefi.

# Fifteen

Stefi felt so good—cool, refreshed, and relaxed. The Mediterranean Sea was heavenly.

But after who knew how long in the water, Stefi was starting to shiver, so she knew she should probably get out. She wondered how long that cold feeling running through her would last in this heat. As she headed toward her blanket amid the ever-growing crowd, she wrung out her soaking hair, then tied it up on a knot on her head. The water felt delicious in this humidity.

Stefi lay down on her towel in the shade of the umbrella, not bothering to dry off. The heat would dry her skin soon enough. She closed her eyes, luxuriating in the coolness from the water. It wouldn't be long before she'd need another swim. Just as Stefi was feeling so relaxed she was nearly asleep, three shocking things happened in quick succession.

The first two came from her phone, which suddenly buzzed to life.

The phone was at the bottom of her bag. Without opening her eyes, Stefi lazily felt around for it, digging down to retrieve the thing. Reluctantly, she held the phone above her face, shading it with her hands and trying to read the screen in the blinding sunlight.

Amber.

The message was from *Amber.*

She'd texted Stefi out of the blue and for the first time since Stefi had arrived in Barcelona.

Granted, Amber had texted Stefi about a billion apologies on the day of the Betrayal and all the way up until Stefi's flight was lifting off the ground. She'd called Stefi incessantly too, leaving sorrowful voice messages. "Please, can we talk? I'm sorry. Please. You know I love you and always will." Blah-blah. This was pretty much what Amber had written too, over and over, in a bunch of different ways. There were other things she'd said: "I didn't mean to fall for Jason" and "Jason and I tried so hard not to be with each other." But they were too painful and humiliating for Stefi to allow herself to remember. The message that was missing from the billions? The one Stefi kept waiting for, the one that said, *It was a mistake. What I did with Jason was a mistake*. But that message never arrived.

Jason did the same, texting and begging and calling Stefi. But she refused to pick up the phone when she saw their names and she refused to respond to any of their texts. After she arrived in Barcelona, the calls and messages stopped. Stefi guessed the two had talked it over and decided to give up on Stefi, because obviously their relationship with each other was more important than either of their relationships with her. Which was probably what had led to the cheating in the first place. The photos she'd seen online of the two of them confirmed this, in addition to making the wound in her heart open all over again and bleed like it would never stop.

But now, seeing Amber's name on her phone after so much silence made Stefi's stomach do a flip and a flop. Not what she needed on the hottest day of the year. She had just been feeling so good after her swim.

**I know you probably hate me.**

**But.**

**I was hoping we could talk?**

All kinds of thoughts and feelings coursed through Stefi as she read Amber's words over and over. Some were full of rage. Some were full of confusion. But a few were sad. If Stefi was totally honest, she was starting to feel lonely without Amber in her life. Stefi's break from Amber and Jason had turned out to be a break from everyone else at school too. It was as though Amber and Jason were Stefi's only doorway to life at home. To get to everyone else, Stefi had to go through them, so Stefi wasn't communicating with anyone. People from school must know by now what Amber and Jason had done to Stefi, and she couldn't bear to face their questions. Not yet.

The other night when Stefi returned home after making out with Xavi in that dark corner of El Gótico, she'd considered texting Amber. Stefi was dying to talk to someone about Xavi, and for the entirety of her life, the first person Stefi always told every single thing was Amber. Amber knew every gory detail about Stefi's life: the good, the awful, the embarrassing, the exciting. When Stefi realized how badly she wished she could call up Amber and tell her about Xavi, it caused a pain inside her that was sharp and piercing and oh so hurtful. Stefi almost wanted to forgive Amber just so they could go back to the part where they told each other everything, and she could get Amber's advice on Xavi. But that could never happen, Stefi realized. There was no way.

For Stefi to be able to tell Amber everything again, Stefi had to be willing to reciprocate on the listening front, and Stefi wasn't—she'd *never* be ready for that. How could Stefi be the person Amber told the details of her relationship with Jason? Which would obviously involve their sex life.

No. No way. There was no going back. Stefi was still and would always be too humiliated by what they'd done to her—by what Amber, specifically, had done to her.

The screen of Stefi's phone faded to black and she set it down on the towel.

But it immediately buzzed to life again.

Stefi assumed it was Amber leaving another message, but when she swiped the screen, her second moment of shock arrived. Stefi peered through her sunglasses at the phone she once again held above her face, moving it into the shade of the beach umbrella so she could better read what was there, and saw it was someone else entirely who'd texted.

Someone equally on her shit list.

Jason. Jason!

*What was going on?*

**Stefi.**

**I know.**

**You're still angry.**

*Angry?* Stefi thought. Angry was not the word for what Stefi still felt. She wasn't sure what the exact word was, but she didn't have time to decide because Jason was still typing and a new message appeared, then another.

**But I really want to talk to you.**

**There's something I need to say.**

To hear first from Amber and now from Jason sent fireworks of confusion off in Stefi's brain. Had the two planned this? Had they decided to begin their Stefi-relationship rehabilitation once more? Or . . . or . . .

Another thought traveled through Stefi.

Was there trouble in paradise? Had they gotten into a little fight, or even a big one, and this was what had prompted today's attempt to reach out? Had they even—Stefi swallowed—broken up? And if they had, how did Stefi feel about it? By now the fireworks finale of confusion was crackling and booming through her mind so loudly and blindingly that Stefi lost track of where she was and what she was doing. She was staring so hard at the screen so she could actually read these messages from Jason and Amber and decode their meaning that she had not only forgotten where she was but she also lost sight of the fact that she was wearing her bikini bottoms and nothing else. Scandalously scantily clad. So when the third shock arrived right as Stefi remembered she was literally half naked in public, boy did the scandal of this hit her like a spectacular belly flop off a diving board.

"Hello."

The sound of a boy's voice floated through the air to Stefi. Followed by a pause.

A shiver rolled through Stefi. Was that hello for her?

No, she decided. If it was for her, then he would repeat—

"Hello? Ah, Stefi?"

Another chill ran across Stefi's body at the sound of her name. Especially when she recognized the owner of the voice that was decidedly close. Standing right above her, in fact.

She set aside the phone.

Oh my God.

She blinked up at Xavi. How long had he been there?

"Hi, Xavi, it's so nice to see you! I hoped we might run into each other again!" Stefi said overly cheerfully, doing her best to be casual and also not to grab for her shirt, her bikini top, a towel, the umbrella, a pile of sand, two conveniently large shells—really, anything to cover herself, even her palms would do. At least she could hide behind her sunglasses. Stefi knew she needed to act normal. Xavi was from Barcelona, he wasn't like one of the dumb guys she knew from school who—in addition to making some stupid comment to Stefi—would likely go and tell every single other dumb guy from school that he had run into a topless Stefi at the beach. For Xavi, who surely came to this beach all the time, this was not a big deal. Nothing to see here. Nothing but Stefi's boobs.

"Nice to see you too," Xavi said. Or, rather, croaked.

Stefi breathed out, she breathed in. She did her best to nonchalantly sit up so she could better talk to Xavi. Who, by the way, had possibly the nicest, tannest body Stefi had ever seen, so nice Stefi forgot herself and nearly kept rising all the way to standing like she might be about to make out with him again like some kind of possessed person. But she managed to resist doing this and stayed put on the towel.

"Beautiful day, isn't it?" Stefi patted the spot next to her. "Would you like to join me?" She was doing so well, given the situation. It had taken Stefi a full nine months of dating before she allowed Jason to remove both her shirt and her bra, and yet here Stefi was, mission accomplished with Xavi and in full view of everyone at this European beach. This was a more daring version of Stefi, for sure.

Xavi sat down. He stared at the sea and not at Stefi.

Stefi stared at the sea and not at Xavi.

A silence fell between them. But it wasn't an awkward one. More like a silence so charged, it could cause a blackout throughout the entire city.

So far, Stefi had never known Xavi to be speechless. She wondered if Xavi was thinking what she was thinking, which was about the two of them kissing the other night, which made her want to kiss him right now. Also, this was totally the type of situation that would happen in one of her romance novels, the kind of sexy chance meeting that would prompt the heroine and hero to finally get together for real, even if there were many more complications to come before their eventual happy ending. But in the romance-novel version, the heroine and hero would clasp one another in a sexy embrace and run off to make love somewhere, unable to resist one another after this very public encounter of temptation.

At least Xavi wasn't with Santiago, Stefi thought. She wasn't sure if she could bear seeing Xavi's cousin on top of Xavi right now, flustered as she was. Then again, Stefi reminded herself that she was dressed like almost every other woman and girl at this beach. She had nothing to be ashamed of. After all, hadn't she just decided this was going to be an excellent opportunity to build her self-esteem and become more comfortable in her own skin? Then again, she hadn't imagined Xavi being involved in this particular growth opportunity.

Xavi finally spoke, eyes still locked on the sea. "I meant to get your phone number the other night."

"I meant to give it to you," Stefi replied.

Xavi turned to her. He opened his mouth, then closed it. He was clearly trying to keep his eyes on Stefi's face, but behind her sunglasses, she could see they kept roaming elsewhere. This made Stefi unbearably nervous. Also unbearably thrilled. Her skin was prickling all over. Once again, she wondered what Xavi was thinking, then decided it was best not to try and imagine what was going through his brain.

Oh, Lord.

"I'm sorry my cousin can be such an idiot," Xavi said.

Stefi managed to laugh. "He definitely is determined not to let you out of his sight."

"No kidding," he said. Then: "Can I see you again? This time on purpose?"

"I'd like that."

"Good."

"Great."

Xavi and Stefi locked eyes, and another silence fell between them. Stefi thought she could see sparks sizzling and crackling into the air, defying the humidity. Then Xavi's face was tilting forward and his lips were brushing across hers. Stefi responded with a sigh. The kiss was gentle, but the situation was, well, anything but subtle.

Xavi pulled back suddenly. He shifted, dug into a pocket, and came out with his phone. He offered it to Stefi. "Before I forget again, your number. Please?"

Stefi tapped it onto the screen. She looked up as she handed it back to Xavi. What she wanted was to kiss him again. What she wanted was to throw her arms around his tan, muscular self and clasp it to her own self and maybe run her fingers through that hair. Then maybe go for a swim. Then maybe repeat the rest. In the water.

But Xavi turned away. "I've got to go," he said.

Before Stefi could even say, *See you later*, Xavi was up from Stefi's towel and had taken off across the sand. She watched as he raced down the crowded beach, slightly off balance, running his hand again and again through his hair, stomping along the edges of people's blankets now and then, people turning to glare at the handsome boy zigzagging haphazardly toward the boardwalk. It was only after Xavi was completely gone from view that Stefi realized how hard her heart was pounding and also that, in the middle of their encounter, she'd nearly forgotten the messages that had arrived from Amber and Jason. She laughed out loud and thought to herself, *Amber and Jason who?*

# Sixteen

Xavi stumbled back through La Barceloneta on his way home in a daze. He barely registered the fact that Santiago was walking behind him and had likely just witnessed his entire encounter with Stefi. Xavi passed the ice cream shops and all the people sitting outside eating their paella and their giant gambas and so many other kinds of seafood. He was usually tempted to stop in El Rey de la Gamba—literally "the King of the Shrimp"—and order a tapa of the shellfish that gave the famous old restaurant its name, but today he barely noticed it as he passed.

Santiago was finally trying to talk to Xavi after their long bout of not speaking, but Xavi wasn't listening.

"Chaval," Santiago called, but Xavi didn't stop. "Hey! Wait up!"

No matter how hard Xavi tried, he could not stop thinking about running into a sunbathing Stefi on the beach, replaying Stefi's every movement like a video in his mind: Stefi emerging out of the water as the waves rolled past her, smiling up into the sun like some kind of goddess. The initial sight of her had rooted Xavi to the sand, and all he could do was stare at the incredible view before him. He'd finally found it in himself to move again, and when he did, his feet took him closer and closer to Stefi, all the way up to the edge of the blanket and umbrella she'd set out for herself. That image of her lying there on her towel, skin glistening from her swim, burned bright in his mind. She'd looked so beautiful, Xavi was at a loss for words, and it took him longer than he'd like to admit to finally say hello and announce his presence.

On top of this, Xavi's usual sense of humor had failed him, replaced by something else, an electricity sparking between him and Stefi so alive that Xavi thought it might short-circuit his brain and so intense that, if he was honest, it kind of scared him. He barely remembered what was said between them because all their words had been overshadowed by that kiss, during which Xavi had kept his hands firmly planted on the towel below like his life depended on it, despite how badly those same hands wanted to meander elsewhere. And yet, their kiss had been brief, almost chaste, and Xavi wondered if he might have hallucinated it in this heat. But no, it was real. He could practically still taste Stefi on his lips, salty and sweet from her swim.

Xavi shifted toward the side of the boulevard that ran along La Barceloneta, where there was some shade from the trees. He needed shelter from the sun so he could clear his head. He could hear Santiago trailing after him, still calling his name, but as usual, Xavi was ignoring him. His mind was too full of Stefi.

He wished he hadn't left Stefi in such a hurry, but Xavi felt he had no other choice. If he'd stayed, he would have kissed her again, and their kissing would have led to other things that shouldn't happen on a public beach. If Xavi was going to further explore his interest in Stefi, he was not going to do it with a million tourists and locals swirling around them. He would do it in private, like the attentive and considerate gentleman Marta had taught Xavi to be. Besides, Xavi didn't want to cause a scandal. Santiago would be proud to know—though Xavi was not going to tell him—that somewhere between leaning forward and kissing Stefi and Stefi's wonderful, enticing sigh, Xavi realized that if he hooked up with Stefi on the beach and someone randomly took a photo of them making out and then later realized it was a photo of the prince of Spain, the scandal would be everywhere and Stefi would be embroiled in it. Much more of Stefi than she would ever want to publicly reveal, surely. Xavi knew he had to protect Stefi from something like this, however unlikely it was to happen. With rumors swirling around already about a Spanish prince in Barcelona, Xavi couldn't be sure and he didn't want to risk it.

At least he'd gotten Stefi's number.

Xavi wondered when it would be considered too soon to text her to see if she wanted to hang out. Was now too soon, for instance? Did Xavi even care if he would be showing Stefi his cards so clearly? No, Xavi decided, he didn't. He wasn't one to play games. That was Isabel. He halted in a patch of shade.

Santiago nearly crashed into him for the second time that day. "Xavi, you need to get ahold of yourself."

"What?" Xavi was too busy pulling out his phone and searching for Stefi's info to pay attention to Santiago's comment.

Santiago peered over his shoulder. "You're going to text her *now*? You just saw her and said goodbye! Maybe give it a minute."

"Maybe I don't want to" was Xavi's reply.

The shade from the tree wasn't strong enough for Xavi to see the screen, so he moved closer to one of the buildings. There. Now Xavi tapped out a series of messages.

**Do you want to come to my house tomorrow morning?**

**We can watch the running of the bulls together.**

**The festival in Pamplona!**

**It's an event not to be missed.**

Santiago was still peering over his shoulder. "Chaval." He sighed.

Xavi stared at the screen and the messages there. He had apparently just invited Stefi over for breakfast. He nearly laughed at this odd invitation for a date. But maybe she'd come and they could spend the day together. And then the evening together. Maybe a breakfast date would somehow make up for their steamy moment on the beach, cool things down to a bearable temperature, at least temporarily. Xavi didn't want Stefi to think he wanted to see her only to make out, and he worried that if he asked her to meet him tonight, she would get that idea. Xavi did want to make out with Stefi, but he didn't want only this. He wanted to get to know Stefi too. Breakfast and the running of the bulls was the perfect opportunity. They could do something together that was very culturally Spanish, spend the morning talking over coffee, then see where things went from there. Maybe Xavi would take her to one of the famous Gaudí houses afterward, if she hadn't already been to them, or perhaps the Picasso museum in El Born? He would prove to Stefi that he was not just some guy who wanted to—

Mierda. He'd forgotten Stefi's morning pastry class at Hofmann.

He was about to type out a new message when a text from Stefi pinged on his phone. She'd written back already—probably to tell him she couldn't make it. But when Xavi read her response, a thrill went through him.

Perfect, my pastry teacher canceled class for tomorrow because of the heat wave.

And the next day too, until this heat wave passes.

Guess she doesn't want anyone else to faint like today?

What time should I be there and what's your address?

Xavi typed out the info and hit Send.

See you tomorrow, bright and early, Stefi wrote back, along with a few smile emojis and one that looked like a cow, which she obviously meant to be a bull.

Xavi laughed. He looked up from the phone and smiled at Santiago like he was thrilled to realize he was standing there. He was finally going to have a date, a real one, with the American girl who'd shown up that day at La Buena and had filled his mind and haunted his dreams ever since. This was perfect. Stefi was perfect. She was going to help Xavi enjoy the last few precious weeks he had before his entire life was altered forever. Stefi wasn't in a position to have a relationship, as she'd made that crystal clear to him the other night, and neither was Xavi, so he was glad they were both on the same page about this. He could just relax and have fun. Both of them could. Xavi was so happy that he even gave Santiago a hug. "Let's go check in on my mother and see if she was serious about that vacation."

"Anything that gets us out of this heat is okay by me," Santiago said.

Xavi adjusted his sunglasses, and the two young men battled the heat and sun the rest of the way along the boulevard until they reached the edge of El Gótico and, finally, the building where Xavi and Marta lived and where Santiago occupied their spare room. Xavi was in such a good mood that when he remembered his current spat with the royal guard he laughed. Recently Santiago had started to seem more like a brother than anything else—a brother with whom Xavi sometimes had disagreements, sure, but they would get past them because that's what brothers did.

When they arrived home, the apartment was completely silent.

"¡Mamá!" Xavi called. Maybe she'd gone to the beach herself?

But then Xavi saw an envelope on the kitchen table addressed to him in his mother's handwriting. He picked it up, tore it open, and began to read.

"I guess my mother took that vacation," Xavi said, incredulous. In all the years he had been old enough to know his mother's whereabouts and decisions, she'd never picked up and left like this. She'd never closed La Buena at the height of summer and given herself a break. It was a good thing, he knew, but he also wondered what could have provoked this unusual behavior. Could Jordi have finally gotten up the courage to ask his mother out? But Xavi immediately knew that couldn't be it. It was one thing to ask someone to dinner and something else entirely to go away with them.

Xavi turned to Santiago and saw a strange expression on his face. Xavi tried to read it and couldn't. "Do you know something about my mother that you're not telling me?"

Santiago shrugged. "Why would I? You know her better than me."

Xavi narrowed his eyes. He didn't know if Santiago's words of denial matched the look in his eyes, which was somewhat mysterious. "Listen, I'm sorry I've been giving you so much trouble lately. I'm just, I don't know, I'm not used to this situation. Being accompanied everywhere. I can't believe this is going to be my life, and this is barely even a taste of what it will be like."

Santiago nodded and seemed to accept Xavi's apology. "It's a big adjustment. But really, we can figure this out together, if only you'd trust me. This doesn't have to be a battle between us."

"Okay, fine. Let's figure it out, then."

"All right."

"So this means we're good?" Xavi asked.

The royal guard hesitated. But then he said, "Yeah, we're good. And I get it. Love makes us do all kinds of things." Santiago's tone suggested he knew a thing or two about the complications of love.

Xavi was startled by Santiago's use of this word—both for what this meant for Santiago and what it meant for himself. Xavi knew it was obvious he had a thing for the American girl, but this was all in fun. Xavi wasn't in a position to get involved with someone seriously this summer, his last as a normal civilian. Love would be too complicated for his predicament, and he planned on avoiding it at all costs. It would be stupid for him not to. Look what had happened to his own mother when she'd fallen for Xavi's father. He would never forget that letter the king had sent his mother when he was still a prince, breaking things off so permanently and talking about duty. Though a part of him couldn't help but wonder if times had changed enough to make it a little less difficult for a prince like him to have a normal dating life.

But now, Xavi only shrugged and said, "Who said anything about love?"

Santiago laughed. The look in his eyes turned disbelieving. "Xavi, you didn't have to."

# Seventeen

When Santiago opened his eyes the next morning, his heart flip-flopped, then fluttered, then flip-flopped again. It was pounding so hard he placed a hand over his chest as though his palm might silence it. He knew his only thought should be of Xavi, of his responsibility to him, but he could barely force himself to think of Xavi at all. The day before, Santiago and Xavi had come to an agreement. And after that, Santiago and Xavi and Diego had come to an agreement. Santiago thought it was a good deal. In fact, he was pretty thrilled about it.

While Xavi was in the house, Xavi could do whatever he wanted without any interference from his royal guard. In fact, Xavi could leave the building and go to any of the neighboring restaurants he liked to frequent as long as he warned Santiago ahead of time and didn't take off somewhere without notifying Santiago first. The public didn't know who Xavi was yet, and there was safety in this—even Santiago could agree to that fact. But if Xavi moved beyond the neighborhood, say, to take Stefi to a museum, Santiago at least needed to be nearby.

"Don't you think Stefi is going to think it's strange if I bring you on our date?" Xavi had protested. "Or whatever it is that we'll be doing?" he added quickly.

Santiago shook his head. "I've already thought of that."

Xavi crossed his arms and stared at Santiago with a very full dose of skepticism. But Santiago was ready with a plan, and boy, the one he'd come up with was good for both of them.

"This is what we're going to do," Santiago said. "To start, we're going to tell Diego the truth about you." Xavi's jaw immediately fell open, but Santiago barreled on before Xavi could get out any words of surprise or resistance. "Diego is your best friend, he's trustworthy, and he's going to find out soon anyway. I think it will be good for you to test the waters with your big news, and I am confident that Diego is someone who will be able to handle it. And then you won't be alone in this anymore."

Xavi went to the fridge and pulled out two tiny frosty cans of Coca-Cola. He popped the lids, handed one to Santiago, and took a long sip as he pondered this. Then Xavi went and sat down at the kitchen table, the two young men taking refuge in the darkness of the room, the wooden shutters closed against the sunlight. In Barcelona, it was common for people to close their apartments to the sun during the day, then open the windows and doors to the cooler air around ten thirty p.m. The summer days were long in this city.

"I'm listening," Xavi said.

Santiago joined him at the table, the cold drink in his hand only a small relief in the heat. He wasn't sure what Xavi would think of part two of this plan. "And then, when you want to go out in the city with Stefi, like to take her to a museum tomorrow as you mentioned, Diego and I will come with you. Third-wheel problem solved."

Xavi finished his Coke in one long gulp then crushed the can in his hand. Tiny rays of sunlight filtered through the cracks in the wooden shutters and lit up thin lines across the table. "But then I'd have both a third and a *fourth* wheel. So how is that going to help?"

Santiago closed his eyes, preparing himself to spill the final part of his plan. When he opened them, he let the words tumble out. "We wouldn't exactly be a third and fourth wheel because it would be more like, um, well, a double date? Because after we tell Diego, we'll also ask how he feels about pretending he and I are together. So then when you want to go out somewhere with Stefi, Diego and I will both have a pretense to be there, and we can also leave you enough alone, because we will obviously also have to pretend to be occupied with one another." Santiago slammed his eyes shut again along with his mouth, afraid to see Xavi's reaction. He knew he was rambling, but he couldn't seem to stop talking and trying to justify his plan. Now, hearing it out loud, he worried he sounded overly obvious, that his plan was ridiculous, that this was the dumbest idea ever. On top of that, he had basically just revealed his feelings for Diego to Xavi.

"Santiago, open your eyes, please. Come on."

"I know it's a stupid idea—"

Xavi put a hand over the one Santiago had placed flat on the kitchen table.

Santiago's eyes fluttered open.

"My turn," Xavi said. "First of all, I've been wondering if you've got a thing for Diego. So tell me the truth: Would pretending to be with Diego really just be pretend?"

Santiago was touched by, well, Xavi's touch, that he had taken Santiago's hand as a gesture of understanding and solidarity. It nearly made him tear up. Santiago leaned his other elbow on the table. He sighed heavily. "It has to be pretend. I could never actually date your best friend. It would be unprofessional and against all expectations of my role as your guard. I'd have to resign."

Xavi removed his hand from Santiago's and leaned back in his chair. He folded his arms across his chest, and studied the guard in the dim light. "That's not really an answer. I'm asking as your friend, Santiago. Do you like Diego? Yes or no."

Santiago studied Xavi hard in return. The young prince had used the word *friend* in reference to him. He had to admit, he was as moved by Xavi calling him a friend as he had been by Xavi taking his hand. The king had requested that Santiago become just this to the prince—a friend. So Santiago decided to give Xavi an honest answer. "I do like Diego," he said, and groaned. "I've been trying not to, but I can't seem to help myself."

A great big smile broke out on Xavi's face. "But this is fantastic! Diego is a great guy and so are you and I'd love to see two people as great as you make each other happy. I have my suspicions about what Diego feels too."

"You do?" Santiago couldn't stop the hope from entering his tone.

Xavi was nodding enthusiastically. "I've known Diego since we were little kids and I've known him during every crush and relationship he's ever had, since the very first one back when we were eleven and he fell for the new defender, Jacques, on our school's fútbol team. All this to say, I know when Diego likes someone and I've seen the way he looks at you. I'd say Diego has a crush."

Santiago knew he was swooning and he knew that this was not how this conversation was meant to go, but he also found that he didn't care. "Really?" he asked.

"Oh, yeah."

"Joder."

"Nah," Xavi said, brushing aside Santiago's worry like it was nothing, "This is good news." Xavi was still beaming. He leaned forward and clapped Santiago on the shoulder. "This 'pretending' to be on double dates with me and Stefi is a great idea. I'm all for love between my friends. Consider me in."

But Santiago was shaking his head. "Wait a minute—there is no love here. This really has to be a cover. I can't actually date Diego. It's not allowed."

"Ha! Says the man who just accused me of loving Stefi."

"But that's different—"

"Oh, is it? How so?"

"You can at least be with Stefi until the announcement," Santiago said, hearing the strangled tone in his voice. "But I can't have Diego at all."

"Who says?"

"It's not up for discussion. I'm a royal guard, my assignment is you, your best friend is Diego. Enough said."

Xavi's expression grew serious. "Maybe once I'm officially the prince, I can bend some of these unfortunate rules. For both of us."

Santiago stared at Xavi. Once again, he was struck by Xavi's kindness. Struck by the fact that Xavi was a good person deep down, despite the swagger and the long hair and the cavalier attitude he displayed to the world. Xavi's happy, supportive reaction to Santiago's confession about Diego told Santiago everything he needed to know about Xavi as a person. In this moment, he thought about how the entire country of Spain was going to adore its new prince. Santiago knew he was right too, that Xavi would charm them all, even the inevitable doubters who would come out of the woodwork when the news was announced.

"But . . ." Santiago started, then stopped. He wasn't sure how to finish the sentence.

Xavi proposed a compromise. "How about this: You and I can promise to keep each other in line. For now, I'll keep you from falling for Diego, and you can keep me from falling for Stefi. If either one of us seems to be letting things go too far, the other will intervene to put a stop to things. No matter what. That's the deal."

Santiago found himself nodding. "All right."

"All right."

The two young men stood up from the table and shook hands. But then they pulled each other into a long hug in the middle of the kitchen.

Xavi grabbed his phone. "Let's call Diego now."

Santiago's heart soared with excitement, then plunged with anxiety. He wondered what Diego would say—about Xavi being the prince, of course, but also about the other part of their plan. Because it was true—now Xavi and Santiago had the apartment all to themselves for four whole days. Marta wouldn't be back until the end of the week, Santiago knew, not until after the heat wave was supposed to break. At the thought of Marta, he glanced at Marta's son and knew that at some point between now and Marta's return, Santiago and Xavi were going to have to have a talk about where Marta had gone. He'd managed to convince Xavi not to worry about his mother—she was a grown woman who could take care of herself—but he had a feeling that Xavi would raise the subject of his mother's disappearance again.

But he hadn't yet. For now, they had plenty of time.

And a lot could happen in four days.

Santiago rose from his bed, sauntered to the bathroom, undressed, and got into the shower. He thought about Diego's reaction when they'd told him their plan. After Diego had gotten over his initial shock at learning that not only were the rumors about a prince in Barcelona true but they were about his best friend from childhood, Diego had proved Santiago right. He said that of course he would keep this secret for Xavi, that he was honored they'd trusted him with this important information. And when Xavi told Diego the other part of their plan, the part that involved Diego and Santiago being on double dates with Xavi and Stefi, Diego enthusiastically agreed to this as well. As far as Diego was concerned, he was in.

Santiago sang in the shower when he was happy. Xavi had made fun of him for this in the past, since it wasn't exactly a large apartment, but he started singing now, louder than ever. He wondered if Xavi could hear him down the hall, but for once he didn't worry about what Xavi might think about Santiago belting out his favorite boleros, the traditional romantic ballads Santiago listened to when he was crushing on someone. He was too excited about the day ahead to be quiet. He had a date with Diego, and whether it was faux or not, he couldn't wait for it to begin.

# Eighteen

Stefi was having her best day yet in Barcelona, despite the heat.

It started early at Xavi's apartment. They'd watched the running of the bulls over cafés con leche and a good deal of shrieking on Stefi's part, though she also found the encierro thrilling from start to finish. The bulls were so big and so fast and there were so many people running. It was a shock to see something so dangerous and exciting live. This kind of event would never happen in the United States, Stefi thought, which was one reason why she loved it. Spain had traditions and rituals that were utterly unlike the kind she was used to at home, and when she looked at Xavi next to her, she thought the same about the men in this country. Xavi was not like anyone she'd ever met, and he had sparked something inside Stefi that she wasn't sure how to describe. Ineffable, indefinable, a need or craving or desire that, once born, Stefi wasn't sure how to control or even if she could. It scared her, but she also liked it.

After watching the encierro in Pamplona, Xavi, Diego, Santiago, and Stefi moved on to the Picasso museum, which Stefi had never been to despite her abuela urging her to go. And this afternoon, they'd landed at the architect Gaudí's famous unfinished cathedral, La Sagrada Familia. This was where Xavi and Stefi stood now, staring up in awe at its magnificent ceiling.

"Gaudí designed it so it would make people feel like they were in a forest," Xavi said as he pointed out the many stunning details soaring above them. "The columns are meant to be like the trunks of a tree, the buttresses like their branches, and you see how the sunlight shines through the gaps in the ceiling? It's meant to be like light filtering through the leaves to the ground so people sitting in the church feel like they're in nature."

Stefi couldn't speak. It was so beautiful, she was at a loss for words.

Xavi and Stefi were standing close enough that their arms were touching through Stefi's cardigan. Xavi had warned Stefi to bring a sweater to put over her sundress because she wouldn't be let into the churches of Barcelona unless her shoulders were covered, heat wave or no heat wave. When Stefi decided to give her poor neck a rest and lower her gaze, she found Xavi watching her with this look in his eyes like maybe he found Stefi as beautiful as the cathedral. She blinked at him and wondered if he could really feel this about someone like herself. Sometimes seeing Xavi stole Stefi's breath too, this gorgeous specimen of boy before her who was funny and kind at the same time and who seemed to want her as much as she wanted him.

Was it wrong to be lusting after someone inside a church?

Probably, but Stefi couldn't help it.

The many tourists visiting the cathedral swirled around the couple standing there in the middle of the sanctuary as though they were alone in admiring this magnificent feat of architecture and beauty.

"Should we go and find Diego and Santiago?" Stefi made herself ask, breaking the silence—or was it more like a spell that had been cast on them? What was it about Xavi that did this to Stefi? This was nothing like what she'd felt about Jason, not even when they first started dating. She tugged at the neck of her cardigan. "I'm melting." It was cooler within the thick stone walls of the cathedral but not cool enough to wear a sweater for long.

"Yeah, probably," Xavi said and sighed.

As Xavi and Stefi wandered through the church, searching the nave and the various chapels that bordered the sanctuary, their fingers unwove and wove together again.

With Stefi's free hand, she pointed. "There they are."

Diego and Santiago were sitting side by side in one of the pews, staring at the front of the church. Stefi wondered what they were thinking about. Was it the beauty of this place all around them? Or was it the attraction the two boys felt for one another when they were close? A little of both? Stefi had been curious about those two, and now her suspicions were confirmed. Stefi had seen the disappointed look on Diego's face when Santiago had finally found Xavi and Stefi making out in El Gótico the other night. Disappointed enough that Stefi wondered if Santiago and Diego had also been making out earlier.

As she and Xavi got closer, Stefi noticed the two boys were holding hands.

Xavi walked up and tapped Santiago on the shoulder, and he startled.

Stefi observed that everyone seemed to have fallen under the same kind of romantic spell. This cathedral did seem like it held magic within it, so maybe this wasn't surprising. Maybe it was what this building did for all who entered it.

Santiago looked like he was trying to pull his hand from Diego's, but Diego held on tight.

*Good for Diego*, Stefi thought.

"Should we head out and get some food?" Xavi asked. "A drink, perhaps?"

Diego stood and pulled Santiago up with him. "I could use a tapa or two, maybe a beer."

The foursome began to walk to the exit, maneuvering around the many people staring up at the ceiling, careful not to knock anyone over.

Stefi glanced at Diego. "What is with all the beer drinking here? I mean, people drink it during breakfast."

Diego shrugged. "It's either that or bottled water. Since people don't drink water from the tap, the two are pretty interchangeable in this city. Besides, this isn't America, where people drink beer to get drunk. Here, people drink beer to be refreshed."

Xavi took a left and headed through the giant cathedral doors, and everyone else followed. "But it's also true," he said, "that eventually, if you drink enough beers consecutively, drunkenness does occur, like it would in any country."

Santiago laughed. "Yes. But because you've been hanging out drinking those beers for so long and you've been enjoying the conversation so much, you barely notice the fact that you've become mareado."

Outside, the heat along with the brightness of the sun was brutal. The second they were on the sidewalk, Stefi was pulling off her sweater. The group sought the shady side of the street as they headed to their next destination. They took their time; it was too hot to hurry. Stefi liked a lot of things about this city, especially the slower pace, whether it was while eating or wandering or even sipping a drink over a long talk with friends.

They arrived at a restaurant. Outside, there were barrels around which people sat on stools, eating and drinking in the shade of the buildings. But inside it was dark and cool, the windows pulled shut to indicate the place had AC. Stefi loved the way so much of everything happened outdoors in Barcelona, but today she was grateful for the air. Xavi led them to a dark wooden table in the far corner. Stefi and Xavi sat on the bench against the wall, and Santiago and Diego took the two chairs across from them.

Underneath the sweater Stefi had shoved into her bag, her phone buzzed. It had been buzzing all day, but she was ignoring it. Now she gave in and pulled it out to check it. The messages from Amber to Stefi had continued.

**Stefi, I need you.**

**Stefi, please.**

One by one, Stefi had been erasing them as they arrived. But this morning before Stefi left for Xavi's, she'd gone to Amber's and Jason's profiles and seen that they'd taken down their photos with one another. This made Stefi nearly certain there was trouble between them. A part of her felt triumphant, and another part was more enraged. They'd gone and destroyed two relationships, both with Stefi, and for what? A few weeks of sex? She owed Amber nothing.

Stefi erased the newest messages and turned her phone off. Then she shoved her phone back in her bag and looked at the three boys she was with at this table in a city so far from home there was an entire ocean between them. It hit Stefi hard but in a good way: she was making a life for herself in Barcelona. Somehow, over the course of just a couple of weeks, she'd made new friends and maybe even had a boyfriend. Or something like that, she thought, as Xavi raised his very attractively muscled arm to call over the waiter. Stefi liked this new version of herself, and other people liked it too, she realized. Maybe this was the real Stefi, but because of Amber and Jason, this Stefi had been buried or made overly small so she could fit herself between them.

She pressed herself closer to Xavi on the bench.

When the waiter arrived, even Stefi ordered a beer. "I like that the goal here isn't drinking," she said after the waiter left, "but hanging out. You're right, at home it's usually the opposite."

"Americans." Diego sighed in an exaggerated way and with a laugh.

Stefi rolled her eyes at him. "We're not all bad."

"I like Americans," Xavi said, leaning toward Stefi. "Certain ones, at least," he added in a low voice just for Stefi, close to her ear, his hair brushing her neck.

Stefi shivered. She searched for something to say back, but words failed her. The beers arrived frosty and fizzy and Stefi took a sip of hers gratefully. She really needed to cool down.

# Nineteen

Santiago was on cloud nine. The four of them had an amazing afternoon, hopping from bar to bar, eating tapas and sipping beers and, frankly, having more fun than Santiago could ever recall having. Best of all, each time they moved from one place to another, Diego grabbed his hand as they walked.

Following all of this, they returned to Xavi and Marta's apartment, at which point Stefi and Xavi promptly went off to Xavi's room. That left Santiago and Diego finally and blissfully alone in the darkness of the living room. They'd yet to open the shutters and doors because the sun was still high and wouldn't set for a few more hours.

Santiago arched his eyebrows at Diego, who was sitting next to him on the couch. "More?" he asked, holding the bottle of ratafia over Diego's tiny glass, ready to pour more of the catalán liqueur that Santiago had learned to enjoy during his time in this part of Spain.

"Of course," Diego said and watched as Santiago filled his glass, the sound of ice cracking and shifting from the warm liquid breaking the silence of the room. Then he filled his own.

Santiago returned the bottle to the coffee table and sat back against the cushions, his ratafia in hand. A single lit lamp gave everything a lovely glow. The streets below the apartment were alive with people defying the heat.

"Salud," Santiago said, and clinked his glass with Diego's.

Santiago had wondered what would happen with Diego once they returned to Marta and Xavi's place. Would Diego stop pretending to be on a date with Santiago? Would he no longer take Santiago's hand? But Santiago now had his answer, and though it concerned the royal guard part of himself, it thrilled the teenage-boy part for sure. Diego hadn't stopped flirting with Santiago. And for once, Santiago was letting himself enjoy this crush, and his heart soared. But he was also extremely nervous and not only because he was breaking protocol.

Santiago had a secret. Kind of a big one: He'd never had a boyfriend.

In fact, he'd only ever kissed one boy, back in Madrid, and that kiss nearly didn't count. It was over practically as soon as it began. Santiago barely remembered it because he had been uncharacteristically drunk at the time. Growing up at the palace under the watchful eyes of the king and the rest of the royal guard did not exactly afford a young man much privacy. Or opportunities to date. When he'd accepted this assignment with Xavi, it had never occurred to him that he might end up with a pretend boyfriend, much less a real one. Someone he might kiss for real. Among many other possible things he could and would like to do with Diego.

But Santiago was getting ahead of himself.

"I still can't get over that Xavi's a prince," Diego said. "*The* prince."

Santiago put a finger to his lips. The apartment wasn't that big. At any moment Stefi might appear looking for something—a glass of water, the location of the bathroom, another bottle of wine. It made sense Diego had more questions. Of course he did. He'd known the news for only twenty-four hours. "There isn't any doubt," Santiago said. "There were DNA tests, of course."

Diego took a sip of his ratafia, the ice moving and clinking as he did, and Santiago was transfixed. He wondered if tonight he would kiss those lips. "It's just . . . it seems impossible," Diego said. "Like some kind of crazy story you'd read in a novel or see on the news happening to someone else, but never to someone you actually know."

Santiago took a sip from his glass and enjoyed the cold, bitter liquid going down his throat. "Trust me, those who know at the palace—and there are still only a select few, to prevent the possibility of leaks—found it hard to accept it too. But honestly, the person who most readily, even eagerly, accepted the news was the king himself."

"Really?"

"Really."

"Why do you think that is? I'd expect the king to be the most suspicious of all."

Santiago debated shifting closer to Diego on the couch. But they had time. They had the whole night ahead of them if they wanted. "Yes, you'd think so. But the king was the person who handled it better than anyone."

"Huh," Diego said with a shrug.

Santiago was fairly sure he knew why this was the case. This conversation was making him wonder what Marta was doing this evening. If, perhaps every person who lived in this apartment was enjoying a bit of romance tonight. Because what Xavi didn't know and what Marta had made Santiago promise not to tell her son was where she'd gone when she so suddenly closed La Buena to take an impromptu and mysterious vacation.

Santiago knew exactly where Marta went because he'd arranged the trip himself. He was surprised and pleased when Marta came to him with her request. He immediately told her to start packing her bags and soon found out he was right to honor her wishes. Of course the answer was yes. So within the hour, Marta was on her way to the airport, suitcase in hand.

To see the king.

Right then, Diego took it upon himself to move closer to Santiago on the couch, which made Santiago forgot all about Marta, kings, being a royal guard, and all kinds of other palace intrigue in favor of the beautiful boy sitting before him.

But his bliss lasted for only about three minutes.

Santiago hadn't even tasted Diego's ratafia-stained lips yet when he was knocked right off that wonderful cloud and sent plummeting down, down, to the earth again. A sinister-sounding alarm had suddenly erupted on his phone, one that held dire implications for himself and certainly for Xavi and maybe even for Stefi too.

# Twenty

Xavi and Stefi were on the terrace outside his room, side by side on the sun beds and shaded by the umbrella. The sun was finally going down over the city, providing the people of Barcelona a small bit of relief from the heat. Though even without the sun, it was still pretty steamy.

Leaning back, legs stretched out and crossed, Xavi and Stefi stared up into the sky, which was turning all kinds of different colors—pink, orange, turquoise. The spires of the Barcelona Cathedral were visible in the distance along with those of another of the beautiful medieval churches of Barcelona, San Just. Every fifteen minutes, the cathedral bells would punctuate their conversation. One, two, then three bells at a quarter to, followed by chimes that tolled the hour.

Xavi listened as Stefi told him about her life in the U.S., about going to school there and all the many things that were different, and about her family, whom she clearly loved.

Stefi was animated as she spoke. "So my father was studying abroad in college, which is how he met my mother, Ana. They dated while he was in Barcelona, but then he went back to the U.S. and they broke up because they were both young and lived on separate continents."

Xavi wondered if Stefi saw any parallel between herself and her father, given that she would likely be going home at the end of the summer, whereas she thought Xavi would be staying in Barcelona. But maybe Stefi wouldn't leave after all. Hadn't she said something about her family possibly staying longer? A pang of regret sounded in Xavi's heart, much like the bells chiming into the evening, that at the end of summer, Xavi's life would no longer be his own. But he decided not to focus on the future when Stefi and he had the entire evening ahead. He might as well enjoy things while he could. He would worry about the monarchy's outdated dating norms later. "But then obviously your parents found their way back to one another," Xavi said.

This caused Stefi to roll her eyes and laugh. "Yes. They apparently couldn't live without one another, so my father saved up money from his restaurant job and sent my mother a plane ticket over the summer—"

"That's awfully romantic."

"Tell me about it." Stefi changed the cross of her ankles on the sun bed, and Xavi tried not to let the sight of those long, lovely legs distract him from her story. "And, well, my mother went to the U.S. to see my father, and somehow she never left. It was a whirlwind-romance kind of thing. They were engaged by Christmas that same year and the rest is history. They're still madly in love too. It's pretty gross to witness, trust me."

The sky was turning a magnificent fiery blue. "But that is nice," Xavi said. "I wish my mother would find love in her life. I hate that she's been alone all these years."

"Why is that? Marta is so beautiful. And talented. Though . . ." Stefi hesitated.

"Though what?"

Stefi seemed to debate her answer. "Your mother . . . it was like, after she saw us talking that first day, she didn't want me to come back to La Buena ever again." Stefi's eyebrows arched at Xavi as she spoke. "Like, she didn't want me to see you."

Xavi shook his head. He would have to talk to his mother about this when she returned. "My mother is just protective."

Stefi tucked a lock of hair behind her ear. "She thinks I'm not good enough for you. Because I'm American?"

"No," Xavi said quickly. "More like she's protective of both of us."

A look of confusion appeared on Stefi's face. "But why—"

"Anyway, you were talking about your parents," Xavi cut in. "Who are now back in Barcelona, the place where they met. Also very romantic."

Xavi watched as Stefi poured herself some agua con gas, not answering right away. She'd told Xavi earlier she needed to pace herself with the wine. She wasn't used to the way people drank wine like it was water here. Xavi had laughed—this was true, everyone did tend to drink all day, including everyone their own age. Children grew up drinking vermut and wine their whole lives, so Xavi and his friends were used to it. Speaking of, he poured himself more cava from the bottle on the table sitting between the two sun beds. He hoped Stefi took his hint and didn't turn the conversation back to Marta.

Thankfully, she did. "Yes, my whole family is here, which makes my grandma very happy."

Xavi took a sip from his glass, enjoying the chill of it. "For how long? Just the summer?" Even if the end of summer would change life as Xavi knew it, he still wanted this information from Stefi.

"The summer and maybe the whole next year," she said.

"But what about school for you?"

Stefi tilted her chin up, eyes seeking the night sky above them. It was too hot and hazy to see the stars, but the city glowed from below. "Well, that is the question. If my parents choose to stay, I'll spend my last year of high school somewhere new."

"How do you feel about that?"

"Not as bad as you'd think," Stefi said, and turned toward Xavi. She seemed to debate what to say next, but then plunged forward. "Remember I told you I went through a breakup?"

Xavi nodded. He had to admit, he was probably as curious about Stefi's ex as Stefi was about Isabel. Xavi wanted to know what kind of guy would end a relationship with the girl before him, a girl who was friendly and interesting and also extremely beautiful. Part of Stefi's appeal was how unconcerned she was about her appearance. Whereas someone like Isabel was what people in Spain called producida. As in Isabel "produced" her beauty, with a combination of nature, the most stylish of clothing, and perfect makeup and hair. But Stefi was gorgeous even when sweaty and sticky and covered in butter from her pastry-making class.

"I remember, yes," Xavi said.

"Well, it was a pretty bad breakup. Like, to the tune of my best friend from childhood, Amber—your equivalent of Diego—hooking up with my long-term boyfriend behind my back. I'd dated Jason, my ex, for almost three years. I walked in on them making out and who knows what else."

Xavi sat up. "Oh, wow, really?" He turned toward Stefi and planted his feet on the terra-cotta floor of the terrace.

Stefi shifted so her knees were pointed up. "Yeah. A sad but true story."

"Cabrón de mierda," Xavi said.

"Agreed," Stefi said, laughing.

"Asshole of shit" was the literal translation of this phrase.

"So are you . . ." Xavi started, then stopped.

"Am I . . . what?"

He decided just to ask. "Are you heartbroken?"

Stefi reached for the bottle on the table and poured some cava into the glass Xavi brought onto the terrace for her. "I was," she said, and took her first sip of wine that evening. "I am still, sometimes."

Xavi studied Stefi's face. Streams of bubbles rose to the surface of both their glasses. "Only sometimes?"

"It's probably the most devastating, humiliating thing that's ever happened to me. I lost my best friend and my boyfriend all at once." Stefi locked eyes with Xavi. "But being in Barcelona has turned out to be a pretty good cure for heartbreak."

"Oh. Really?"

Stefi nodded. "So far, yes. I'm having fun."

"Me too." Xavi couldn't bear it any longer. He was too far from Stefi, so he got up from his sun bed and joined Stefi on hers. She shifted a bit so he could sit down. He remembered the deal he'd made with Santiago about not letting things get out of hand with Stefi. But then Xavi was saying, "I really want to kiss you," and Stefi was replying, "I was really hoping you would at some point," and soon Stefi had shifted again so she was sitting upright next to Xavi, her lips so deliciously close that suddenly Xavi was actually kissing them.

Unlike yesterday when they'd kissed so quickly at the beach, this time their kiss lingered, and soon they'd moved from kissing to full-on making out. Xavi couldn't seem to merely kiss Stefi. He could only inhale her, as if without her mouth, he might die of thirst, and without her body, ideally in his arms, he might starve to death. Xavi suddenly understood the term comerse la boca, which was the Spanish equivalent for making out but literally translated to "eating each other's mouths." And unlike when they were at the beach, this time Xavi let his hands roam wherever they wanted. As things between them grew more heated, all Xavi wanted was to lay Stefi back on that sun bed and climb on top of her. Xavi wanted Stefi more than he'd wanted any other girl in his life.

But then something stopped him cold.

The word *love* passed through Xavi's heart and up to his brain like a whisper, echoing what Santiago had said only yesterday. He needed to slow this down before it got out of hand. So once again, as he'd done at the beach, Xavi forced himself to pull away.

"I should probably walk you home," he said suddenly.

"You should? Ah, okay. Sure, yes, I suppose," Stefi replied, not sounding at all sure. Sounding very much like a disappointed person. She looked away. As she did, she adjusted the straps of her sundress and pulled the skirt of it down over her thighs.

Xavi didn't want Stefi to be disappointed or embarrassed, and he definitely didn't want her to think, well, that he didn't *want* her. Because, boy, did Xavi want her. "I'd actually like for you to stay . . ."

"But?"

"But the last time I let things go too far too quickly with someone, it didn't end well." This was true, so Xavi felt okay saying it. His real reason was something other, though. He hated that he couldn't tell Stefi the truth about himself, but such was his life now. Hiding things from people he cared about. And, for better or worse, he was starting to care for Stefi. Once again Xavi wondered if there was a way to make this work beyond the summer, if he could fight the Spanish royal tide pulling him away from someone like Stefi. After all, there were other monarchs around the world who were doing just this, though with varying levels of success and scandal.

"You mean you let things go too fast with Isabel," Stefi supplied.

"Yes."

Xavi watched as Stefi's expression darkened and her gaze shifted away, out into the Barcelona night. "I can't compete with someone like Isabel," she said. "She's . . . like an actress out of a movie. She's beautiful and rich and glamorous . . ."

Xavi reached out and touched Stefi's cheek. "You have that wrong."

She turned back, blinking at Xavi as she waited for him to explain. "Wrong how?"

Xavi's heart stirred in his chest as he stared into Stefi's eyes. So many different thoughts collided in his head even as so many different feelings collided in his heart, including the wish that the end of summer wouldn't bring the changes in Xavi's life he knew were ahead, changes that would make it impossible for him to do anything normal again, like fall in love with a beautiful American girl like he was some kind of normal catalán boy. Or, at least, make it very, very difficult. But the one feeling that rose to the top and won out over all the others was the one he expressed to the girl who sat there, waiting for him to speak.

"Stefi, it's Isabel who can't compete with someone like *you*," he said, and as he heard the words emerge from his mouth, he knew they were true.

# Twenty-One

Santiago was careful to arrive for this meeting at the appointed time. He pushed all the other thoughts pulsing in his mind to the back of it. Like his worry about leaving Xavi alone. Reason told him Xavi would be fine, that he probably wouldn't notice Santiago's absence because of Stefi, that Stefi would likely distract Xavi from even leaving his room. And Santiago tried valiantly to forget the look on Diego's face when he'd abruptly told the boy he needed to go right when everything between them was just about to begin. His heart hurt to have left Diego there, confused and alone and, disappointingly, still never-been-kissed. At least not by Santiago.

But now Santiago forged ahead. His presence was requested at the restaurant of the private club high up on Diagonal above the Eixample, where the wealthiest of Barcelona were members.

The doorman ushered Santiago into the grand lobby.

"Gracias," Santiago said, and the doorman nodded solemnly.

Santiago already hated the place. It was stuffy and formal and exclusive, which was why it could get away with such old-fashioned drab decor. Dark wood on the walls, gilded mirrors, opulence, yes, but the kind that had long gone out of style. A total contrast to the newer restaurants and bars always popping up around the city, with their floor-to-ceiling windows and doors that opened onto the street and chandeliers and tiny lights that invited passersby inside. This was the kind of institution that kept people, except for the chosen few, out.

The elevators opened on the top floor and Santiago stepped into the lobby.

The maître d' was as stuffy and unsmiling as the establishment. He greeted Santiago with only raised eyebrows.

"I'm here to see Isabel de Luna," Santiago announced.

The cryptic message that had interrupted his tryst with Diego and sent ripples of stress down Santiago's spine had come from Xavi's ex-girlfriend. It included only a time, a place, and a short but foreboding message, one that sent Santiago hurtling away from the boy of his heart and barreling up, up, up, and across the entire city into the belly of the rich.

**If you value Xavi's secret, you'll be here soon.**

Without a word, the maître d' ushered Santiago down a dark hall and into the dining room. At least it was well air-conditioned in here, Santiago thought as he followed the man, wiping the sweat from his brow after all that rushing to arrive on time.

At the end of the room, wearing a white silk sundress that embraced her every curve and made her look like she'd just walked off a Paris runway, sat Isabel. Erect, poised, and exquisitely beautiful, Isabel perched on her chair like a glittering bird, a candle flickering at the center of the table for two, and a chair waiting for Santiago. There was a practiced glamour to the scene she'd created for this meeting, a setting that only the richest of the rich could contrive. On top of everything else, Isabel was perfectly framed by a magnificent Goya on the wall behind her.

As Santiago neared the girl, it crossed his mind that she'd make a beautiful princess. But just as quickly, Santiago regretted every charitable thought he'd ever had for Isabel, for her supposed broken heart because of

Xavi, for Santiago's idea that because Isabel's parents were a marqués and a marquesa, she would be a good match for him. Attempting to blackmail a royal guard immediately knocked Isabel off Santiago's list of eligible partners for the young prince. Because that's what this was, blackmail. He just didn't yet know what it would entail.

Santiago arrived at the table. "Hello, Isabel."

"Sit," she ordered.

Santiago complied. A waiter swooped by to fill his water glass.

A bottle of cava sat chilling next to the table, Isabel's champagne flute nearly empty. A half-eaten salad was on Isabel's plate. Santiago wondered how long she'd been waiting for him.

"What is this about?" he asked without preamble.

"So impolite," Isabel tsked. "Wouldn't you like something to drink? To eat?"

The waiter appeared like magic and refilled Isabel's glass of cava; he offered to fill Santiago's too, but Santiago placed a hand over the top of it and shook his head.

"I'd take it if I were you," Isabel advised. "My guess is you're going to want it."

Santiago kept his hand over the flute and eventually the waiter returned the bottle of cava to the silver bucket of ice and scurried off. Another waiter appeared and deposited a basket of bread on the table. Neither one of them moved to touch it. "Just out with it, Isabel," he said.

She sighed. "Bueno. I'll be direct. First, I know you are not Xavi's cousin. It didn't take me that much digging to find out you're a member of the king's royal guard. There are plenty of pictures of you floating around online; all I needed to know was to look."

Despite all attempts to keep his gaze steady, Santiago felt his eyes widening. But he didn't ask Isabel how she figured out she should look in the first place.

Isabel had no trouble keeping her gaze steadily on him. "Well, in truth, I didn't do the digging—my contact at ¡Qué Fuerte! did. I just offered Leonora a few leads, a photo here and there, and set her on the right path."

Santiago sighed. "Leonora Valdez?"

Leonora was behind the initial rumor about Xavi posted on the gossip site. She had over a million followers and was part of the jet-set crowd of Spain because of this. She fed on their need to be photographed and admired by the less lucky masses, and they in turn invited her to their glitzy parties and onto their private jets. All this, and Leonora was barely out of high school. She'd risen to influencer fame quickly and was currently dating the youngest-ever Formula 1 driver. Santiago knew this because he followed Formula 1 like everyone else in Europe, including the king.

But apparently Isabel wasn't interested in discussing Leonora. "Here's what else I know," she continued. "You grew up at the palace, your father was once the head of the king's royal guard, and you've recently joined its ranks." She picked up her fork and it dangled elegantly in her delicate, manicured hands. "It didn't take a math genius to put two and two together and figure out that you had something to do with the king, despite this bullshit story about you being Xavi's cousin." Her eyebrows arched, and she stopped.

For a moment, Santiago was hopeful. Could it be Isabel knew only about his relationship to the king? Maybe she had no idea about Xavi. Should he acknowledge the truth of his background and hope she didn't know the rest? Then again, Isabel had basically revealed she was behind the viral post about a secret prince of Spain residing in Barcelona. Santiago decided to play half dumb and partially truthful. He shrugged. "I'm affiliated with the palace. So? Why would that preclude me from being Xavi's cousin? It's not like you dated him long enough to know that kind of thing about your ex." He landed heavily on that last syllable, meaning for it to hit just as heavily on Isabel's haughty attitude.

But she didn't falter. "I also know you have no legitimate reason to be spending the summer with Xavi and Marta. And, listen, Santiago, you're lucky that I've held Leonora off as long as I have." She used the fork in her hand to stab a cucumber on her plate and lift it into the air between them. She pointed the cucumber at Santiago. "She's dying to post what she has on Xavi, and you know how influencers are. She's not going to hold back for much longer, not without a good enough reason." Isabel popped the cucumber into her mouth.

Santiago's heart was racing. Isabel knew Xavi's secret, and Santiago knew that she knew. He used the time it took for Isabel to chew and swallow to think. Meanwhile, he plucked Isabel's glass of cava from the table, raised it to his lips, and drank it down. She was right; he should have let the waiter fill his glass. The bubbles fizzed and burned in his throat as he waited for even the smallest dash of calm to spread through his body. It didn't.

What did Isabel want with him? What, exactly, was this *good enough reason* that would hold Leonora back from whatever she planned to post? Santiago knew this was going to be about damage control. The question was, how much damage had already occurred? Maybe if Santiago gave Isabel some satisfaction, it would win him some points. "So how did you figure it out?"

She blinked. "How did I figure what out?"

Santiago just stared and waited. He could tell Isabel wanted her moment of triumph.

The waiter came by and plunked a new flute on the table before Isabel, filled it to the brim with cava, then refilled the empty glass in Santiago's hand. "Xavi practically told me he was the prince of Spain himself," Isabel began once the waiter left. "But don't worry, it was before you arrived. As I'm sure you know, Xavi never drinks to the point of getting drunk, but on one rare occasion at a party I threw, he did drink too much—and this was back when he and I were still on again, off again. He was probably drowning his sorrows about our most recent breakup."

Santiago opened his mouth to make a sarcastic remark, but Isabel got there first.

"Then again," she went on, "it was your arrival that made me suspicious about something Xavi told me that night. He made this bitter remark that one day both my social-climbing mother and I would find out who he truly was and regret the way I'd discarded him from my life like garbage." She shook her head. "At first, I had no idea what he meant, but then you showed up out of the blue and I did a little digging. All that was left was a phone call to one of the influencers who's been dying to get close to me for ages, and voilà!"

A bubbling rage surged in Santiago as if he himself were a champagne glass filling up with cava. "So what do you really want, Isabel? Why am I here?"

"I am going to throw a party," Isabel said. "Tomorrow. And you will bring Xavi."

Santiago leaned back in his chair and crossed his arms over his chest. "That's it?"

Isabel took a dainty sip from her water glass, then dried her lips with her napkin. "Yes."

Santiago narrowed his eyes. "Yes. *And?*"

Isabel narrowed her big blue eyes in return. "Just make sure the American girl comes with him."

At the mention of Stefi, Santiago's stress level shot up. "Why? What are you going to do to Stefi?"

"I'm not going to do anything. Nothing that will do lasting damage, at least." Isabel lowered her gaze. "Hearts do mend eventually after they're broken, as anyone who's been in love knows." She dug into her salad again. "The party will be at the W. I've reserved the entire pool deck, and there will even be special cocktails."

As Isabel spoke of her party plans and all they entailed, Santiago's brain was exploding. This sounded like the kind of party that was more likely to push Xavi farther away from Isabel than endear her to him again, if that was part of her plan. What was Santiago missing? "Isabel, Xavi is not the kind of person who'd care about any of this. He's not going to be impressed. You already know this."

Isabel's eyes frosted over. She pulled her phone out of a very expensive-looking bag, swiped the screen a few times, then handed the phone across the table to Xavi.

**Look what I saw the other night on the streets of El Gótico. Not to mention one afternoon at the beach.**

The text was from Leonora. Below the message was a series of photos. Santiago scrolled through them, and his heart sank like a fat olive dropped into a glass of vermut. Santiago felt all control slipping away as quickly as the second glass of cava he'd drained from the champagne flute in his hand. Apparently, Leonora or one of her photographers had been tasked with following Xavi around town. That person had followed Xavi as he'd walked straight into the arms of Stefi.

Santiago went through the photos again, one by one. There were photos of Xavi and Stefi kissing passionately, Stefi's back pressed against one of the tall stone walls along a narrow street of El Gótico. Each image showed their kisses becoming, well, more involved. The worst were the photos of Xavi and Stefi on the beach, angled so that Xavi's arm was blocking Stefi's chest, but any viewer could tell she was topless. For any normal couple, these would simply be a series of romantic images that captured two attractive people clearly into one another. But given Xavi's secret identity, these images were dangerous. They could make someone a fortune; they held the power to multiply someone's followers threefold. All Xavi's hopes to have one last summer of anonymity would vanish instantly.

But even more than this, these photos—especially the ones from the beach— could change Stefi's life, and likely not in a way she'd want. Xavi was not the only one who would immediately lose all anonymity; Stefi would too. Paparazzi would follow her everywhere and dig up all the dirty details of her past—not that she necessarily had any, but if she did, they'd find their way into the public eye. Her life would never be the same, at least not for a while, especially if her family remained in Barcelona like she said they might.

Worse, Stefi would know Xavi had lied. Or at least that he'd withheld extremely important information from her and in doing so risked destroying Stefi's currently nice, normal life.

What a mess.

This was exactly why Santiago should have worked harder to stop Xavi from getting involved with anyone romantically this summer. He knew exactly how high the stakes would be, and now look what had happened. This was all his fault.

"You can't allow anyone to release these," Santiago said. "They could ruin Stefi's life. She's not like . . . you."

Isabel rolled her eyes. "Don't worry, I'm not planning on allowing these to be posted. It's not in my interest either to have these out in the world. I should be the one at Xavi's side when he's announced as the prince. Even you must see that I'm a better fit. My family is royal, but I've also lived in the public eye my whole life and I know exactly how to handle it. I even enjoy it. It's in my blood in a way that it will never be in that American girl's." Isabel took a sip of her cava. "Besides, I promised Leonora something far more juicy in her future if she holds those photos back."

What could be juicier than the secret prince of Spain kissing an unsuspecting American girl on the streets of El Gótico? Or sitting with that same nearly naked girl on the beach? "I'm listening," Santiago said.

Isabel smiled for the first time since Santiago arrived. "Here's what I need you to do."

# Twenty-Two

Stefi kept deleting Amber's messages, but Amber kept sending them, even at eight a.m. when she and her parents sat down to watch the second day of the encierro in Pamplona. Silvia refused to watch with them, she said it was too upsetting and stressful, but Stefi's father, James, was the most game among them. He hooted and hollered the entire two minutes and forty-eight seconds of the bull run. Her dad especially enjoyed the many slo-mo replays of all the goring and trampling incidents and the ritual of the reading of the injuries that followed the morning's run.

"I am going to watch this every single day," her father had said to his wife.

Ana sighed. "You've created a monster, sweetheart," she said to her daughter.

But Stefi grinned. She was glad she had a willing Pamplona partner in her father. It figured that it would be the two Americans in the house who most wanted to watch.

During the replays, Stefi got another message from Amber.

**Are you even getting these?**

By Stefi's calculations, it was just after two a.m. for Amber. Which meant Amber was now sending Stefi middle-of-the-night texts.

She deleted it anyway. But she was starting to feel guilty about not responding.

The encierro now long over, Stefi was drying her hair in front of the mirror in the bathroom when yet another message arrived on her phone. She was getting ready for the party Xavi was taking her to this afternoon, thrown by his ex-girlfriend, no less. She dreaded seeing what was waiting there on the screen, assuming it must be from Amber, so she decided not to look. For now, at least.

Stefi didn't know what to do, what was right and what was wrong anymore with respect to her oldest friend. What she really wanted was to spend her time thinking about the exciting boy who'd shown up in her life, this person who'd gallantly walked her home last night rather than ravishing her out on his terrace like she'd been hoping he might. She understood why Xavi wanted to take things slow and knew that he was trying to be a gentleman, but she wished he would be a little less gentlemanly. This was her summer fling, and she wanted to fling herself into being with Xavi rather fully.

And kissing Xavi? God, it was amazing.

Like, the best kissing Stefi had done in her life so far.

Also, well, it made Stefi want things. It made Stefi want to *do* things. Last night, it had made Stefi want to remove all her clothing and see what happened next with Xavi. But even the new Stefi couldn't make herself be that forward. She had only ever had sex with Jason. They'd dated all through high school, and because Stefi—unlike Jason—wasn't the type to cheat, she had never had sex with anyone else. Besides, it took ages for Stefi to feel ready to take that step with Jason. It had all been fine too—fine sex. But Stefi always wished for fireworks, and so far, the sky had yet to reply with sunbursts across her vision.

She had high hopes for this where Xavi was concerned, though. When she was kissing Xavi, all her powers of decision-making seemed to go out the window, her body taking over completely to guide Stefi toward what it wanted next. Sex with Xavi was now very high up on Stefi's summer bucket list, and she was hoping to check it off that list ASAP.

Stefi stood in front of her closet, hair dry, in a T-shirt and shorts, trying to decide which outfit for the party would best communicate to Xavi that he was welcome to take it off her.

A dress, definitely. But which one?

As Stefi debated what to wear, it occurred to her that if she had sex with someone new, maybe the sharp sting of Jason and Amber's betrayal wouldn't be quite so sharp. Then Stefi remembered seeing Xavi on the beach, the muscles that rippled across his stomach, how well defined they were. The memory automatically made Stefi wonder what it would be like to trace those lines with her fingers. The thought of doing this made her heart jump and her skin go all tingly. A promising sign, she decided.

Stefi settled on a green spaghetti-strap dress the same color as her bathing suit. It was short but flowy, pretty but simple. She wore only a pair of tiny pink lace underwear underneath it. She automatically imagined Xavi slipping it off her later tonight, and a thrill raced through her.

Sex with Xavi would be different than it was with Jason.

In this moment, she'd bet her life on it.

And maybe in a mere few hours, she'd find out if she was right.

By the time Stefi finished getting ready for the party, more messages had arrived on her phone, and she couldn't resist checking them. Yes, they were all from Amber, and Stefi wondered if Amber had been up all night. This was becoming torture and Stefi didn't like it. She wanted to feel free to enjoy herself with Xavi, no distractions from home intruding. Maybe she'd leave her phone at her abuela's. Maybe that was the easiest thing for her to do. Stefi made her way down to the other end of the hall. She needed help.

It was silent behind the door of her parents' room. She knocked.

"Yes?" came her mother's voice.

Stefi was relieved Ana answered. "Mom? Can you talk?"

In half a second the door was open and Ana was standing there. "Of course. Always, my darling."

"Where's Dad?" Stefi asked, hoping he was not inside the room too.

"He went with your abuela to the market to help her shop," Ana said. "He worries about her dragging around that giant heavy roller cart."

"I do too," Stefi said.

"She's stronger than you think," Ana said with a smile. "You look nice, by the way."

Stefi felt herself blushing. She hoped her outfit didn't reveal to her mother what she hoped it would reveal to Xavi. Ana had always been open with Stefi about sex and had helped her go on the pill when she started having sex with Jason, but still. Stefi had limits. "You think?" was all Stefi replied.

Ana smiled again. "You're lovely." Her mother gestured toward the stairs. "Let's go down to the kitchen and you can tell me whatever you like. It's been ages since we've really talked, Estefanía."

Stefi swallowed and followed Ana. She took a seat on one of the stools at the island and watched as her mother packed espresso into the cafetera and set it on the stove to heat. Ana pulled down cookies from one of the higher cabinets. "I bought these the other day at Brunells."

Stefi heard the guilt in her mother's tone. Brunells was the competition for Hofmann.

"But Mom," she groaned.

The bag crinkled as her mother opened it and peered inside. "I know, sweetheart, but they are also *very* good. You should try them."

"Never," Stefi protested, and Ana laughed.

Even though it was hot enough to burn her feet on the stone streets outside, Stefi missed her pastry class. She hoped next week it would start up again. She hoped for a lot of things, and now she remembered why she'd knocked on her mother's bedroom door in the first place. While her mother set cookies on a plate, Stefi began to talk. "So a lot has happened that you don't know about, Mom."

Ana glanced at her daughter sideways, then turned her attention to the stove. The water was already starting to bubble up into the top of the cafetera. "I'm aware, darling. I've known for a while something was going on, but I figured you would tell me when you were ready."

Despite her earlier protests, Stefi reached for one of the tiny cookies and popped it into her mouth. God, it was buttery and almondy and it immediately made her reach for another. She had to admit, Hofmann's competition or not, they were delicious. "I'm ready now."

Ana prepared their cafés con leche and pushed the two cups toward the other side of the island. She sat down on the stool next to Stefi's. "You can tell me anything, sweetheart. I mean it. *Anything*."

Given the way her mother said this, Stefi wondered if Ana not only knew there was something wrong but that the something was about Amber and Jason. Maybe she'd seen one of the photos Amber and Jason had put up on their profiles. Stefi plunged onward anyway. She stared into her coffee cup as she blurted out the worst of it. "A couple of days before we came here, I walked in on . . . Amber and Jason." She swallowed. "Um, together."

Ana's eyes widened. "Oh, sweetheart! Oh, honey."

Okay, so her mother hadn't known.

Ana placed a hand over her daughter's. "I wondered, but I didn't realize . . . oh, darling. I'm so sorry. That must have been awful. Okay. Okay." She seemed to gather herself. "Tell me everything. Well, as much as you want. I've got all day, sweetheart. For you, always."

Her mother's concern and this outpouring of love made Stefi tear up. She didn't want to cry, and for once, she'd put on mascara. But in this moment, she remembered how wonderful her mother could be. What a relief to confess this humiliating secret to her mom; it was like having poison drawn from a wound. Now she was no longer alone in it, and she knew her mother would help take away the sting, because that's how Ana had always been. Stefi was lucky in the mother department.

Stefi took a deep breath, and over their cafés con leche and one delicious cookie from the enemy after another, Stefi told her mother all of it. About what she'd seen at Amber's house, how betrayed and devastated she'd been, and everything she'd been doing and feeling since arriving in Barcelona. About Xavi and Diego and Santiago and even Xavi's ex-girlfriend Isabel and about how much she liked Xavi and how quickly she'd started falling for someone after Jason, surprising even herself in the process. Eventually Stefi came around to the other issue at hand, which was what to do about Amber's messages.

Ana listened patiently to every word of her daughter's story, getting up only once to make them more coffee. When Stefi finished, her mother remained quiet for a moment.

"That's a hard one, darling," she said after a long silence. "You and Amber have been friends since you were little. It's a terrible betrayal she put you through. But you're both so young. Love appears sometimes when we least expect it."

A surge of shock went through Stefi. "Are you taking her side, Mom?"

"No, sweetheart, no," Ana said quickly, placing a hand on her daughter's arm. "It may be that a friendship can never recover after something like what Amber did. You may never be able to trust her again. But you may find in time that you have things you'd like to say to Amber. And you also may find there comes a time when you want to hear Amber out."

Stefi thought about this. She knew her mother was probably right. She was already tempted to text Amber back. Even though she kept deleting Amber's messages, each time a new one came in, she kind of wanted to respond. "Maybe I will. Maybe soon, but just not yet."

"You get to take your time on this one. Amber will have to be patient." Her mother ate a cookie, took a sip of her coffee, then continued. "We've been talking only about Amber. But what about Jason—do you miss him?"

"Sometimes," Stefi said automatically. But even as this word came out, she wasn't sure it was true anymore. Not since she'd started hanging out with Xavi.

Ana inhaled deeply. "I'm going to tell you something, Estefanía, and I hope it doesn't make you angry at me."

"What, Mom?" she said, eyeing her mother cautiously.

"I've never liked Jason for you. Not long term. One of the reasons I thought it would be good for our family to come to Barcelona was to give you some space from him."

"Mom!"

Ana kept her gaze steady on her daughter despite Stefi's protest. "I know, I know. But you know what else, darling?"

Stefi was still taking in what her mother had confessed. She wasn't sure she was ready for more, but she knew her mother would tell her regardless. "Oh no, what else?"

Ana looked her daughter up and down as she sat there on the stool, coffee cup in one hand. "Sweetheart, I've never seen you happier. You're positively glowing here, and it's not just the heat wave. Barcelona is good for you." Her mother's smile turned mischievous. "And maybe this Xavi person is good for you too?"

At the mention of Xavi's name, Stefi's heart gave a flutter. A smile crept onto her face. She knew it was the thing putting a smile on her mother's face too. Her mother loved romance and had gotten lucky with Stefi's dad, and she'd always wanted the same for Stefi. "Maybe."

Ana clapped her hands gleefully. "When can I meet him?"

"Oh my God, Mom," Stefi said, rolling her eyes. "I don't know. Today, maybe? He's coming to pick me up soon."

"Perfect! Today it is, then." Ana got down from her stool and stood before her daughter. "But before we do anything else, I need to give my daughter a giant hug. I love you, sweetheart."

Stefi let her mother take her into her arms, and as she did, Stefi closed her eyes. She was glad she'd told Ana today. It was always a relief when a person was no longer alone in something terrible. Stefi had to remember this for next time.

"You can always come to me, mi amor," her mother said as though reading Stefi's mind. "No matter what it is, I'm here for you."

# Twenty-Three

The news about Isabel's party spread like lightning. It would be the party of the summer, apparently. Xavi did not want to go, but for some reason, Santiago was determined they would all go together, Stefi too; he argued that Diego wanted to be there so Santiago wanted to be there and that Xavi should think of Stefi, that maybe she'd like to experience an Isabel de Luna party extravaganza while in Barcelona.

So it was settled. Xavi would go—for a while. But he had other plans for later this evening. Plans he'd been hatching all day as he awaited the hour they'd all head down to the beach and the W, make their appearance for however long was necessary, and then take off.

Xavi rang the bell downstairs at Stefi's apartment. Then he stepped back to peer up to the top of the building. He'd passed it many times before, but this would be his first time inside. Diego and Santiago were sitting at a little café half a block away while Xavi fetched Stefi. As Xavi waited for someone to answer on the intercom, he checked his phone again. What was going on with Marta? She'd yet to respond to his most recent message, and the whole time she'd been away, her replies had been sporadic. Normally, Marta responded to Xavi's texts nearly immediately, as though she were always waiting for her son to say hello. But these past two days, there were times it had taken Marta several hours to reply to a simple *Just saying hi, mamá, everything all right?* The longer it took

Marta to respond, the more Xavi wondered if his mother had a secret boyfriend. He'd considered reaching out to Jordi to see where he was on this sudden summer vacation from La Buena. Boy, when Marta got home, Xavi was going to grill her. He looked forward to it, since finally the tables would be turned.

"Helloooo?" came an unfamiliar woman's voice through the speaker.

Not Stefi and not her abuela, Xavi guessed. Older than Stefi but not so old she could be a grandmother. "Hi, it's Xavi. I'm here for Stefi."

"Come on up," the voice said excitedly, and the door buzzed open.

Xavi began the long climb of staircase after staircase, but he was used to it. The apartment he shared with Marta was also a walk-up; they were common in El Gótico, given that buildings as old as these weren't exactly designed for elevator installation. Some buildings' central staircases were so narrow, you felt like you were ascending the inside of a shell, coiled tightly and perfectly.

A door opened above and Stefi's voice floated down to Xavi. "Um, warning, the whole family is here! I'm sorry ahead of time."

Xavi finally reached the landing and did his best not to check Stefi out too obviously, given that suddenly three other people were standing in the doorway to greet him. Xavi put on his best smile. He was good at parents. Well, unless they were Isabel's. Hers were the only exception. "Hello, I'm Xavi."

Everyone beamed back at him in the doorway.

"Silvia," the abuela said.

"Ana, Stefi's mother!" This was obvious, given that she looked like an older version of Stefi.

"Encantada," Silvia and Ana said at once.

Stefi's father, on the tall side, stood at the back of the group. "I'm James."

"Nice to meet you all," Xavi said, and he turned to Stefi, who looked like she wanted to die.

"Come in," Silvia said, beckoning Xavi into a beautiful old catalán apartment, one Silvia had obviously kept up carefully over the years, with its long wood beams across the ceiling and beautiful terra-cotta floors. Marta would love this place. Maybe if things worked out with him and Stefi . . . but no. That was not an option, so Xavi shouldn't allow himself these kinds of thoughts.

Ana talked to Xavi as she walked him across the living room to the kitchen. "Would you like a coffee? A vermut? Some cava?"

Stefi followed. "We really need to go," she said impatiently. "We're expected at a party, Mom."

Xavi glanced at Stefi. She shook her head no, but he already liked this family, liked how normal they were, how welcoming, how different than the families of his friends from school. "Maybe we have time for one vermut?"

Stefi groaned, and Xavi laughed; Ana and Silvia beamed, and James chuckled.

Xavi immediately felt at home.

"Have a seat," James said, pulling out a chair at the round table near the kitchen island and offering it to Xavi.

Before Xavi took his seat, he offered to help Silvia with the vermuts. She answered him in a stream of catalán, and Ana chimed in to ask how he liked it, orange slice or lemon? And suddenly he was next to Silvia in the kitchen, knife in hand, carving up the orange carefully and using tiny tongs to pluck olives from the jar and plop them into the catalán cocktails, chatting with Stefi's mother and grandmother. Occasionally, he looked over to grin at Stefi.

"Oh, fine." Stefi sighed, giving in and sitting herself down at the table.

Xavi wondered if he would be in trouble with Stefi later. No, he decided. She was nervous, but these people loved her and she loved them. Xavi could tell. He filed this tidbit away along with all the others that were adding up to become a girl Xavi had more feelings for than he wanted to admit. Way too many. Dangerously many.

"Have fun!" Ana called as the door clicked shut behind Stefi and Xavi a full hour after he'd arrived at the apartment. Her family had asked Xavi all kinds of questions, and in addition to enjoying the conversation, he was pleased to realize that Stefi had obviously been speaking about him to Ana and Silvia. Ana, especially, seemed to know a whole lot about him.

"Oh my God," Stefi said. "My family."

Xavi laughed. "They like you a lot, obviously. And you like them."

Stefi and Xavi kept talking as they descended the stairs. "I think it's that you're the first new guy I've, well, gone out on a date with pretty much since the beginning of high school. Since Jason. So for my mother, this was, like, a big event. And my abuelita, well, she just wants me to be happy."

"I hope I passed the test," Xavi said, realizing he really did hope this.

They picked up Santiago and Diego at the café, and Diego immediately led them out to Via Laietana so they could catch a cab to the hotel. The heat was unbearable. The walk down to the W would be too, Diego argued. "At this hour, it will be about twenty-five full minutes of direct sun," Diego said when Xavi resisted a taxi. Xavi never took taxis; they were a waste of money.

"I've got it," Santiago said, and Xavi shrugged. Fine, let the king pay for their taxi.

In the car, Santiago was squeezed in on the other side of Xavi and Stefi, and he seemed more nervous than usual. Xavi could feel Santiago studying him when, really, he wished it were Stefi's eyes on him now.

"Chaval, how are you? Are you all right?" Santiago asked for about the tenth time that day.

Xavi gave him a quizzical look. "Cálmate, everything is fine."

Santiago lowered his voice to a whisper. "Promise that you will not sneak off without me at this party." His royal guard's eyes were full of worry.

Xavi patted Santiago on his knee. "Try to enjoy yourself today. You're the one who wanted to go to this party, not me."

Santiago made a strangled sound in response.

This must be about Diego, Xavi decided. Santiago seemed to really like him. Xavi smiled. He was glad for both of them. Professional conflict or not for his royal guard, Xavi could tell Diego was very happy, which made Xavi happy on his best friend's behalf.

When the group emerged from the barely air-conditioned car in front of the W, Santiago and Diego led the way into the hotel lobby and all four of them stopped to bask in the coolness.

"God, that feels good," Diego said.

The lobby was bustling with people. Some staying at the hotel, surely, but definitely also people headed to Isabel's party out on the deck. Girls in bathing suits and expensive, flowing cover-ups, boys in swim trunks, ready to take advantage of the W's magnificent pool, which overlooked the Mediterranean. There were other partygoers dressed to the nines, some of the girls in heels so high and spindly it made Xavi dizzy to watch them walking. The W lobby was like a lair for gilipollas, wealthy guys who used their money to impress women, and there were plenty of women ready to let themselves be impressed. Not Xavi's scene. But even he had to admit the place was beautiful. The bar curled all around the lobby; beautiful lanterns hung from the ceiling, and there were many nooks for sitting and gorgeous couches and lounges and little tables on which to place your expensive cocktails and wine.

Xavi wondered what Stefi thought of this place. When he turned to her, she was holding her arms out, head tilted up, as though she were bathing herself in the sunlight, but in here it was the frosty air all around them. Stefi had on a simple bright green dress and she wore her hair long and loose and flowing over her shoulders. Xavi took advantage of this moment to admire her. After spending so much time with her these past few days and now meeting Stefi's family, Xavi was convinced he and Stefi were more alike than not. It worried him that when he officially took on his role as prince, Stefi was the kind of person Xavi wasn't meant to be with, someone he'd be expected to avoid. Because apparently becoming prince required Xavi to be someone else, someone he'd never been and never wanted to become.

Stefi dropped her arms to her sides and opened her eyes. She looked at Xavi and smiled. "I'm ready to be wowed by an Isabel de Luna party," she said. "I'm already wowed by the lobby."

*Isabel who?* Xavi thought. He could barely remember what Isabel looked like with Stefi standing before him in that dress. Xavi reached for Stefi's hand; he would enjoy being with her while he could. "Pues, ven conmigo entonces," he said, and braced himself to do the thing he'd promised himself he'd never do again after the last time, when he ended up drunk and regretful—attend a party thrown by his ex. One never knew what might happen at an Isabel de Luna party, and Xavi already had enough going on to last him the rest of his life.

# Twenty-Four

Santiago looked around the party. He was in trouble in more ways than one this afternoon, and time seemed to be passing unnaturally quickly.

First, there was Diego.

They'd danced on the deck until they'd thought they would melt. The party was packed with people from school and influencers Santiago had seen only online, the kind normally barred from royal events. There were even young celebrities from some of his favorite TV shows. The deck was teeming with guests; the pool was wall to wall. Balls bounced aimlessly across the many hands that pulsed in the air. There was even a special cocktail the W bartenders had mixed for the occasion, naming it, aptly, the Ola de Calor, the Heat Wave. Packed with ice and rum and mint, it tasted suspiciously like a mojito yet was still its own thing, and the drink went down all too easily. Santiago was trying not to drink too many.

But maybe he already had?

The entire afternoon, as Diego and Santiago alternated between the bar and the dance floor, Santiago was keeping an eye on Xavi. At the moment, Xavi was on the other side of the dance floor with Stefi. Santiago still hadn't said a word to him about what Isabel expected by the end of this evening. Santiago knew he had to tell Xavi something soon, but the right moment never seemed to arise and now time was slipping through his fingers. Other things kept getting in the way and distracting him.

Things like Diego arriving with another set of frosty cocktails.

"Otro Ola de Calor," Diego announced gleefully, handing Santiago one of the glasses.

Santiago took it and raised it up between them. "¡Salud!"

"Salud," Diego said in return, holding Santiago's gaze in a way that made him woozy.

They clinked glasses and kept dancing, sipping their drinks as they did.

Ample shade was on offer for the partygoers, the entire deck strung up with fluttering sails that rose high above them. The breeze coming off the water helped quell the heat, but the biggest help was the sun eventually beginning to set behind the hotel's other side. The people on the dance floor jumped and swayed and sang at the top of their lungs to celebrate this relief, waving their hands high and giving themselves over to the pulsing music.

Santiago had to admit it: Isabel de Luna knew how to throw a party.

Speaking of Isabel, Santiago glanced around. He'd yet to see Isabel at her own party. Which was another reason why Santiago was in such trouble. Isabel's absence allowed him to forget about her or at least pretend that she didn't exist, that last night at Isabel's family's club was all an unpleasant hallucination, and that the only thing Santiago had to worry about right now was finding a way to kiss the handsome boy in front of him before the evening's end.

Diego's eyes were closed as he moved his body to the music and he leaned into Santiago. Santiago did the same and leaned back.

Maybe Isabel wouldn't come to her own party? Maybe she'd decided against going through with her plan? Maybe someone had kidnapped her?

If only.

Santiago knew he had a painful choice to make and that the clock was ticking; soon he'd have to pick a path and go down it one way or the other.

The stakes for Xavi and Stefi were higher even than the arc of the W hotel reaching up into the Barcelona sky.

Isabel had tasked Santiago with somehow convincing Xavi—in exchange for her protecting Stefi's identity and not publishing those scandalous photos—to call everyone together at the height of the party and make two official announcements. First, Xavi would reveal his true identity, allowing Leonora to scoop and photograph the entire, shocking moment and publish it online. Then Xavi would make a special toast to Isabel de Luna, his girlfriend and longtime love, who had kindly thrown this incredible party for the very special occasion of Xavi, her boyfriend, announcing to the world he was the prince of Spain. Leonora, of course, would also photograph the moment that he kissed Isabel in front of everyone.

Especially in front of Stefi.

On top of all this, Isabel wanted Xavi to break up with Stefi right before his big announcement. And after the toast Xavi made to Isabel, thanking her for this wonderful night, they would sit down with Leonora to do an exclusive interview about plans for their future.

This, or Leonora would simply out Xavi as the prince herself and publish those photos of Xavi with Stefi. *All* of them.

Diego danced even closer to Santiago, oblivious to the turmoil bouncing inside of Santiago's brain like the beach balls around the pool deck.

What was Santiago going to do?

Time was running out, but he didn't want to tear himself away from Diego.

Santiago decided he would let himself enjoy a few more songs before he dealt with Xavi.

Last night, Santiago had protested to Isabel that these were impossible expectations, that Xavi would never go for any of it, especially not the part about presenting Isabel as his official and longtime love in front of Stefi and capitulating to Isabel's clear designs on becoming Spain's princess-to-be. But inside, Santiago wondered if—given the choice—Xavi might be willing to give Isabel all she wanted to protect Stefi's identity, if not her heart. So, intentionally or not, Isabel had given Santiago a choice too—to tell Xavi or not to tell him and let the chips fall where they may. A small, idiotic part of Santiago didn't want to offer Xavi these terrible options. He almost preferred to see what would happen if it all just came out, and everyone had to face the consequences: Xavi and Stefi, Isabel herself, who'd see she couldn't always get her way, and even Santiago with respect to Diego.

Or maybe this was all those Olas de Calor speaking?

The only choice Santiago seemed to be saying yes to without any reservation was the one that involved the person he was currently clutching like his life depended on it as a ballad came over the speakers and slowed everything down.

Santiago hadn't danced like this since, well, maybe ever.

He let himself sink even further into this moment at the expense of all else.

Santiago's entering the Guardia Real at such a young age meant he'd taken on a lot of responsibility very early. Everything about his life at the palace had always held a subdued quality, so Santiago never did things like this—attend lavish parties at hotels smack on the beach and the sea of Barcelona. Or let loose to the point where he'd sweat through his shirt so thoroughly that, like the many guys around him, he simply took it off. Diego had taken his off too, and why not? It was a pool party, it was a Barcelona heat wave, and they were outside dancing on a hotel deck by the sea. And God, Santiago thought to himself, Diego was such an amazing dancer. Santiago decided their respective heights were perfect, too, because Diego could practically fit right under Santiago's chin, which allowed them to dance especially close. And Santiago wanted Diego close. Diego being so close was helping Santiago convince himself that he might have simply hallucinated the whole situation with Isabel.

So when Diego looked up at Santiago and said, "Do you want to cool off? Go for a swim?" Santiago told him, "Definitely," without hesitation.

Diego could have said, *Do you want to go skydiving?* and Santiago would have said yes to that too. He was pretty sure he'd say yes to anything Diego asked in this moment.

Santiago also knew he was headed right off the deep end into unknown territory—territory that could blow up in his and Xavi's and the monarchy's faces. But at this very second, the deep end looked a lot like the hotel pool of the W, and he was being invited to jump into it by this very handsome person.

He glanced over at Xavi and Stefi, who were still dancing away. Then he glanced at his watch. Sixty minutes. He had sixty minutes before he was supposed to meet Isabel and potentially ruin Xavi's happiness. And Stefi's along with it.

"Are you coming?" Diego had turned and beckoned when he realized Santiago wasn't following him.

Santiago plucked a pair of rolled-up towels from a nearby shelf. "I am," he said, deciding that for the next fifty-nine minutes, or maybe fifty-eight, to be safe, what he would choose for once was his own happiness. He would put himself and Diego above his duty to the monarchy and to Xavi and to Isabel de Luna and her stupid connections to the gossiping influencers and paparazzi that were always threatening to shred the peace and well-being of the Spanish royals.

No, for just over fifty minutes. He was allowed fifty additional minutes of joy, right? Besides, the less time Xavi had to think about what Isabel wanted him to do, the better. It would be like ripping off a Band-Aid.

Diego continued through the throng on the deck and Santiago followed him.

He'd assumed Diego wanted them to somehow fit into the packed pool and was surprised when Diego led him beyond the pool toward the beach below. He took one last glance at Xavi, who seemed lost in the music and in Stefi's arms, then headed down the steps. It was like the partygoers had forgotten that the Mediterranean Sea stretched out before them, barely a few feet away.

Soon Santiago found himself wading into the turquoise water, which was already warm for July, Diego next to him. The two boys dove under.

Santiago came up and shook out his hair. "This was a good idea," he said as a voice inside him fairly shouted, *Chaval, what are you doing? Go and find Xavi!*

"The water does feel amazing," Diego said. "I love to dance but I needed to cool off."

"Me too," Santiago said, but as he did, he was thinking he definitely meant this comment in more ways than one. His brain was spinning, his heart was pounding, and Santiago focused all his attention on whether or not he might get to kiss Diego tonight. They'd come close on the dance floor, but so far they hadn't. As Diego floated next to Santiago in the beautiful sea, Santiago tried to convince himself to just do it, to lean forward in the water and finish what they hadn't last night when Isabel de Luna had so cruelly called him away.

This was what Santiago was thinking when Diego spoke.

"I want to ask you something," he said. "And I want you to answer me honestly."

"You can ask me anything," Santiago said and meant it. He was busy pretending that nothing else existed in his life at this moment. The only thing that existed for his heart was the boy in the water so close he could wrap his arms around him if only he could muster the courage.

Diego moved closer, beads of water dotting his eyelashes. "What are we doing here, Santiago? I mean, apart from Xavi. I guess I'm asking, what are *you* doing here with *me*?"

The water lapped softly around them as Santiago debated how to answer, how much of the truth he should admit to. But then he threw caution to the wind and decided to tell Diego the whole of it. "I'm here because I've liked you since the moment we met. Even though I'm not supposed to. But I can't seem to stop myself."

"Okay," Diego said.

Disappointment nipped at Santiago all over, like some kind of sea creature scuttling across the sand below the water. "Just okay?"

Diego nodded. But instead of explaining himself with words, Diego suddenly put his arms around Santiago's neck and got up on his toes, his mouth rising toward Santiago's for a kiss, the effect of which was to immediately erase from Santiago's mind every other thought that had been coursing through it.

Santiago wasn't sure how long he and Diego had been kissing.

They'd gotten out of the water and made their way back to the beach, at which point they kissed in between laying out their towels on the sand and sitting down on them. Then they kissed some more and more and more. It was as if the entire Barcelona night were theirs alone, as though no one else could see them and the most packed party of the summer was not occurring just above them on the teeming nearby deck.

Santiago sighed.

Diego's lips were soft, they were perfect, they were delicious.

Kissing Diego was incredible. Kissing Diego made Santiago forget all else—Xavi, Stefi, conniving ex-girlfriends, the fact that life as Xavi knew it, and as Santiago knew it too, would soon end if Isabel had her way or if Leonora went ahead with all of her threats. But if things were about to go down and fast, at least Santiago would go down kissing this exceedingly handsome, wonderful boy in his arms. It was an excellent way to go, he decided, and he gave into it fully.

Diego seemed to have read Santiago's mind, because right then, he pulled away and said, "Kissing you is amazing," rather breathlessly.

Joy and relief poured through Santiago. He felt the same way, but given Santiago's limited romantic past, he'd had no idea how he measured up. After all, Diego had clearly enjoyed having boyfriends over the course of his entire life so far, whereas Santiago had not.

"I agree completely," Santiago said. "Though, I don't have much experience to go on," he admitted, then groaned and looked away. What he didn't say out loud was that he might like *all* the experience he could have with Diego as soon as humanly possible. The amount of want coursing through Santiago was significant. It was wonderful and also totally terrifying.

He tried to breathe and found that he couldn't. Was he falling in love? Was that what this was? His heart was jumping, his mind was spinning, he couldn't get ahold of anything inside him.

Santiago felt a gentle hand on the side of his face as Diego shifted Santiago's gaze back to himself. "All that really matters is chemistry, and that we have plenty of." Diego leaned forward and kissed Santiago deeply before pulling back and leaving Santiago breathless again.

"Obviously," Santiago concurred.

Diego planted another kiss on Santiago's mouth. "Why don't we take advantage of this . . . chemistry of ours and go back to my house? My parents are away."

All kinds of thoughts coursed through Santiago's brain at this invitation. It was suddenly like La Noche de San Juan inside his head, with fireworks going off left and right and front and center all across the city. One side of his brain lit up with the possibility of all he and Diego could do if they were finally alone, *really* alone, but the other side was showing him all the dangers and pitfalls of what might happen if Santiago dared to say yes. But then Diego kissed him again and kissed him hard as though to emphasize his desire that they get away from this party to be in private.

"Come on," Diego whispered. "Xavi will be fine."

Oh, yeah. Xavi. *That* guy.

The spell Diego had put on Santiago was suddenly broken. His brain began to function again, but this time the half of his brain that finally clicked on belonged to the royal guard.

A river of worry entered Santiago's bloodstream and flowed violently through his veins.

Joder. What time was it?

It finally occurred to Santiago to think about the time. He checked his watch, and a wave of relief crashed over him like the salty sea he'd so recently bathed in. There was still fifteen minutes before the appointed hour. Santiago had fifteen minutes to find Xavi and tell him everything!

"We need to find Xavi and Stefi right now," Santiago said, jumping up from the towel. He gazed into those beautiful blue pools peering back at him and it hurt his heart to think of all that joy being behind him. He wanted to turn back the clock so he could live through the most wonderful, beautiful, perfect hour of his whole life again, but of course, he couldn't. "I need your help with Xavi. We need to find him. It's kind of an emergency, actually. An Isabel de Luna–size emergency."

Diego studied Santiago a beat, seeing the desperation in Santiago's eyes. "Of course," he said, getting up to join him.

Without another word, the two young men took off in a hurry toward the pool deck, both boys sending texts to Xavi as they went.

The crowd at the party was even more dense than when they'd left. It was as though half the city of Barcelona had shown up at the W.

Santiago searched and searched the dancing masses but Xavi and Stefi were nowhere he could see. Diego and Santiago ran from nook to nook among the hotel's many bar areas, inside and out, disturbing tangled couples who were very unhappy to have their privacy disrupted. They tried the winding lobby next and even the taxi stand beyond it.

It was no use. Xavi and Stefi were gone. Like, gone completely from the W.

Santiago was going mad.

"Joder," he cursed loudly over the sounds of the DJ.

This was bad. This was horrible.

This was what Santiago got for messing up so royally—pun intended.

Worse still, the price for his failure would be paid by not only Xavi, but Stefi too.

He looked at Diego next to him, still searching the crowd for his best friend since childhood, and all Santiago wanted to do was take Diego into his arms and pick up where they'd left off a few minutes ago. If only he could.

"Joder," he said once more.

Diego studied the royal guard next to him. "What aren't you telling me, Santiago?"

"Ah, well, there's a bit of a situation." Santiago swallowed. "With the gossip site ¡Qué Fuerte! And possibly a Spanish influencer."

"So this would count as a level-five royal emergency, then, if you know what I mean?" Diego asked.

Santiago nodded.

Diego pulled out his phone, tapped a message with lightning speed, and sent it off. "When Xavi and I were boys, we came up with a call sign of sorts. A code red," he added. "I haven't used it since we were, I don't know, maybe nine?"

Santiago wanted to kiss Diego on hearing this, but this time he refrained. Look where kissing Diego had gotten him tonight.

They waited for a response, and Santiago realized he was holding his breath.

He didn't have to hold it for long.

Nearly immediately, a response pinged on Diego's phone. Diego held up the screen and Santiago saw that Xavi had replied, **Everything okay? I'm with Stefi.**

Diego typed out, **Obviously, but where? Can we come find you?**

Three dots appeared, then disappeared. Xavi was hesitant to share his whereabouts.

Another message arrived on Diego's phone.

**Sorry, you were busy getting cozy with Santiago on the beach**, Xavi wrote.

**I didn't want to interrupt.**

**But I didn't want to stay at the party either. Not my scene.**

**Is something wrong? I'm not exactly close by.**

Santiago's heart sank as he read. He checked the time. Then he looked around for Isabel. He looked around for Leonora too.

"Joder, joder, joder." Santiago was obviously undeserving of his position, of his role in the royal guard. If his father were still alive, he'd be ashamed of him, Francisco Hernández would be ashamed of him, and the king would be too. Santiago was ashamed of himself. He'd failed miserably at his duties and he kept failing at them, risking the prince of Spain's anonymity and his family's secret and his own position in the process. What's more, now he'd failed Stefi. He was an embarrassment to the crown. He was an embarrassment, period.

This was going to be a shitshow.

Santiago tried to swallow and couldn't. "This is all my fault. I should have told Xavi the truth, then he never would have taken off," he said to no one in particular, mainly himself.

But Diego was standing there, of course. "Told Xavi the truth about what, exactly?"

He let out a long, helpless breath. "Xavi doesn't realize that—"

"Xavi doesn't realize what?"

Santiago turned around.

Behind the two young men stood Isabel de Luna in an outfit that a gossip site like ¡Qué Fuerte! might fittingly caption: *As pretty as a princess*.

Fate had finally found Santiago. Jo-der.

"Hi, Isabel," he said to the beautiful woman who was currently Xavi's ex and apparently would remain so, and got ready to beg.

# Twenty-Five

Stefi was having the best night of her life. It was making her question *everything*.

The country where she belonged, the place she might be happiest, the people she'd be happiest with. Whether her family should stay in Barcelona well beyond the summer and for the entirety of her senior year.

So many new possibilities unfolded before her, including enrolling as a student at Hofmann for real. Maybe her parents would allow Stefi to do a gap year of sorts, but in her senior year of high school instead of on her way to college? Also, why in the world had Stefi stayed with Jason so long? Clearly, she hadn't realized what might lie ahead if she just let him go. That what lay ahead of Stefi might be someone like Xavi, this very handsome person who was, incidentally, currently engaged in cooking Stefi a late-night dinner at his family's tiny restaurant in the darkness of La Boqueria market.

Stefi sat on one of the stools at the counter watching Xavi make tapas magic.

He was taking something out of the narrow deep fryer in the tiny kitchen of La Buena. "Wait till you eat this, you're going to die," he said as he set the giant sizzling ball of mysterious goodness onto a paper towel placed across a plate.

She was already salivating. "I can't wait," she said. For the food Xavi was making for her, sure, but also for the cook himself.

Stefi looked around. La Boqueria was so quiet and empty. She and Xavi were alone. Blissfully so. No Santiago, no Diego, no Isabel or anybody else to intrude. Stefi was so glad they'd taken off without bothering to say goodbye to Xavi's very sticky cousin Santiago.

"Are we going to get in trouble for being here?" she had asked just thirty minutes ago when Xavi walked right up to the padlock on the tall iron gates at the entrance to La Boqueria.

"Nah, we'll be fine," Xavi had replied, pulling out the key and clicking the lock open. "This market has always been my second home, and I love coming here when I have it all to myself." The chain fell away and Xavi slid the heavy gate open wide enough for the two of them to slip inside. "My mother used to bring me here, just the two of us, when I was little," he went on as he relocked the gate behind them. "I'd be in my pajamas and she'd cook for me and it felt like such a treat, like this whole beautiful place was all for us."

Stefi had loved the image this sparked in her mind of Xavi when he was small.

Then he'd maneuvered them through the empty stalls with their canvas shades pulled down over their wares, some of the stalls with steel-slatted doors closing them off. "Besides, if someone came in and asked what you and I were doing, I could just say I'm here to do some special prep work at La Buena. I've known the guards that come through my whole life too. My mother has been a part of this place for decades. It's one big family for us."

"One a.m. is definitely early to be doing prep work, though," Stefi had whispered. She felt like she should keep her voice down, like the stalls and the many things they held might be sleeping.

Xavi flashed Stefi a grin as he led her through the circle at the center of the market, empty now of all the magnificent fish that would be arriving in just a few hours. "The worst that would happen is whoever found us might tell my mother I was here on a date."

Stefi had already figured this was a date—Xavi had come to pick her up at abuela's apartment to take her to a fancy party, after all—but it was still exciting to hear him say this out loud and so casually.

Now Xavi placed a plate of boquerones on the countertop in front of Stefi, their first tapa of the night. Next to them, he added a plate with pan con tomate to eat with the long, vinegary fish. He'd sprinkled chopped onions and pickles on top of them.

"This is for while we wait for the bomba to cool," Xavi explained, referring to the giant fried ball of mashed potatoes and spicy meat sitting on the paper towel.

"Pickles, really?" Stefi inquired as she took in what seemed, at least to her, a strange garnish for the boquerones. She watched as Xavi took a piece of the tomato bread and draped a fish across it, then scooped some of the pickles and onions over the top.

He took a bite. "Hmm, it's the pickles that make this, I swear. Just try it."

Stefi did what she was told—she was very pliable when it came to obeying someone who offered excellent culinary advice. Pickles, onions, and vinegary fish would not normally be high on Stefi's list of food pairings, but she took a big bite of the concoction. Then she closed her eyes. "Oh my God."

When she opened them again, Xavi was grinning. "See, La Buena may be famous for the tortilla, but there are lots of other wonderful things on the menu. I want you to try them all."

Stefi grinned back. "I'm willing try whatever you make," she promised. Then she took another giant bite of her tapa and thought of her abuela. "You have to cook for my abuela. And my parents. My mother would love this. She'd love that you not only know your way around a kitchen, but, well . . ." Stefi gestured above her toward the sign announcing La Buena Tapas Bar to the market's visitors. "She'd love this place especially."

Xavi threw several handfuls of tiny green peppers into a hot iron skillet to sear them, the flames underneath leaping into the pan. Stefi studied Xavi as he cooked, his hair pulled back in a ponytail. This whole situation was unbelievably romantic. This would never happen to Stefi in the U.S. It wouldn't because it couldn't. There weren't places like La Buena at home. Places like this only existed in magical European cities like Barcelona. There weren't boys like this in the U.S. either.

Soon Xavi was pouring the contents of the skillet into a bowl and sprinkling large flaky salt over the top of the peppers. He placed the bowl between them on the counter. "I will cook for your family anytime." He took one of the tiniest peppers, its skin blistered and shining, and ate the whole thing to the stem. "Okay, now you pick," he told her. "Careful, some of them are spicy. That's the fun of this dish. You never know when your pepper is going to be picante."

Over the course of the next hour, Stefi ate everything Xavi offered, from the pimientos de Padrón to the bomba once it cooled to the teeny-tiny clams Stefi had never seen before that Xavi steamed in garlic and wine that made Stefi moan with delight, they were so delicious.

After the two of them had eaten all they could, Xavi came around the counter and sat on the stool next to Stefi's. Xavi's shirt was dirty and sweaty, and his hair was pulled back in a messy ponytail, and Stefi thought he had never been so attractive.

Xavi poured each of them a glass of wine and raised his. "To being alone in the city," he said.

"Salud," Stefi replied. They clinked glasses. "Thank you for cooking for me. That was . . . really special."

"I'm glad you enjoyed it." He smiled.

"Did you do this for Isabel too?" Stefi asked before she could stop herself.

The smile left Xavi's face at the mention of his ex. He shook his head. "No. I would never do this with her. This part of my life was always a problem for Isabel."

Stefi looked around at the tiny restaurant, the countertop and the stools, the jars of artichokes and tins of sardines and other preserved things lining the shelves above the stove, this place that's so bustling during the days and where Xavi had grown up and socialized with all their regulars. "But this *is* your life. It's your family."

"Exactly," Xavi said. "Isabel and I were always too different in just about every fundamentally important way."

"You and I are different too," Stefi said.

Was Stefi imagining it, or did Xavi's eyes cloud over even further at this observation? She couldn't decide. She hoped not. She *really* hoped not. Stefi decided not to press things when, instead of replying to Stefi in words, Xavi leaned forward to kiss her. She chose to kiss him back.

The romance of the marketplace in the middle of a Barcelona night sparked and flared around them, and Stefi slid off the stool so her feet were on the ground and she could press her whole body against Xavi's. Just like the other times they'd been alone, soon the couple was kissing like the end of the world was near and only the two of them making out might save it. But unlike those other nights, this time Xavi did not hold back, and Stefi finally found what it was like to have Xavi's hands in places she'd fantasized about them going. The experience was definitely *not* disappointing. It was making Stefi sigh.

But then Xavi pulled back for one breathless moment. "Should we leave?"

Stefi was nodding. "I know you want to take things slow, but you should know, I *really, really* don't," she said, surprising herself by how forward this sounded.

Xavi brushed a kiss across Stefi's neck, which sent a shiver through her body. "What I meant is, should we go back to my apartment? Since no one is there. At least I hope not."

A thrill went through Stefi. "Yes, definitely. That sounds perfect."

At this, Xavi closed up La Buena and unlocked the market doors so they could leave. Soon they were out in the street again, stealing through the Barcelona night on their way to Xavi's. The city was alive with revelers, with couples leaving candlelit restaurants among the labyrinth streets, so many people still sitting outside in the terraces of El Gótico's bars and plazas. Stefi's heart pounded and her mind raced. Halfway there, Xavi pulled Stefi into a dark corner to kiss her as if he couldn't possibly make it any farther without having more of Stefi before they continued onward. Then they pulled apart and raced the rest of the way to Xavi's, practically taking the stairs to his apartment two at a time, winding their way up the last of the steps in the stairwell of his building. As they reached the door and Xavi took his keys out to unlock it, Stefi suddenly wondered if she'd been wrong about what she'd been telling herself ever since she first laid eyes on this boy.

Maybe Stefi *was* ready for more than just a summer fling.

Maybe she was ready to fall in love with someone new.

Maybe she was *already* falling in love with him.

Maybe Xavi was already falling in love with Stefi too. There was something about the way that he kissed her. There was something about the way he looked at her. There was just *something*, and Stefi felt it from the tips of her toes to the tips of her fingers and running all the way up her back and her neck to the very tiptop of her head.

Xavi opened the door and peeked inside the apartment. "Hello?" he called.

No one answered.

He turned to Stefi with a grin. "All ours. Adelante." Stefi went inside and Xavi led her straight to his room and shut the door tight behind them. They were both still breathless from their climb. He took a step closer and looked into Stefi eyes, and she knew—she *knew*—that Xavi was feeling the same way she was. She could see it written all over his face.

"Stefi," Xavi said then.

"Xavi," she said right back.

And she thought, *Yes*.

She watched as Xavi pulled off his shirt so Stefi's fingers could wander across all those muscles she'd wanted so badly to touch and which she let herself do now, and enjoyed doing so immensely. Then Xavi was slipping the straps of Stefi's dress over her shoulders and the rest of the way down her body until it was only a pool of green silk at her feet on his bedroom floor. Next Stefi was helping Xavi out of his jeans and he was sliding Stefi's underwear over her hips so it could join her dress, and the two of them were climbing onto his bed.

Once again, Stefi was not disappointed.

In fact, she thought she might be in heaven.

"Xavi," Stefi whispered in his ear as she clasped him to her.

"Stefi," he whispered back as he pressed himself to Stefi like he couldn't possibly get close enough and needed to be even closer.

The faint sounds of the streets of Barcelona reached inside the windows of Xavi's bedroom and punctuated their night, occasionally reminding Stefi for a moment where they were, and that they were not, in fact, thousands of kilometers from the rest of civilization. It was strange to think there was an entire city just outside when it was as though Stefi and Xavi were in a world of their own making, one that was theirs and theirs alone to enjoy.

# Twenty-Six

Leonora Valdez didn't think overly much about what she was about to post.

Well, that wasn't true. She *did* think about all the new followers she would amass once the news got out. About the lucrative new endorsements that would surely follow, not to mention all the invitations to fabulous parties and island paradises for new hotel openings. But she did not give a single worried thought to the havoc she was about to cause for the crown or the way she was about to upend the life and anonymity of the young prince of Spain and, in the process, blow up the life and anonymity of several others around him. Leonora hadn't become an influencer specializing in gossip to make friends. She loved the notoriety. She ate it for breakfast, lunch, and dinner and drank it down with matcha.

She dialed her media manager.

The woman picked up nearly immediately. "Leonora, hello! What can I do for you?"

Leonora studied her glossy nails. "Isabel de Luna, shockingly, did not come through as she promised." Leonora sighed. Then she smiled to herself. "But either way, I win."

There was a pause. "Yes, either way you're in possession of the gossip of the year," the woman affirmed in a voice that was smooth and assertive, despite the middle-of-the-night hour. "Take whatever you've got and post it," she added. "You've delayed releasing this long enough."

"Of course," Leonora said, then hung up.

She sat back in her chair and stared at the giant screen of her production studio, at the two posts ready to go live, side by side on the big monitor. Normally, her assistants would handle crafting these and the texts and links that would go with them, but this kind of priceless information was for Leonora's eyes only—she couldn't risk letting it get into anyone else's hands.

One post linked to a tell-all about Xavi, led by a photo of the young prince and some girl he was kissing on the streets of Barcelona. Well, kissing was an understatement. They looked like they were about to swallow each other whole. Whoever she was, she should consider herself lucky Leonora had charitably decided to hold back the photos of her on the beach with the prince. Even Leonora had limits. She had gone so far as to imagine herself in this unsuspecting girl's place and decided topless photos should be published only by the girl who was the subject of those photos.

Leonora was not a monster.

But the other post featured Isabel de Luna, Xavi's ex-girlfriend, and led to another tell-all, replete with images of the pair at parties earlier this year as well as a couple of Isabel on her own.

The teaser read: *Isabel de Luna, Our Future Princess?*

This post claimed Isabel had recently enjoyed a romantic reunion with the prince, and they had imminent plans to jet off to the palace in Madrid together and live happily ever after and blah-blah-blah. Isabel de Luna was lucky she had enough . . . *resources* to convince Leonora to throw Isabel this bone, even after the girl failed to produce the young prince for the grand party announcement or the exclusive interview and selfie session Isabel had promised Leonora she'd have with Xavi afterward.

As Leonora stared at the screen before her, she had to admit Isabel did possess the beauty to become royalty. Certainly the attitude as well. But when she compared Xavi to Isabel, she shook her head. The notion these two would work out was misplaced, in her view. Anyone who looked long enough into their eyes could see this—the hardness in the gaze of one, the playful joy in the gaze of the other. Isabel and Xavi were never going to work, if Leonora had to bet. And she should know—a person didn't amass as many followers as Leonora without being very, very ruthless.

Leonora turned back to the photo of the girl who was kissing the prince. She was beautiful too, though in a very different way than Isabel. If Leonora had to bet on one of them, she'd choose the mysterious girl in the prince's arms.

Now Leonora yawned, stretching her arms high toward the ceiling. It was nice being alone for once and not having her influencer-wannabe assistants scurrying around like pesky mice.

Leonora's finger hovered over the button that would make all the gossip she'd worked so hard to gather this summer public. That finger descended.

Listo.

She stood up and shut off everything in her studio. She needed sleep before her day turned crazy with inquiries and requests for interviews and the wave of reposts and new followers. At least a couple of hours to get her to early morning.

PART THREE

# The Prince of Spain

# Twenty-Seven

Xavi woke to doors slamming inside the apartment.

He rolled over in bed. A sleepy smile appeared on his face as he remembered his night and, well, also his morning with Stefi. With *all* of Stefi. What a stupid boyfriend she'd had back home, to let someone like her go. But Xavi was happy to benefit from his idiocy.

Another door slammed.

It must be an angry Santiago trying to disturb Xavi's peace. He felt a little bad that he ditched Santiago again last night, but it was for a good cause and he'd enjoyed the results. He could still hear Stefi's voice sighing his name as if she were with him right now.

Xavi rolled over again and adjusted his pillow. His main concerns this morning were when he could see Stefi again and if there was any way this prince situation didn't have to mess up what they'd started. Maybe times had changed enough for a monarch to have an untitled American girlfriend—and why not? Xavi deserved to have a normal love life just like anyone else.

*Love life*. This phrase floated through Xavi's mind, reached the end, and was on its way back, flashing rather brightly. Was Xavi falling in love with Stefi? Was he already in love with her?

He'd certainly never felt like this. Like he wanted to plant himself firmly in Stefi's mind and heart, sear himself across her memory in a way she could never forget, become the boy against whom she measured all other boys, the person who erased all thoughts of her ex. And yet, when this whole thing started, it was only supposed to be a summer fling. But Xavi could no longer lie to himself about this. Even more, he needed to stop lying to Stefi. Because last night certainly felt something like love.

Mierda. His heart pounded relentlessly.

If indeed he was in love with Stefi, this meant he'd been lying to this girl he supposedly loved since the day they met. Though maybe lying was too strong a term. Withholding the truth. A very big, splashy truth. Which he needed to tell Stefi ahora mismo. ASAP.

What would she say when she found out?

Xavi would only know the answer once he spoke to her.

Another door slammed, this time louder. There really was a lot of banging around happening in the apartment. Xavi was just about to close his eyes for a few more minutes of sleep when Santiago flung open his bedroom door, a look of sheer madness on his face.

Xavi lifted his head from the pillow. "Can you at least knock before barging in? I could have been in here . . . *not* alone. Also, why do you have that giant suitcase?"

Santiago threw the suitcase onto Xavi's bed and unzipped it. "We need to talk."

"About your night with Diego or my night with Stefi?" Xavi asked, grinning. But Santiago was clearly not in the mood to joke. "Hey. What's wrong?" At the sound of the gentle concern in Xavi's question, the royal guard halted for a moment, letting the suitcase fall closed. Santiago seemed near tears, but he still wasn't speaking. "Oh no, did something bad happen with Diego?" Xavi wondered. "I thought you guys were hitting it off."

Now Santiago really looked like he might cry. "I'm glad you were able to have one last night with Stefi," he said. "I hope you made it a good one."

A chill pierced Xavi's heart. "Wait—why one last night?"

"I might have fucked up, Xavi. No, I definitely did. And I'm likely about to get relieved of my position because of it. If you'd kept your phone on, you'd already know."

Xavi shot up in bed. "What are you talking about?"

Santiago began opening Xavi's drawers and throwing their contents haphazardly into the suitcase. "See for yourself," he said, sounding strangled.

For once, Xavi obeyed. He opened the drawer in his bedside table where he'd shoved his phone away. He turned it on, and the second the screen came to life, it nearly exploded with messages, alerts, notifications, missed calls. "I don't even know where to start," Xavi said.

"Oh, just try any of them, I'm sure they all lead to the same place."

Xavi randomly tapped one of the notifications, which took him to the homepage of ¡Qué Fuerte!. His eyes grew wide at the headline, which announced clearly and in large boldface letters that Xavier Bas—aka him—was the prince of Spain who had been living in secret. His heart, his stomach, his every internal organ seemed to drop like rocks to the floor and all the way to the bottom of the building, then right on through to the Roman ruins below.

"Joder," he said.

Santiago slammed one of Xavi's drawers shut. "Joder is right."

Xavi was fixated on the lead photo. It was an unbelievably laser-focused image of him with Stefi, the two of them kissing. For a second, his heart leaped at the sight of himself passionately embracing this girl with whom he was falling in love, and his brain cycled back to memories of their wonderful night together. In the photo, they looked so good together. They made a lovely couple.

But: *Joder, joder, joder.*

This photo had been published on Spain's most notorious gossip site, the page people turned to each day when they were bored and seeking entertainment. Not only had Stefi gotten pulled into the article announcing Xavi's true identity, something that had surely already gone viral far and wide, but Stefi would soon realize Xavi had lied to her. Or, as he preferred to think of it, had withheld this awfully big truth. Xavi would probably never have the chance to be with Stefi again because of his stupidity. He hadn't warned Stefi—and truly hadn't really worried either—about the risks of being with someone like him if his secret slipped out. Worldwide notoriety for one, and paparazzi following Stefi and her family everywhere they went, the nosy press digging up her past and everyone in it. For the first time, Xavi understood the enormous cost a person might have to endure to date him.

This was horrible.

He also finally grasped why Marta might want to chase someone like Stefi out of his life.

Marta. He needed his mother. Where in the world was she? He checked his phone again. Amid the gazillion messages and notifications, there must have been thirty missed calls from his mother. *Gracias a Dios*. Marta would know how to handle everything and, most important, she'd know what Xavi should say to Stefi. Maybe she'd know how to fix this. Maybe his mother could find a way through to something like a happy ending for both of them. Xavi was about to call his mother back but something else nagged at him. Xavi watched Santiago frantically moving about his room, still throwing clothes into the suitcase.

"Why is all this *your* fault?" Xavi asked.

Santiago came and stood next to Xavi. His gaze shifted all over—left, right, up, down—before his eyes landed on the prince's. "I had a chance to prevent this situation. And I screwed it up."

Something began to sink again inside of Xavi. "What do you mean?"

Santiago was biting his lip so hard, Xavi wondered if he might draw blood. "Isabel de Luna is behind all this."

At the mention of Isabel, Xavi's stomach began to churn. "Why didn't you tell me?"

His royal guard looked stricken. "You were so happy with Stefi, and I was holding off ruining your time with her. Isabel, as I'm sure you might imagine, had—no, has—great expectations for herself. Well, for the two of you together."

Xavi took this in. He almost didn't want to know the details. All that mattered in any case was that Isabel's scheme *did* ruin things. And might have ruined Stefi's life. Or, at a minimum, made it highly difficult.

Santiago seemed to be reading Xavi's mind. "At least the photo doesn't include Stefi's name in the caption," he said. "They just dubbed her 'Mystery Girl.'"

Xavi gazed at Santiago hopefully. "Do you think it will stay that way?"

Santiago shrugged, then shook his head. "Probably not. You know how people are; they'll go sleuthing and come up with it eventually. There's already an entire Twitter account dedicated to finding out Mystery Girl's identity. I can show you if you want to see."

This made Xavi groan. "I need to talk to Stefi." But before he could pull up Stefi's text chain and send her a message, Santiago snatched the phone away.

"No," he said.

"But I—"

"Life as you knew it is over, Xavi. Or, I should say, Your Royal Highness. The word is out, your summer fling has been flung, and whether you and I like it or not, we're headed to Madrid to deal with the fallout and so you can officially assume your role as prince, ASAP."

"But Stefi—"

Santiago stared at Xavi in this way that told him there was no use. "Stefi will just have to get over you when she (a) finds out who you really are, (b) realizes there are photos of herself in flagrante with a monarch-in-hiding going viral across Spain, and (c) figures out that soon the paparazzi will be camping on her abuela's doorstep. You know how people are. I won't even tell you the very unfeminist modifiers people are using to describe Stefi online. And never mind the fact that I've been outed in the middle of all this."

"Joder." Xavi reached for the phone again, but Santiago was too tall. "Give it back!"

Santiago scrolled to something, then angled the phone so Xavi could see the new photo he'd pulled up. Xavi studied the image. It was of Xavi at the party last night, but not far in the background, Santiago could clearly be identified—Santiago together with Diego. The two of them were kissing. Like, full-on making out.

Santiago stuffed Xavi's phone into his own pocket and continued packing Xavi's things. "When you get to the palace, you'll be getting a special encrypted phone, so consider this one officially out of commission. And luckily, after today, I won't have to worry about you escaping me again, since I'll be out of a job." Santiago laughed ruefully.

"I'm so sorry," Xavi said, a wave of guilt pulling him under. "I truly am." The tall young royal guard paused to wipe his eye.

Xavi sighed. He had never felt so out of sorts and helpless. If this was what it was like to be royalty, he definitely did not like it. "Can I at least call my mother?" Xavi asked. "She's been trying to reach me. I'm sure she's going out of her mind, and getting harassed herself."

Santiago stared at Xavi in a way that made him wonder what he was missing. "Where do you think Marta went on her little vacation?" he asked. "Are you really that dense?"

A bright ray of sun came through the gap in the shutters and shone over Xavi, lighting up the confusion on his face. "What are you talking about? Did my mother tell you where she was going?"

"Xavier Bas, I arranged her trip. Marta is already in Madrid. She and I have been in touch, and yes, she's worried, and yes, she wants to talk to you. But you can talk to her in person the second we arrive."

Xavi finally got up and out of the bed. "Wait, is she in Madrid with Jordi or something?"

Another pile of Xavi's shirts got dumped into the seemingly bottomless suitcase. "No, she's not with Jordi," Santiago said. "She's with your father, you dumbass. Marta went to see the king so they could 'talk things over'—as in maybe reconcile? That man is still in love with your mother and if I had to bet, I'd say she's still in love with him. So hurry up and get in the shower so we can be off to Madrid and the three of you can be one big, happy royal family."

With that, Santiago zipped up the suitcase and went to pack his own things. Xavi did as he was told and went to get in the shower. In addition to everything else, he was yet again at a loss on hearing this other head-spinning news Santiago had just sprung upon him.

His mother was with the king?

But this question was soon eclipsed when Xavi's thoughts returned to Stefi. He tried to imagine what she must be going through and was overwhelmed with the need to be in touch with her immediately. What if she hated Xavi now and this ridiculous situation had ruined everything between them? Xavi was desperate to explain and beg for forgiveness and even more desperate to tell Stefi how he felt. Stefi deserved to know that Xavi was falling in love with her. Being the heir to the Spanish throne didn't change this fact.

He had to find a way to speak with her.

A cool breeze flowed through the open bathroom window. Somewhere in Xavi's frenzied mind, he realized the heat wave had finally broken.

Along with his entire life.

# Twenty-Eight

Ana was in Stefi's bedroom, shaking her daughter. "Stefi, Stefi, wake up!"

Stefi was having trouble opening her eyes. After all, she'd gotten home at five a.m. and couldn't have slept for very long. A few hours at most.

"Mom, I'm sleeping," she mumbled. "So tired." She rolled over, away from the door and the sound of her mother's voice. She wasn't ready to get up; she was still enjoying the aftereffects of her dreamy night with Xavi. The thought that she was falling in love with him wafted across her brain. The words even hovered on her lips when Xavi kissed her goodbye at the door of her grandmother's building after walking her home. She wondered if they'd hovered on his as well. How could they not after their magical night?

The weight on the other side of Stefi's bed shifted as Ana sat down. "Stefi!" Her mother was practically shouting. "Wake. Up!"

"Jeez," she protested, forcing her eyes open. She let out a heavy breath and lifted her head off the pillow. Ana had a look of sheer panic on her face. "Oh my God, what's wrong—is it abuela?"

Ana's expression softened. "No, my love. Your abuela is totally fine. Though she's worried about you. We all are."

Something fluttered in Stefi's chest. They were worried about her? "What's going on, Mom?"

Ana studied her daughter's face. "You really don't know?"

*Don't know what?* Stefi's mind sifted through the events of the past twenty-four hours, which in Stefi's estimation included some of the best hours of her life. She wondered what could have happened between her going to sleep and waking up to make her mother act like this. She suddenly thought of Amber. Could something be wrong with her former best friend? Was that why Amber was sending so many texts? When Stefi was falling asleep, she'd actually thought she might be able to forgive Amber and Jason. If they hadn't betrayed her, Stefi might have missed out on Xavi. Stefi even promised herself she would contact Amber first thing when she woke up. But maybe she was too late?

Stefi sat up and rubbed the sleep from her eyes. "Mom, just tell me."

"Oh, sweetheart," Ana sighed.

Stefi's mother was not one to overreact, and some of her mother's panic seemed to transfer to Stefi, flying around inside her like a bat caught in the attic of a house. She watched as Ana got up from the bed and opened the shutters one by one, followed by the windows.

A cool breeze flowed inside the room.

"The heat wave is over," Ana said.

"Mom, stop stalling or I'm going to have a heart attack at age seventeen!" was Stefi's reply.

Ana stood at the end of Stefi's bed, the sun pouring over her. "Well. Did you know your boyfriend, Xavi—though, *is* he your boyfriend? I know you met rather recently."

Oh no, had something terrible happened to Xavi? "What about Xavi, Mom?"

Ana's eyebrows arched high. "Did he possibly mention to you that he was the . . . ah, the prince of Spain?"

Stefi threw back the covers and crawled on top of them to the end of the bed. Relief flooded through her and she started to laugh. This was obviously a joke. "The prince of Spain? Like, the *prince* of Spain? Like, the son of the king of Spain?"

"Yes, like all of that," her mother confirmed.

Stefi wondered if her mother had been drinking some vermut to start her day and was a bit tipsy. "Um, no, he didn't, Mom, because why would he, since he's none of those things?"

Ana was nodding like this all made sense when none of it made sense. "Okay, I figured he might not have told you."

Stefi studied her mother's face, which was deadly serious. Ana had never been one for melodrama. Stefi's mind went back to her time with Xavi this morning. Had she been having sex with the prince of Spain? Ha! Right, sure. Absolutely. Royal sex. "Mom, is this some prank you and Dad came up with? If it is, it's not funny. I really like Xavi. A lot."

Ana sat down on the bed again. "I am not joking, Estefanía. I would never do that to you. I could see it yesterday that you both liked one another. It made me happy." Her mother pulled out her phone and swiped the screen to life, tapping it a few times. "It was announced this morning, honey. Though it looks more like Xavi's identity was outed and then confirmed. Or at least, not officially denied by the royal family." She handed the phone to her daughter.

Stefi stared at the screen and saw the photo and the headline.

A very handsome Xavi was leaning against the countertop at La Buena, arms crossed. Above the image, in all caps with boldface letters, it said, *Xavier Bas, the Secret Prince of Spain?*

A strangled laugh erupted from Stefi's chest. "This is fake news." She set her mother's phone on the covers and reached for her own on the bedside table.

Her mother stopped her, pulling Stefi's arm away. "I wouldn't do that," she said.

"But I need to text Xavi. I'm sure he's laughing about this crazy mistake, Mom. There's just no way. His mom owns a tapas restaurant at La Boqueria! They're as normal as normal gets. They're like us, Mom." Stefi thought back to Xavi cooking for Stefi at La Buena and all they'd talked about. "Besides, he would have told me. He would never lie about something like this. It's too . . . big. And too impossible. Practically hilariously absurd."

Ana inhaled deeply, then let out a big breath. "I'm pretty sure it's not a rumor. It's real, Estefanía. The royal family—the king—called a press conference for this evening. The news is everywhere and even the reputable papers have picked it up."

Stefi's heart was starting to contract. "Why won't you let me have the phone, Mom? What else aren't you telling me?"

"There's also a photo of you circulating," Ana said.

"Of me," Stefi said flatly.

"Of you and Xavi kissing."

"Okay," she said. "Is that a crime?"

"Of course not, sweetheart, but you know how people are these days."

Stefi swallowed. "No, why don't you tell me how they are, Mom?"

"I just think it's best if you—"

"Mom, just let me see!"

"I don't think that's a good idea, oh, sweetie, no—"

Stefi grabbed for her mother's phone at the edge of the bed and immediately scrolled down the article about Xavi. That was when she saw it. Whoa. In truth, Stefi's heart did a serious pitter-patter as she took in the image. The photo was taken from the side; her back was pressed to a wall, and Xavi was, um, pressed to Stefi. It was quite the passionate embrace. If someone had given Stefi this photo to keep for herself, she would have been happy to have it. She kind of loved it. But obviously this was not hers to keep in private; it was making the rounds online. She looked up at her mother, slightly embarrassed.

"Mom, you know I'm careful, that I would never do anything stupid—"

"Oh, sweetheart," Ana cut in, "I'd never judge you for this photo or for kissing Xavi. Or for anything else, for that matter," she added.

Stefi's gaze dropped back to the screen and she kept scrolling.

Oh. Her mother was worried about Stefi seeing the comments.

Slut. Puta. Whore. And many other creative versions of this theme in not only English and Spanish but also French and what looked to be Italian.

Stefi gasped as she kept reading. There were some positive comments, people saying she was pretty and that the prince seemed into her. A few even claimed that she had nice legs. But those rolled off Stefi, whereas the others were absorbed by her suntanned skin and sank right into her center like sharp spikes. Shame bloomed through her.

Stefi felt a gentle finger under her chin, lifting it up.

Ana's gaze was full of sympathy. "You can't let what people say get to you. People online forget they are commenting on a real person—a beautiful, kind, smart, funny person who is the daughter I love very much and of whom I will always be proud." Her mother's hand cupped Stefi's cheek before she pulled it back. "This is a lot to take in, I know."

Stefi's gaze sought the safety of the bedspread. "Please tell me Dad hasn't seen what people are saying? And abuela?"

"I can't tell you that, sweetheart." Ana combed her fingers through her daughter's hair, something Stefi loved. Her mother was trying to soothe her, but no gesture would help relieve the turmoil inside of Stefi. She loved her mother for trying, though. "Honey, no one is upset with you. We are all upset at ¡Qué Fuerte! and that awful influencer who posted the photos. And there is a bit of good news." Ana brightened slightly. "They didn't use your name. Maybe they don't know it."

Stefi could hear a *but* coming in her mother's tone. "Okay? But what?"

"Well, if Xavi wasn't famous yesterday, he's certainly famous now," Ana said. "That photo is going to send reporters and all sorts of people trying to get information about you. And probably about everyone you know. Even people from home."

Stefi didn't know how to internalize any of this. All she wanted to do was talk to Xavi, to have him call her or message her or *something* so he could tell her this was all a mistake. *But what if it really isn't?* This question whispered through her. "Mom, how did you find out about the article? It's not like you to read gossip sites."

Ana got up from the bed and began smoothing her hand across the covers, fixing them. "One of abuela's friends recognized you in the photo and sent the article to her," she said.

Stefi could tell that Ana was trying to sound casual. "Who else do you think has seen it by now?"

"Ah, well, the article, it's all gone a bit viral." Her mother moved on to picking up the clothes Stefi had left on the floor and stuffing them into the laundry basket. "This is big news, sweetie, but don't worry, we'll get through it together."

If these rumors were true, then the boy Stefi thought she was falling for had withheld an extremely important truth, one that was right now upending Stefi's life. Did Xavi truly not care enough to tell her? Maybe she'd been wrong about him.

The breeze from the open windows didn't provide Stefi any relief, and she shivered. The temperature might have finally dropped, but with it, Stefi's world had bottomed out.

Tears pressed into the back of her eyes, and she wiped them away.

"There is one other bit of good news, darling," her mother said, full of forced cheer.

A tiny seed of hope sprouted inside of Stefi. "Oh?"

"Because the heat wave broke," Ana said, "your pastry class is back on!"

# Twenty-Nine

Santiago was miserable. The long black Escalade maneuvered him and Xavi out of the Casco Antiguo, the narrow streets at the heart of Barcelona, across the wider boulevards, and finally onward to the highway and heliport where transportation to Madrid awaited them. They inched forward on the highway in the morning traffic. The two boys sat in silence, each one lost in his own private storm of regrets. The only good thing about their morning was that the paparazzi hadn't yet figured out Xavi's home address, so they'd been able to leave their apartment building quietly and secretly. At least Santiago had been able to get Xavi safely to the car. But aside from this? He was a total failure.

Xavi lifted his head from the dark tinted window. "Do you want to talk about it? I know I'm not the only heartbroken person in this car. It's written all over your face."

Santiago let out a heavy sigh. Did he want to talk about it? Yes. And no. And yes.

Last night, Santiago had lived the best—and worst—hours of his life. How could the two collide together like this? Why did they have to? Santiago was desperate to discuss the finer details of the prior evening with a friend and to ask a million questions of that person to get an opinion about this and that and the other thing. He wished Xavi were just a normal civilian and not also Santiago's professional responsibility.

"Santi?" Xavi pressed.

Santiago looked over at the boy next to him. Xavi had used his nickname, and Santiago knew he'd done it intentionally—to communicate that he saw Santiago as a friend. It nearly made Santiago want to burst into tears again. For all Xavi's maddening behavior, underneath it, Santiago knew he could be trusted. As though to emphasize this, Xavi raised the glass partition between the back seat and the driver up front to give them privacy.

"I really like Diego," Santiago admitted. "Like, maybe-I'm-falling-for-him like him. But it's hard to tell. I mean, I don't know." He covered his eyes with his hands. "I've never had a boyfriend before." He groaned. Santiago peered at Xavi through a gap in his fingers.

Xavi's eyes grew soft. "Listen, you don't need to feel embarrassed—like, please do not be. All of this disastrous mess aside, I'm really happy you and Diego like each other. I want Diego to be with someone great, and you definitely fit that description."

"Really?" Santiago let his hands fall from his face to look at Xavi directly. "But you know I can't be with him. Not in real life, at least. It's against my job description to fraternize with the person I'm guarding or any of their associates." He gave a bitter laugh. "Then again, it's not likely I'll have a job after today."

Xavi scooted closer to Santiago on the soft leather seat. "But life is not only work. Sometimes you've got to put a relationship first."

"If only life were so simple." Santiago sighed.

"Sometimes it is. Or it could be if we let it."

Santiago leaned his head back against the seat. "Says the person whose life is the very opposite of simple."

"Hey, don't try and turn the subject back to me," Xavi said. "We were talking about you."

The traffic eased, and the Escalade sped up. Soon they'd arrive at the heliport and then they would be on their way to Madrid. Santiago turned to the window, watching the city recede, taking him farther and farther from Diego. He wondered if he'd ever come back to Barcelona and, if so, when.

Xavi nudged Santiago's arm. "Did you and Diego manage to actually discuss how you feel? I mean, you don't have to give me the details. But if you want, you can talk to me about it."

Could he really talk to Xavi about kissing Diego like the world might end and about how much Santiago wished Diego could be his first boyfriend? About how being ripped from the arms of this person so soon after kissing him was splintering Santiago's inexperienced heart into a million jagged pieces? Santiago didn't want to embarrass himself.

"Whatever you decide, you should know," Xavi went on, "that Diego has been my best friend for forever, and I wouldn't want him to be with anyone less worthy. I wouldn't want you to be with someone less worthy either. You guys deserve each other."

A tear rolled down Santiago's cheek, then another. He could no longer hold them back.

Xavi covered Santiago's hand with his own and squeezed. "We'll figure this out. For both of us. Right?"

Santiago could hear the way Xavi's voice cracked and found himself nodding in agreement. He even found himself considering giving Xavi his phone back so he could contact Stefi. Then he began telling Xavi all the things he'd wanted to discuss since the moment Diego's lips first touched his own. As the two young men talked and talked some more, Santiago again thought how lucky his country was to have found such a worthy prince. It really was a shame that being heir to the Spanish throne was going to cost Xavi the life he'd always known and loved plus one particular American girl named Stefi. But Santiago just couldn't see a way around so many obstacles. Not for either one of them.

# Thirty

For the second time today, Xavi was gliding along in an Escalade, but now they were pulling up in front of the royal residence, La Zarzuela, just outside of Madrid. The driver practically had to run over the swarm of paparazzi waiting in front of the gates. The sight of them shouting his name and shoving cameras against the windows made Xavi's heart sink yet again this morning.

Dios. A couple of posts and his life in Barcelona was over.

Santiago turned to him. "It's going to be okay," he said. "You're going to be great at this. It will just take some getting used to."

Xavi didn't respond. Their earlier heart-to-heart receded as reality set in. One loud helicopter ride was only the beginning of this new life Xavi was finding difficult to grasp. Maybe he was going into shock, though he wasn't sure which part was more shocking—that he went from anonymity to public celebrity in a matter of hours right after one of the most romantic encounters of his existence, or that in the process of being whisked away to Madrid, he'd learned his mother was "vacationing" with the king of Spain for old times' sake. Speaking of Marta, there she was in the doorway of the palace residence, a worried look on her face. The world was seriously upside down.

The Escalade came to a stop. Before the driver could hop out and open the doors in the back, Xavi had already exited the car and was running up the stairs to his mother.

"Oh, Xavi," she cried, stepping onto the esplanade and drawing him into an enormous hug. "I'm sorry I didn't tell you where I was going. And I'm sorry all this has happened so quickly for you. I know you wanted one final summer of peace, and, well . . ."

Xavi hugged his mother back. But he didn't know what to think about how she'd withheld her whereabouts. Especially when those whereabouts had everything to do with how Xavi had ended up in this particular situation in the first place. He pulled away and looked at Marta. "Why didn't you tell me, mamá? Don't you trust me?"

"Mi amor, of course. But I wasn't sure how things would go and I didn't want to make anything worse between you and your father."

Xavi studied his mother as she stood in front of this grand residence. He took in the opulence of the entrance and the magnificent fountain arcing water high into the air behind them. Both mother and son were so out of place. Xavi turned around to look for Santiago, wanting some reassurance, but he was already gone. Xavi faced his mother again. "Mamá, right now, I'm just glad you're okay. But I need to be honest and tell you that I'm worried. I don't want to see the king break your heart all over again."

Marta wiped a tear from her eye. "Why don't we sit and talk?"

Xavi glanced at the marble esplanade below their feet. "Here?"

His mother nodded. "This is your house too. I think you should be able to sit wherever you want, and as your mother, I should as well. These are technically your front steps." She squinted at the shadow cast by the residence. "Besides, it's nice and shady over there."

It was reassuring that Marta might be a guest of the king at the royal palace but she was still Marta and they were still themselves—a mother and son who would sit on some stairs to catch up, even if those stairs were marble and they led up to a palace. So Xavi walked to the edge of the esplanade and plopped down on one of the steps. He stretched out his long legs. His mother soon joined him.

One of the guards came hurrying over. "Ma'am? Your Highness? Would you like to—"

Xavi looked up at this person in his fancy gold-tasseled uniform. "We're good, thanks."

Marta nodded. "Really. Don't worry about us."

The guard seemed torn about what to do, but eventually he wandered back toward the entrance doors, leaving them in peace.

"You first," Xavi said to Marta, eyebrows arching.

His mother's gaze left his own and sought the safety of the beautiful gardens. "Well, as you know, Alfonso and I did not speak for many years. But then, after I finally told him about you, he kept wanting to talk. Initially I refused, but if I'm honest, there were some things I'd left unsaid that it was time for me to share and for him to hear."

Xavi wondered if his mother was referring to the letter and if this was the moment for him to confess that he'd gone through her things and read it.

But Marta looked at her son again and continued on before he had the chance. "So one night we talked on the phone until morning about everything—specifically, what had happened to drive us apart—"

"Mamá, I know about the letter Alfonso wrote to you," he interrupted. There; Xavi had finally told her.

His mother blinked. "Xavi! But that would mean—"

"That I went through your desk, I know," he said. "I did go through it and I'm sorry. I shouldn't have but I was so angry."

"But Alfonso never wrote that letter!"

Xavi tried to take this in. He had never considered the possibility that the letter had been forged. Then again, he was new at palace intrigue. "And you believe him?"

Marta was nodding. "I do, because there wasn't just one letter. There were two."

"What do you mean?"

"The second one was from me to Alfonso," she said.

"I didn't know you'd written him a letter."

"That is the thing, mi amor. I didn't! He didn't write the letter I received, and I didn't write the letter he received. He showed me the one he'd gotten and it looked so real, exactly like my own handwriting, my signature, all of it. The things it said were terrible. No wonder he never reached out to me ever again."

Marta's words revealed nothing short of a royal conspiracy, one whose consequences had reverberated down the line for decades, nearly denying Xavi knowledge of his father's existence permanently. As this began to sink in, he realized the gravity of it all. "Who wrote it, then?"

Marta shook her head. "We don't know. Alfonso is looking into it. Obviously it was someone who really didn't want us to be together, who'd go so far as to forge those letters and break us up for good. Or so that person thought."

"Qué increíble, mamá."

"Yes. When Alfonso and I figured out what had truly happened, we were both shocked. And greatly saddened at the pain and heartbreak we've suffered because of this and that it had deprived him of you."

Xavi studied his mother, a new question burning inside him. "So what does that mean for you and the king?"

"Well, Alfonso apologized for not being stronger and coming to Barcelona to find me, despite the contents of the letter and so we could talk in person. And I apologized to him for keeping you a secret, and he told me he understood why I had, given what I thought he'd wanted and demanded of me. And we forgave each other . . . " Marta trailed off.

But Xavi knew there must be more. "And?"

His mother clasped her knees with her hands and looked off into the distance. "Alfonso confirmed that he didn't ever marry because he could never get over me. That he was still in love with me."

"Okay, all right," Xavi said, trying to take in this particular new tidbit. "But . . . what about you? How do *you* feel?" he asked, even though deep down, he was pretty sure he knew the answer. All those years with Marta never dating anyone, all those years she'd raised him alone.

Marta looked at her son, eyes glassy. "I still care for Alfonso very much, yes."

Xavi wasn't exactly sure how to handle all of this new information and the twists and turns that it involved, but he loved his mother and knew he needed to support her. This also meant he needed to make amends with the man who was his father. His mother wanted to be with him, and he had to confess to Alfonso that the letter forged to Marta was behind the way Xavi had acted on his only other visit to the palace. But Xavi also thought about Stefi and what Santiago had said about Xavi being expected to date someone titled, and he wondered if this meant that maybe circumstances weren't actually as they seemed. "But what about the other reasons that kept you and the king apart? That you were a commoner and the king was meant to marry someone titled. Does this mean they no longer matter?"

His mother sighed. "Xavi, those issues don't go away, of course. But Alfonso and I are much older, and we've lived nearly two decades without being with anyone else. The things that seemed impossible before, Dios, I'm not sure we care about them anymore." Marta gave Xavi a look she'd been giving her son his entire life, the one that told him she could see right into his soul and knew when her son was holding something back. "Are you angry with me?"

Xavi took his mother's hands. "Mamá, I could never be angry at you for . . . for following your heart. You've given so much of your life to raising me, and all by yourself. It's true, I'm surprised, but I'm not angry. I want you to do what makes you happy."

A smile crept onto Marta's face. "Alfonso and I want to give things a try, regardless of what the press may think. Or the rest of the royals of Spain, I suppose. And whoever had those letters forged, if that person is still alive."

Xavi nodded. So his mother was really going to date the king. He hated the thought of people saying awful things about her online and in the press, and yet another part of Xavi filled with hope. What if Alfonso could make his mother truly happy?

A bird landed on the branch of one of the nearby trees and began to sing. A promising sign?

Once again, Xavi was desperate with the need to be in touch with Stefi, to tell her everything he should have told her from the very second they'd met. But for the first time, there was a spark of hope that maybe Stefi and Xavi had a chance. *If* she was willing to forgive him.

Marta seemed to read Xavi's mind. She took her son's hand and clasped it in her own. "It's going to be okay, mi amor. We're going to figure this out for the both of us, ¿vale? No matter what, I'm still your mother and I will always protect you. You may be a tall and handsome prince, but you're still my beautiful boy." And with that, she pulled Xavi into another hug.

# Thirty-One

Stefi was once again folding layers of butter into pastry at Hofmann.

The long, thin rolling pin in Stefi's hands was dusty with flour. She carefully pressed it along the delicate rectangle of dough on the cutting board and felt more herself than she had in days. Maybe weeks. She was glad to be back in the kitchen and that the heat wave was over. She was glad she'd convinced her father she should be allowed to come to class, that just because some dumb influencer posted a photo of her didn't mean she should stop living her life. Besides, so far her name was still a secret. There'd been no word from Xavi, but she shooed away from her brain the dismay that accompanied this reality.

Instead, Stefi sighed with satisfaction as she executed another perfectly buttered layer by folding the dough in half and went to put it in the freezer. This was how croissants were made—layer, fold, freezer, butter, new layer, fold, freezer. Each time she opened the freezer door, the cold air that wafted out made her shiver. She eyed the rectangle of dough with pride before closing it inside for the next five minutes. When she turned around to return to her station, she ran smack into one of the other students. His name was—Enric? No, Oriol, if she remembered correctly.

He was staring at her, eyes narrowed.

"Hi, Oriol," Stefi said cheerfully.

The heat wave had arrived so quickly that Stefi barely had time to meet her fellow Hofmann students. The way Oriol was looking at Stefi made her nervous. Then Oriol pulled out his phone and shoved it in Stefi's face, and her nerves gave way to full-on anxiety.

"Is this you?" he asked. "This is you, isn't it!"

Stefi blinked as she stared at the screen. The photo of her and Xavi kissing stared back at her. Oriol had magnified it so Stefi's face was blown up at the center. She felt her cheeks coloring; she opened her mouth to respond, but no words came. She wasn't sure what to say or do. Should she just confirm that yes it was her or try and evade the truth somehow?

Apparently, she hesitated too long.

"It *is* you!" Oriol yelled to the rest of the pastry class working at their various stations, "I told you guys it was her!" He swiveled to face Stefi again. "Is he really the prince of Spain? Are you his girlfriend? Or just some random American he fucked?" He snickered at this last part.

Stefi swallowed in shock. When she recovered, she shouted back at Oriol, "That's none of your business, you gilipollas! Don't you wish *you* could be my random fuck!" Stefi surprised even herself at the way she was fighting back after Oriol slut-shamed her.

The three other women in the class erupted into applause. One of them—Stefi tried to remember her name; maybe Susana?—was already clearing the pastry station next to her own. Susana and one of the other women began moving Stefi's things as far from Oriol's station as they could get.

Chef Arzak appeared next to Stefi and Oriol, breathing fire. She snatched Oriol's phone from his hand. "I will not have any of my students harassed in my class!"

Oriol's contempt turned to dismay and maybe a little fear. "I'm sorry, I didn't mean—"

Chef slipped his phone into her pocket. "Don't tell *me* sorry, tell *Stefi* sorry. You owe her an apology!"

Oriol turned to Stefi. "I'm sorry. I shouldn't have done that. Or said those things."

Chef looked at Stefi. "Stefi, you are free to accept Oriol's apology or not. Either way, he will no longer be in our class, so you have plenty of time to decide how you feel and whether you're inclined to be forgiving."

Oriol blinked at Chef. "Wait, what? You're kicking me out? Seriously?"

Stefi's pastry teacher pointed to the door. "Pack up and go."

A few of the other students whistled.

Stefi wanted to hug Chef.

As Oriol put his things away and left the kitchen, Stefi finished moving her rolling pin and other pastry tools next to Susana. "Thank you," she whispered to her new pastry-making friend.

"It was nothing," Susana said and smiled warmly back.

Stefi was still staring at the exit through which Oriol had disappeared. Chef turned around to look at Stefi sternly. "Now go get that dough from the freezer! You don't want it to be a hard block and impossible to work, do you?"

"No, Chef," Stefi said and happily did as she was told.

# Thirty-Two

Santiago was pacing his palace bedroom. It was strange to be back in this familiar place, his home since he was a small boy. It was big for a guard, but only because his father had been given his pick of rooms for his young son, and the king was softhearted about such things. There was a small private bathroom adjoining it, a large closet, and two sets of French doors with balconies that faced the palace gardens. It was located on the highest floor because that was where the palace staff had their rooms, as per tradition. This place had changed so much over the course of Santiago's lifetime. Once it had been full of picture books and toys and a brightly painted mural; now the walls were painted a light gray with dark wood bookcases full of Santiago's favorite novels, books about famous artists, and histories of the Spanish royals across the centuries. One book in particular about the Guardia Real had an inscription from his father, a gift for Santiago after one of their last conversations.

Santiago pulled the heavy tome from the shelf. He held it carefully, remembering the first time he'd read it, how his hands were those of a small boy. It was one of his most prized possessions. Over the years Santiago had read and reread this book, each time understanding a little more about who his father was and what he did and then, as Santiago got older, who he would become as he followed in his father's footsteps. But the question now at hand was this: Would Santiago continue in his footsteps or would he veer in another direction and take a different path?

Along the far wall of Santiago's bedroom was his closet.

He went to it now and opened the door. Hanging inside was the special uniform of the Guardia Real, the version worn by the guards of the highest rank who protected the royal family. Santiago hadn't worn it since he left Madrid so many months ago. Next to his uniform, inside a clear protective cover, was the uniform of his father, Santiago's other most prized possession. The afternoon when Santiago went to pick up his own uniform after earning the right to wear it was one of the proudest moments of his life. He remembered how he carefully hung it up, pressed and ready for the following day, right next to his father's. He'd understood by then the sacrifices wearing it would require of him.

Santiago ran a hand along the fine material of the uniform's jacket, the sleeve, the cuffs.

More than anything else, he wanted to honor his father, his family's legacy, and the king who treated him like his very own son. If Santiago had to choose between love and honor, so be it.

He dug his phone from his pocket and called up the message chain between himself and Diego that they'd so recently started. He steeled himself to look at it.

**Santi?**

**Santiago?**

**Can you pls just write me back?**

**Are you okay? Is Xavi?**

**Talk to me.**

**Come on.**

**Seriously, Santi, where are you?**

**What's going on?**

All these pleas for contact were tugging Santiago's heart so hard, he wondered if it might push right on through his rib cage to the outside of his body. But the latest messages were the hardest to read.

**Kissing you last night was amazing, and I think you feel the same way.**

**I like you, Santi, like, more than like you.**

**I don't want this to be the end. Are you really going to let it be?**

**Can't we figure this out?**

A tear escaped Santiago's eye and rolled down his cheek.

He wiped it away.

He couldn't seem to stop himself from crying today.

Santiago began to tap a message back to Diego, to say all the things he'd put off telling Diego because he dreaded saying them.

**Diego, kissing you was amazing for me too, and you are right.**

**I do feel the same way about you.**

**I don't want this to be the end either, but**

Santiago stopped typing. He couldn't bring himself to keep going.

A new message from Diego immediately popped up on the screen.

**But what, Santi?**

He stared at Diego's question for a long moment.

Then he put his phone away again.

Santiago let out a sigh of sadness, frustration, *confusion*.

He had always known the deal with his job, and the deal was this: Much like being a part of the royal family came with certain social expectations and therefore restrictions, becoming a Guardia Real at the level of Carlos, Santiago's father, came with sacrifices and restrictions. It wasn't that

Santiago couldn't fall in love and be in a relationship—of course he could have a partner, *if* he found the exact right person. The exact right person was *not* an associate of the person he was guarding and definitely not the best friend of that person.

He also knew there was another way to be with Diego. But it would require a different kind of sacrifice on Santiago's part, one that would cost him all he'd imagined for his future as a guard. Santiago could accept another posting, for instance, but it would need to resolve the conflict of interest Diego posed. Given that Xavi was the prince, and the king was his father, and they were the very heart and soul of the Spanish crown, this would mean Santiago would have to give up his life in Madrid and the dream of being like Carlos.

Could Santiago give up everything for a boy he'd so recently met?

Someone he barely knew?

And then, what could he ask of Diego?

If Santiago accepted a new assignment outside of the palace, it likely would not end up being in Barcelona. So this would mean a long-distance relationship for the two of them or Santiago would have to ask Diego to move to wherever Santiago landed. Their romance was barely a few hours old, and Santiago could not imagine expecting something so big of Diego so soon. No matter how strongly they felt for one another. Right?

Santiago studied his father's uniform once more and remembered how proud he'd always been to see his father in it, how honored he was to wear it for the first time himself. His heart was pulling him in two opposite directions and he knew he would have to choose one way or the other. Santiago dropped his gaze to the message chain one last time, his heart practically screaming for him to reach out to Diego and tell him all the ins and outs of the agony he was feeling and ask what Diego thought and wanted in the middle of it. But then his brain reminded him once more that their first kiss was not even twenty-four hours ago and his heart was making him think irrationally. So, delicately, as though he were touching something fragile and precious, Santiago lifted the hanger from the closet and carried his uniform over to the bed.

He began to get dressed.

# Thirty-Three

Xavi barely had time to wash his face in a fancy bathroom near the entrance of the palace before he was summoned to see the king. Everything was urgent today, apparently.

He arrived at the round table in the informal dining room of the royal residence—as informal as things got in a royal residence, he supposed. Every single thing in every room glittered or glinted or sparkled or shone or was covered in frescoes painted by old Spanish masters with elaborately carved crown molding to frame it. But this time, it wasn't only Xavi's father, the king, waiting for him. Sitting next to the king at the table, which was covered with plates heaped with jamón ibérico, Manchego, olives, pickled artichokes, a bowl of fruit, a basket of bread, and several dishes piled with cookies, was his mother. What's more, he caught Marta pulling her hand from the king's quickly, perhaps believing her son hadn't noticed.

Xavi definitely had.

Marta practically jumped out of her chair as Xavi approached, and Alfonso's adoring gaze followed her as she moved across the room.

Whoa.

For so many years Xavi had wished Marta would find someone, but in all his imaginings about the suitor who might suit his mother best, the king of Spain never made his list.

Marta glanced back at Alfonso, and the king nodded. "I'll leave you two to talk," she said to Xavi.

"Mamá—"

"I'll be in the kitchen just down the hall, making us tortilla for later. The staff here could learn a thing or two about the filling." At this, she disappeared through what looked to be a secret door in the wall.

Alfonso watched her go. "Your mother is quite something. At first, the staff wasn't sure how to handle her barging into the kitchen, but she's won them over." He turned to Xavi, and his smile faltered. The king—no, Xavi's father—gestured for him to sit. The French doors around the room were open and a breeze flowed through them, buffeting the gauzy curtains.

Xavi exhaled and sat down. He gripped the glass of water at his place so tightly, he worried it might shatter. The food the staff had laid out didn't appeal to him, despite the bounty of it. He needed to keep his eye on the ball. "I want my mother to be happy," he declared, deciding this was as good a place as any to start.

Alfonso's expression grew hopeful. "I do as well. And I don't want to do anything to jeopardize her happiness. Or yours. I know you are as protective of her as she is of you."

"Yes," Xavi said. At least they could agree on this. It was a solid beginning. "I want to apologize for how I acted during my first visit here."

The king's lips parted with surprise. "This is not what I was expecting you to say. But thank you for saying it. I want so badly for us to find a way toward a relationship. And I can understand why you might hate me—"

"My mother told me that the letter you sent her was forged," Xavi interrupted before the king could say anything else. "And about the forged letter to you. Just before I came to La Zarzuela the first time, I found the letter you sent"—he stopped to backtrack—"that *someone* sent, and I was so angry that you had discarded my mother like that and me in the process. And I don't hate you. Someone might have wanted to prevent the three of us from ever having a relationship, but that doesn't mean they get to win in the end."

Xavi's father—because this was how Xavi needed to start thinking of the king—wiped a tear from his eye. Alfonso took a sip of coffee and returned the cup to its saucer, blinking quickly. "Life doesn't often give us second chances. Your mother is willing to give me one, and I was hoping you might as well. But this is far more than I could have expected. I am so glad to hear you feel this way."

Xavi nodded. He tried to take in all that had happened in a few short hours. Between the article and everything with Stefi, then finding his mother at the royal residence, Xavi didn't know how to feel, never mind what to say. But Xavi could hear sincerity in the king's voice and the admiration he felt for Marta. And Xavi was surprised by how calm the king was in the face of the morning's disaster. "You're not angry with me about what happened in the press?"

Alfonso shook his head. "Not angry, no. It's more that I'm sad."

This, Xavi was not expecting. "Sad?"

Alfonso's eyes traveled across the room to an enormous painting on the far wall. A portrait of his own father with his two beloved sheepdogs, Ginger and Soda, who stood obediently by his side. Xavi knew—because everyone in Spain knew—that after Alfonso's father died, the young king never went anywhere without Ginger and Soda. He kept those two goofy, affectionate sheepdogs with him as though they might stave off the grief of such loss and all the responsibility that came with his father's death. But once Ginger and Soda were gone, Alfonso refused to get another dog, even though breeders from all over the world offered to send him sheepdog puppies.

A sharp pang of sorrow pierced Xavi. How alone this king must have been all these years and then how heartbroken in his own right about Marta because of the forged letter to him. For the first time it occurred to Xavi that Alfonso was not only a king but a person too. A human who perhaps tried to shield himself from further grief by refusing to raise another pair of dogs he would eventually lose, and who refused to marry if he could not be with the woman he truly loved despite such tremendous public pressure. Xavi already knew from a few hours of being in the public eye how isolated being the prince could make a person.

The king's eyes returned to his son. "I wanted you to enjoy these last few weeks of privacy, and now you've lost them. I'm sorry for this. Truly."

This touched Xavi. For the first time since he learned the truth of his heritage, he was beginning to believe that he and the king—no, he and his father—would be able to get beyond their rocky start and move toward something like a real relationship.

Xavi let out a breath he didn't realize he was holding. "Can I ask you something?"

Alfonso looked at Xavi, eyes pleading. "Anything."

Xavi had been turning over this question in his mind since he'd learned where Marta was. He couldn't understand why two people who claimed to be in love would part ways just because of titles, tradition, and ceremony. Love seemed too much to give up. "Is it really still expected for members of the royal family to date only people who come from certain families? Haven't times changed? I mean, you and my mother are considering defying this."

The light in the king's expression dimmed. "Well, it's not easy being royal, Xavier, as you likely know a bit about from this morning's uproar. It's especially difficult being royal when the entire public feels it's their right to comment on your choice of life partner."

Xavi couldn't read the king. "And? So?"

Alfonso sighed and looked away. "Even now, Xavier, if your mother chooses to pursue a relationship with me, it will require great sacrifices, and it will lead to a lot of difficulty. But she and I both agree that it's worth it for us to try again. Growing older changes a person. Things we felt were nearly impossible when we were young seem different now."

The breeze from the windows was getting stronger and the curtains billowed into the air. Xavi's thoughts snagged on one specific word the king used in reference to his mother. "What kind of sacrifices are we talking about for my mother?"

Alfonso's eyes clouded over. "Your family's tapas place will have to shut down, at least for a time," he began, and Xavi's chest contracted. "Every single thing your mother has ever been and done, every photo that can be dug up—it will all come out. But this would also have happened because she is your mother and you are my heir, and she kept you from me and therefore the entire monarchy and the whole of Spain. And we don't know yet who forged those letters and we may never find out who did, and the public might not believe it anyway. But in addition to all of this, Marta is catalán, she's been to catalán independence marches. You've been to them too. This is likely to cause some scandal. As you know, there is tension between Madrid and Catalunya." He swept a hand across the magnificent room. "To live here is small recompense for the loss of one's privacy, and I should know. You will know now as well. The wonder of anonymity is something we take for granted until it is gone."

Xavi wasn't sure how to comprehend the first part of what the king had suggested. Could his mother really give up La Buena? Close it, even for a time? He couldn't imagine her agreeing to this. But Xavi supposed he hadn't really thought through what would happen at the end of this summer—he'd expressly avoided doing this. He'd been so stupid and selfish. He should have thought of Marta and her life, but he was too busy thinking of his own. Xavi wasn't sure which fate was worse, shutting down their family's restaurant or watching his mother ripped apart online. Maybe Marta *needed* the king. Maybe the fact that Alfonso and Marta still loved each other after all these years was serendipitous. As they endured all that was to come, at least they'd be together. Maybe they'd all be together, as a family.

His father was staring down at his empty plate. Neither one of them seemed able to eat any of the food set out on the table for them.

Xavi thought of Stefi again; he couldn't help it. He worried for her and the price she'd pay because he'd been so self-centered. How long would it be before people figured out her name and began doing the same deep dive as they would with Marta? He could suddenly understand the cost of being with someone royal and why a person might give up someone they loved—to save that person from such a fate. Xavi had seen only a sliver of the comments about Stefi on Santiago's phone, and they made him want to put his fist through walls and people's faces. Xavi wondered if she could ever forgive him for omitting this tiny detail about his identity.

Could he even ask her to? Did he have that right?

"I know this is a lot," Alfonso said. The king met Xavi's eyes with sincerity. "But I want to do whatever it takes to make this work between all of us. Sometimes love is worth the sacrifice, no matter how steep. My hope is that by me standing by Marta, members of the public will eventually see how lucky they are that the prince's mother is so wonderful."

Xavi was starting to wonder if one day he might even be grateful that Alfonso was his father. "Can I ask you something else?"

The king reached for a piece of ham, apparently finding a bit of appetite. "Anything."

Xavi reached for a wedge of cheese. "If you could go back and do things over with my mother, would you ask her to stay with you, come what may, regardless of letters forged or otherwise?"

Alfonso studied his son hard. "I think so, yes."

Xavi wondered if the king knew he wasn't really asking about his mother anymore. Regardless, Xavi had gotten his answer. Maybe it shouldn't be up to him or Marta or Santiago or the king or anyone else at the palace to make a decision that should be Stefi's alone. Maybe if Xavi had just told her who he was, they could have talked things through and they wouldn't be in this mess. "Um, is there a phone I could use? I really need to make a call."

The king nodded. "Yes, of course. Within a couple of days, the staff will be setting you up with your new encrypted phone and explaining the parameters of communication at the palace."

"A couple of *days?*" Xavi asked.

The king gulped down coffee and reached for a cookie. "Well, yes. At the moment, you're under a media blackout. After this morning's articles, I'm sure you can understand why. But don't worry, soon you'll receive the necessary media training and learn all the palace protocols and you can be in touch with your friends again. If they're truly your friends, they'll be more than willing to forgive a few days of silence. I'm sure they'll understand why this had to be the case."

More silence was not what Stefi needed from Xavi.

Xavi raked his hair with his fingers, then did this again. "What if it can't wait?"

The king regarded his son. "It must."

Xavi tried to allow this to sink in, to accept that this was just the way things were now.

But he couldn't. He really needed his phone back. Or something.

A messenger pigeon?

# Thirty-Four

Stefi still hadn't heard from Xavi, and the joy of her pastry-making triumphs from this morning was receding quickly. She'd vanquished a nasty bully in Oriol, and her croissants were getting ever better, plus Chef Arzak had been generous with her praise. But Stefi could distract herself for only so long with Hofmann and pastries and female empowerment.

Now she was sitting on her bed in her room, staring down at her phone, the message chain between her and Xavi staring back. Ana had reluctantly returned the phone to Stefi after making her daughter promise she wouldn't read any more of the comments under the photo of her kissing Xavi. Her name hadn't yet been leaked, but Stefi knew things were bound to get a lot worse.

The message chain ended just after Stefi had gone to sleep in the wee hours of this morning. The time stamp was 4:55 a.m. **I already can't wait to see you again.** This was what Xavi wrote. Not even twelve hours had passed since he'd sent this message.

"Come on, Xavi, talk to me!" Stefi said to the screen. Maybe if she stared long enough, she could will Xavi to text her and explain everything. She took one last look, then set the phone on her bed and went to the windows of her room.

Xavi might not be speaking to her, but Barcelona always did.

The streets were alive with chatter, with people sitting outside at the café in the plaza below, drinking their afternoon cafés con leche and catching up with one another, laughing and telling each other stories. Across the way, a neighbor spoke to her plants as she watered them on the balcony. The seagulls were talking too, squawking overhead as they journeyed inward from the beach, and soon the cathedral bells were speaking as well, chiming out the hour. As usual, the guide who always led crowds of tourists up to the medieval church in front of Stefi's bedroom was telling everyone about its beautiful stained-glass window that lit up in the evenings with shining color.

A sharp pang pierced Stefi's heart. She hated that she wished she were standing here taking all of this in with Xavi, but she couldn't help it. ¡Dios! Was it her summer destiny to be betrayed not once but twice? How could Xavi have lied to her about something so enormous? He'd had so many chances and chose not to tell her. Shame flooded Stefi, her cheeks burning despite the breeze coming off the water and floating up to El Gótico. Had Xavi just been using her? Her skin flamed hotter. Was she some final conquest before the world found out he was a prince?

Stefi laughed out loud. The whole idea of Xavi being a prince was just ridiculous. Though he was certainly handsome enough to be royalty. Her heart swooped and then plummeted at this thought, and she wished she could reach inside her chest and calm it.

The guide led his tourists away, and in the distance, Stefi could hear whistles and drums, a protest moving through the streets. One group or another was always protesting something here. The taxi union. The nursing union. The *scuba divers* union. If Stefi had a whistle, she'd take to the streets herself and protest conniving Spanish princes.

Stefi leaned on the railing of the balcony and continued looking out onto the afternoon.

A cat from a nearby apartment peered back at her as he sunned himself.

There was a royal press conference scheduled for later this evening, and Stefi would be in front of the TV to watch it. She wouldn't believe the gossip until she heard it confirmed by someone official, ideally the king himself. It was only hearsay until then as far as she was concerned.

Though there was a *teeny* part of Stefi that was *slightly* thrilled by the thought that Xavi was royalty. It would be more than a little like a fairy-tale romance if it was true. Stefi had come to Barcelona with her family after one of the most humiliating moments of her life, and she'd fallen for a local who was not only exceedingly handsome and charming but who also happened to be a prince?

Stefi wondered if there was a way for Xavi to make things right.

If he ever spoke to her again.

Stefi left the windows and grabbed her phone once more, willing Xavi to text already. She stared harder and harder until a video call came in—which she was definitely not expecting, and it was definitely not from the person she wished to talk to. The phone continued to ring.

Stefi took a breath and accepted it.

"Stefi!" Amber's familiar face stared back at her. "I'm so glad you picked up. I didn't know if you would, and I didn't think you would, actually. I'm so happy to see you—oh, I've missed you! Oh, Stefi!"

Stefi didn't reply. She pressed her lips into a tight line and stared at her best friend—her former best friend—observing that Amber was the same as always, with her long fiery hair, pale freckled skin, beautiful face, and those big green eyes. But she was also different. Because those eyes of Amber's looking at Stefi right now? Stefi could see they were filled with sadness.

"Stefi, please! Say something?"

"Hi." Stefi's voice was flat.

"Okay," Amber said. "'Hi' is a start."

Stefi could see the familiar wallpaper in Amber's room behind her, the shelf of stuffed animals from when she was little; the photo collage they'd made of their favorite images from all the years they'd known one another was still tacked up next to her bed. An enormous pang of missing hit Stefi. So many pangs were poking through her insides today, she felt like Swiss cheese. "I'm glad you called," she found herself saying.

Amber's eyes widened. "Are you really?"

"Yeah. *Yes*," Stefi admitted. "I've thought of writing you back. I guess I just wasn't ready."

"I understand. I do. I did something terrible. Something unimaginable. The worst thing ever, and I almost can't believe it myself and I'm so sorry, Stefi. I'll be sorry forever. I'll do anything to make it up to you. I was wrong and I wish I could go back and have a do-over."

Stefi stared into the eyes of the girl who'd been her best friend since she was small and saw the sincerity there. Amber meant everything she said. It sent a wave of relief through Stefi, soothing the hurt a little. "Okay," she said and nodded.

Amber wiped the corner of her eye. "Okay? 'Okay' is also a start."

"You and Jason broke up," Stefi stated next because she knew in her heart this must be true and at least part of why Amber was calling.

Amber wiped another tear from her cheek. "Yes. We should never have been together, Stefi. It was all such a big mistake. I still can't believe what I did to you, all for—"

"Love?" Stefi supplied.

Her friend's face filled with surprise. "Yes," she whispered. "Well, I thought it was love. Obviously I was wrong."

"I'm sorry to hear that," Stefi said, startled to realize she was speaking yet another truth. She *was* sorry for Amber, sorry that Amber thought she'd found love—admittedly not in the best of circumstances, but still—

and it hadn't worked out. Stefi could understand what that was like, since she'd gone through it twice now in a single summer. "I know a thing or two about love not working out the way you thought it would."

Once again, Amber's face fell. "I know you do. And I know it's my fault that you do. Oh, Stefi, tell me what I can do to fix things between us."

A tear dropped down Stefi's cheek and she wiped it away, then nearly laughed. The two best friends had always joked their hearts were tied together with string. When one heart was tugged, the other one was too, so if one of them cried, the other inevitably ended up crying as well.

"This apology is a good start," Stefi said and sniffled.

Amber sniffled in reply.

Then the two girls did laugh, together and out loud.

This made Stefi think—and maybe even believe—that all was not lost between them. That there was a path forward for them to reconcile. She could almost see it unfurling. Maybe Stefi didn't need boys in her life after all; they were so much trouble. She would have Hofmann and making croissants and her best friend back. Stefi and Amber would rebuild what they'd lost and move forward together, leaving the boys that hurt them in the dust.

Stefi wiped her eyes and both her cheeks and sniffled some more. "I'm glad you reached out and that you didn't take my silence as a final answer."

"I'm glad I kept trying too," Amber said. "It's so good to talk to you. I've missed you so much."

Tears kept filling Stefi's eyes amid the laughter. Yes, things were going to be okay. It would take work and persistence, but their friendship was worth it, and they'd get through this. "Me too, Amber." Stefi suddenly felt the urge to tell Amber everything. "There's so much we need to talk about." She tapped the screen until the photo of her and Xavi kissing appeared. "Take a look at what I just sent you."

Stefi watched as Amber studied the image.

Amber looked up. "Wow, Stefi. I see you've moved on from Jason."

"Well, yes. And also no. It's complicated," she began and was already feeling better. She needed to tell someone about Xavi, someone other than her mother. "But Amber, the weird thing is . . ." She stopped.

"The weird thing is what?" Amber pressed.

"The weird thing is that you and Jason almost did me a favor." She'd had this thought before, but now she knew it was true. "Maybe Jason and I should have broken up a long time ago. I mean, I'm not happy with how things ended. But it freed me to be with someone new.

Amber was staring at the photo again. "Do you like him or is this just . . . a kiss?"

"I more than like him." Stefi groaned. "I don't even know where to start, honestly—"

"Hey, before you say anything more," Amber interrupted, then took a deep breath. "There's something important I need to tell you. It's part of why I called and, well, called again and again. I'm guessing it's not going to come as the best of news, so prepare yourself."

Stefi didn't like the ominous tone in Amber's voice. "Uh-oh. What?"

"It has to do with Jason."

Anxiety fluttered in Stefi's chest. "Amber, just tell me."

"Brace yourself."

"I'm braced, okay? Just say it."

Amber was doing that thing where she picked at the little stitches covering the quilt on top of her bed as she stalled. "All right. So it's possible that Jason is on a plane to Barcelona to beg for forgiveness and try to get you back."

"Oh my God. On a plane right now?"

"Yup, definitely now, and definitely, yes, he is. It's probably just taking off. I wanted to warn you. I felt I should even if you still hated me." Amber checked the time. "Let's see, he has a stopover, I think, so you've got about fourteen hours to prepare."

Stefi looked at the clock on her phone and did some math. By her calculations, she had three hours until the big press conference this evening and then one fitful night ahead until her ex-boyfriend arrived at BCN airport. Fantastic. Could this day get any more complicated? For about the hundredth time since she'd woken up this morning, Stefi's stomach bottomed out.

# Thirty-Five

Turmoil raged inside Santiago. The SUV driver, Mateo, wound along the narrow streets of Madrid on their way to the center of it. Santiago had been summoned to a meeting with the jefe of the royal guard, Francisco Hernández, at the Palacio Real. It would be the first time he'd seen the man since he was given the assignment to guard Xavi way back when.

He gripped the armrest tighter. He worried he was on his way to his doom.

Francisco might have been like an uncle to him, but Santiago was still one of his guards, and Francisco could be harsh when it came to protecting the crown and the royal family.

As they got closer to the heart of Madrid, Mateo kept having to stop and wait for the metal barriers embedded in the cobbled streets to lower, or he'd get out and move them himself, pass through, then stop the car again to put the heavy posts back. The streets in Madrid's Casco Antiguo were restricted to pedestrians, and only cars with special access were allowed entry. All the starting and stopping and winding around the medieval center was making Santiago's stomach churn. They advanced little by little, street by street, barrier by barrier. Even though Santiago had been to the Palacio Real a million times, this trip seemed to be taking forever.

The inside of this SUV was freezing and Santiago shivered.

Or maybe the texts from Isabel de Luna were responsible for the icy cold running through his veins. His phone pinged again.

**You really fucked up,** Isabel wrote.

**I fucked up? You outed Xavi! And me!**

**Cue the tiny violin. You had your chance to prevent this and didn't take it.**

**You're just bitter because you drove Xavi away and now you know he's the prince.**

**You still have an opportunity to salvage this situation, Santiago.**

**Salvage what? There's nothing left to save! All of Spain knows about Xavi. You made me look like an idiot, Isabel.**

**You'll see what's left in just a few minutes, royal guard. ¡Nos vemos!**

Santiago waited for her to explain but she didn't.

**Isabel?**

**Isabel, tell me what you're talking about?**

**What do you mean, "a few minutes"?**

**What's happening in a few minutes?**

"¡Joder!" Santiago shouted and Mateo glanced at him.

"Are you all right?" the driver asked.

Mateo was new at the palace and perfectly nice, but Santiago wished one of the drivers he'd grown up with were at the wheel, someone to whom he could at least admit he was having a tough day. "Perdona, yes, thank you," he said back to be polite.

But of course Santiago wasn't all right.

He stared at the phone in his hand, reading and rereading Isabel's last message. What, exactly, had she meant? He looked out the windows, left, then right, then left again, like something might spring at the car from the shadows. Assassins? A parade of models? Isabel had said he'd know what she meant in a few minutes, but how many minutes? Three, five, fifteen, sixty? What could Isabel possibly be up to now? *Nos vemos* meant they'd "see each other," and Santiago wondered if she was saying that in a general sense, as in one day, eventually, if he ever returned to Barcelona, or if she meant something specific, like they were going to see each other very and worrisomely soon.

Mateo finally came to a stop in front of the Palacio Real. "We're here."

*Deep breaths,* Santiago told himself. "I know . . . I just need one more minute."

"Take all the time you want," Mateo replied. "Besides, there's a line of cars waiting to reach the entrance. You can hang out until we pull up to the doors if you like."

At least Santiago could postpone his fate for a few additional seconds.

He looked ahead through the windshield of their car. Guests were arriving for the reception the palace advisers had thrown together that would take place after the press conference tonight. The makeshift event was meant to present Marta and Xavi to people within the king's inner circle, and also to begin the work of gaining the mother and son acceptance by those in the press who'd decide if they would sink or swim. Marta and Xavi were the newest and most important members of the royal family, so the scrutiny would be merciless. The task ahead for everyone would be difficult, to say the least.

As far as Santiago knew, he would not be attending the press conference or the party.

He watched as a tall palace guard rushed out to the car in front of theirs and opened the door for the guests inside. The guard bent low and peered at its occupants.

Then Santiago saw one long, perfectly toned leg stretch out into the street, a glittering five-inch heel at the end of it.

"Dios," he muttered. Santiago knew exactly whose heel was planting itself on the ground without even a wobble.

The palace guard offered his hand to the woman emerging from the vehicle. She took it gracefully, manicured nails shining, long diamond earrings swinging from her ears, the epitome of elegance and style.

Isabel de Luna stood there in all her glory, her hand still held by the admiring guard.

She'd told Santiago a few minutes and she'd certainly meant it.

Exactly four; Santiago did the math.

Isabel wore a high-necked floor-length Cortana dress in the gauziest of linen. It was sleeveless but uncharacteristically conservative, he thought, except for the slit up the side that nearly reached her hip. Santiago didn't know whether to roll his eyes or scream. The color was white, and Isabel surely intended to evoke the image of a wedding gown, because Cortana, the haute couture Spanish fashion house, was famous for its wedding gowns. She'd obviously come to snag her prince.

Isabel rose onto her toes and whispered something into the palace guard's ear. The man immediately flushed.

Santiago had never hated anyone more than he hated Isabel in this moment. She was the person who had ruined everything—for Xavi and Stefi but also for him and Diego. He grabbed the door handle to get out of the car and confront her, but then he stopped.

Isabel was turning back, and the same guard was peering inside the car again, talking to someone else. Apparently, she'd arrived accompanied by someone. Maybe her mother? That would make sense, given that her mother was a marquesa. When Santiago thought about it, of course the de Lunas would be invited to the press conference and the reception to follow. But the new leg emerging and stepping onto the ground was that of a man.

Santiago swallowed, he blinked, he gasped for air.

His whole body shivered, his heart pounded, his skin tingled, his mouth went dry.

Diego.

There he was, standing in front of the very car in which Santiago sat watching, in all his compact perfection. This boy that just last night he'd held in his arms and never wanted to let go of, this person whose lips he'd tasted and thought there could not possibly exist anything as sweet again in his life. Had Diego come to get him in a grand romantic gesture? Santiago counted the hours since they'd been exchanging messages and concluded that Diego must have already been on his way to Madrid. As Santiago stared through the windshield at his beautiful, adorable almost-boyfriend, his heart threatened to burst. He wanted to cry with joy and weep with grief at once. It took everything inside him, every ounce of strength, not to race from the car, pick up Diego, twirl him around, and ask him to be his alone. Santiago would do anything, absolutely anything, for the chance to plant his lips on Diego's delicious mouth one more time. This was what the staccato beating of his heart was telling him with so much urgency.

Then a dissenting voice echoed inside his brain.

*Really, you'd do anything at all, Santi?*

In the end, Santiago didn't leap from the car to proclaim his love. He didn't move at all, didn't even let Diego know that he was a mere few meters away. Instead, he braced himself against these urges and watched as Diego gallantly offered Isabel his arm and Isabel delicately place her hand atop it. He remained utterly still as the two of them walked under the soaring stone archway to the entrance of the Palacio Real and disappeared inside. Diego must be hoping to see Santiago at the reception. He wanted to run after them, calling Diego's name, then strip off his tasseled uniform jacket and toss it to the floor in the grandest romantic gesture of his own life. But he didn't do this. It was a lie to claim that he'd do absolutely anything to kiss Diego again. Because he wouldn't. Not if it involved no longer following in the footsteps of his beloved father.

Santiago finally got out of the SUV.

He inhaled the air and stood tall, shoulders back.

The sun was gloriously bright. The Palacio Real was alive and bustling and as beautiful as ever, just like Madrid. Santiago was home again and he felt it all the way to his center. He headed toward the side entrance for staff.

Away from Diego.

Toward duty and honor and the hope of preserving the life he'd always wanted.

# Thirty-Six

Xavi stepped out onto the large veranda attached to his bedroom. His new bedroom in the *palace*.

A breeze flowed through the air; his mother was somewhere nearby. It was as though it was just another afternoon in Barcelona. Except that now, everything felt different, because it *was* different. Xavi wasn't in Barcelona, he was in Madrid, trying to get through his first official day as the prince of Spain.

The giant marble esplanade where Xavi stood—because that's what it was, a huge marble terrace fit for a prince—made the one attached to his bedroom in Barcelona seem like a pauper's. This terrace boasted every kind of fruit tree—fig, lemon, mandarina, peach, even olive. Xavi had his choice of places to sit, since there were couches and lounge chairs galore, plus a table for dining with eleven of his closest friends. The only thing missing was a pool. Save for that, he could be on Isabel's rooftop, except here was even more beautiful than her family's place, if that was possible.

Everywhere Xavi turned, there was art. Portraits painted by Spanish masters, contemporary works that would normally hang in a museum, artisanal stonework, woodwork, glasswork. Crystal chandeliers and gold filigreed trim on mirrors.

But so far—aside from making amends with his father earlier today—Xavi's life as the prince had sucked.

He was about to endure his first-ever press conference, after which there'd be a so-called small gathering of a hundred people, called together by Alfonso to make the first significant introductions of him and Marta. Who knew how many press conferences and receptions the prince of Spain would be required to preside over during the course of his lifetime? Certainly more than Xavi wanted to think about at the moment. Maybe eventually he'd grow used to all of this. But at least tonight he only had to stand next to the king and show his face alongside his mother's. Soon he would have to make a formal statement to the country, but this would not occur before he'd endured his "training" for handling the media.

Xavi shook his head. Until now, the only training he'd ever needed had been provided by Marta and typically involved knife techniques for chopping vegetables or how to heat the oil in a pan so it was hot enough but not so hot that it burned. Those were the days.

Xavi turned and headed back into his room.

He needed to get dressed.

It was time to put on the formal regalia of the prince of Spain. The staff had taken it out for him and displayed it in the corner of the room. It looked like an elaborate military uniform, with its gold braids on each shoulder, its sashes and tassels. The valet—because apparently Xavi now had a personal valet and his name was Luis—reluctantly allowed Xavi privacy this evening, but only after Xavi insisted. He'd never needed help getting ready before and he told Luis he didn't need it now. Only after Marta intervened did the man finally agree to leave Xavi in peace. This peace would not last, so Xavi knew he might as well enjoy it while it did.

Xavi tossed his hair. The staff had wanted to cut it today, but he refused. He would continue to refuse if it was the last thing he did. He wanted to retain at least one defining feature of his former self.

Piece by piece, Xavi put on the regalia. After buttoning the very last button and fastening the elaborate cuff links at the end of the sleeves, he stood in front of the floor-to-ceiling mirror and studied his reflection.

It looked to Xavi like he was wearing some kind of costume.

Then again, Xavi supposed it *was* a costume. The old Xavi would be ready with some crack about how not everybody could pull off tassels and brocade like he could. But the new Xavi felt flat, like someone had steamrolled all the laughter out of him. In the mirror's reflection, he saw the opulent four-poster bed that awaited him later, with its pile of downy pillows and its soft duvet. His mind automatically supplied an occupant with whom he'd love to enjoy that beautiful bed. If only.

Xavi was desperate to get a message to Stefi. He went to the bedside table, opened the drawer, and took out the letter he'd started to write after he'd shooed away the staff fussing around his room. Without a phone for who knew how long, he had no choice but to write to Stefi the old-fashioned way. He went over to the desk across the room and sat down in the opulent chair before it, then picked up a pen to finish. *I know I should have told you who I was from the beginning, and I am so sorry that I did not. When we met, I had no idea who you would soon become to me. Stefi, I . . .* His hand stopped moving. He wiped his brow. This uniform was far too hot to wear in the summer. Xavi stared down at his unfinished sentence, his unfinished *sentiment*, and knew that heat was not the problem. If there was ever a time to pour out his heart, this was it. Once more, he guided the pen across the page.

Stefi, I am falling in love with you.
Can you ever forgive me?

He wrote the final sentence and set the pen on the desk. Then he folded the letter carefully, slipped it into an envelope, and sealed it. He tucked it inside the pocket of his jacket, the final piece of his outfit. But how to get it to Stefi? Xavi might be the prince of Spain and living in a palace, but he couldn't leave the room without someone noticing him or following him or asking what he needed and where he planned to go. He would have to figure something out; he just wasn't sure what. Bribery? He was considering pocketing one of the many priceless objects around the room when there came a knock on his door.

He answered it.

Marta stood there beaming at her son. "¡Qué guapo!"

All thoughts of bribery and theft vanished as Xavi took in his mother. She wore a column gown of navy blue silk, simple, but Marta didn't need elaborate clothing to draw attention. She was as lovely pouring eggs into a tortilla pan and sweating at La Buena as she was dressed for a press conference and private party at the Palacio Real.

"Hola, mamá. You look beautiful too."

"How are you doing, mi amor?" she asked.

Xavi's gaze shifted away from his mother to the elaborate tiled floor. He couldn't lie to her. "Every minute has been hard," he admitted. "I don't know how to be myself here."

She got on her toes and planted a kiss on her son's cheek, then wiped off the lipstick she'd left. "We'll get through this together. Little by little, okay?"

Xavi nodded. He knew it was getting late and that they needed to get to Madrid soon for the press conference. He gestured down the hall. "Shall we?" He stepped out of the room and waited for Marta to take his arm.

The two of them began the rather long journey navigating the halls of the royal residence to where the cars would whisk them off to the Palacio Real. Blue silk shimmered along the floor behind his mother. The palace staff appeared at just the right moments to point their way at each turn. Yet another thing Xavi supposed he needed to get used to. Xavi took in the portraits of former kings on the walls, the chandeliers hanging above them, the expensive carpets underneath their fancy shoes. It was a lot to absorb. But the letter burned in his pocket, distracting him.

Maybe his mother could help him get it to Stefi?

"¿Mamá?"

Marta squeezed his arm. "¿Sí?"

"I really need to get in touch with Stefi. She must be wondering why I haven't messaged her after everything this morning and—"

"—Oh, Xavi," she interrupted, turning to him. "I know this is difficult, but you must resist."

Xavi halted, a match struck inside him. "But why? You and Alfonso aren't!" Xavi could hear his frustration and it surprised him. He almost never got upset with his mother.

"Xavier, right now your only job is to get your feet underneath you." The stern tone in Marta's voice also surprised her son. "Alfonso and I are much older, so we can make a decision with a lot of hindsight. Even so, it comes with tremendous consequences." Marta reached up, gently turned Xavi's face in her direction, and met his eyes. Everything about her softened again. "Look what's already happened. If you dated this girl as the prince, her life would be turned upside down."

"But we could find a way—"

"No, Xavi, don't even think about it. You aren't going to be able to date whomever you want anymore. I hate to say this but it's true. Every time you go out with someone, you will have to take care to protect their identity. To make something public will require an entire team of handlers and fixers! Whichever girl it turns out to be will be discussed across the country and maybe even the world as a possible future princess. That is a lot to ask of someone. Too much to ask of someone you just met a few weeks ago. It might sound like a real-life fairy tale at first, but believe me, it isn't. Just think about what Alfonso and I went through, having someone conspire to keep us apart!"

Xavi didn't speak. The words that wanted to come, he knew his mother wouldn't like.

Marta seemed to take his silence as acquiescence. She linked her arm through his again. "I love you with all my heart and I know this is hard, but it's for the best. For you and for Stefi. You need to trust me."

"I love you too," Xavi said, which was true and which Xavi hoped would make up for the fact that, for maybe the first time in his life, he did not agree with his mother. He supposed there was a first time for everything, including disobeying Marta's wishes.

They arrived in the foyer, and the palace staff ushered them into the cars that waited outside. The king was already at the Palacio Real practicing his speech and would meet them there.

On the ride into Madrid, mother and son were uncharacteristically quiet.

Perhaps Xavi's mother was contemplating what lay ahead once it came out that she was involved with the king. But what swirled in Xavi's mind was that he would find a way to get this letter to Stefi if it required him to walk all the way back to Barcelona to hand-deliver it. Xavi's heart was pulling him in the opposite direction of where his mother wanted him to go. And the heart wants what it wants, as they say, regardless of whether that heart belonged to the prince of Spain or a catalán boy who made a mean Spanish tortilla and who just yesterday was as ordinary as drinking vermut on a Sunday afternoon in Barcelona. Though maybe not so ordinary to one particular American girl who Xavi hoped might find it in her heart to forgive him this small transgression of failing to mention that he was the prince of Spain.

# Thirty-Seven

Stefi was alone in her room, sitting on her bed. She turned up the volume on her laptop, tapping the button so hard she was lucky it didn't break. The press conference was about to begin. A woman from the royal palace appeared at the podium and got ready to introduce the king. She was poised and smooth in her movements, everything about her was polished.

In Stefi's other hand she gripped her phone; she stared at the screen, giving Xavi till the very last minute to be in touch and explain, hoping he might do just this. The urge to talk to Xavi helped stave off the anxiety Stefi was suffering about Jason's imminent arrival. But she would figure out Jason later. She had until morning to determine what to do. Now was the time to focus on Xavi.

All afternoon, Stefi kept making deals with herself: She would listen to Xavi with an open mind and heart if he would just message her in the next hour. When that hour passed, she renegotiated the terms, giving Xavi one more hour, then thirty minutes, then another thirty, then an additional fifteen. Soon it was ten more minutes, then five and five more, all the way up until now, as the press conference was beginning and no minutes remained for Xavi to contact her.

Stefi bit her lip, trying not to cry. The moment of truth arrived, and Xavi's silence gave Stefi all the answers she needed. The reality hurt far more than the end of a summer fling should. Her parents and abuela tried to convince Stefi to watch the press conference with them in the living room, but Stefi wanted to be alone. She was glad they couldn't see how upset she was.

Just before the elegant woman spoke into the mic, a message lit up the screen of Stefi's phone. Her heart flipped and flopped and then deflated.

It was Amber.

**I'm watching the press conference online. Are you okay?**

She couldn't bear to give Amber a response, so she set the phone aside. Earlier she'd confessed the events that had led up to this morning with Xavi, though she left out a few key details. Stefi wasn't yet ready to tell Amber absolutely everything again.

The woman introduced the king, then stepped aside.

Stefi tapped the volume button again but it was as loud as it could go.

King Alfonso XIV walked out to the clicks of what sounded like a hundred cameras. He towered over everything. He looked up, straight into the lens, and in that moment, Stefi knew the rumors were true. It wasn't that she hadn't seen photos of the king—she had. But before today, she hadn't really looked at the man or looked for anything familiar in him. Now she could see Xavi in the king's face. She recognized his soulful eyes.

"Xavi is the prince," Stefi said into the air of her room, trying out these words in her mouth. Trying out the idea that the boy she'd met this summer, the boy she'd kissed so cavalierly for the first time not so long ago, was royalty. An actual prince. The heir to the Spanish throne.

Seriously? *Seriously?!*

Stefi shifted on the bed, crossing her legs, uncrossing them, then drawing her knees up to her chin, then sitting on her heels. She couldn't get comfortable as she waited for the king of Spain to confirm or deny the claims of this morning's article announcing he had a secret son who'd been living in Barcelona for nearly two decades. And who had recently been dating an American girl who was learning to make croissants at Hofmann, to be totally exact.

The king cleared his throat. "Tonight, I want to address the rumors circulating about the royal family and, in particular, whether or not I have a son." His words were slow and careful. "First, I want to say how unfortunate it is that our society has given such prominence to gossip and such little respect to privacy. I make this claim with full awareness of the tremendous responsibility and privilege I occupy in my role as monarch of this great country. I love our country, and I am grateful to be its ruling monarch. But I want to remind everyone listening that members of the royal family are still people, with all the challenges that come with our shared humanity." Here, Alfonso paused.

Stefi used this time to finish translating all he'd said in her head to make sure she understood his meaning clearly. It sounded like he was starting by asking for forgiveness for whatever he was about to announce next—or, really, asking for mercy.

The king inhaled, ready to continue.

Stefi swallowed, remembering to breathe.

"Over my years as king, it has been a concern, a debate, and a worry among citizens and the royal family that I do not have an heir. I understand this is why the rumor that I might have a secret son has caused such a stir far and wide." Alfonso gripped the sides of the podium, looking straight into the camera. "I'm here to confirm that the rumor is true."

Stefi pressed a hand to her heart, which felt like it might beat right out of her chest.

"Recently, I learned I am lucky enough to have a son. I was thrilled by this news," the king went on. "I want the citizens of Spain to know I have welcomed this wonderful young man into the royal family along with his mother. For those of you with questions about the truth of this claim, all the requisite DNA testing has been carefully done, and there is no doubt of his heritage. He is my son. It was a wonderful surprise at this stage of my life to realize I have a child. At this juncture for the royal family, it is also serendipitous."

Alfonso looked to the side and beckoned to someone.

The camera followed the direction of the king's arm.

Stefi blinked and waited; she thought she might have a heart attack. "Oh my God."

There was Xavi. And his mother next to him.

At first Xavi didn't move, but then he seemed to come to life. He went and stood beside the king.

His *father.*

Holy shit. *Holy shit.*

The king of Spain was Xavi's father. For real.

It was difficult to believe, but Stefi had to accept this as truth, because obviously it was.

The camera zoomed in on the newly minted prince.

Xavi's face was a blank. He didn't smile; there was no laughter in his eyes. He was Xavi but he was someone else. Stefi supposed this made sense, because apparently he *was* someone else, not the carefree boy she'd met earlier this summer. He was dressed in the formal attire that Stefi imagined only a prince would wear, which was much like the king's. Gold braids at his shoulders, gold brocade at his cuffs, with a light blue diagonal sash across a dark blue formal jacket like that of a military uniform. A wide red band marked his waist, with long tassels hanging off the end of it.

What was Xavi thinking about? Stefi wondered. Was he thinking about her at all? Was he regretting not telling Stefi the truth from the very start?

The king was winding down his remarks. "I want to ask the press and the citizens of Spain to respect the privacy of this young man whose life has changed drastically in a matter of hours and the privacy of his mother as well. In the very near future, he will address you himself, but until then, he will not be making a statement. Thank you for your cooperation. Viva España, and good night."

On the screen, Stefi watched as the reporters erupted into chaos, shouting questions after the royal trio as the king, Xavi, and Marta disappeared from the room through a large, carved wooden door. A sharp pang pierced Stefi's heart as she watched Xavi go.

But then the camera panned across the audience, and Stefi saw a familiar face in the front row. The camera lingered on her, because of course it would—she was gorgeous, she was perfect, she was elegant. The epitome of royal. She practically screamed future princess. She was also Xavi's ex-girlfriend and rather infamous herself in all the gossip pages.

Stefi's heart squeezed again, this time in pain.

Now the tears flowed freely down her cheeks to her chin, where they proceeded to drop onto the bedspread below. She wondered if this had been Xavi's plan all along: Have a fling with the American girl, then get back together with the wealthy Spanish one after his big announcement. Maybe Xavi and Isabel had planned it together. Stefi had seen the article on Isabel de Luna that dubbed her Spain's future princess and chronicled her past relationship with Xavi. She had hated seeing all those pictures of them together. Maybe the entire romance with Stefi was a ruse to distract from Isabel until Xavi's identity was announced. Well, at least Stefi had her answer about Xavi, even if it wasn't one she liked. She wouldn't be hearing from him again, not to explain and certainly not to beg her forgiveness. He had moved on to his royal life without a backward glance at Stefi. Right on and back to Isabel.

A sob escaped Stefi. Then another.

For the second time this summer, she'd been betrayed.

In between sobs she heard a knock on the door and managed to hiccup a "Come in!"

The door creaked open.

Abuela stood there holding a tray full of food. Two giant steaming artichokes rose up from their individual bowls, and two big goblets of red wine stood next to them. Plus there was a little bowl of lemon juice for dipping the leaves. "Oh, mi niña," abuela said, full of feeling.

Stefi choked out a laugh of gratitude and wiped her face with the back of her hand. Then she got up to take the tray from abuela. Of course she would try and soothe her granddaughter's heart with their favorite snack. Stefi set the tray on the bed, and the two women climbed onto it, facing one another, the food between them. Stefi plucked a single artichoke leaf, dipped it into the bowl of lemony liquid, and ate it. Then she washed it down with a big gulp of wine and felt a bit better. "Thank you, abuela."

The older woman nodded. "Estefanía, what a boy to fall for while in Barcelona."

"I know." Stefi sighed and sniffled.

Abuela looked at her hard, eyebrows arching. She raised her glass, and Stefi raised her own. "Salud to that," abuela said, and they clinked goblets.

"What a disaster," Stefi said. "I hope I didn't embarrass you with your friends. I know one of them recognized me from the photo."

"Nooo!" abuela cried out. "Nunca. You could never embarrass me, mi amor, and you have nothing to be ashamed about."

Stefi stuffed her face with artichoke leaves, one after another, to try and stem the feelings of shame colliding inside her despite her grandmother's reassurances. "I let myself get carried away with someone I just met, and now I'll probably never hear from him again." The humiliation of this rushed to the surface of Stefi's skin, and the burn was intense. "God, I'm so stupid!" She tried to blink back the tears that wanted to come once more.

Abuela held the glass of vino tinto in her hand and looked at Stefi thoughtfully. "I know this has come as a shock and you have every right to be upset," she began, "but Xavi may have no control over who he's in touch with at the moment. The royal family must be dealing with a firestorm of paparazzi and press. I bet he has publicists and handlers and all sorts of palace people controlling every word. If you can find it in your heart to give the boy a little time, you may hear from him still. He may be just as shocked and disubicado as you are, cariño."

Her grandmother said this with such confidence, like she knew exactly what she was talking about, that Stefi nearly believed her. She wanted to believe her, that was for sure. "You think so?"

Abuela took another sip of wine and looked Stefi in the eye again. "You like him a lot, yes?"

Stefi nodded.

"You think he likes you too, yes?"

As painful as this was, Stefi allowed herself to remember her night with Xavi and their goodbye at the door of abuela's building just this morning. "I do think so, yes, or I did before."

Her grandmother nodded with confidence, like she really did know what was occurring inside the heart of the prince of Spain with respect to Stefi. "You just need to be patient, then, Estefanía. He's going to reach out to you the first moment he gets. I just know it." At this, her gaze dropped to the artichoke in her bowl. "Now, let's finish these before they're cold. They did come out very well, I think."

"They always do when it's you who makes them," Stefi said, and decided to put her faith in her abuela, who had never failed her before. Stefi hoped for her own sake that her grandmother's words would prove to be as true as the feelings that went into cooking the artichokes abuela made for Stefi with all the love she had in her heart.

# Thirty-Eight

Francisco Hernández gestured for Santiago to sit on the other side of his desk. The young royal guard obeyed. Francisco's thick hair was graying as he aged, and it gave him a distinguished appearance. On one wall of Hernández's office, a television screen was tuned to the press conference, which was coming to an end. It made Santiago nauseated to watch, so he did his best to avert his eyes. He had been waiting for what felt like hours for this meeting that would determine his fate, and now it was here.

Francisco looked at Santiago. "Tell me what happened," he said, and he did not sound friendly.

Santiago hung his head. He almost didn't want to take in the familiar sights around the room, the shelves with the many books from Spanish poets, because Francisco was a lover of literature. His collection of tiny Real Madrid figurines, which he displayed on a table, always boasted a full roster of players, as he liked to tell people who visited him here. The newest figurine of a futbolista on Madrid's team was always a good gift for Francisco, so he could add it to his collection. One entire wall was filled with commendations and medals Francisco had earned over the years as head of the guard, and amid the framed photographs of him and the king at events he'd attended was a single image of Francisco with Carlos, Santiago's father.

Santiago felt the weight of his father's gaze like never before; Carlos's long shadow had eclipsed his son completely. He forced himself to meet Francisco's eyes. "I guess I wasn't ready for such an important posting," he admitted. "I let you down, I let the king down, I let down the prince and the entire Guardia Real in the process. I do not deserve this position or your trust, and I am so sorry to have failed you and this worthy institution. I am prepared to offer my resignation."

Francisco got up and came around to the other side of his desk. He shifted one of the visitor's chairs so it faced Santiago. Then he sat down and leaned forward, hands clasped. "Perhaps it is I who failed you, Santi."

Santiago opened his mouth, then closed it. This was not what he was expecting to hear from this prestigious important jefe. "What are you talking about? How can you say that, when—"

Francisco stopped him from continuing by putting up a hand that meant *Wait*.

So Santiago waited.

"I see now that I put you in an impossible position. The king and I should have brought his son to the palace immediately once he was confirmed as the rightful heir. But the king desperately wanted to give Xavier a last few months of normalcy because, as we both know, the king is far too generous about such things. I knew the risks, however, knew that the prince's anonymity might not last long, especially after his visit to meet the king earlier this year and especially given Xavier's resistance to assuming his position in the royal family. Yet I sent you to Barcelona to be with him regardless." Francisco shook his head. "You were placed in the middle of a losing situation. And I'm sorry for putting you there."

Santiago stared at the jefe in disbelief. "So I'm not fired?"

Francisco leaned back in his chair and crossed his arms over his chest. "No."

Santiago blinked back tears of gratitude. A bead of hope grew in his chest and began to knock around in his heart, this way and that, like the tiki-taka of the ball in a lively Madrid-Barça game. He wanted to hug the man before him. "I don't know what to say."

A smile appeared on Francisco's face, but one that was difficult to read. There was something . . . a bit off about it. "Say that you'll continue as a member of the guard. We will put this behind us and start afresh. The prince needs this for his role as a central member of the royal family and the future heir. And both Alfonso and I discussed it and want to give you an opportunity to start over and set you up for success."

Relief soared across Santiago like a perfectly executed gol by Madrid. He would continue as a guard! He and Xavi were being given a chance to start over together! His mind spun with possibilities and even forgiveness for Isabel. How wonderful that she'd brought Diego to the palace tonight so Santiago could see him again. He would invite Diego for a tour of the Palacio Real that only a guard like himself could offer, and he knew exactly where he'd bring the handsome boy so they could kiss once more. Santiago's brain exploded with thoughts of romance and the promise of future love.

But then Francisco took Santiago's burgeoning hopes and dreams and crushed them. "I think you're going to love living in Seville," he said. "It's rather hot in the summer but I'm certain you'll be very comfortable in the palace residence there, Real Alcázar. It's very beautiful, and you'll get to see Xavier now and again when he makes an official visit."

Santiago's heart skidded to a stop. "Seville?"

"Yes, I've arranged for you to take on a wonderful new posting there."

His mouth gaped open. He tried to breathe; he tried not to cry; he tried once again to be grateful for the second chance that deep down he still believed he didn't deserve. "So it's not an option for me to continue working with the prince here in Madrid?"

Francisco shook his head. "I'm sure you can understand. This is for the best, for both you and Xavier. This distance between you will allow this scandal in the press to recede more quickly."

"Yes, of course I understand," he said. The thing is, he did. It made sense Xavi would begin his new palace existence with a different guard. And that Santiago would be exiled to a city many hours from Madrid and on the complete other side of the country from Diego. "Thank you very much, señor," he said formally. "I am grateful for this opportunity." Santiago got up to leave.

Francisco stopped him. "One other thing."

Santiago turned back. "Yes?"

"Just so we're clear, for you to continue in the guard, any conflicts of interest will have to be resolved," Francisco said, his voice growing icy cold. "Do you understand my meaning?"

Once again, Santiago told him, "Yes, of course," because once again he did. All too well. Without saying it directly, Francisco Hernández was telling Santiago—no, he was ordering Santiago—to tie up any loose ends he might still have related to Xavi. Which really meant Diego.

Francisco stood up. "Before you leave to pack, you're welcome to say your goodbyes at the reception. I am sure Xavier will want to see you and say his goodbyes as well."

"Thank you, señor," Santiago said again, and he turned on his heel to walk out, wondering if his heart was still in one piece in his chest or if he was trailing the shards of it behind him.

In a daze Santiago maneuvered himself through the labyrinth of the Palacio Real to the grand room where the reception was being held. A thought was trying to form in his brain about the end of his conversation with Francisco, but he couldn't quite hold it together, so Santiago let it go in favor of the permission he'd been given to make his goodbyes. The closer he got to the party, the more his heart pounded at the thought of seeing Diego. But Santiago had just been given a second chance and he needed to take it. He'd been born to be a Guardia Real like his father.

Hadn't he?

Santiago turned another corner. Ahead of him, the reception was in full swing. He could already hear the guests milling about, laughter spilling from the open doors, glasses clinking in toasts to the young prince's health. Nearing the entrance, he slowed his pace. Once again Santiago threw back his shoulders, preparing himself to walk inside. He imagined reaching inside his chest and removing his heart so he could leave it behind. It was better this way, Santiago decided. No, it was the only way.

# Thirty-Nine

Many surprises awaited Xavi at his first royal reception, not all of them unpleasant. In fact, several turned out to be wonderful.

The moment he walked into the party, all the guests seemed to stop eating and chatting and drinking to watch the handsome young prince enter the room in full regalia. But Xavi barely noticed how the people gaped because he saw something that made him think he must be imagining things. Good, familiar things. He walked straight to the tables laid out with lavish amounts of food for the guests.

"Jordi, is that you?" Xavi said to a man standing near a member of the palace staff who was carefully and expertly carving a leg of jamón ibérico. The man held a small plate in his hand, but the plate was bare, since he was eating the jamón as fast as the staff could serve it. At the sound of his name, he turned, and Xavi saw it was indeed their prep chef from La Buena.

"Xavi!" he returned enthusiastically. He set the plate on the table and opened his arms wide. Jordi laughed. "Or should I call you Príncipe now?"

Xavi's heart rose in his throat. He let himself be pulled into a big hug by this person he'd worked next to chopping potatoes and onions since he was a young boy.

When Jordi let Xavi go, Jordi immediately grabbed his plate again and gestured at the person serving the famous Spanish ham. "I'm ready for more whenever you have it," he said to the ham carver. Then to Xavi: "You need to try this, it's the best jamón ibérico I've ever had in my whole life. They must have fed this pig some extra-special acorns to make him turn out so delicious."

"Don't be offending me now, Jordi," a nearby woman piped up. "My jamón ibérico is just as good as what they're serving here tonight."

Xavi turned toward yet another familiar voice. "Josefina!"

"Perdona, señora," Jordi said and kissed the old grandmother from La Boqueria on her cheek.

Josefina laughed and put her hand out to Xavi. "Qué guapo, this one, eh?"

Xavi bent low to kiss her on both cheeks and let himself be hugged again. "I can't believe you both are here. How—"

Before his question could be answered, he saw yet more familiar faces and they all surrounded him, laughing and chatting and snacking on the incredible goodies laid out for the party. There was Bonnie the Scot from the neighborhood, and Lis from the bar everyone went to en El Gótico. Soon Marta joined their group and everyone was talking and catching up as though they were not at a reception at the Palacio Real thrown by the king but instead sitting around the counter at La Buena. The only difference was they were dressed in their finest and surrounded by the upper echelons of Spanish society and members of the royal family. Which somehow now included Xavi.

Marta leaned close to her son and whispered, "Alfonso thought it might be nice to surprise you with a little taste of home tonight. And surprise me with it as well."

Xavi nodded. He was overwhelmed as he looked at these people who'd been his family since he was small.

Jordi raised his eyebrows at his fellow prep chef. "Granted, we were all a little stunned by the news about you, Xavi, but we plan on keeping you grounded." He clapped Xavi on the shoulder. "I want to assure you that I am going to take good care of everything at La Buena until your mother decides what to do with it."

Xavi turned to his mother and she nodded. He blinked back tears. "Jordi, I don't know what to say. I'm so relieved. And grateful."

Josefina patted Jordi's arm. "We're all going to help out, cariño."

Bonnie smiled. "You may be a prince, but you're still ours, love."

Xavi almost couldn't believe any of this. For the first time since he'd woken up this morning and his world came crashing down, he started to feel hopeful. Like maybe being prince would change a lot of things but not *every single thing*. He wiped a tear from his cheek. Xavi almost expected Stefi to appear through one of the doors and stride toward him in some gorgeous dress with a glass of cava in her hand.

Alas, this did not occur.

At the thought of Stefi, Xavi remembered the letter in his pocket and his determination to get it to her as soon as a prince on strict phone lockdown could manage. Lucky for Xavi, he was now surrounded by potential couriers from the neighborhood. The question was, which one could best keep the secret? It wasn't as though his neighbors were known for their secret-keeping talents. They were rather known for the opposite, since they all excelled at the gift of the gab.

Before Xavi could choose the one least likely to blab, a member of the staff fetched him to join the king in a receiving line. *Cue the royal duties*, Xavi thought and sighed. He said his goodbyes for now and went to stand next to his father.

"He does clean up nice," someone commented to another guest as he passed.

"The likeness to the king is truly remarkable," said a woman in reply.

Alfonso watched Xavi approach with a look of concern. "Are you all right?"

Xavi's smile for the man was genuine. "I want to thank you for inviting our friends from home. It's truly . . . a gift to my mother and me."

Relief entered the king's eyes and he placed a warm hand on Xavi's shoulder. "It was a small thing to do. I want to make things easier wherever I can. I want to make you—and your mother—feel at home."

"But it wasn't small at all," Xavi said, his eyes trying their best to communicate his gratitude. Then he took his place and stood tall next to his even taller father. His first receiving line as prince began, and it snaked all around the room.

One after the other, the king welcomed the guests and introduced them to Xavi, at which point Xavi said hello and thanked them for coming. As Xavi greeted all of these people, it occurred to him to wonder whether one of them was behind those devastating letters to Alfonso and his mother. Maybe they would never find out who it was, and maybe it didn't even matter now that his mother and his father had resolved their terrible misunderstanding, Xavi thought to himself as the never-ending line continued. But eventually something else began to nag at him—something that had been bothering him all afternoon. He glanced up at Alfonso. "Where's Santiago? I haven't seen him since I arrived."

His father hesitated, but another guest awaited greeting and he only replied, "I'm sure he'll be here soon."

Xavi worried about his former "cousin." Guilt for all the trouble he'd caused Santiago was starting to get to him again. His mind was spinning in all sorts of directions about where his currently MIA royal guard could be when he noticed someone else he knew intimately making her way toward him. His eyes widened and not from admiration. He watched as Isabel de Luna began chatting away with the king like she was already family.

Isabel looked as beautiful as ever, but her charms no longer worked on Xavi.

"My mother, the marquesa, sends her regards. She's so sorry not to make it tonight but would be happy to make the trip at your earliest convenience," Isabel gushed, fluttering her eyelashes at Alfonso in the process. "I'm sure we'll be seeing plenty of one another, given my, well, connections with the prince." She smiled brightly at Xavi now and placed a gloved hand on his arm.

Xavi's smile was frozen on his face. It took everything in him not to jerk away from her. "Isabel," he said.

She leaned toward him, but Xavi couldn't bring himself to give Isabel the traditional kiss on each cheek in greeting. Instead, he turned to the king. "Excuse me, but I want to catch up with my friend Isabel for a minute in private."

The king looked at Xavi and smiled kindly. "Of course, take your time. It was very nice to meet you," he said to Isabel, who flashed another glittering smile in return.

But Xavi was not having this charade. He led Isabel to the far corner of the room where they were slightly hidden by a tall marble statue of one of Spain's former queens. Xavi couldn't tell who at first, but when he figured it out, he nearly laughed. He'd dragged his ex-girlfriend right over to the queen who was her namesake, Isabella II, the powerful monarch who had ruled Spain for thirty-five years in the nineteenth century. Along the way, Xavi had grabbed a glass of cava from one of the waiters holding trays full of elegant flutes of Spain's answer to champagne. He took a long drink of it now and nearly finished the glass in one gulp.

Isabel stood there, aloof as ever, like the caricature of a monarch who would never mingle with the likes of Xavi's friends from the La Boqueria.

She was clearly preparing herself to be the recipient of Xavi's anger. "You can't even be polite to me tonight, Xavier?"

Xavi didn't respond. Instead, he finally took in her attire and realized she was wearing white like some kind of bride-to-be. "You are unbelievable," he said. "After all the havoc you've caused and people you've hurt? I can't even comprehend that there was a time I was falling for you."

A tiny gasp escaped Isabel's perfect mouth, and the smallest crack appeared in her haughty facade. "Falling for me?" she whispered. "As in falling in love with me?"

The shock in her voice almost made Xavi feel bad for her. When they were in their on-again, off-again state, Xavi wondered on more than one occasion whether Isabel had ever known what it was like to be loved, even by her own parents, or if she was simply impervious to feeling. "Yes, I was, Isabel," he said. "*Was*, past tense. If you had stopped conniving for once, you might have noticed how much I cared for you. We might even still be together."

Isabel's eyes filled with tears. "Oh," she whispered, and closed her eyes, lashes glistening. "But instead, now you hate me."

A heavy sigh emerged from Xavi. "I don't hate you."

Isabel opened one lovely eye. "You don't?"

Xavi shook his head. "No."

Isabel reached up and seemed about to throw her arms around him as though Xavi had just confessed he'd love to give their romance another chance, but he took a big step away before she could. He might not hate Isabel, but he'd certainly developed a massive allergy to her presence given all the damage she'd done to him and to Stefi. Not to mention Santiago and everyone else Xavi loved. "I don't hate you, but I need you to hear me, Isabel: You and I are over for good. If your showing up today was some kind of effort to get me back, it failed. If you think that because I am a prince and you come from a titled family, we are somehow meant to be, I can tell you right now that you're wrong. ¡Qué Fuerte! and all the gossip influencers in Spain can publish on their websites that you and I are to be married for all I care, but that isn't going to make it happen."

Another waiter appeared and offered the couple more cava.

Xavi exchanged his empty glass for a full one, and Isabel removed a flute from the tray for herself. She immediately took a sip. Xavi watched as the old Isabel composed herself before his eyes, the tears disappearing and her gaze hardening once more.

"With time, you may change your mind, Xavi." Isabel swept a hand across the room and all the posh people in it. "I saw your friends from La Boqueria, which I am sure is nice for you and your mother, but soon you'll realize they don't belong in a place like this, with people like this—with royalty like yourself. You'll want to be with someone who knows how to handle such situations."

"Isabel, I don't agree—"

"Just you wait and see," she said, unwilling to let him finish. "I'll be anticipating that day and I look forward to being there for you when it arrives."

Xavi didn't like the rueful warning in Isabel's voice, and in truth, it made a bead of dread form in his middle. He hoped she was wrong and that he was right, but he didn't want to stay and argue about it. "I think you should leave," he found himself saying, wanting to banish Isabel, and the thoughts she was trying to plant in him, from the room.

Isabel downed the rest of her cava. "Well, you can't send me away. Don't forget, I'm titled too, and you'll have to get used to me at future events because I don't plan on missing any."

Xavi was about to reply that there was nothing Isabel could ever do to redeem herself with him at this point, but his comment died away as he noticed Diego striding toward them.

Isabel narrowed her eyes. "Don't say I never cared for you, Xavi," she said as Diego joined them. She gestured at Xavi's best friend. "Case in point—I brought Diego here for you," she added, then stalked off.

Xavi wondered if this was true or just another manipulation tactic.

"Chaval, I told Isabel you were a lost cause as far as she was concerned," Diego said by way of greeting. "I don't think she'll ever give up, though, now that she knows you're the prince. Isabel will settle for nothing less than queen, I think."

The two young men looked at each other and started to laugh, then they hugged.

Diego leaned against the statue of Isabel's namesake. "I do think she cares for you deeply, and she does have a heart somewhere underneath all that couture." Diego gave Xavi's outfit a once-over. "You look awfully princely, I have to say."

Xavi laughed again. "Regardless of my feelings about Isabel, I'm glad she brought you to Madrid tonight."

"Just for the record, while I did come to see you, I'm really here in the hopes of seeing a certain royal guard," Diego admitted. His eyes darkened. "Have you seen or heard from Santiago? He stopped responding to my messages," he added with a sigh.

"No, I haven't seen him since we arrived at the palace," Xavi said. "I'm actually worried he's in trouble." Xavi was the one sighing now. "I hope he'll still remain my royal guard after today."

It was as though the two young men had conjured Santiago, because suddenly he was there, walking through the doors of the party and heading their way. Xavi glanced at Diego, who was watching Santiago approach like he had never seen anyone more handsome in his life. This pleased Xavi. He wanted their romance to work out. Someone should get a happy ending today. If it wasn't Xavi, he wanted it to be someone that he loved.

As Xavi took in Santiago's uniformed self, he was flooded with relief. "So you still have your job? And you look great in that getup, by the way."

Santiago nodded gravely. "I do still have my job, yes. Though after this reception I will be heading for Seville immediately."

Diego's thrilled expression vanished. "Seville? But—"

"But that was the price of the day's events. Seville or . . ." Santiago shrugged.

Xavi eyed his two friends, both standing carefully apart from one another. "Long-distance relationships can work, you know. And I'm sure I can help out with the logistics—"

"Xavi, there will be no long-distance. Not for me with, ah, any of your associates." Santiago looked away, his gaze seeking the open door onto the terrace.

"Santi." Diego sighed and tried to reach for Xavi's former guard, but Santiago stepped away.

Xavi shook his head. "You can still choose to return to Barcelona, you know."

"But I can't," Santiago said quietly and firmly. "This is my life."

Diego's eyes immediately filled with tears. He blinked them back, croaked, "Santi," then gave Santiago a desperate look and walked away abruptly, shaking his head. Xavi supposed he was too upset to speak or maybe he wanted to avoid a scene.

Santiago and Xavi watched him disappear through the doors to the terrace.

Xavi turned to his royal guard again—no, his former royal guard—

and his hope from earlier turned to dust. He wanted to scream. This was all so unacceptable—he wasn't with Stefi, and Diego and Santiago apparently couldn't be together. But of course, they could, *if* Santiago was willing to make the choice that would allow him to be with Diego.

He let out a long, frustrated breath. "Let's be honest here, Santiago, you can leave the guard if you want to." All the feelings inside him came pouring out. "I'm the one who doesn't have options. I'm the one who has this ridiculous birthright to honor, one that apparently is not so easy to abdicate. But you don't have any obligation to the royal family. Not really. You do not have to live some life according to tradition and bloodline. You can just go. You can quit and be with . . . whomever you want in peace. Blissful, anonymous peace." Xavi sighed.

Santiago was shaking his head. "It's not as easy as that for me either, Xavi. I do have my own birthright to consider, whether you understand that or not. My father . . . he was a hero to the palace and the king and I want to . . . no, I need to honor him. It's always been my dream, Xavi."

The two young men regarded one another for a long moment.

At this, all the fight went out of Xavi. He did understand why this choice was not so simple for Santiago, that it was anything but, and that it in fact came with as many familial expectations and griefs as his did. But then Xavi had an idea. Perhaps he was in a position to give one last gift to both his former royal guard and his best friend since childhood, plus get this letter to Stefi in the process.

Santiago seemed to sense Xavi was hatching some kind of plan. "Uh-oh, what is going on in your head? I can tell it's the kind of thing likely to jeopardize my job yet again."

Xavi was nodding, though not at Santiago's words. "What if I asked you to do something as your final act as my royal guard, something that only you are equipped to accomplish? Something that might also come with the opportunity of one long goodbye with Diego?" Xavi saw a little beam of hope enter Santiago's eyes and could tell that he was intrigued. A part of Xavi hoped that if Santiago agreed to do this, maybe Diego would have the time to convince Santiago not to take the posting in Seville. To follow his heart instead of his duty for once.

But Santiago groaned. "Like what, exactly?"

Xavi leaned closer. "Like deliver a note to someone important in Barcelona. And perhaps return my best friend home again, since I think he suddenly needs to get back urgently. And you, chaval, will have all those hours to talk to him, the entire drive from here to Barcelona to say whatever you need to before parting ways . . ."

Santiago was staring at Xavi. "You want me to *drive* to Barcelona? That will take all night."

Xavi put a firm hand on Santiago's shoulder. "Exactly. You are my royal guard, after all, and I am asking you, specifically, to do this for me."

"But I'm not actually your royal guard anymore," Santiago said.

"Maybe, but no one has told me this officially. Besides, what if I demanded that you go get the rest of my things in Barcelona and refused to take no for an answer? Because I think I may need my things immediately. I really want to feel at home here in the palace residence, as I'm sure you understand. Everyone else will understand too, since I'll convince them."

Santiago inhaled a long, hoarse breath. He held out his hand to Xavi. "Give me the note. I will get it to Stefi. But I'm not going to change my mind about anything else because of this scheme of yours."

Xavi shook his head. "I would never dream of that happening." He removed the official-looking envelope from inside his coat, and a spark of gratitude mixed with hope lit up inside him. Santiago was a good person; Xavi was lucky to know him. He made a wish that somehow over the long drive to Madrid, Santiago might have a change of heart about his own future with Diego.

Xavi handed the letter to Santiago, who put it inside his own jacket. Then Xavi glanced around the room and said, "Nos vemos, chaval. Off you go."

Santiago gave the prince one last long and meaningful look. "I won't forget this, Your Royal Highness," he said, then went to fetch Diego so they could be on their way.

# Forty

The next morning, Stefi, along with her mother, watched from the balcony above the plaza for Jason's taxi to arrive. It was another sunny day in Barcelona, but this time, the sun failed to warm Stefi's heart. She'd tossed and turned all night; sleep had refused to come. Her mind had spun and spun some more: Xavi. Jason. Xavi. Isabel. Jason. Amber. Croissants. The prince of Spain. ¡Qué Fuerte! and that photo. Isabel becoming the princess. Xavi, Xavi, Xavi. And maybe back to croissants again. Because Stefi had class at Hofmann today and she didn't plan on missing it. Especially not after the debacle with Oriol and especially not for Jason.

"Jason's plane must have landed late," Ana said, turning to her daughter.

Stefi was checking her phone again, and it wasn't to see if Jason had texted. She looked in case Xavi had contacted her, but the answer was still a depressing no. The more time that passed without Stefi hearing from Xavi, the more she knew she should wash her hands of the boy. Besides, now that she knew Xavi was actually the prince of Spain, the notion that he would choose to be with Stefi was beyond ridiculous. It not only was inconceivable, it meant he belonged with someone exactly like Isabel de Luna. But Stefi's heart still hurt at the thought Xavi had gotten back together with his beautiful ex. It hurt even worse at the thought that Stefi might never hear from him again, not even to break things off officially.

Stefi stared at the church across the plaza, her eyes traveling all the way up to its bells, which were about to chime out the time. Then her gaze fell lower and she searched the neighboring streets for a cab that might be Jason's. There was still no sign of him.

The hurt spreading through Stefi was like butter melting in a microwave. It made a teeny part of her wonder if she should hear Jason out once he arrived. But most of her knew to squelch this urge. Jason was not a worthy consolation prize. How could he be, after Xavi? Stefi sighed.

The bells chimed the hour, scattering the birds throughout the blue Barcelona sky with the noise. She was due at Hofmann in fifteen minutes.

Ana reached for her daughter's hand and squeezed it. "Sweetheart, you shouldn't wait. I'm glad you were able to reconcile with Amber, but you have no obligation to that boy. I'll speak to him when he arrives and explain that you and he can talk after you get back from class."

Another minute was already passing and the clock marched toward the time Stefi was due at Hofmann. Chef Arzak did not tolerate lateness. Students who arrived even one minute past the beginning of class weren't allowed to enter.

Ana pulled her daughter closer. "I know you're hurting, my Stefi, which is why it will be good for you to go and make some pastry. Baking always makes you feel better."

"I know," Stefi said.

With that, Stefi left the balcony and the apartment. She made her way through the narrow streets of El Gótico and onward into El Born. She hoped Ana was right, that a little baking might work its magic on her wounded heart, as it had always managed to in the past. And the very moment Stefi arrived in the sweltering kitchen with its shiny, metal surfaces, its canisters full of flour and sugar, and its fridges packed with giant blocks of butter, a kind of peace flowed through her body. It was a feeling she seemed to experience only while making cakes and tarts and muffins and, yes, even now as she attempted the croissant at the famous Hofmann culinary school after the prince of Spain had broken her heart.

Chef Arzak smiled and nodded at Stefi on her way in, which Stefi took as a positive sign. "It's good to see you again, Estefanía," she said warmly.

Yes, the day was already getting better.

"Thank you, Chef, you too," Stefi answered, and took her place at the station next to her new friend and croissant-making peer Susana. "Buenos días," Stefi said to her neighbor and began to set up her things.

Susana answered with a smile. "Glad you came back. I was a little worried Oriol's behavior might have scared you off."

"I might not be here if it weren't for you," Stefi told her gratefully.

Susana waved this off. "We women have to stick together in culinary school. Also, Oriol is an asshole. I'm glad he's gone." She nodded at their classmates around the room. "So is everyone else. He wasn't nice to anyone, really."

Ana had been right to send Stefi off to bake. The longer Stefi rolled butter into dough, doing her best to perfect her pastry layers, working hard and sweating harder, the lighter she felt. Happiness was returning, despite all the chaos of her life. This was another one of the things she'd always loved about baking. It was predictable, it was exact, it was based on the order of things—often quite literally, the order in which you put things into a bowl, the order in which you added the ingredients that would affect the outcome of their chemistry. Stefi might have made mistakes with respect to the romantic chemistry in her life, but she didn't make mistakes when it came to the chemistry of flour and water and baking soda and butter. What a relief!

But after Stefi put her dough into the freezer to cool for the requisite five minutes and returned to her station, Susana nudged her.

"So, there's a guy at the door," she said. "He's staring through the window at you."

For one glorious second, Stefi's heart lifted as it beat out Xavi's name. But then that same heart plummeted as hard as a soufflé near a pair of stomping feet.

Jason stood outside, a giant bouquet of flowers in his arms.

Their eyes locked.

He saw her see him.

An icy cold shot through Stefi. How had Jason known where to find her? Her mother would never have sent him to interrupt Stefi's class. She tried to remember if she'd told Jason her plans for Hofmann this summer. She didn't think she had. Could Amber have told him?

"You'd better see what he wants before Chef Arzak notices him," Susana advised.

Stefi glanced at Chef, who was busy with another student who'd left his pastry dough in the freezer so long, it was frozen stiff. Stefi ran quickly to the door, hoping Chef would assume she was headed to the bathroom. After yesterday, Stefi didn't want any more disruptions in class on her behalf. Her presence here seemed delicate enough already.

Jason's eyes lit up the moment she emerged. "Stefi!"

She put her finger to her lips and clicked the door shut quietly behind her. She beckoned Jason to follow her down the hall so they could talk and not be heard inside the kitchen. They arrived at a nook with chairs and tables where students hung out on their breaks.

Stefi turned to face Jason. She studied this person who'd been her boyfriend for so many years and tried to decide how she felt about him now. The strangest thing was how, earlier in the summer, after she'd caught Jason with Amber and as she was arriving in Barcelona, Stefi had fantasized about a moment just like this one. Jason would surprise her by making the trip here to ask Stefi to get back together because he'd realized what a grave mistake he'd made by cheating. And like in some kind of movie, her fantasy was coming true, yet she felt no satisfaction about it.

"Hi, Jason," was all Stefi managed to sigh.

Jason stood there waiting for her to say more, and Stefi found that she saw him with new eyes. Here was this person she'd thought she'd been in love with. But had she really? She'd cared for him, of course, but when they'd gotten together way back when, they were both so young; they'd barely started high school. Stefi hadn't really known who she was, and in so many ways, dating Jason had prevented her from figuring this out, from searching inside herself to discover her own likes and desires. Instead, her wants had conformed to Jason's, her interests to his own. This wasn't all his fault either. Stefi had happily allowed this to happen; she had even welcomed it.

Once again, she had the thought that Jason and Amber did her a favor.

Meanwhile, Jason was staring at Stefi like he had never seen her before either. He seemed to have forgotten the flowers in his arms. The roses drooped in the heat of the Barcelona day and the petals were turning black at the ends. This seemed rather fitting, Stefi decided, both for the situation with Jason and for the state of her heart post-Xavi. The longer Stefi's silence went on, the more worried Jason's eyes grew.

Now he was the one to sigh. "Stefi, I can understand why you don't want to talk to me," he began. "I came all this way because there are things I need to say that should only be said in person. The first of which is, I'm so sorry for what happened. And I really wanted to look you in the eye when I told you this. I'm sorry," he said again, staring at her hard. Then he waited.

But what was he waiting for, exactly? Stefi wondered.

For Stefi to say, *Hooray, I never stopped loving you*?

She could hear that Jason's apology was from the heart, though. "I just wish you'd broken up with me before you got together with Amber. Then maybe we could have found a way to be friends."

The hope that had entered Jason's eyes after his plea to Stefi faltered. "Just friends?" Jason hung his head. "You're right, but Amber and I . . . we . . . I guess I didn't know how to tell you I wanted to be with another girl and that girl was also your best friend."

Stefi wasn't going to let Jason excuse away what he did so easily. "Yes, but it still would have been better to find out because you told me, not by walking in on you two hooking up."

Jason raised his gaze to Stefi's again. "I know, and I'm sorry for being so totally stupid." Jason seemed to remember the flowers and he held the giant dying bouquet of roses out to Stefi.

She didn't take them—she didn't want them. She put her flour-caked fists on her hips in answer. "You can keep your flowers, Jason."

The look in Jason's eyes was of shock. His whole demeanor was starting to make Stefi angry.

"But I crossed an ocean to give you these and apologize," he said, as though he'd truly believed Stefi was going to take him back without much convincing.

This reminded Stefi of all the other anger she'd felt earlier this summer, and now her insides began to boil. She shook her head no and gestured back and forth between them. "There is nothing you can say or do, no flowers in the universe that would make me say yes to being your girlfriend ever again, Jason." He retracted his arm when it was clear Stefi really wasn't taking the flowers. But Stefi wasn't finished. "And you should have asked me if I wanted to see you before you got on that plane. My life here is complicated enough already."

The flowers were getting crushed underneath Jason's arm, petals dropping to the floor in a shower of disappointment. "I tried to tell you I was coming but I gave up! You weren't writing me back."

"That should have been your answer," Stefi said. She did her best to tamp down the frustration surging higher and higher within her. "You should go back home and try and make amends with Amber, not me. I know she cares for you a lot."

"But I didn't come all this way to be rejected," Jason said.

Enough was enough. Stefi could put her whole self into the industrial freezer in the pastry lab and it wouldn't make a dent in her emotional temperature. "Are you not listening to anything I've said? I don't want you back! I've moved on, Jason, and I need you to accept this!" Stefi lowered her voice. She didn't want Chef Arzak to come out and find her arguing with her ex-boyfriend. "Jason, you cheated on me with my best friend," she hissed. "But that doesn't even matter because I don't want you anymore."

"And I told you I was very sorry! *Really* sorry."

"Just because I appreciate the apology doesn't mean I still love you!"

Jason seemed to hear Stefi's words like they were a slap. "But Stefi, we have so much history!" He was the one hissing now. "You can't just throw it all away!"

Stefi glanced down the hall toward her class; she really needed to get back inside. Her dough was probably frozen. "Yes we do, Jason, and you are the one who threw it all away the moment you hooked up with Amber."

There was a trash can nearby and Jason walked to it, shoved the flowers inside the bucket, then turned around again to Stefi. "This is because of that other guy, isn't it," he snapped.

His comment startled Stefi. Could Amber have told Jason about Xavi? No, she wouldn't do that after everything. Besides, as far as Stefi knew, Jason and Amber weren't speaking. But then Stefi recalled that Jason had somehow found her at Hofmann today. For the second time this morning, her heart sank like a doomed soufflé. "Wait a minute," she said. "How did you know I'd be at this pastry class?"

Jason stared at her like he knew something she didn't. "It wasn't that difficult."

"Humor me and explain."

"I saw the photo, Stefi," he said.

Stefi swallowed. "What photo do you mean?"

"*The* photo. Stop playing dumb. The one of you making out with that guy who's supposedly a prince? And right." Jason huffed. "Like he's actually the prince of Spain."

"Oh my God." Stefi's heart was skipping beats and she thought she might faint. "But who sent you that picture?"

Jason's expression turned bitter. "It was pretty much the first thing that came up on my phone when my plane landed. Some guy from your class here did some kind of tell-all about you that appeared in a Spanish gossip paper this morning? Oriol somebody? He gave your full name, this location. He practically put a pin in a GPS map and Google translate was particularly helpful. So after I read the interview, I came straight here in a taxi to talk to you."

Stefi nearly plopped down on the floor, her legs were so rubbery. After Chef kicked Oriol out yesterday, he must have decided to get revenge.

"I'm not the only one who knew how to find you either." Jason glanced behind him.

"What are you talking about?"

"Stefi, you seriously don't know?" he asked.

Stefi didn't. Chef prohibited phones in class. Which had been a relief, since at least she would stop checking her phone for messages from Xavi for the duration.

Jason gestured in the direction of the main doors of the building.

"There's probably a hundred paparazzi on the street waiting for you to come out after class. When I arrived, they were already gathered there. I just pretended I was a student to get in." Jason sat down on one of the chairs and put his head in his hands. "Just go outside and check. I'm not lying, Stefi."

Stefi closed her eyes. Could her life get any crazier? No, she decided. It couldn't.

This was how Stefi found herself taking Jason's advice to go and check for herself. She wound her way along the hall toward the school's main entrance. She peered outside and immediately saw that Jason was telling the truth. Up and down the streets, crowded in this dark corner of El Born, dozens of people with cameras waited. It was a veritable paparazzi-fest.

Before Stefi could think, before she could remember she was still wearing her apron, that Jason was sitting inside Hofmann waiting for her to return and finish their conversation, that she was sweaty and covered head to toe in flour and butter, she pushed through the doors and into the cobbled street. She needed to get home; she needed to get away. She hoped that the paparazzi wouldn't pay any attention to the girl caked in dough wearing a chef's hat, her hair shoved in a knot underneath it. Maybe they wouldn't recognize Stefi if she acted fast. She elbowed her way through the crowd with determination.

"Con permiso," she squeaked, yanking her chef's hat lower.

At first, her plan seemed to work. No one recognized her. She got through the crowd and was about to turn to the right and around the safety of the corner when she heard someone shout. "¿Es ella? ¡Sí, es ella! ¿Stefi? ¡Stefi! ¡Stefi!"

Now she took off in a run.

# Forty-One

Santiago gripped Diego's hand across the gearshift like he might never let it go. Diego's palm was smaller than his; it was soft and warm and fit perfectly within his own. He pulled off the highway heading toward the center of Barcelona at the tail end of their very long drive. At a red light, Santiago glanced over at the boy next to him, his eyes full of love.

Diego returned his loving stare right back.

Santiago's heart grew so big, he thought it might expand beyond his chest.

"What are you thinking, Santi?" Diego asked.

Santiago didn't speak—not at first. He watched the cars coming down the hill through the Eixample as they idled on Gran Vía, thinking a whole traffic jam of conflicting things. Among them were that Diego looked so handsome in his semiformal reception attire, though he'd removed his tie over the course of their long drive. He thought Diego was one of the sweetest, smartest, most charming people he had ever met, that he was kind and generous to his friends, and, most important of all, that Diego had posed a grand gesture of a question to Santiago in the wee hours of the morning. It immediately set off fireworks of joy in Santiago's heart and at the same time was like an ominous bomb exploding in his brain. He knew, too, that the moment to give Diego an answer had arrived. This whole summer, Santiago's head was yanking him in one direction while his heart pulled him in the opposite one in an ongoing tug-of-war about his future and what it was meant to be.

But the jefe of the Guardia Real had been crystal clear with him, and he knew this.

Diego leaned toward Santiago from the passenger seat and planted a gentle kiss on his cheek.

Santiago closed his eyes at the soft press of Diego's lips against his skin.

When Diego pulled away, he spoke. "I think I already know your decision, and it's okay, I understand. It's wrong for me to ask you to give up so much for a relationship so recently begun."

Santiago turned toward Diego, but Diego was staring straight ahead through the windshield at his home city stretching out before them. The sun was already high in the sky, and though the heat wave may have passed, the day promised to be a hot one.

"It's better this way anyhow," Diego went on. "If we had let things drag on between us in secret, it would only be more difficult later. I'm glad we had this drive together so we could at least say goodbye." Diego seemed to be having a conversation with himself, and yet Santiago wasn't stopping him. "A clean break is best, so after you drop me off at home, I think we should stop talking. No calls, no messages. Maybe one day we can be friends again, but it will take me a while before I'll be ready for that. I hope you can understand and respect this."

The cars behind them began to honk their horns. The light had turned green, but Santiago had no idea how long it had been that way. He broke his stare with Diego to step on the gas, and their SUV jerked forward.

"No," Santiago cried out. "No, no, no!"

Diego seemed startled by his shouts. "No, you can't respect my wishes?"

Now Santiago was flying through the green lights one after the other, across Gran Vía, past the end of Rambla Catalunya, and onward around the fountain at the center of Passeig de Gràcia. Soon they'd take the right down Via Laietana toward El Gótico and Stefi, and their long night and morning of driving would come to an end. "No, no, no—"

"But Santi, I don't think it's too much for me to ask—"

"No, Diego, stop. Wait. *Wait*. You're misunderstanding my no!"

The light at the corner of Pau Claris turned red and Santiago slammed on the brakes. Both young men flew forward but were restrained by their seat belts; their breaths coming quickly and unevenly.

Two hearts were on the line, after all.

"Perdona," Santiago said to Diego and checked to make sure that he was all in one piece, that his unpredictable driving hadn't caused any bruising to the boy's perfect skin or other damage. Diego was absolutely flawless as he was, and Santiago would never forgive himself if he was responsible for altering this.

Diego was blinking quickly and staring into his lap. "Perdona for stopping short or for your inability to respect my wishes about not talking after today?"

As Santiago stared at an ever sadder Diego in the passenger seat, his heart finally and decisively won the battle with his brain. Because Santiago's words were all a jumble inside him, he did the only thing he could to try and clarify what he meant—and what he wanted.

He took both his hands and turned Diego's face his way.

Then he pulled Diego closer.

Santiago kissed him. He kissed this perfect and perfectly handsome person like he was the only boyfriend Santiago could ever dream of having and like he was falling in love with Diego because he absolutely was. Diego's mouth was sweet on Santiago's own and he never wanted to pull away, not even when the cars behind them once again began to protest loudly. So amid the brass band of angry traffic at the center of Barcelona, Santiago finally pulled back from the boy of his dreams and said, "I'm falling in love with you, Diego, and I don't think I can be without you. I've made my decision. I'm not going to Seville. I'm going to leave the guard." Santiago's brain skidded in protest at this news but his heart beat triumphant in his chest.

Then he grabbed the wheel again and made the right turn down Via Laietana.

Now it was Diego's turn at silence.

Was Santiago too late with his decision? With this news of his commitment to stay?

Soon Santiago heard a sniffle.

He glanced over and saw a tear rolling down Diego's cheek.

"Is that a tear of happiness or of regret?" he asked.

Diego sniffled again. "Are you sure about this, Santi?"

Santiago's brain once again signaled down to his chest and tried to short-circuit his heart, but once more his brain failed to do so. In truth, Santiago wasn't certain about his decision, and he worried one day he'd regret giving up everything he'd ever wanted for the boy sitting in the passenger seat of this royal vehicle. But it was a risk Santiago knew he needed to take. Either way, he might have regrets—if he went to Seville his heart would be broken, and if he didn't he was choosing not to follow in his father's footsteps. Yet for the first time in Santiago's life, he would let his heart lead the way and it was leading him straight to this person next to him, so close he could take his hand. Santiago knew that if he went to Seville, he would not only sacrifice his ability to weave Diego's fingers between his own whenever he liked but also forfeit the chance to press his lips to Diego's again when his whole body yearned to do this and only this as many times as Diego would allow.

Santiago sped through another green light on his way down the hill.

"But that means you're going to give up your job as guard," Diego said.

"Yes, I am. And I want to. For you. I can't remain a royal guard if I am dating the prince's best friend after everything that's happened, and what I want most is to date the prince's best friend. Which would be you, Diego."

Diego sighed. And then he inhaled and was about to say something more, but Santiago never found out what it was because other, urgent matters suddenly called for their attention.

The two boys saw a familiar American just ahead, on the corner of a tiny street, Joan Massana, where it met Via Laietana at the entrance to El Born.

Diego pointed. "Is that—"

"Stefi?" Santiago finished. "I think so."

"She looks a bit panicked," Diego observed.

And very disheveled, Santiago thought to himself.

He slowed the car, and the two boys stared at the American girl who was covered in flour, her T-shirt smeared with butter and grease, and a chef's hat nearly over her eyes. She was waiting for the walk sign so she could cross, but she also seemed to be debating running straight into the road and trying to dodge the cars. Santiago was about to laugh, remembering another time not so long ago when he and Xavi had run into Stefi in a similar state, when he noticed the crowd emerging from down the street and behind her.

"Joder," Diego said.

"Paparazzi!" Santiago swerved across the traffic, causing all the surrounding vehicles to honk at him in protest for the third time in barely twenty minutes, then pulled up in front of Stefi. Diego had already scrambled over the seats into the back and was reaching for the door handle.

Stefi stared in horror at the SUV now blocking her from crossing Via

Laietana. She looked like she was about to run left, down the hill toward La Barceloneta, when Santiago lowered the dark tinted window on the driver's side and called to her, "Stefi, stop, it's us!"

Diego flung open the back door, shouting, "Come on, get in!" and beckoning Stefi inside.

Given the oncoming traffic, not to mention the approaching paparazzi flying up the street in an ever-larger mass, Santiago hoped Stefi would hurry. The paparazzi were shouting for Stefi to stop and yelling her name and asking all kinds of invasive, demanding questions.

"Stefi! Give us a smile!"

"Are you in love with the prince?"

"Are you and the prince having sex?"

"Is the prince a good kisser?"

"Stefi, is that butter you're wearing?"

Between these deeply personal questions plus the growing sound of clicking cameras, Stefi made her decision. Santiago watched with relief as Stefi dove into the back seat. Diego quickly slammed the door behind her just as the paparazzi reached the car and began to surround it, pounding on the windows and trying to snap images of Stefi and whoever she was with. Good thing that from the outside, the windows were practically as dark as the SUV itself.

"Go, go, go!" Diego shouted to Santiago, blocking Stefi's body with his own.

Oh so heroically, Santiago thought.

Santiago's foot hit the gas and they zoomed back up the hill that was Via Laietana as the paparazzi ran through the street after them. Santiago watched the crowd of camera-toting men and women clogging one of Barcelona's most trafficked roads, snapping photos of the escaping car.

Stefi was crouched near the floor and panting. Santiago could hear her behind the driver's seat. "Stefi, it's safe. Nobody is following us." He turned down a tiny deserted alley and came to a stop. He opened the glove compartment and pulled out an ornate blue glass bottle. "Water?" he offered, handing it over the back seat.

Her chest still heaving, Stefi took it, opened the cap, and gulped some down.

Santiago and Diego exchanged a glance and some raised eyebrows.

Even though Stefi was a mess, Santiago could see why Xavi was so taken with the girl. She was pretty, certainly, but she was also real. He had always thought that Xavi dating Stefi was a royal disaster waiting to happen—and in a way, it had turned out to be just this. But for the first time, he found himself doing an about-face where Stefi was concerned. Maybe it was because Santiago had so recently decided to follow his own heart, but he suddenly hoped Stefi would forgive the prince for his errors of omission and give him another chance. If Santiago got to be happy, shouldn't Xavi get to be happy too? And with the girl he truly liked, regardless of her background? And Stefi was obviously a lovely, down-to-earth person, much like Xavi and also much like Marta. Exactly the kind of girl who deserved to date royalty. Their story could become Spain's own royal fairy tale, if they could only get through the slightly challenging complication they faced at this moment.

The two young men watched as Stefi finished the water, wiped her mouth, and suddenly seemed to realize where she was and who she was with.

"So, ah, hello again," she finally said. She looked from one to the other. "Diego. Santiago."

"Surprise?" Diego tried.

"I see you haven't stopped taking your pastry class," Santiago observed, gesturing at her floury attire. She even had dough caked on her knees.

Stefi raised her chin. "And why should I?"

"I can also see why Xavi likes you," Santiago said quietly.

Hearing Xavi's name seemed to cause Stefi to wince. "I wouldn't know. It's not as though he's been in touch. It's also not as though I even knew him it all, as it turns out."

"Stefi," Diego said. "Why do you think Santiago and I are here? We came to find you."

"You couldn't have just called? Or texted?" Stefi asked.

Santiago and Diego exchanged another glance.

"The past twenty-four hours have been complicated," Santiago said.

Stefi studied Santiago in the driver's seat. She crossed her arms over her chest. "I'm listening."

Santiago heard a tiny bit of hope enter Stefi's voice. It was time he gave her Xavi's letter. He reached inside his jacket and pulled the envelope from the pocket. "I'm here to present you with a letter, Stefi." He held it out to her. "From the prince."

Stefi sat there staring at it, unmoving.

He pushed the letter closer. "Take it. Diego and I drove all the way from Madrid overnight on Xavi's orders to deliver this to you. He's desperate to be in touch. You can at least read what he has to say."

At this, Stefi uncrossed her arms and reached for the letter.

Diego and Santiago watched hopefully as Stefi opened the envelope. The stationery was almost too beautiful to touch, and yet Stefi's buttery fingers were already staining the paper.

Just before she started reading, Stefi looked up and asked, "What could Xavi possibly say after everything that's happened? 'Sorry I didn't mention the part about how I'm the prince of Spain, and oh, by the way, I've gotten back together with my ex, Isabel'?"

Santiago shook his head. "Whatever Xavi says, that's between you and him. But I can promise you, Isabel is not in the picture where Xavi is concerned." With that, he turned around, started the car, and made his way slowly down the narrow street once more. He rounded one corner, then another. He'd drive in circles all over Barcelona until Stefi made her decision about what to do. No, until Stefi decided she was willing to at least hear Xavi out.

Santiago really was hoping for a happy, romantic ending for everybody in his life.

Diego and Santiago exchanged another adoring glance, this time in the rearview mirror.

Stefi dropped her gaze and began to read.

Though Xavi hadn't told Santiago the exact words he'd written to Stefi, he knew this much:

The letter contained an invitation to the palace.

# Forty-Two

Xavi didn't know how much longer he could stand to wait without any word from Stefi or Santiago or anybody else. He paced his opulent bedroom and then he paced the terrace outside it, eyes on the fountain below and the drive that led up to the palace. It was getting dark, and soon the light would be gone from the sky. Stefi's name had gotten into the press today, and photos of her were already popping up all over on the gossip sites, plus various people were talking about her to the press, claiming to know all sorts of things about Stefi and her family. He hated the thought of her going through this all alone.

Xavi wondered if Stefi had read his letter yet.

He wondered, too, if during the long ride to Barcelona, Santiago had decided to follow his heart. He would be thrilled for Diego and Santiago if they found a way to be together. At least two people in his life deserved to have their romance, and these were two people Xavi would be glad for if they got their happy ending.

But would he and Stefi too?

He needed his damn phone back already!

Xavi leaned over the carved stone railing of the terrace looking out at the darkening evening. A long black Escalade was coming up the gravel drive, kicking up pebbles as it approached. Xavi's heart flipped inside his chest.

The vehicle came to a stop at the palace entrance.

He peered into the darkness and saw that it was his mother and the king, returning from their date. Xavi thought he should probably look away and give his parents their privacy, but he found that he couldn't. Alfonso jumped out from the back of the car and ran around to the other side to open the door for Marta. Her laughter floated up through the air to where Xavi stood watching. His mother's face was radiant. She let Alfonso take her hand and help her out.

"Tonight was wonderful," she told his father.

Who beamed back at Marta.

Then his mother rose on her toes to kiss the king.

Now Xavi turned away.

So many thoughts collided in his brain. The sheer fact that his mother had been on a date with his father, for one, a father he had only recently learned existed and almost equally recently had started to like and trust. But this also meant his mother was on a date—was dating?—the king of Spain. Right. What would happen if they kept on dating? Then Marta would become the king of Spain's girlfriend. Now Xavi wondered when and if they would announce this to the public and how that public would react when they did. And then what if things between them progressed even further? What if they decided to get *married*? There would probably be a royal wedding. It might even be televised. No, of course it would be televised! Then Marta would become the king of Spain's *wife*! Which would make her the queen of Spain?

Xavi shook his head. His mother, the famous tortilla-making owner of La Buena, becoming the queen of Spain seemed an impossibility. Then again, so did Xavi being the prince of Spain, and yet he was exactly this. He sincerely hoped the person behind the forged letters was dead by now. If not, they likely weren't at all happy about Marta and Alfonso finding their way back to one another for a date, never mind one day soon getting married. But Xavi was getting ahead of himself and ahead of his parents too.

It was too early to predict such a future for his mother. Xavi promised himself, though, that no matter what happened with his mother and Alfonso, if they wanted to be together, he would be happy for his parents. Marta deserved happiness wherever and however it arrived, even if she had to become the queen of Spain to find that happiness.

The magnitude of this turn in his mother's life distracted Xavi for a few blissful minutes and kept him from thinking about Stefi. Xavi knew it was futile to watch the gravel drive that led up to the palace's front entrance in the hopes that Santiago would arrive, toting Stefi along with him, but Xavi couldn't help himself. He had been keeping an eye on it off and on all night.

Now he parked himself on the elaborately carved chair in front of his desk. Seconds later he stood up again and crossed the room to the silk brocade upholstered couch on the other side. And then he got up once more and climbed onto the bed, unable to sit still or get comfortable. Finally there was a knock on his door and he raced to answer it. He took a deep breath, preparing to see Santiago on the other side but hoping it might be Stefi instead. When he opened it, his eyes were not met by Stefi's or even Santiago's.

His valet, Luis, was standing there, looking as grave as always. "Sir, you have some small friends who want to see you," he said.

At this, two adorable sheepdog puppies bounded into the room and circled Xavi's legs, sniffing and jumping. How could Xavi's spirits not be lifted by such wonderful, enthusiastic visitors? He crouched down and let them lick his face all over, laughing as they did.

Luis was still very erect in the doorway. "May I leave Vermut and Oliva with you or should I take them away?"

The two puppies that Alfonso decided to name after the popular catalán aperitif as a gesture to Marta and Xavi's heritage were still busy licking Xavi's cheeks. He glanced up at Luis and nodded. "Thank you for bringing them. Yes, of course they can stay."

The valet closed the door and left Xavi with his furry guests.

The puppies had been Xavi's idea, a gift he hoped Alfonso would appreciate. He knew about Alfonso's love for his own father's dogs when he was younger, and Xavi hoped that the father and son raising these puppies together could be a bond they'd share as they moved forward getting to know one another. Plus, what could be better than silly, floppy, furry sheepdogs with love for everyone who came into the room to lighten up the mood of a palace?

Vermut plopped himself onto the floor and lay his head on Xavi's thigh while Oliva ran back and forth underneath the massive bed, sniffing as she went. Xavi scratched behind Vermut's ears and felt as soothed by this as he hoped Vermut was.

Xavi sat there petting Vermut and laughing at Oliva's endless energy as he waited for news about Stefi to arrive and found himself wishing he could go back to the start of summer for a redo. If only he could meet Stefi for the first time again. The moment an opportunity arrived, he would tell her he was the prince of Spain. That the royal institutions of this country were old and antiquated and outdated but that one of the things he planned to do as soon as he assumed his royal birthright was change some of the expectations for royals. For example, he would ensure that a prince like himself could date an untitled American girl like Stefi without it being such a big deal.

Then again, things at the palace were already in the process of changing without Xavi. Just look at his mother and the king.

Hours seemed to pass, and eventually Xavi got up from the floor and climbed onto the bed; the puppies settled around him on top of the comforter. He stretched out his legs, his back against the headboard, trying to stay awake, but his eyelids were drooping.

Then a knock sounded, startling Xavi.

He looked around, confused—had he fallen asleep?

The clock on the wall said three a.m.

Oliva lifted her head, then dropped it again, closing her eyes.

Xavi got up from the bed, careful not to disturb the slumbering puppies, and made his way to the door. When he opened it, Xavi blinked, then blinked again.

Standing there was Santiago, but he was alone.

The prince's heart plummeted.

"Chaval," Santiago said by way of hello. He glanced down the hall to his left nervously, then back at Xavi. "Are you awake or what?"

Xavi did his best to breathe. "Stefi doesn't want to see me," he supplied. His chest constricted.

Santiago opened his mouth to respond, but someone else got there first.

The American girl stepped into the doorway. "Stefi is right here," she said, meeting Xavi's eyes. Her hair was rather flat on one side, her T-shirt was wrinkled and stained, her shorts were rumpled, and her legs seemed caked with bits of dough. Flour flecked the skin of her arms and even the side of her neck. Xavi had never seen Stefi more beautiful than she was right now, this minute.

Santiago was staring at Xavi, eyebrows raised. "And FYI, we may have had some run-ins with the paparazzi along the way," he said.

But Xavi wasn't listening to Santiago; his eyes were fixed on Stefi.

"You should have told me, Xavi," Stefi said, and took a single step into his room, glancing to the left and right, up and down, taking in the sight of it.

A single step was better than none, Xavi decided. His heart lifted a bit. "I know," he said. "I should have, and I didn't, and I will be sorry for the rest of my life for not telling you my secret."

At this, Santiago left, closing the door quietly behind the couple so they could talk in private.

Xavi and Stefi were finally alone, after all the chaos of the past forty-eight hours.

She looked above her at the frescoed ceiling and then all around at this gilded, opulent place, so different than the bedroom where Xavi had slept his whole life in Barcelona. She shook her head like she might be seeing things, then met his eyes. "I can't believe you're really the prince of Spain" was all she said.

"But I'm still Xavi, the person you met at La Buena cooking tortillas."

Stefi cocked her head, studying him. "You are and you aren't." She sighed.

Xavi examined the contents of his heart and knew it was now or never. He had to say the words he had been rehearsing on the off chance that she would accept his invitation to the palace. "Stefi . . ."

She took another step closer. "Yes, Xavi?"

"I meant what I said in the letter," he began.

Stefi raised a single, skeptical eyebrow. "Which part?"

Now it was Xavi who took a step closer to Stefi, so close he could nearly reach a hand out to touch her. And oh, how badly he wanted to do just this. "The part in the letter where I said I was falling in love with you." Xavi took a breath. There. He'd said it. "And that I am hoping you will give me—us—a second chance."

The expression on Stefi's face was unreadable.

A long silence passed, and Xavi thought his heart might fall out of his chest from anticipation. He'd had so much time to think in the past couple of days, and during most of it he'd assumed that being with Stefi was a lost cause for him. And the thought of losing her made Xavi realize so many important things about how he truly felt about Stefi. The biggest realization of all was that he might not simply be falling for Stefi, he might have already fallen and hard. Xavi wanted this very down-to-earth, croissant-making girl standing before him with all the desire within him.

"Before I can make a decision," Stefi finally said, "I need to know something first."

"Anything," Xavi said.

Her eyes narrowed. "I need to see if the prince is a good kisser. The tortilla-making guy of my summer fling definitely was, but the guy who lives in this place?" She looked around again. "I'm not so sure. It's a bit stuffy."

Xavi bit his lip, trying not to smile. "I think that could be arranged."

Stefi fought back her own smile and said, "Oh, yeah?"

"Definitely," Xavi said and closed the distance between them, a distance that had begun with rumors and viral photos and paparazzi chases and helicopter rides and long, long drives back and forth from Madrid to Barcelona and the possibility that this young Catalan and this pastry-making American might never see one another again.

But that is not how their story was coming to an end, at least not at the moment, because Xavi and Stefi were right here, together, in the same palace room, and best of all, now they were together in each other's arms, and nothing else could possibly matter—not even all the photo-snapping paparazzi publishing a thousand photos of the couple on every gossip site in the online universe. Or even a million.

As Xavi pressed his lips to Stefi's, his heart leaped and it flew.

Stefi was giving him a second chance.

Like his father with Marta, Xavi wouldn't waste it. As his kiss with Stefi deepened and he pulled her even closer, the prince of Spain knew that this flour-covered, dough-caked girl was the only one for him. He couldn't wait to make the rest of Spain fall as hard for Stefi as he had on his one final summer before his country found out that they indeed had an heir to the throne, and a very handsome one at that.

# Epilogue

## Stefi and the Prince of Spain

## THE NEXT MORNING

Stefi blinked up at the frescoed ceiling of the palace room. Stars dotted it like the night sky, mapping out the constellations. The residence was quiet except for the occasional church bell chiming the hour because La Zarzuela had its own chapel. A gentle breeze moved through the air from the open terrace doors. Correction, the open veranda doors, Stefi decided, because anything that big and made of marble could not be deemed a simple terrace. Priceless paintings dotted the walls, and expensive vases adorned different surfaces. There was even a regal-looking statue in the corner that Stefi supposed had been carved by some famous Spanish artist.

She stretched out her arms and legs, the sheets fine and soft against her skin.

Then she turned to her left.

The one other thing that adorned this beautiful room, the most important one of all, was the young, handsome prince who lay snoozing in the bed next to Stefi. She took this opportunity to study Xavi as he slept: The sloping curve of his shoulder and the shape of his arm thrown out on top of the billowy comforter. The beautiful, smooth skin of Xavi's torso, the sharply carved muscles of his chest, that wild hair fanning across the pillow. The look on Xavi's face was of complete and utter peace and slumber. She wondered if Xavi had any idea how seductive he was, just lying there and not moving. She wanted to kiss his lips so badly.

Stefi looked down at her own attire, the polka-dotted pajama pants and matching button-down pajama shirt that were far too big for Stefi's frame because they were Xavi's. Her own dirty, sweaty clothes were in a pile on the floor of the most beautiful bathroom Stefi had ever seen. Its blue and white traditional tiles were hand-painted.

Unlike Xavi, Stefi had not slept a wink. How could she?

How was she even in this gigantic bed next to a boy who was actually the heir to the Spanish throne? Just yesterday, Stefi had to face her ex, Jason, who'd flown all the way from the United States in order to try and win her back, after which Stefi somehow went straight from her pastry class at Hofmann to this palace residence in Madrid, with paparazzi chasing after her, to see her summer fling who had turned out to be royalty. Whose spare pajamas she changed into after showering in that magnificent bathroom, because remaining in her pastry-making attire even another minute was untenable. All this in a mere few hours. On the ride from Barcelona, Stefi had called her family and managed to convince them not to worry about her, at least not yet, and to give her some time to figure this out with Xavi. But Stefi knew she'd only temporarily held off the many complications that had suddenly befallen her life and everyone in it. Eventually—as in very soon, likely even today—she would have to begin sorting them out.

Last night, after one initial, glorious kiss of reunion, Stefi and Xavi sat down face to face on the carpet at the foot of his enormous bed, Stefi's hair still wet from her shower. And they had talked. They talked and talked until they were both so sleepy, they climbed up onto that bed to nap before they got up and talked some more. So far there was only the one kiss, because an unspoken agreement had unfolded between them—if and when they kissed again, this would occur only after they figured out a few crucial details about who they were to one another and who they were willing to become for the rest of the citizens of Spain.

The stakes were low, in other words, Stefi thought to herself sarcastically.

A raw vulnerability opened inside her as she and Xavi talked about all the obstacles that stood between them and the possibility of their being together. They'd exchanged so many what-ifs and what-abouts during those long hours of conversation, it made Stefi's head spin to remember.

What if Isabel plotted her revenge?

What about the fact that Stefi was not royal?

What about Stefi's abuelita and her family?

What about Marta, Xavi's mother—what would she say and want for her son?

What if the king didn't want Xavi dating a commoner?

What if the king didn't want Xavi dating an *American* commoner?

What if the people of Spain didn't accept Stefi?

Because what if they didn't want their prince dating an American commoner?

What if being with Xavi turned Stefi's life, and the life of everyone she loved, upside down?

What if being with Stefi made Xavi's initial time as prince more difficult?

What if, what about, what if, what if?

At one point, Stefi cried out, "Why couldn't you just turn out to be a regular boyfriend?"

This caused Xavi to smile. "So you do want me to be your boyfriend?"

Stefi looked at Xavi from under half-lidded, sleepy eyes.

"Maybe." She sighed.

But inside, her heart knew the answer, and that answer was a clear and loud *yes*.

A million other questions still simmered between them, however, and very few answers. So many questions it caused that same heart in Stefi's chest to pound with dismay. But they could ask all they wanted, and truly, only time would tell. They would need to live through whatever came their way and see how it all turned out. The only thing they didn't wonder was about their feelings for one another. Those, at least, were as clear as the blue of Xavi's eyes.

Stefi tore her own eyes from Xavi now, lay back on the pillow, and stared up at the ceiling. The stakes were high not only for her and Xavi but also for Santiago and Diego. The officially-together boyfriends had spent the rest of *their* morning enclosed in Santiago's own palace room.

On the ride from Madrid, the two young men explained their whole story to Stefi, that Santiago was going to give up his post as a royal guard to follow his heart all the way to Barcelona to be with Diego. She wondered how that would go and hoped for their sake it all worked out. But she also took note—it was impossible not to—that being involved with the royal family seemed to raise the stakes for everyone on everything, complicating every decision and act. Grand gestures were constantly required, and Stefi wondered what, exactly, she would be asked to give up in the future if she and Xavi managed to make their relationship work.

But then, as with all the other questions that swirled around the young couple like a summer storm, Stefi didn't need to worry right this minute. She should approach this like one of her pastry recipes—one step at a time, one ingredient at a time. Eventually she would find out if the recipe that was their relationship was a delicious success or a flop. Besides, as long as Stefi stayed in this room, it felt like she and Xavi could hold the world at bay. This, plus a very handsome shirtless prince was sleeping peacefully on the other side of Stefi in the bed. Or at least he had been.

Xavi's eyes fluttered open.

He turned to look at Stefi.

Once again, Stefi longed to kiss him.

"Where are Vermut and Oliva?" Xavi asked.

“I let them out a while ago,” she said, allowing herself to enjoy at least one question with an easy answer.

Xavi’s eyes lazily perused the girl next to him in bed. “I like you in my pajamas.”

“I like being in them,” she admitted, and wondered if Xavi wanted to kiss her as much as she wanted to kiss him. And maybe also get her out of those pajamas.

Soon she had her answer.

Xavi reached for her in the bed and pulled her close. She sighed as his mouth touched hers and her whole body came alive, every inch of skin tingling. Stefi couldn’t help but wrap her arms around Xavi. Soon their legs were tangled together and Stefi’s fingers were roaming the beautiful, smooth skin of Xavi’s back and his fingers were busy undoing the buttons of the pajama top she was wearing. *One, two, three*, she counted as each one popped free. Soon he’d have them all undone and Stefi could barely wait. She already wanted more. She wanted *all* of Xavi.

But then the church bells chimed the hour.

Stefi forced herself to count them, all the way until ten.

The prince and the American girl pulled themselves apart, panting.

Xavi’s turned to her. “I think it’s time, Stefi,” he said.

She nodded. She began redoing all those buttons.

He watched with sadness as she did.

“So, are you ready to meet my parents?” Xavi asked. “Do you want to?”

What Stefi really wanted was to lean forward and kiss Xavi again and go back to running her fingers all over that beautiful skin, but this was not what he was asking. “Well, I already met your mother,” Stefi stalled. “I’m nervous about what she’s going to think of me being here. But I suppose you really mean your father, the king?” At this, Stefi shook her head, because it was all so outlandish.

Xavi's eyes clouded over. "I can still sneak you out of the palace. You can go back to your life in Barcelona like I was never there," he said, then backtracked. "Well, almost. Eventually the press will die down around you and it really can be like I was never there. If that's what you want."

Stefi's heart squeezed dramatically in protest. The idea of her life without Xavi in it—she didn't even want the thought to cross her mind. Once and for all, Stefi pushed it away and asked Xavi, "So, when the two of us show up at the breakfast table, what are you going to tell your parents to explain this?" Stefi gestured back and forth between them.

Now Xavi's expression grew hopeful. "That you are, well, my girlfriend, regardless of what they or anyone else might say. Which brings me to my next question: *Are* you my girlfriend?"

Stefi nearly laughed at the absurdity. Did she want to be the prince of Spain's girlfriend? She was already sitting in the bedroom of a Spanish palace, in a borrowed pair of pajamas provided by the prince, on the bed with the prince himself. After all the ups and downs of falling for Xavi and Xavi's identity upending her life and then being whisked to Madrid to speak with him, this prince was officially asking her to be his girlfriend.

"On one condition," Stefi said.

Xavi reached for Stefi's hand. "And what is that?"

She studied their fingers entwined together, then raised her gaze to meet Xavi's. "I'm finishing my pastry class at Hofmann this summer," she said.

The remaining clouds left Xavi's eyes and a smile crept onto his face. "I would never let the monarchy stand in the way of your lessons in perfecting the croissant."

"Okay, then," Stefi said, nodding.

"Okay, then, what?"

"I'll be your girlfriend," she confirmed.

Xavi's smile grew into a grin and Stefi found herself blushing. She thought Xavi had never been so handsome as he was right now. For a split second, the momentousness of Stefi's decision expanded inside her and caused everything about her to falter. She wondered what people from home would think about this girl who'd always been known as Jason's girlfriend and Amber's best friend now becoming known as the prince of Spain's girlfriend. Once more, Stefi would be in someone's shadow. But then, who was to say this couldn't be reversed? Xavi could become known as the boyfriend of Stefi, the American croissant-maker extraordinaire, who also happened to be the prince of Spain.

The unease creeping into Stefi's heart dissipated.

It also nearly made her laugh.

"What's so funny?" Xavi asked.

Stefi's eyebrows arched. "Let me rephrase what I just said."

"Okaaay," he answered, sounding nervous.

"I'll agree for you to be *my* boyfriend."

Xavi began nodding enthusiastically. "I can definitely agree to being an aspiring pastry chef's boyfriend."

Stefi's heart and body and mind were doing all kinds of separate, opposing things. Her heart was like a butterfly, fluttering with joy; her mind was spinning, trying to take in the meaning of all that had befallen her in the past forty-eight hours; and her entire body was aching with want for Xavi. But most of all, Stefi was happy.

"All right, then," she said. "We have a deal, Xavier Bas."

At this, the newly minted boyfriend and girlfriend sealed their relationship with a kiss.

The church bells chimed once, signaling that it was a quarter past the hour.

"We don't have to go down to breakfast *yet*," Xavi said suggestively.

At the moment, Stefi was very open to suggestion. "No?"

His eyes filled with mischief. "I think I can eat whenever I want around here."

"I do love a good brunch," Stefi agreed, nodding. "Breakfast is overrated."

"Besides, brunch at the palace is probably amazing," Xavi said, laughing now.

Stefi smiled at the handsome, grinning young man before her who might have been the prince of Spain but who was also just Xavi, her boyfriend. "Why don't we find out together, then?" she proposed. Then she leaned forward once more and kissed her prince.

# Acknowledgments

My heartfelt gratitude goes out to Tara Weikum, my editor. I am so very thankful to you that *Stefi* exists.

I was actually meant to do a totally different book than this one—sad, dramatic, tragic. Tara and I worked out the details over the course of many months. Then my father died unexpectedly just before I was about to begin, and I knew I wouldn't be able to write the book we discussed. So after all our back and forth, I asked Tara, pretty please could I write a rom-com that takes place in Barcelona instead? Tara said yes, and she has been nothing less than amazing the entire time I've worked on this story. I needed an escape from so much grief, and rom-coms are such a good recipe for getting through sadness.

Thank you, Tara, for being so flexible and understanding. *Stefi* has been a bright spot for me in an otherwise very difficult time.

I want to thank everyone at Harper, especially Sarah Homer and Chris Kwon; Vi-An for the totally inspired art on the cover, which I love. And Miriam, my longtime agent, of course, who has been a wonderful cheerleader for *Stefi*.

Most of all, I am so grateful to Barcelona, my favorite city in the world, and for all my neighbors in El Gótico, where Stefi just *happens* to live in this story and where my husband and I also live for half of every year. My neighborhood and everyone in it is special in so many ways. I hope you all enjoy your cameo appearances in this novel. Barcelona has been my happy thought these last few years and I am so lucky and grateful to call this city my part-time home. It has the brightest, sunniest days and the yummiest of food, and my heart is here alongside Stefi's.